'Think about what I [...]
You can reclaim your [...]
to being a carefree stu[...]
pointed out, his persua[...] insidious.
'No more scrubbing floors or serving drinks.'

'Stop!' Poppy said, leaping to her feet to walk restively around the room while she battled the tempting possibilities he had placed in front of her.

Gaetano studied her from below heavily lashed eyelids. She would surrender—of course she would. As a teenager she had been ambitious, and he could still see that spirited spark of wanting more than her servant ancestors had ever wanted glowing within her.

'And of course *your* ultimate goal is becoming CEO of the Leonetti Bank—and marrying me will deliver that,' Poppy filled in slowly, her luminous green eyes skimming to his lean darkly handsome features in wonderment. 'I can't believe how ambitious you are.'

'The bank is my life. It always has been,' Gaetano admitted without apology. 'Nothing gives me as much of a buzz as a profitable deal.'

'I'll give you an answer in the morning.'

Gaetano slid fluidly out of his seat and approached her. 'But you already know the answer. You like what I do to you,' he said huskily, with blazing confidence, running a teasing forefinger down over her cheek to stroke it along the soft curve of her full lower lip.

Lynne Graham was born in Northern Ireland and has been a keen romance reader since her teens. She is very happily married to an understanding husband who has learned to cook since she started to write! Her five children keep her on her toes. She has a very large dog who knocks everything over, a very small terrier who barks a lot, and two cats. When time allows, Lynne is a keen gardener.

Books by Lynne Graham

Mills & Boon Modern Romance

The Secret His Mistress Carried
The Dimitrakos Proposition
A Ring to Secure His Heir
Unlocking Her Innocence

The Notorious Greeks

The Greek Demands His Heir
The Greek Commands His Mistress

Bound by Gold

The Sheikh's Secret Babies
The Billionaire's Bridal Bargain

The Legacies of Powerful Men

Ravelli's Defiant Bride
Christakis's Rebellious Wife
Zarif's Convenient Queen

A Bride for a Billionaire

A Rich Man's Whim
The Sheikh's Prize
The Billionaire's Trophy
Challenging Dante

Visit the Author Profile page at
millsandboon.co.uk for more titles.

LEONETTI'S HOUSEKEEPER BRIDE

BY
LYNNE GRAHAM

MILLS & BOON

Published in Great Britain 2016
By Mills & Boon, an imprint of HarperCollins*Publishers*
1 London Bridge Street, London, SE1 9GF

© 2016 Lynne Graham

ISBN: 978-0-263-92099-4

Our policy is to use papers that are natural, renewable and recyclable
products and made from wood grown in sustainable forests. The logging
and manufacturing processes conform to the legal environmental
regulations of the country of origin.

Printed and bound in Spain
by CPI, Barcelona

LEONETTI'S HOUSEKEEPER BRIDE

CHAPTER ONE

GAETANO LEONETTI WAS having a very bad day. It had started at dawn, when his phone went off and proceeded to show him a series of photos that enraged him but which he knew would enrage his grandfather and the very conservative board of the Leonetti investment bank even more. Regrettably, sacking the woman responsible for the story in the downmarket tabloid was likely to be the sole satisfaction he could hope to receive.

'It's not your fault,' Tom Sandyford, Gaetano's middle-aged legal adviser and close friend, told him quietly.

'Of course it's *my* fault,' Gaetano growled. 'It was *my* house, *my* party and the woman in *my* bed at the time who organised the damned party—'

'Celia was that soap star with the cocaine habit you didn't know about,' Tom reminisced. 'Wasn't she sacked from the show soon after you ditched her?'

Gaetano nodded, his even white teeth gritting harder.

'It's a case of bad luck…that's all,' Tom opined. 'You can't ask your guests to post their credentials beforehand, so you had no way of knowing some of them weren't tickety-boo.'

'Tickety-boo?' Gaetano repeated, his lean, darkly handsome features frowning. Although he was born and raised in England, Italian had been the language of his home and he still occasionally came across English words and phrases that were unfamiliar.

'Decent upstanding citizens,' Tom rephrased. 'So, a handful of them were hookers? Well, in the rarefied and very privileged world you move in, how were you supposed to find that out?'

'The press found it out,' Gaetano countered flatly.

'With the usual silly "Orgy at the Manor" big reveal. It'll be forgotten in five minutes…although that blonde dancing naked in the fountain out front is rather memorable,' Tom remarked, scanning the newspaper afresh with lascivious intent.

'I don't remember seeing her. I left the party early to fly to New York. Everyone still had their clothes on at that stage,' Gaetano said drily. 'I really don't need another scandal like this.'

'Scandal does rather seem to follow you around. I suppose the old man and the board at the bank are up in arms as usual,' Tom commented with sympathy.

Gaetano compressed his wide sensual mouth in silent agreement. In the name of family loyalty and respect, he was paying in the blood of his fierce pride and ambition for the latest scandal. Letting his seventy-four-year-old grandfather Rodolfo carpet him like a badly behaved schoolboy had proved to be a truly toxic experience for a billionaire whose investment advice was sought by governments both in the UK and abroad. And when Rodolfo had settled into his favourite preaching session about Gaetano's womanising lifestyle, Gaetano had had to breathe in deeply several times and resist the urge to point out to the older man that expectations and values had changed since the nineteen forties for both men *and* women.

Rodolfo Leonetti had married a humble fisherman's daughter at the age of twenty-one and during his fifty years of devoted marriage he had never looked at another woman. Ironically, his only child, Gaetano's father, Rocco, had not taken his father's advice on the benefits of making an early marriage either. Rocco had been a notorious playboy and an incorrigible gambler. He had married a woman young enough to be his daughter when he was in his fifties, had fathered one son and had expired ten years later after over-exerting himself in another woman's bed. Gaetano reckoned he had been paying for his father's sins almost from the hour of his birth. At the age of twenty-nine and one of the world's leading bankers, he was tired of being continually forced to prove his worth and confine his projects to the narrow expectations of the board. He had made millions for the Leonetti Bank; he *deserved* to be CEO.

Indeed, Rodolfo's angry ultimatum that very morning had outraged Gaetano.

'You will *never* be the chief executive of this bank until you change your way of life and settle down into being a respectable family man!' his grandfather had sworn angrily. 'I will not support your leadership with the board and, no matter how brilliant you are, Gaetano, the board *always* listens to me… They remember too well how your father almost brought the bank down with his risky ventures!'

Yet what, realistically, did Gaetano's sex life have to do with his acumen and expertise as a banker? Since when were a wife and children the only measure of a man's judgement and maturity?

Gaetano had not the slightest interest in getting married. In fact he shuddered at the idea of being anchored to one woman for the rest of his life while living in fear of a divorce that could deprive him of half of his financial portfolio. He was a very hard worker. He had earned his academic qualifications with honours in the most prestigious international institutions and his achievements since then had been immense. Why wasn't that enough? In comparison his father had been an academically slow and spoiled rich boy who, like Peter Pan, had refused to grow up. Such a comparison was grossly unfair.

Tom dealt Gaetano a rueful appraisal. 'You didn't get the old "find an ordinary girl" spiel again, did you?'

'"An ordinary girl, *not* a party girl, one who takes pleasure in the *simple* things of life,"' Gaetano quoted verbatim because his grandfather's discourses always ran to the same conclusion: marry, settle down, father children with a home-loving female…and the world would then miraculously become Gaetano's oyster with little happy unicorns dancing on some misty horizon shaped by a rainbow. His lean bronzed features hardened with grim cynicism. He had seen just how well that fantasy had turned out for once-married and now happily divorced friends.

'Perhaps you could time travel back to the nineteen fifties to find this ordinary girl,' Tom quipped, wondering how the era of female liberation and career women had contrived to pass Rodolfo Leonetti by so completely that he still believed such women existed.

'The best of it is, if I did produce an *ordinary* girl and announce that I was going to marry her Rodolfo would be appalled,' Gaetano breathed impatiently. 'He's too much of a snob. Unfortunately he's become so obsessed by his conviction that I need to marry that he's blocking my progression at the bank.'

His PA entered and extended two envelopes. 'The termination of contract on the grounds of the confidentiality clause which has been breached and the notice to quit the accommodation that goes with the job,' she specified. 'The helicopter is waiting for you on the roof, sir.'

'What's going on?' Tom asked.

'I'm flying down to Woodfield Hall to sack the housekeeper who handed over those photos to the press.'

'It was the *housekeeper*?' Tom prompted in surprise.

'She was named in the article. Not the brightest of women,' Gaetano pointed out drily.

Poppy leapt off her bike, kicked the support into place and ran into the village shop to buy milk. As usual she was running late but she could not drink coffee without milk and didn't feel properly awake until she had had at least two cups. Her mane of fiery red-gold curls bounced on her slim black-clad shoulders and her green eyes sparkled.

'Good morning, Frances,' she said cheerfully to the rather sour-looking older woman behind the counter as she dug into her purse to pay.

'I'm surprised you're so bright this morning,' the shop owner remarked in a tone laden with suggestive meaning.

'Why wouldn't I be?'

The older woman slapped a well-thumbed newspaper down on the counter and helpfully turned it round to enable Poppy to read the headline. Poppy paled with dismay and snatched the publication up, moving on impatiently to the next page only to groan at the familiar photo of the naked blonde cavorting in the fountain. Her brother, Damien, had definitely taken that photo on the night of that infamous party. She knew that because she had caught him showing that particular one off to his mates.

'Seems your ma has been talking out of turn,' Frances remarked. 'Shouldn't think Mr Leonetti will appreciate that…'

Glancing up to meet the older woman's avidly curious gaze, Poppy hastily paid for the paper and left the shop. That photo? How on earth had the newspaper got hold of it? And what about the other photos? The heaving, fortunately unidentifiable bodies in one of the bedrooms? When invited to join the party by a drunken guest, had Damien taken other, even more risqué pictures? And her mother…what insanity had persuaded her to risk her job by trashing her employer to a tabloid journalist? Poppy's soft full mouth down-curved and her shoulders slumped as she climbed back on her bike. Unfortunately Poppy knew exactly why her mother might have been so foolish: Jasmine Arnold was an alcoholic.

Poppy had once got her mother to an AA meeting and it had done her good but she had never managed to get the older woman back to a second. Instead, Jasmine just drank herself insensible every day while Poppy struggled to do her mother's job for her as well as doing her own. What else could she do when the very roof over their heads was dependent on Jasmine's continuing employment? And after all, wasn't it *her* fault that her mother had sunk so low before Poppy realised how bad things had got in her own home and had finally come back to live with her family again?

It was very fortunate that Gaetano only visited the house once or twice a year. But then Gaetano was a city boy through and through and a beautiful Georgian country house an inconvenient distance from London was of little use or interest to him. Had he been a more regular visitor she would never have been able to conceal her mother's condition for so long.

Poppy pumped the bike pedals hard to get up the hill before careening at speed into the driveway of Woodfield Hall. The beautiful house had been the Leonetti family home in England since the eighteenth century when the family had first come over from Venice to set up as glorified moneylenders. And if there was one thing that family were good at it, it was making pots and pots of money, Poppy reflected ruefully, shying away from the challenge of thinking about Gaetano in an any more personal way.

She and Gaetano might have virtually grown up in the same household but it would be an outright lie to suggest that they were ever in any way friendly. After all, Gaetano was six years older and had spent most of his time in posh boarding schools.

But Poppy knew that Gaetano would go crazy about the publication of those photos. He was fanatical about his privacy and if his idea of fun was a sex party, she could perfectly understand why! Her spirits sank at the prospect of the trouble looming ahead. No matter how hard she worked life never seemed to get any easier and there always seemed to be another crisis waiting to erupt round the next corner. Yet how could she look after her mother and her brother when their own survival instincts appeared to be so poor?

The Arnold family lived in a flat that had been converted from part of the original stable block at the hall. Jasmine Arnold, a tall skinny redhead in her late forties, was sitting at the kitchen table when her daughter walked in.

Poppy slapped down the paper on the table. 'Mum? Were you out of your mind when you talked to a journalist about that party?' she demanded, before opening the back door and yelling her brother's name at the top of her voice.

Damien emerged from one of the garages, wiping oil stains off his hands with a dirty cloth. 'Where's the fire?' he asked irritably as his sister moved forward to greet him.

'You gave the photos you took at that party to a journalist?' his sister challenged in disbelief.

'No, I didn't,' her kid brother countered. 'Mum knew they were on my phone and she handed them over. She sold them. Got a pile of cash for them and the interview.'

Poppy was even more appalled. She could have excused stupidity or careless speech to the wrong person but she was genuinely shocked that her mother had taken money in return for her disloyalty to her employer.

Damien groaned at the expression on his sister's face. 'Poppy…you should know by now that Mum would do anything to get the money to buy her next drink,' he pointed out heavily. 'I told her not to hand over the photos or talk to the guy but she wouldn't listen to me—'

'Why didn't you tell me what she'd done?'

'What could you do about it? I hoped that maybe the photos wouldn't be used or that, if they were, nobody of any importance would see them,' Damien admitted. 'I doubt if Gaetano sits down to read every silly story that's written about him… I mean, he's never out of the papers!'

'But if you're wrong, Mum will be sacked and we'll be kicked out of the flat.'

Damien wasn't the type to worry about what might never happen and he said wryly, 'Let's hope I'm not wrong.'

But Poppy took after her late father and she was a worrier. It was hard to credit that it was only a few years since the Arnolds had been a secure and happy family of four. Her father had been the gardener at Woodfield Hall and her mother the housekeeper. At twenty years of age, Poppy had been two years into her training at nursing school and Damien had just completed his apprenticeship as a car mechanic. And then without any warning at all their much-loved father had dropped dead and all their lives had been shattered by that cruelly sudden bereavement.

Poppy had taken time out from her course to try and help her mother through the worst of her grief and then she had returned to her studies. Unhappily and without her knowledge, things had gone badly wrong at that point. Her mother had gone off the rails and Damien had been unable to cope with what was happening in his home. Her brother had then got in with the wrong crowd and had ended up in prison. That was when Poppy had finally come home to find her mother sunk in depression and drinking heavily. Poppy had taken a leave of absence from her course, hoping, indeed expecting, that her mother would soon pull round again. Unfortunately that hadn't happened. Although Jasmine was still drinking, Poppy's one consolation was that, after earning early release from prison with his good behaviour, her little brother had got his act together again. Sadly, however, Damien's criminal record had made it impossible for him to get a job.

Poppy still felt horribly guilty about the fact that she had left her kid brother to deal with her deeply troubled mother. Intent on pursuing her chosen career and being the first Arnold female in generations *not* to earn her living by serving the Leonettis, she had been selfish and thoughtless and she had been trying to make up for that mistake ever since.

When she returned to the flat her mother had locked herself in her bedroom. Poppy suppressed a sigh and dug out her work kit and rubber gloves to cross the courtyard and enter the hall. She turned out different rooms of the big house every week, dusting and vacuuming and scrubbing. It was deeply ironic that she had been so set against working for the Leonettis when she was a teenager but had ended up doing it anyway even if it was unofficial. Evenings she served drinks in the local pub. There wasn't time in her life for agonising when there was always a job needing to be done.

Disturbingly however she couldn't get Gaetano Leonetti out of her mind. He was the one and only boy she had ever hated but also the only one she had ever loved. What did that say about her? Self-evidently, that at the age of sixteen she had been really stupid to imagine for one moment that she could ever have any kind of a personal relationship with the posh, privileged scion of the Leonetti family. The wounding demeaning words that Gaetano had shot at her then were still burned into her bones like the scars of an old breakage.

'I don't mess around with staff,' he had said, emphasising the fact that they were not equals and that he would always inhabit a different stratum of society.

'Stop coming on to me, Poppy. You're acting like a slapper.' Oh, how she had cringed at that reading of her behaviour when in truth she had merely been too young and inexperienced to know how to be subtle about spelling out the fact that should he be interested, she was available.

'You're a short, curvy redhead. You could never be my type.'

It was seven years since that humiliating exchange

had taken place and apart from one final demeaning encounter she had not seen Gaetano since, having always gone out of her way to avoid him whenever he was expected at the hall. So, he didn't know that she had slimmed down and shot up inches in height, wouldn't much care either, she reckoned with wry amusement. After all, Gaetano went for very beautiful and sophisticated ladies in designer clothes. Although the one who had thrown that shockingly wild party had not been much of a lady in the original sense of the word.

Having put in her hours at the hall in the ongoing challenge to ensure that it was always well prepared for a visit that could come at very short notice, Poppy went back home to get changed for her bar work. Jasmine was out for the count on her bed, an empty bottle of cheap wine lying beside her. Studying her slumped figure, Poppy suppressed a sigh, recalling the busy, lively and caring woman her mother had once been. Alcohol had stolen all that from her. Jasmine needed specialised help and rehabilitation but there wasn't even counselling available locally and Poppy had no hope of ever acquiring sufficient cash to pay for private treatment for the older woman.

Poppy put on the Goth clothes that she had first donned like a mask to hide behind when she was a bullied teenager. She had been picked on in school for being a little overweight and red-haired. Heck, she had even been bullied for being 'posh' although her family lived in the hall's servant accommodation. Since then, although she no longer dyed her hair or painted her nails black, she had come to enjoy a touch of individuality in her wardrobe and had maintained the basic style. She had lost a lot of weight since she started working two jobs and she was convinced that her Goth-style clothes did a good job of disguising her skinniness. For work she had teamed a dark red net flirty skirt with a fitted black jersey rock print top. The outfit hugged her small full breasts, enhanced her waist and accentuated the length of her legs.

At the end of her shift in the busy bar that was paired with a popular restaurant, Poppy pulled on her coat and waited outside for Damien to show up on his motorbike.

'Gaetano Leonetti arrived in a helicopter this evening,' her brother delivered curtly. 'He demanded to see Mum but she was out of it and I had to pretend she was sick. He handed over these envelopes for her and I opened them once he'd gone. Mum's being sacked and we have a month's notice to move out of the flat.'

An anguished moan of dismay at those twin blows parted Poppy's lips.

'I guess he did see that newspaper.' Damien grimaced. 'He certainly hasn't wasted any time booting us out.'

'Can we blame him for that?' Poppy asked even though her heart was sinking to the soles of her shoes. Where would they go? How would they live? They had no rainy-day account for emergencies. Her mother drank her salary and Damien was on benefits.

But Poppy was a fighter, always had been, always would be. She took after her father more than her mother. She was good at picking herself up when things went wrong. Her mother, however, had never fully recovered from the stillbirth she had suffered the year before Poppy's father had died. Those two terrible calamities coming so close together had knocked her mother's feet from under her and she had never really got up again. Poppy swallowed hard as she climbed onto the bike and gripped her brother's waist. She could still remember her mother's absolute joy at that unexpected late pregnancy, which in the end had become a source of so much grief and loss.

As the bike rolled past the hall Poppy saw the light showing through the front window of the library and tensed. Gaetano was staying over for the night?

'Yeah, he's still here,' Damien confirmed as he put his bike away. 'So what?'

'I'm going to speak to him—'

'What's the point?' her brother asked in a tone of defeat. 'Why should he care?'

But Gaetano *did* have a heart, Poppy thought in desperation. At least he had had a heart at the age of thirteen when his father had run over his dog and killed it. She had seen the tears in Gaetano's eyes and she had been crying too. Dino had been as much her dog as his because Dino had hung around with her when Gaetano was away at school, not that he had probably ever realised that. Dino had never been replaced and when she had asked why not in the innocent way of a child, Gaetano had simply said flatly, 'Dogs die.'

And she had been too young to really understand that outlook, that raising of the barriers against the threat of being hurt again. She had seen no tears in his remarkable eyes at his father's funeral but he had been almost as devastated as his grandfather when his grandmother passed away. But then the older couple had been more his parents than his real parents had. Within a year of becoming a widow, his mother had remarried and moved to Florida without her son.

Poppy breathed in deep as she marched round the side of the big house with Damien chasing in her wake.

'It's almost midnight!' he hissed. 'You can't go calling on him now!'

'If I wait until tomorrow I'll lose my nerve,' she said truthfully.

Damien hung back in the shadows, watching as she rang the doorbell and waited, her hands dug in the pockets of her faux-leather flying jacket. A voice sounded somewhere close by and she flinched in surprise, turning her head as a man in a suit talking into a mobile phone walked towards her in the moonlight.

'I'm security, Miss Arnold,' he said quietly. 'I was telling Mr Leonetti who was at the door.'

Poppy suppressed a rude word. She had forgotten the tight security with which the Leonetti family surrounded themselves. Of course, calling in on Gaetano late at night wouldn't go unquestioned.

'I want to see your boss,' she declared.

The security man was talking Italian into the phone and she couldn't follow a word of what he was saying. When the man frowned, she knew he was about to deliver a negative and she moved off the step and snapped, 'I *have* to see Gaetano! It's really important.'

Somewhere someone made a decision and a moment later there was the sound of heavy bolts being drawn back to open the massive front door. Another security man nodded acknowledgement and stood back for her entrance into the marble-floored hall with its perfect proportions and priceless paintings. A trickle of perspiration ran down between her taut shoulder blades and she straightened her spine in defiance of it although she was already shrinking at the challenge of what she would have to tell Gaetano. At this juncture, coming clean was her sole option.

Poppy Arnold? Gaetano's brain had conjured up several time-faded images. Poppy as a little girl paddling at the lake edge in spite of his warnings; Poppy sobbing over Dino with all the drama of her class and no thought of restraint; Poppy looking at him as if he might imminently walk on water when she was about fifteen, a scrutiny that had become considerably less innocent and entertaining a year later. And finally, Poppy, a taunting sensual smile tilting her lips as she sidled out of the shrubbery closely followed by a young estate worker, both of them engaged in righting their rumpled, grass-stained clothing.

Bearing in mind the number of years the Arnold family had worked for his own, he felt that it was only fair that he at least saw Poppy and listened to what she had to say in her mother's defence. He hadn't, however, thought about Poppy in years. Did she still live with her family? He was surprised, having always assumed Poppy would flee country life and the type of employment she had soundly trounced as being next door to indentured servitude in the modern world. Touching a respectful forelock had held no appeal whatsoever for outspoken, rebellious Poppy, he acknowledged wryly. How much had she changed? Was she working for him now somewhere on the pay roll? His ebony brows drew together in a frown at his ignorance as he lounged back against the edge of the library desk and awaited her appearance.

The tap-tap of high heels sounded in the corridor and the door opened to reveal legs that could have rivalled a Vegas showgirl's toned and perfect pins. Disconcerted by that startlingly unexpected and carnal thought, Gaetano ripped his attention from those incredibly long shapely legs and whipped it up to her face, only to receive another jolt. Time had transformed Poppy Arnold into a tall, dazzling redhead. He was staring but he couldn't help it while his shrewd brain was engaged in ticking off familiarities and changes. The bright green eyes were unaltered but the rounded face had fined down to an exquisite heart shape to frame slanting cheekbones, a dainty little nose and a mouth lush and pink enough to star in any male fantasy. The pulse at Gaetano's groin throbbed and he straightened, flicking his jacket closed to conceal his physical reaction while thinking that Poppy might well get the last laugh after all because the ugly duckling he had once rejected had become a swan.

'Mr Leonetti,' she said as politely as though they had never met before.

'Gaetano, please,' he countered wryly, seeing no reason to stand on ceremony with her. 'We have known each other since childhood.'

'I don't think I ever *knew* you,' Poppy said frankly, studying him with bemused concentration.

She had expected to notice unappetising changes in Gaetano. After all, he was almost thirty years old now and lived a deskbound, self-indulgent and, by all accounts, *decadent* life. By this stage he should have been showing some physical fallout from that lifestyle. But there was no hint of portliness in his very tall, powerfully built frame and certainly no jowls to mar the perfection of his strong, stubbled jaw line. And his dense blue-black curly hair was as plentiful as ever.

An electrifying silence enclosed them and Poppy stepped restively off one foot onto the other, her slender figure tense as a drawn bow string while she studied him. Taller and broader than he had been, he was even more gorgeous than he had been seven years earlier when she had fallen for him like a ton of bricks. Silly, silly girl that she had been, she conceded ruefully, but there was no denying that even then she had had good taste because Gaetano was stunning in the way so very few men were. A tiny flicker in her pelvis made her press her thighs together, warmth flushing over her skin. His dark eyes, set below black straight brows, were locked to her with an intensity that made her inwardly squirm. He had eyes with incredibly long thick lashes, she was recalling dizzily, so dark and noticeable in their volume that she had once suspected him of wearing guy liner like some of the boys she had known back then.

'Do you still live here with your mother and brother?' Gaetano enquired.

'Yes,' Poppy admitted, fighting to banish the fog that had briefly closed round her brain. 'You're probably wondering why I've come to see you at this hour. I'm a bartender at the Flying Horseman down the road and I've only just finished my shift.'

Gaetano was pleasantly surprised that she had contrived to speak two entire sentences without spluttering the profanities which had laced her speech seven years earlier. Of course, right now she was probably watching her every word with him, he reasoned. A bartender? He supposed it explained the outfit, which looked as though it would be more at home in a nightclub.

'I saw the newspaper article,' she added. 'Obviously you want to sack my mother for talking about the party and selling those photos. I'm not denying that you have good reason to do that.'

'Where did the photos come from?' Gaetano asked curiously. 'Who took them?'

Poppy winced. 'One of the guests invited my brother to join the party when she saw him outside directing cars. He did what I imagine most young men would do when they see half-naked women—he took pictures on his phone. I'm not excusing him but he didn't sell those photos… It was my mother who took his phone and did that—'

'I assume I'll see your mother in person tomorrow before I leave. But I'll ask you now. My family has always treated your mother well. Why did she *do* it?'

Poppy breathed in deep and lifted her chin, bracing herself for what she had to say. 'My mother's an alcoholic, Gaetano. They offered her money and that was all it took. All she was thinking about was probably how she would buy her next bottle of booze. I'm afraid she can't see beyond that right now.'

Taken aback, Gaetano frowned. He had not been prepared for that revelation. It did not make a difference to his attitude though. Disloyalty was not a trait he could overlook in an employee. 'Your mother must be a functioning alcoholic, then,' he assumed. 'Because the house appears to be in good order.'

'No, she's not functioning.' Poppy sighed, her soft mouth tightening. 'I've been covering up for her for more than a year. I've been looking after this place.'

His lean, darkly handsome features tightened. 'In other words there has been a concentrated campaign to deceive me as to what was going on here,' he condemned with a sudden harshness that dismayed her. 'At any time you could have approached me and asked for my understanding and even my help—yet you chose not to do so. I have no tolerance for deception, Poppy. This meeting is at an end.'

A hundred different thoughts flashing through her mind, Poppy stared at him, her heart beating very fast with nerves and consternation. 'But—'

'No extenuating circumstances allowed or invited,' Gaetano cut in with derision. 'I have heard all I need to hear from you and there is nothing more to say. *Leave.*'

CHAPTER TWO

POPPY TOOK A sudden step forward. 'Don't speak to me like that!' she warned Gaetano angrily.

'I can speak to you whatever way I like. I'm in my own home and it seems that you are one of my employees.'

'No, I'm not!' Poppy contradicted with unashamed satisfaction. 'I donated my services free for my mother's sake!'

'Let's not make it sound as if you dug ditches,' Gaetano fired back impatiently. 'As I'm so rarely here there can't be that much work concerned in keeping the house presentable.'

'I think you'd be surprised by how much work is involved in a place this size!' Poppy snapped back firely.

Anger made her green eyes shine blue-green like a peacock feather, Gaetano noted. 'I'm really not interested,' he said drily. 'And if you donated your services free that was downright stupid, not praiseworthy.'

Poppy almost stamped an enraged foot. 'I'm not stupid. How dare you say that? I could hardly charge you for the work my mother was already being paid to do, could I?'

Gaetano shrugged a broad shoulder, watching her tongue flick out to moisten her red-lipsticked mouth, imagining her doing other much dirtier things with it and then tensing with exquisite discomfort as arousal coursed feverishly through his lower body. She was sexy, smoulderingly so, he acknowledged grimly. 'I'm sure you're versatile enough to have found some way round that problem.'

'But not dishonest enough to do so,' Poppy proclaimed with pride. 'Mum was being paid for the job and it was done, so on that score you have no grounds for complaint.'

'I don't?' An ebony brow lifted in challenge. 'An alcoholic has been left in charge of the household accounts?'

'Oh, no, that's not been happening,' Poppy hastened to reassure him. 'Mum no longer has access to the household cash. I made sure of that early on.'

'Then how have the bills been paid?'

Poppy compressed her lips as she registered that he truly did not have a clue how his own household had worked for years. 'I paid them. I've been taking care of the accounts here since Dad died.'

'But you're not authorised!' Gaetano slammed back at her distrustfully.

'Neither was my father but he took care of them for a long time.'

Gaetano's frown grew even darker. 'Your father had access as well? What the hell?'

'Oh, for goodness' sake, are you always this rigid?' Poppy groaned in disbelief. 'Mum never had a head for figures. Dad always did the accounts for her. Your grandmother knew. Whenever your grandmother had a query about the accounts she had to wait until Mum had asked Dad for the answer. It wasn't a secret back then.'

'And how am I supposed to trust you with substantial sums of money when your brother was recently in prison for theft?' Gaetano demanded sharply. 'My accountants will check the accounts and, believe me, if there are any discrepancies I will be bringing in the police.'

Having paled when he threw his knowledge of Damien's conviction at her, Poppy stood very straight and still, her facial muscles tight with self-control. 'Damien got involved with a gang of car thieves but he didn't actually *steal* any of the cars. He's the mechanic who worked on the stolen vehicles before they were shipped abroad to be sold.'

'What a very fine distinction!' Gaetano derided, unimpressed.

Poppy raised her head high, green eyes flashing defiance like sparks. 'You get your accountants in to check the books. There won't be any discrepancies,' she fired back with pride. 'And don't be snide about my brother.'

'I wasn't being snide.'

'You were being snide from the pinnacle of your rich, privileged, feather-bedded life. Damien broke the law and he was punished for it,' Poppy told him. 'He's paid his dues and he's learned his lesson. Maybe you've never made any mistakes, Gaetano?'

'My mistake was in allowing that party to be held

here!' Gaetano slung back at her grittily. 'And don't drag my background or my wealth into this conversation. It's unfair—'

'Then don't be so superior!' Poppy advised. 'But maybe you can't help being the way you are.'

'Do you really think hurling insults at me is likely to further your cause?'

'You haven't even given me the chance to tell you what my cause is,' she pointed out. 'You're so argumentative, Gaetano!'

'*I'm*...argumentative?' Gaetano carolled in disbelief.

'I want you to give Mum another chance,' Poppy admitted doggedly. 'I know you're not feeling very generous. I know that having your kinky party preferences splashed all over the media has to have been embarrassing for you—'

'I do not have kinky preferences—'

'It's none of my business whether you do or not!' Poppy riposted. 'I'm not being judgemental.'

'How very generous of you in the circumstances,' Gaetano murmured icily.

'And if you're not being argumentative, you're being sarcastic!' Poppy flared back at him with raw resentment. 'Can you even *try* listening to me?'

'If you could try to refrain from commenting about my preferences, kinky or otherwise,' Gaetano advised flatly.

'May I take my shoes off?' she asked him abruptly. 'I've been standing all night and my feet are killing me!'

Gaetano shifted an impatient hand. 'Take them off.

Say what you have to say and then go. I'm bored with this.'

'You're so kind and encouraging,' Poppy replied in a honeyed tone of stinging sweetness as she removed her shoes and dropped several crucial inches in height, unsettled by the reality that, although she was five feet eight inches tall, he had a good six inches on her and now towered over her in a manner she instinctively disliked.

As she flexed those incredible long legs sheathed in black lace, Gaetano watched, admiring her long toned calves, neat little knees and long slender thighs. A flash of white inner thigh as she bent in that short skirt and her small full breasts shifting unbound below the cling-ing top sent his temperature rocketing and made his teeth grit. Was she teasing him deliberately? Was the provocative outfit a considered invitation? What woman dressed like that came to see a man at midnight with clean intentions?

'Talk, Poppy,' he urged very drily, infuriated at the way his brain was rebelling against his usual rational control and concentration to stray in directions he was determined not to travel.

'Mum has had it tough the last few years—'

Gaetano held up a silencing hand. 'I know about the stillbirth and of course your father's death and I'm heartily sorry for the woman, but those misfortunes don't excuse what's been happening here.'

'Mum needs help, not judgement, Gaetano,' Poppy argued shakily.

'I'm her employer, not her family and not a therapist,' Gaetano pointed out calmly. 'She's not my responsibility.'

In a more hesitant voice, Poppy added, 'Your grandfather always said we were one big family here.'

'Please don't tell me that you fell for that old chestnut. My grandfather is an old-fashioned man who likes the sound of such sentiments but somehow I don't think he'd be any more compassionate than I am when it comes to the security of his home. Leaving an untrustworthy and unstable alcoholic in charge here would be complete madness,' he stated coolly.

'Yes, but…you could give Mum's job to me,' Poppy reasoned in a desperate rush. 'I've been doing it to your satisfaction for months, so you've actually had a free trial. That way we could stay on in the flat and you wouldn't have to look for someone new.'

Discomfiture made Gaetano tense. 'You never wanted to do domestic work… I'm well aware of that.'

'We all have to do things we don't want to do, particularly when it comes to looking out for family,' Poppy argued with feeling. 'After Dad died I went back to my nursing course and left Damien looking after Mum. He couldn't cope. He didn't tell me how bad things had got here and because of that he got into trouble. Mum is my responsibility and I turned my back on her when she needed me most.'

Gaetano, who was unsurprised that she had sought a career outside domestic service, thought she had a ridiculously overactive conscience. 'It wouldn't work, Poppy. I'm sorry. I wish you well and I'm sorry I can't help.'

'*Won't* help,' she slotted in curtly.

'You're not my idea of a housekeeper. It's best that you make a new start somewhere else with your family,' he declared.

No, he definitely didn't want Poppy with her incredibly alluring legs in his house, even though he didn't visit it very often. She would be a dangerous temptation and he was determined that he would never go there. *Never muck around with staff* was a maxim etched in stone in Gaetano's personal commandments. When a former PA had thrown herself at him one evening early in his career he had slept with her. For him it had been a one-night stand on a business trip and nothing more, but she had been far more ambitious and it had ended messily, teaching him that professional relationships should never cross the boundaries into intimacy.

'It's not that easy to make a new start,' Poppy told him tightly. 'I'm the only one out of the three of us with a job and if I have to move I'll lose that.'

Gaetano expelled his breath on an impatient hiss. 'Poppy… I am not going to apologise for the fact that your mother breached her employment contract and plunged me into a scandal. You cannot lay her problems at my door. I have every sympathy for your position and, out of consideration for the years that your family worked here and did an excellent job, I will make a substantial final payment—'

'Oh, keep your blasted conscience money!' Poppy flung at him, suddenly losing her temper, her fierce pride stung by his attitude. He thought that she and her mother and her brother were a sad bunch of losers and he was so keen to get them off his property that he was prepared to pay more for the privilege. 'I don't want anything from you. I won't *take* anything more from you!'

'Losing your temper is a very bad idea in a situation like this,' he breathed irritably as she bent down to scoop up her shoes and turned on her heel, her short skirt flaring round her pert behind.

Poppy turned her head, green eyes gleaming like polished jewels. 'It's the only thing I've got left to lose,' she contradicted squarely.

Gaetano threw up his hands in a gesture of frustration. 'Then why the hell are you *doing* it? Put yourself first and leave your family to sort out their own problems!'

'Is that what the ruthless, callous banker would do to save his own skin?' Poppy asked scornfully as she reached the door. 'Mum and Damien are my family and, yes, they're very different from me. I take after Dad and I'm strong. They're not. They crumble in a crisis. Does that mean I love them any less? No, it doesn't. In fact it probably means I love them *more*. I love them warts and all and as long as there's breath in my body I'll look after them to the best of my ability.'

Gaetano was stunned into silence by her emotive words. He couldn't imagine loving anyone like that. His parents had been both been weak and fallible in their different ways. His father had chased thrills and his mother had chased money and Gaetano had only learned to despise them for their shallow characters. His parents had not had the capacity to love him and once he had got old enough to understand that he had stopped loving them, ultimately recognising that only his grandparents genuinely cared about him and his well-being. For that reason, the concept of continuing to blindly love seriously flawed personalities and still feel a duty of care towards them genuinely shocked Gaetano, who was infinitely more discerning and demanding of those closest to him. He had seen Poppy Arnold's strength and he admired it, but he thought she was a complete fool to allow her wants and wishes to be handicapped by the double burden of a drunken mother and a pretty useless kid brother.

He went for a shower, still mulling over the encounter with a feeling of amazement that grew rather than dwindled. Rodolfo Leonetti would have been hugely impressed by Poppy's speech, he acknowledged grimly. His grandfather, after all, had wasted years striving to advise and support his feckless son and his frivolous daughter-in-law. Rodolfo had overlooked their faults and had compassionately made the best of a bad situation. Gaetano, however, was much tougher than the older man, less patient, less forgiving, less sympathetic. Was that a flaw in him? he wondered for the very first time.

Thinking of how much Rodolfo would have applauded Poppy's family loyalty, Gaetano reflected equally on her flaws that Rodolfo would have cringed from. Her background was dreadful, the family unpalatable. Mother an alcoholic? Brother a convicted criminal? Poppy's provocative clothing and use of bad language? And yet wasn't Poppy Arnold an ordinary girl of the type Rodolfo had always contended would make his grandson a perfect wife?

Having towelled himself dry, Gaetano got into bed naked and lay there, lost in thought. A sudden laugh escaped him as he momentarily allowed himself to imagine his grandfather's horror if he were to produce a young woman like Poppy as his future wife. Rodolfo was much more of a snob than he would ever be prepared to admit and it was hardly surprising that he should be for the Leonettis had been a family of great wealth and power for hundreds of years. Yet the same man had risked disinheritance when he had married a fisherman's daughter against his family's wishes. Gaetano couldn't imagine that kind of love. He felt no need for that sort of excessive emotion in his life. In fact the very idea of it terrified him and always had.

He didn't want to get married. Maybe by the time he was in his forties he would have mellowed a little and would feel the need to settle down with a companion. At some point too he should have a child to continue the family line. He flinched from the concept, remembering his father's temper tantrums and his mother's tears and nagging whines. Marriage had a bad image with him. Why couldn't Rodolfo understand and accept that reality? He was just too young for settling down but not too young to take over as CEO of the bank.

The germ of an idea occurred to Gaetano and struck him as weird, so he discarded it, only to take it out again a few minutes later and examine it in greater depth. Suppose he quite deliberately produced a fiancée whom his grandfather would deem wrong for him?

In that scenario nobody would be the slightest bit surprised when the engagement was broken off again and Rodolfo would be relieved rather than disappointed. He would see that Gaetano had made an effort to commit to a woman and honour that change accordingly by giving his grandson breathing space for quite some time afterwards. A fake incompatible fiancée could get him off the hook…

In the moonlight piercing the curtains, Gaetano's lean, darkly handsome features were beginning to form a shadowy smile. Pick an ordinary girl and she would naturally have to be beautiful if his grandfather was to be convinced that his fastidious grandson had fallen for her. Pick a beautiful ordinary girl guaranteed to be an embarrassment in public. Poppy could drop all the profanities she liked, dress like a hooker and tell everybody about her sordid family problems. He wouldn't even have to prime her to fail in his exclusive world. It was a given that she would be so out of her depth that she would automatically do so.

A sliver of the conscience that Gaetano rarely listened to slunk out to suggest that it would be a little cruel to subject Poppy to such an ordeal merely for the sake of initially satisfying and then hopefully changing his grandfather's expectations. But then it wouldn't be a real engagement. She would know from the outset that she was faking it and she would be handsomely paid for her role. Nor would she need to know that he was expecting, no, *depending* on her to be a social embarrassment to get him out of the engagement again. It would sort of be like *Pygmalion* in reverse, he reasoned with quiet satisfaction. Pick an ordinary girl, who was an extraordinary beauty and extremely outspoken and hot-tempered… She would be absolutely perfect for his purposes because she would be an accident waiting to happen.

Poppy barely slept that night. Gaetano had said and done nothing unexpected. Of course he wanted them off his fancy property, out of sight and out of mind! His incredulous attitude to her attachment to her family had appalled her though. And where were they going to go? And how would they live when they got there? She would have to throw them on the tender mercies of the social services. My goodness, would they end up living in one of those homeless hostels? Eating out of a food bank?

She got up early as usual, relishing that quiet time of day before her mother or her brother stirred. Even better it was a sunny morning and she took her coffee out to the tiny square of garden at the back of the building that was her favourite place in the world. Making plants flourish, simply growing things, gave her great pleasure.

A riot of flowers in pots ornamented the tiny paved area with its home-made bench seat that was more than a little rickety. However, her Dad had made that bench and she would never part with it. With the clear blue sky above and birds singing in the trees nearby, she felt guilty for feeling so stressed and unhappy. When she had been a little girl working by her father's side she had wanted to be a gardener. Assuming that that would inevitably mean one day working for the Leonettis, she had changed her mind, ignorant of the reality that there were a host of training courses and jobs in the horti-cultural world far from Woodfield Hall that she could have aspired to. Well, so much for her planned escape, she thought heavily. Now that they were being evicted, she didn't want to leave.

'Miss Arnold?' One of Gaetano's security men looked over the fence at her. 'Mr Leonetti wants to see you.'

Poppy leapt upright. Had he had second thoughts about his decision? She smoothed down the thin jacket she wore over a black gothic dress. She had expected Gaetano to demand to see her mother again and she had dressed up in her equivalent of armour to tell him that her mother would be incapable of even speaking to him until midday. She walked round the side of the building and headed towards the house.

'Mr Leonetti is waiting for you at the helicopter.'

So, he was planning to toss a two-minute speech at her and depart, Poppy gathered ruefully. It didn't sound as though he'd had a change of heart, did it? She followed the path to the helipad at the far side of the hall, identifying Gaetano as the taller man in the small clump of waiting males who included the pilot and Gaetano's security staff. In a pale grey exquisitely tailored designer suit, his arrogant dark head held high, Gaetano looked like a king, and as she moved towards him he stood there much like a king waiting for her to come to him. So, what was new? Gaetano Leonetti didn't have a humble bone in his magnificent body.

No, no, less of the magnificent, she scolded herself angrily. No way was she going to look admiringly at the male making her and her family homeless, even if he did have just cause!

'Good morning, Poppy,' Gaetano drawled, smooth as glass, scanning her appearance in the form-fitting black dress that brushed her knees and what appeared to be combat boots with keen appreciation. The jacket looked as if it belonged to a circus ringmaster and he almost smiled at the prospect of his grandfather's disquiet. Clearly, Poppy always dressed strangely and he could certainly work with that eccentricity. In fact the more eccentricities, the better. And she looked amazingly well in that weird outfit with her freckle-free skin like whipped cream and her hair tumbling in silky bronzed ringlets round her slight shoulders, highlighting her alluring face.

He was not attracted to her, he told himself resolutely. He could appreciate a woman's looks without wanting to bed her. He wasn't that basic in his tastes, was he? The incipient throb of a hard-on, however, hinted that he might be a great deal more basic than he wanted to believe. Of course that was acceptable too, Gaetano conceded shrewdly. Rodolfo was no fool and would soon notice any apparent lack of sexual chemistry.

Poppy thought about faking a posh accent like his and abandoned the idea because Gaetano would be slow to see the joke, if he saw one at all. 'Morning,' she said lazily in her usual abbreviated style.

'We're going out for breakfast since there's no food in the house,' Gaetano murmured huskily.

Poppy blinked, catching the flick of censure but too caught up in the positive purr of his deep, slightly accented drawl, which was sending a peculiar little shiver down her taut spine. *'We?'* she queried belatedly, green eyes opening very wide.

Gaetano noted that her pupils were surrounded by a ring of tawny brown that merely emphasised the bright green of her eyes and said quietly, 'I have a proposition I want to discuss with you.'

'A proposition?' she questioned with a frown.

'Breakfast,' Gaetano reminded her and he bent to plant his hands to her hips and swing her up into the helicopter before she could even guess his intention.

'For breakfast we get into a helicopter?' Poppy framed in bewilderment.

'We're going to a hotel.'

A proposition? Her mind was blank as to what possible suggestions he might be able to put to her in her family's current predicament and, although she was far from entertained by his virtual kidnapping, she knew she was in no position to tell him to get lost. Even so, Poppy would very much have enjoyed telling Gaetano to get lost. His innate dominant traits set her teeth on edge, not to mention the manner in which he simply assumed that everyone around him would jump to do his bidding without argument. And he was probably right in that assumption, she thought resentfully. He had money, power and influence and she had none of those things.

The craft was so noisy that there was no possibility of conversation during the short flight. Poppy peered down without surprise as the biggest, flashiest country-house hotel in the area appeared below them. Only the very best would do for Gaetano, she thought in exasperation, wishing she'd had some warning of his plan. She had no make-up on and not even a comb with her and wasn't best pleased to find herself about to enter a very snooty five-star establishment where everyone else, including her host, would be groomed to perfection. And here she was wearing combat boots ready to cycle to the shop for a newspaper.

Deliberately avoiding Gaetano's extended arms, Poppy jumped down onto the grass. 'You could've warned me about where we were going... I'm not dressed—'

Gaetano dealt her a slow-burning smile, dark golden eyes brilliant in the sunshine. 'You look fabulous.'

Her mouth ran dry and suddenly she needed a deep breath but somehow couldn't get sufficient oxygen into her lungs. That shockingly appealing smile...when he had never smiled at her before. Gaetano was as stingy as a miser with his smiles. Why *was* he suddenly smiling at her? What did he want? What had changed? And why was he telling her that she looked *fabulous*? Especially when his raised-brow appraisal as she'd approached him at the helipad had told her that he knew about as much about her style as she knew about high finance.

At the door of the hotel they were greeted by the manager as though they were royalty and ushered to the 'Orangery' where Gaetano was assured that they would not be disturbed. Had there been a chaise longue, Poppy would have flopped down on it like a Victorian maiden and would have asked Gaetano if he was planning a seduction just to annoy him. But if he had a proposition that might ease her family's current situation she was more than willing to listen without making cheeky comments, she told herself. Unfortunately, her tongue often ran ahead of her brain, especially around Gaetano, who didn't have to do much to infuriate her.

CHAPTER THREE

'THAT...ER...' POPPY hastily revised the word she had
been about to employ for a more tactful one. 'That
remark you made about there being no food in the
house... We didn't know you were coming to the hall,'
she reminded him.

Gaetano watched a waiter pull out a chair for Poppy
before taking his own seat. Sunshine was cascading
through the windows, transforming her bright hair into
a fiery halo. She clutched her menu and ordered chocolate cereal and a hot-chocolate drink. He was astonished
that the vast number of menu options had not tempted
her into a more adventurous order.

'The hall is supposed to be kept fully stocked at all
times,' Gaetano reminded her, having ordered.

Poppy shifted in her seat. 'But this way is much more
cost-effective, Gaetano. When I took over from Mum I
was chucking out loads of fresh food every week and it
hurt me to do it when there are people starving in this
world. Until yesterday, someone always phoned to say
you'd be visiting, so I cancelled the food deliveries...
Oh, yes, and the flowers as well. I'm not into weekly

flower arranging. I've saved you so much money,' she told him with pride.

'I don't need to save money. I expect the house to always be ready for use,' Gaetano countered drily.

Poppy gave him a pained look. 'But it's so wasteful…'

Gaetano shrugged. He had never thought about that aspect and did not see why he should consider it when he gave millions to charitable causes every year. Convenience and the ability to do as he liked, when he liked, and at short notice, were very important to him, because he rarely took time away from work. 'I'm not tight with cash,' he said wryly. 'If the house isn't prepared for immediate use, I can't visit whenever I take the notion.'

Poppy ripped open her small packet of cereal and poured it into the bowl provided. Ignoring the milk on offer, she began to eat the cereal dry with her fingers the way she always ate it. For a split second, Gaetano stared but said nothing. For that same split second she had felt slightly afraid that he might give her a slap across the knuckles for what he deemed to be poor table manners and she flushed pink with chagrin, determined not to alter her behaviour to kowtow to his different expectations. The rich were definitely different, she conceded ruefully.

'I will eat chocolate any way I can get it,' she confided nonetheless in partial apology. 'I don't like my cereal soggy. Now this proposition you mentioned…'

'My grandfather wants me to get married before I can become Chief Executive of the Leonetti Bank. As I don't want to get married, I believe a fake engagement would keep him happy in the short term. It will convince Rodolfo that I am moving in the right direction and assuage his fear that I'm incapable of settling down.'

'So, why are you telling me this?' Poppy asked him blankly.

'I want you to partner me in the fake engagement.' Gaetano lounged lithely back in his seat to study her reaction.

'You and me?' A peal of startled laughter erupted from Poppy's lush pink mouth beneath Gaetano's disconcerted gaze. 'You've got to be kidding. No one, but no one, would credit you and me as a couple!'

'Funny, you didn't see it as being that amusing when you were a teenager,' Gaetano derided softly.

'You are *such* a bastard!' Poppy sprang out of her chair, all pretence of cool abandoned as she stalked away from the table. She had never quite contrived to lose that tender, stinging sense of rejection and humiliation even though she knew she was being ridiculous. After all, she had been far too young and naïve for him as well as being the daughter of an employee, and for him to respond in any way, even had he wanted to, would have been inappropriate. But while her brain assured her of those facts, her visceral reaction was at another level.

A few weeks after his rebuff, the annual hall summer picnic had been held and Gaetano had put in his appearance with a girlfriend. Poppy had felt sick when she'd seen that shiny, beautifully dressed and classy girl who might have stepped straight out of a glossy modelling advertisement. She had seen how pathetic it had been to harbour even the smallest hope of ever attracting Gaetano's interest and as a result of that distress, that horrid feeling of unworthiness and mortification, she had plunged herself into a very unwise situation.

'Poppy...' Gaetano murmured wryly, wishing he had left that reminder of the past decently buried.

Poppy spun back to him, eyes wide and accusing. 'I was sixteen years old, for goodness' sake, and you were the only fanciable guy in my radius, so it's hardly surprising that I got a crush on you. It was hormones, nothing else. I wasn't mature enough to recognise that you were *totally* the wrong kind of guy for me—'

'Why?' Gaetano heard himself demand baldly, although no sooner had he asked than he was questioning why he had.

Poppy was equally surprised by that question. Her colour high, she stared at him, her clear green eyes luminescent in the sunlight. 'Why? Well, I've no doubt you're a great catch, being both rich and ridiculously good-looking,' she told him bluntly. 'You're a fiercely ambitious high achiever but you don't have heart. You're deadly serious and conventional too. We're complete opposites. People would only pair the two of us together in a comic book. Sorry, I hope I haven't insulted you in any way. That wasn't my intention.'

An almost imperceptible line of colour had fired along the exotic slant of Gaetano's spectacular cheekbones. He felt oddly as though he had been cut down to size and yet he couldn't fault what she had said because it was all true. There was an electric little silence. He glanced up from below his lashes and saw her standing there in the bright sunshine, her hair a blazing nimbus of red, bronze and gold in the light to give her the look of a fiery angel. Or in that severe black dress, a gothic angel of death? But it didn't matter because in that strange little instant when time stopped dead, Gaetano, rigid with raw arousal, wanted Poppy Arnold more than he had ever wanted any woman in his life and it gave him the chills like the scent of a good deal going bad. He breathed in slow and deep and looked away from her, battling to regain his logic and cool.

'I still want you to take on the role of playing my fake fiancée,' he breathed in a roughened undertone because just looking at her, drinking in that clear creamy skin, those luminous green eyes and that pink succulent mouth, was only making him harder than ever. 'Rodolfo always wanted me to choose an ordinary girl and you are the only one I know likely to fit the bill.'

Something in the way he was studying her made Poppy's mouth run dry and her breath hitch in her throat. She was suddenly aware of her body in a way she hadn't been aware of it in years. In fact, her physical reactions were knocking her right back to the discomfiting level of the infatuated teenager she had once been and that galled her, but the tight, prickling sensation in her breasts and the dampness between her thighs were uniquely memorable testaments to the temptation Gaetano provided. Falling for a very good-looking guy at sixteen and comparing every other man she had met afterwards to his detriment was not to be recommended

as a life plan for any sensible woman, she reflected ruefully, ashamed of the fact that she couldn't treat Gaetano
as casually as she treated other men.

'An ordinary girl?' she questioned with pleated
brows, returning to the table to succumb to the allure
of the melted marshmallows topping her hot chocolate.
While she sipped, Gaetano filled her in on his grandfather's fond hopes for his future.

Poppy almost found herself laughing again. Gaetano
would never genuinely *want* an ordinary girl and no ordinary girl would be able to cope with his essentially
cold heart.

'So, why me?' she pressed.

'You're beautiful enough to convince him that I
could be tempted by you—'

Guileless green eyes assailed his. 'Am I?'

'Yes, you're beautiful but, no, I'm not tempted,'
Gaetano declared with stubborn conviction. 'When I
say fake engagement I mean fake in *every* way. I will
not be touching you.'

Poppy rolled her eyes. 'I wouldn't let you. I'm very,
very picky, Gaetano.'

Gaetano resisted the urge to toss up the name of that
young estate worker she had entertained in the shrubbery. Odd how he had never forgotten those details, he
conceded, while recognising that such a crack would
be cruelly inappropriate because she was as entitled
to have enjoyed sex as any other woman. His perfect
white teeth clenched together. He loathed the way Poppy
somehow knocked him off-balance, tripping his mind
into random thoughts, persuading his usually controlled

tongue into making ill-advised remarks, turning him on when he didn't want to be turned on. Each and every one of those reactions offended Gaetano's pride in his strength of will.

'You've got to be wondering what would be in this arrangement for you,' Gaetano intoned quietly. 'Everything you want and need at present. Rehabilitation treatment for your mother, a fresh start somewhere, a new home for you all as security. I'll cover the cost of it all if you do this for me, *bella mia*.'

Straight off, Poppy saw that he was throwing her and her family a lifebelt when they were drowning and for that reason she didn't voice the refusal already brimming on her lips. Treatment for her mother. You couldn't put a price on such an offer. It was what she had dreamt about but knew she would never be able to afford.

'You've got to have a selfish bone somewhere in your body,' Gaetano declared. 'If you get your mother sorted out you can get your own life back and complete your nursing training, if that is still what you want to do.'

'I'm not sure I could be convincing as your ordinary-girl fiancée—'

'We'll cover that. Leave the worrying to me. I'm a skilled strategist,' Gaetano murmured, lush black lashes low over his beautiful dark golden eyes.

Her chest swelled as she dragged in a deep breath because really there was no decision to be made. Any attempt to sort out the mess her mother's life had become was worth a try. 'Then…where do I sign up?'

She had agreed. Having recognised that Poppy was pretty much between a rock and a hard place, Gaetano was not surprised by her immediate agreement. In his opinion she had much to gain and nothing at all to lose.

'So…er…' Poppy began uncertainly. 'You'll want me to dress up more…?'

A sudden wolfish smile flashed across Gaetano's lean, darkly handsome features. 'No, that's exactly what I don't want,' he assured her. 'Rodolfo would see straight through you trying to pretend to be something you're not. I don't want you to feel the need to change anything—just be yourself.'

'Myself…' Poppy repeated a tad dizzily as she collided with shimmering dark golden eyes fringed by those glorious spiky black lashes of his.

'Be yourself,' Gaetano stressed, severely disconcerting her because she had expected him to want to change everything about her. 'My grandfather, like me, respects individuality.'

Poppy wondered how it was then that, even in recent years, she had noticed from reading the papers, and catching a glimpse or two of past companions at the hall, Gaetano's women all seemed to be formed from the same identikit model. All were small, blonde and blue-eyed arm-clingers, who appeared to have no personality at all in his presence. The sort of women who simpered, hung on his every word and acted super-attentive to their man. No, Gaetano had definitely never struck her as a male likely to appreciate individuality.

'I would have another request,' she said daringly. 'My brother's a fully qualified mechanic. Find him a job.'

Gaetano frowned. 'He's an—'

'An ex-con. Yes, we are well aware of that, but he needs a proper job before he can hope to rebuild his life,' she pointed out. 'I'd be very grateful if there was anything you could do to help Damien.'

Gaetano's beautifully shaped mouth tightened. 'You drive a hard bargain. I'll make enquiries.'

Almost a full month after that breakfast, Poppy was sitting in the kitchen with her mother. Jasmine was studying her daughter and looking troubled, an expression that had become increasingly frequent on her face as she slowly emerged from the shrouding fog of alcoholic dependency and realised what had been happening in the world around her. Initial assessment followed by several sessions with trained counsellors and medication for her depression had brought about an improvement in Jasmine's state of mind. The older woman was trying not to drink, not doing very well so far but at least trying, something she had not even been prepared to contemplate just weeks earlier. This very afternoon Poppy and her mother were heading to London where Poppy would join Gaetano and take up her role as a fake fiancée while Jasmine embarked on a residential stay in a top-flight private clinic renowned for its success with patients.

'I just don't want to see you get hurt,' the older woman repeated, squeezing her daughter's hand. 'Gaetano is a real box of tricks. I appreciate his help, but I would never fully trust him. He's too clever and he hasn't got his granddad's humanity. I can't understand what's in this masquerade for Gaetano—'

'Climbing the career ladder at the bank—promotion. Seems that Rodolfo Leonetti is a real stick-in-the-mud about Gaetano still being single.' Poppy sighed, having already been through this dialogue several times with her mother and wishing the subject could simply be dropped.

'Yes, but how will it benefit Gaetano when your engagement is broken off again?' Jasmine prompted. 'That's the bit I don't get.'

Poppy didn't really get it either but kept that to herself. How was she supposed to know what went on in Gaetano's multifaceted brain? Apart from anything else she'd had hardly any contact with him since that hotel breakfast they'd shared. He had phoned her with instructions and information about arrangements for her mother and travel plans, but he had not returned to the hall. In the meantime, a new housekeeper had moved into Woodfield Hall and Poppy assumed that the giant refrigerator was being kept fully stocked and vases of flowers were now once again decorating the mansion for the owner who never visited. Gaetano had dismissed Poppy's opinions with an assurance that made it clear that his household arrangements were not and never would be any of her business.

The helicopter picked them up at two in the afternoon. Poppy had packed for both her and her mother, who was being taken to the clinic. Jasmine was nervous and not entirely sober when they boarded and fairly shaky on her legs by the time they landed in London, leaning on her daughter's arm for support.

Gaetano, however, didn't even notice Jasmine Arnold. He was too busy watching Poppy stroll towards him with that lithe, lazy walk of hers. She wore black and red plaid leggings and a black tee, her hair falling in wind-tousled curls round her heart-shaped face. He saw other men taking a second glance at her and it annoyed him. She was unusual and it gave her a distinction that he couldn't quite put a label on but one quality she had in spades and that was sex appeal, he acknowledged grimly, struggling to maintain control of what lay south of his belt. He would get accustomed to her and that response would fade because nothing, not one single intimate thing, was going to take place between them. This was business and he was no soft touch.

The staff member from the clinic designated to pick up Jasmine intercepted Poppy and her mother. The women parted with a hug and tears in their eyes, for the guidelines of Jasmine's treatment plan had warned that the clinic preferred there to be no contact between their patients and families during the first few weeks of treatment. That was why Poppy's first view of Gaetano was blurred because she had been watching her mother nervously walk away and, while knowing that she was doing the best thing possible for her troubled parent, she still felt horribly guilty about it.

'Poppy...' Gaetano murmured, one of his security men taking immediate charge of her luggage trolley.

His lean, darkly handsome features swam through the glimmer of tears in her wide eyes and sliced right through her detachment. He looked utterly gorgeous, sheathed in designer jeans and a casual white and blue striped shirt that accentuated the glow of his bronzed skin colour. For a split second, Poppy simply stared in search of a flaw in his classically beautiful face. At some stage she stopped breathing without realising it and, connecting with dark golden eyes the same shade as melting honey, she suddenly felt so hot she was vaguely surprised that people didn't rush up with fire extinguishers to put out the blaze. Her heartbeat thumped as the noise of their surroundings inexplicably ebbed. A little tweaking sensation in her pelvis caused her to shift her feet while her nipples pinched full and tight below her tee.

'G-Gaetano…' she stammered, barely able to find her voice as she fought a desperate rearguard reaction to what she belatedly realised was a very dangerous susceptibility to Gaetano's magnetic attraction.

Gaetano was taking in the tenting prominence of her nipples below her top and idly wondering what colour they were, arousal moving thickly and hungrily through his blood as he studied her lush pink mouth. 'We're going straight back to my house,' he told her brusquely, snapping back to full attention. 'You've got work to do this evening.'

'Work?' Poppy parroted in surprise as she fell into step by his side.

'I've made up some prompt sheets for you to cover the sort of details you would be expected to know about me if we were in a genuine relationship,' he explained. 'Once you memorise all that we'll be ready to go tomorrow.'

'*Tomorrow?*' She gasped in dismay because seemingly he wasn't giving her any time at all to practise her new role or even prepare for it.

'It's Rodolfo's seventy-fifth birthday and he's throwing an afternoon party. Obviously we will be attending it as an engaged couple,' Gaetano explained smoothly.

Nerves clenched and twisted in Poppy's uneasy tummy. She had probably met Rodolfo Leonetti at some stage but she had no memory of the occasion and could only recall seeing him in the distance at the hall when he had still lived there. She had known his late wife, Serafina, well, however, and remembered her clearly. Gaetano's grandmother had been a lovely woman, who treated everyone the same, be they rich or poor, family or staff. Alongside Jasmine, Serafina had taught Poppy how to bake. Recollecting that, Poppy knew exactly what she would be doing in terms of a gift for the older man's birthday.

Her cases were stowed in the sleek expensive car Gaetano had brought to the airport. Damien could probably have told her everything about the vehicle because he was a car buff, but Poppy was too busy marvelling that Gaetano had taken the time to come and pick her up personally and that he was actually driving himself.

His phone rang as they left the airport behind. It was in hands-free mode and the voluble burst of Italian that banished the silence in the car only made Poppy feel more out on a limb than ever. She had to toughen up, she told herself firmly, and regain her confidence. Gaetano had given her the equivalent of a high-paid job and she planned to do the best she could to meet his no doubt high expectations but secretly, deep down inside where only she knew how she felt, Poppy was totally terrified of doing something wrong and letting Gaetano down.

Gaetano was so incredibly particular, she reflected absently, recalling the look on his face when she'd eaten her chocolate cereal with her fingers. Even little mistakes would probably irritate Gaetano. He wasn't tolerant or understanding. No, Poppy knew it wasn't going to be easy to fake anything to Gaetano's satisfaction. In fact she reckoned she was in for a long, hard walk down a road strewn with endless obstacles. While the animated dialogue in Italian went on for what seemed a very long time, Poppy looked out at the busy London streets. Once or twice when she glanced in the other direction she noted the aggressive angle of Gaetano's jaw line that suggested tension and picked up on the hard edge to his dark-timbre drawl and clipped responses.

'Our goose has been cooked,' Gaetano breathed curtly when the phone call was over. 'That was Rodolfo. He wants to meet you now.'

'Now…like right now, *today*?' Poppy exclaimed in dismay.

'Like right now,' Gaetano growled. 'And you're not ready.'

Poppy's eyes flashed. 'And whose fault is that?'

'What do you mean?'

'You shouldn't have waited until the last possible moment to clue me up on what I'm supposed to know about you,' Poppy pointed out without hesitation. 'Sensible people prepare for anything important *more* than one day in advance.'

'Don't you dare start criticising me!' Gaetano erupted,

sharply disconcerting her as he flashed a look of angry, flaming censure. 'It's more than twenty-four hours since I even slept. We've had a crisis deal at the bank and this stupid business was the very last thing on my mind.'

'If it's so stupid you can forget about it again.' Poppy proffered that get-out clause stiffly. 'Don't mind me. This was, after all, *your* idea, *all* your idea.'

'I can't forget about it again when I've already told Rodolfo I'm engaged!' Gaetano launched back at her furiously. 'Whether I like it or not, I'm *stuck* with you and faking it!'

'Oh, goody…aren't I the lucky girl?' Poppy murmured in a poisonous undertone intended to sting. 'You're such a catch, Gaetano. All that money and success but not a single ounce of charm!'

'Be quiet!' Gaetano raked at her with incredulity.

'Go stuff yourself!' Poppy tossed back fierily as he shot the car to a halt outside a tall town house in a fancy street embellished with a central garden.

'And you're stuck with me,' Gaetano asserted with grim satisfaction as he closed her wrist in a grip of steel to prevent her leaping out of the car. He flipped open the ring box in his other hand and removed the diamond engagement ring to shove it onto her wedding finger with no ceremony whatsoever.

'Oh, dear…ugly ring alert,' Poppy snapped, studying the huge diamond solitaire with unappreciative eyes. 'Of course, it's one of those fake diamonds…right?'

'Of course it's not a fake!' Gaetano bit out, what little patience he had decimated by lack of sleep and her unexpectedly challenging behaviour.

'It's hard to believe that you can spend that much money and end up with something that looks like it fell out of a Christmas cracker.' Poppy groaned. 'I can't go in there, Gaetano.'

'Get out of the car,' he urged, leaning across to open the door for her. 'Of course you can go in there and wing it. Just look all intoxicated with your ring.'

'Yes, getting drunk in receipt of this non-example of good taste would certainly be understandable.'

'You're supposed to be in love with me!' Gaetano roared at her.

'Trouble is, you're about as loveable as a grizzly bear,' Poppy opined, walking round the bonnet and up onto the pavement. 'My acting skills may be poor but yours are a great deal worse.'

'What the hell are you talking about?' Gaetano squared up to her, six feet four inches of roaring aggression and impatience. 'It's time to stop messing about and start acting.'

Poppy lifted a hand and stabbed his broad muscular chest with a combative forefinger. 'But you *said* you wanted me to be myself. What exactly do you want, Gaetano?'

'*Porca miseria!* I want you to stop driving me insane!' Gaetano bit out wrathfully, backing her up against the wing of the car, long powerful thighs entrapping her. 'I will tell you only once. If you can't do as you're told you're out of here!'

'I'm only just resisting the urge to use some very rude words,' Poppy warned him, standing her ground with defiant green eyes. 'This is all *your* fault. You've dragged me here straight from the airport knowing I'm not remotely prepared for this meeting.'

And for Gaetano, whose aggressive need to dominate had emerged in the nursery when he had systematically bullied his first nanny into letting him do pretty much whatever he wanted, that resistance was like a red rag to a bull. Totally unaware of anything beyond the overwhelming desire to touch her while forcing her to do what he wanted her to do, Gaetano snapped an arm round her and kissed her.

His mouth slammed down on hers and it was as if the world stopped dead and then closed round that moment. She was in such a rage with him, it was a reflex reaction for Poppy to close her teeth together, refusing him entry. He shifted against her, all lean, sinuous, powerful male, and the erection she could feel nudging against her stomach sent the most overwhelming awareness shimmying through her like a dangerous drug. The heat and strength of him against her was even more arousing and she unclamped her teeth for him, helpless in the grip of the driving hunger that had captured her and destroyed her opposition.

With a hungry groan, his tongue eased into her mouth and it was without a doubt the most heart-stopping instant of sensation she had ever experienced as his tongue teased and tangled with hers before plunging deep. An ache she had never felt in a man's arms before hollowed almost painfully at the heart of her and she was pushing instinctively against him even as he urged her back against the car, so that they were welded together so tight a card couldn't have slid between them.

Her arms went round him, massaging up over his wide shoulders before sliding up to lace into his luxuriant black hair and then raking down again over his muscled arms to spread across his taut masculine ass. It was a mindless, addictive, totally visceral embrace.

In an abrupt movement, Gaetano stepped back from her, his breathing audible, sawing in and out of his big chest as if he had run a marathon. Poppy was all over the place mentally and she blinked, literally struggling to return to the real world while fighting a shocking desire to yank him bodily back to her. He was so hot at kissing she was ready to spontaneously combust. He might not have an ounce of charm but when it came to the sex stuff he was out at the front of the field, she decided, a burning blush warming her face as she too worked to get her breath back.

'Well…that was interesting,' she remarked shakily, feeling the need to say something, anything that might suggest that she had regained control when she had not.

Gaetano, who never, *ever* did PDAs with women, was horribly aware of his bodyguards standing by staring as if a little Martian had taken his place. In short, Gaetano was in shock but he also knew that if he had been parked somewhere private he would have had Poppy spread across the bonnet while he plunged into her lithe body hard and fast and sated the appalling level of hunger coursing through his lower body. He ached; he ached so bad he wanted to groan out loud. Dark colour etched the line of his high cheekbones.

'Let's go inside,' he suggested in a driven undertone. 'Just take your lead from me, *bella mia.*'

And won't doing exactly as Gaetano tells you be fun? a little devil enquired inside Poppy's bemused head. If it had related to kissing, she would have been queuing up, she conceded numbly. Nobody had ever made her feel so much with one kiss. In fact she hadn't known it was even possible to be that turned on by a man after just one kiss. Gaetano had hidden depths, dark, sexy depths, but she had not the smallest intention of plumbing those depths...

CHAPTER FOUR

'I SAW YOU ARRIVE,' Rodolfo Leonetti volunteered, disconcerting his grandson. 'It looked as though you were having words.'

Poppy almost froze by Gaetano's side, her discomfiture sweeping through her like a tidal wave. Gaetano's grandfather didn't look his age. With his head of wavy grey hair and the upright stature of a much younger man, not to mention a height not far short of Gaetano's, he still looked strong and vital. He greeted her with a kiss on both cheeks and smiled warmly at her before unleashing that unsettling comment on Gaetano.

'We were having a row,' Poppy was taken aback to hear Gaetano admit. 'Poppy doesn't like her engagement ring. Perhaps I should have taken her with me to choose it…'

Rodolfo widened his shrewd dark eyes. 'My grandson left you out of that selection?'

Pink and flustered by the speed with which Gaetano plotted and reacted in a tight corner, Poppy said, 'I'm afraid so…' In an uncertain movement she extended her hand for the older man to study the ring.

'You could see that diamond from outer space,' Rodolfo remarked, straight-faced.

'It's beautiful,' Poppy hastened to add.

'Be honest, you hate it,' Gaetano encouraged, having told the story, clearly happy to go with the flow.

'It's too bling for me,' she murmured dutifully, sinking down into the comfortable seat Rodolfo had indicated. Her nerves were strung so tight that her very face felt stiff with tension. She barely had the awareness to take in the beautiful big reception room, which strongly resembled the splendour of the reception rooms at Woodfield Hall.

'I was very sorry to hear about your mother's problems,' Gaetano's grandfather said while Poppy was pouring the tea, having been invited to do the hostess thing for the first time in her life. She almost dropped the teapot at Rodolfo's quietly offered expression of sympathy. Evidently Gaetano had been honest about her mother's predicament. 'I'm sure the clinic will help her.'

'I hope so.' Poppy compressed her lips as Rodolfo got to his feet and excused himself. As the door swung in his wake, Poppy groaned out loud. 'I'm no good at this, Gaetano—'

'You'll improve. He must've seen us kissing. That will have at least made us look like a proper couple,' he pointed out soft and low. 'Sometimes not having a script is better.'

'I would work better from a script.' She slanted a glance at him, encountering smouldering dark golden eyes, and pink surged into her cheeks.

Rodolfo reappeared and sank back into his seat. He

had a small box in his hand, which he opened. 'This was your grandmother's ring. As all her jewellery will go to your wife I thought it would be a good idea to let Poppy have a look at Serafina's engagement ring now.'

Poppy stared in astonished recognition at the fine diamond and ruby cluster on display. 'I remember your wife taking it off when she was baking,' she shared quietly. 'It's a fabulous ring.'

'It belongs to you now,' Rodolfo said with gentle courtesy and the sadness in his creased eyes made her eyes sting.

'She was a lovely person,' Poppy whispered shakily.

Gaetano couldn't credit what he was seeing. His fake fiancée and Rodolfo were having a mutual love-in, full of exchanged glances and sentimental smiles of understanding. His grandfather was sliding his beloved late wife's ring onto Poppy's finger as if she were Cinderella having the glass slipper fitted.

'I believe she would have been happy for you to wear it,' the old man said fondly, admiring it on Poppy's hand, the giant diamond solitaire purchased by Gaetano now abandoned on the coffee table.

'Thank you very much,' Poppy responded chokily. 'It's gorgeous.'

'And it comes with a very happy history in its back story,' Rodolfo shared mistily.

Gaetano wanted to groan out loud. He wanted his grandfather to disapprove of Poppy, not welcome her with open arms and start patting her hand while he talked happily about his late wife, Serafina. Of course, a little initial enthusiasm was to be expected, he reasoned shrewdly, and Rodolfo would hardly feel critical in the first fine flush of his approval of the step that Gaetano had taken.

Afternoon tea stretched into dinner, by which time Gaetano was heartily bored with family stories. With admirable tact and patience, however, Poppy had listened with convincing interest to his grandfather recount Leonetti family history. She had much better manners than Gaetano had expected and her easy relaxation with the older man was even more noteworthy because few people relaxed around Rodolfo, who was considerably more clever and ruthless than he appeared. If Poppy had been his real fiancée, Gaetano would have been ecstatic at the warmth of her reception. Indeed one could have been forgiven for thinking that Rodolfo had waited his entire life praying for the joy of seeing his grandson bring the housekeeper's daughter home and announce that he was planning to marry her. Only when Poppy began smothering yawns did Gaetano's torture end.

'Time for us to leave.' Gaetano tugged a drooping Poppy out of her seat with a powerful hand.

'Hope we don't have to go far,' she mumbled sleepily.

Encountering the older man's startled glance at his bride-to-be's ignorance, Gaetano straightened and smiled. 'She hasn't been here before,' he pointed out. 'I wanted to surprise her.'

'What surprise?' Poppy pressed as he walked her out of the drawing room.

'Rodolfo had an entire wing of this house converted

for me to occupy ten years ago,' he told her, throwing wide a door at the foot of the corridor. 'All we have to do is walk through a connecting door and we're in my space.'

And even drowsy as she was it was very obvious to Poppy that Gaetano's part of the house was a hugely different space. Rich colours, heavy fabrics and polished antiques were replaced by contemporary stone floors, pale colours and plain furniture. It was as distinct as night was to day from his grandfather's house. 'Elegant,' she commented.

'I'm glad you think so.' Gaetano showed her upstairs into the master bedroom. 'This is where we sleep...'

Poppy froze, her brain snapping into gear again. *'We?'*

'We can't stay this close to Rodolfo and pretend to be engaged *without* sharing a room,' Gaetano fired back at her impatiently. 'His staff service this place as well as his.'

'But you didn't *warn* me about this!' Poppy objected. 'Naturally I assumed you had an apartment somewhere on your own where I'd have my own room.'

'Well, you can't have your own room here,' Gaetano informed her without apology. 'Doubtless Rodolfo would like to think you're the vestal-virgin type, but he wouldn't find it credible that I had asked you to marry me...'

Poppy studied the huge divan sleigh bed and her soft mouth compressed. 'For goodness' sake, there's only one bed...and I'm not sharing it with you!'

'You have to sleep in here with me. There's a downside for both of us in this arrangement,' Gaetano countered grimly.

'And what's *your* downside?' Poppy asked with interest.

'Celibacy,' Gaetano intoned very drily. 'I can't risk being seen or associated with any other woman while I'm supposed to be engaged to you.'

'Oh, dear…' Poppy commented without an atom of sympathy. 'From what I've read about your usual pursuits in the press, that will be a character-building challenge for you.'

Exasperation laced Gaetano's lean, darkly handsome features. He would never ever hurt a woman but there were times when he wanted to plunge Poppy head first into a mud bath. 'There's a lot of rubbish talked about my private life in the newspapers.'

'That line might work with one of your socialites, Gaetano…but *not* with me. I know that party *did* take place and what happened at it.'

Gaetano fought the urge to defend himself and collided with her witchy green eyes and momentarily forgot what he had been about to say. 'I'm going for a shower,' he said instead and began to undress.

Leonetti flesh alert! screamed a little voice in Poppy's head as Gaetano shed his shirt without inhibition. And why would he be inhibited when he was unveiling a work of art? He was all sleek muscle from the vee above his lean hips to the corrugated muscular flatness of his abdomen and the swelling power of his pectoral muscles. Her mouth ran dry. She might not be the vestal-virgin type but she *was* a virgin and she had never shared a room with a half-naked male before. That was not information she planned to share with Gaetano, especially as she pretty much blamed him for the reality that she had yet to take that sexual plunge in adulthood.

At sixteen, after his rejection, she had almost decided to have sex with someone else but had realised what she was doing in time and had called a halt before things got out of hand. She wasn't proud of that episode, well aware that she had acted like a bit of a tease with the boy concerned. Her real lesson had been grasping that going off to have mindless sex with someone else because Gaetano didn't want her was pathetic and silly. While she was at college doing her nursing training she had had boyfriends and occasional little moments of temptation but nobody had tempted her as much as Gaetano had once tempted her. And Poppy was stubborn and had decided that she would only sleep with someone when she really, *really* wanted to. She wasn't going to have sex just because some man expected it of her, nor was she planning to have sex just for the sake of it.

Poppy opened one of her cases and only then appreciated that her luggage had already been unpacked for her. So this was how the rich lived, she thought ruefully, wondering what she was going to use as pyjamas when she didn't ever wear them because she preferred to sleep naked. She had nothing big enough to cover her decently in mixed company and she rifled through Gaetano's drawers to borrow a big white tee shirt that was both large and sexless. He might have forgotten that kiss, that terrifying surge of limitless hunger…but she hadn't and she had no plans to tempt fate.

* * *

Gaetano was thinking about sex in the shower and wondering if Poppy would consider broadening their agreement. He wanted her and she wanted him. To his outlook that was a simple balanced equation and it made sense that they should make the most of each other for the duration of their relationship. It was the practical solution and Gaetano was always practical, particularly when it came to his high sex drive.

A towel knotted round his lean hips, Gaetano trod back into the bedroom. Poppy took one look at all that bronzed skin still sprinkled with drops of water and re-alised that she wanted to lick him like a postage stamp. With a stifled groan at her own atrocious weakness, she pushed past him and went into the bathroom to get changed.

Gaetano pulled on boxers on the grounds that it never paid to take anything for granted with women and that doing so only annoyed them. Poppy emerged from the bathroom wearing what could only be one of his tee shirts because it hung off her slender frame in loose folds. Even so, it still couldn't hide the promi-nent little peaks of her breasts, the womanly curve of her hips or the perfection of the long shapely legs below the hem.

'I have a suggestion to make,' Gaetano murmured huskily.

'Do I want to hear this?' Poppy wisecracked, pushing back the bedding and scrambling into the bed, feeling her limbs settle into an incredibly soft and supportive mattress that was a far cry from the ancient lumpy bed of her youth. Wearing only silk boxers Gaetano was an outrageously masculine presence and very hard for Poppy to ignore. She was trying to respect his space by not looking at him and hoping he would award her the same courtesy of acting as though she were still fully clothed.

'We have to pretend to be lovers,' Gaetano pointed out.

Wondering in what possible direction that statement could be travelling, Poppy prompted, 'Yes…so?'

'Why don't we make it real?' Gaetano drawled, smooth as melted honey.

Her vocal cords went into arrest and respecting his space suddenly became much too challenging. *'Real?'* Poppy exclaimed loudly. 'What exactly do you mean by real?'

'You're not that innocent,' Gaetano assured her lazily as he sprang into bed beside her.

'So, you're suggesting that we have sex because you don't fancy celibacy?' Poppy enquired, delicate auburn brows raised in disbelief.

'We are stuck in this situation,' Gaetano reminded her.

'I can live without sex,' Poppy told him tightly, feeling colour climb hotly towards her hairline because even saying 'sex' in Gaetano's presence made her feel horribly self-conscious.

'I can as well but not happily,' Gaetano told her bluntly. 'We're very attracted to each other. We might as well make the most of it.'

'Any port in a storm?' Poppy remarked without

amusement. 'I'm here in the bed and, as you see it, available, so I should be interested?'

Gaetano leant closer, his stubbled jaw line propped on the heel of his upraised hand as he gazed down at her with absolutely gorgeous dark golden eyes. 'I'm good, *bella mia*. You wouldn't be disappointed.'

Poppy was as frozen with fear as a woman facing a hungry cannibal might be. But insidious heat and dampness were welling in the tender place between her thighs, striving to work their wicked seductive magic on her resistance. In fact she could feel her whole body literally wake up, sit up and take notice of Gaetano's offer. He was offering her what she had once desperately wanted but on terms she could never accept. 'I don't want to be used.'

'I'm surprised you're so narrow in your outlook. Wouldn't you be using me to scratch the same itch?' Gaetano enquired softly.

Her whole face flamed and she flipped over on her side, turning her narrow back defensively on him. Get thee behind me, Satan, she thought helplessly. 'No, thanks,' she said chokily, unsure whether she wanted to laugh or cry at his blunt proposition. 'If I want meaningless sex I imagine I can get it just about anywhere.'

Gaetano stroked a long brown forefinger down her taut spinal cord. 'Sex with me wouldn't be meaningless. It would be amazing. You set me on fire, *gioia mia*.'

Poppy rolled her eyes. He was so slick and full of confidence but that caressing touch lingered with her, lighting up little pockets of melting willingness inside her treacherous body. 'I'll keep it in mind. If my itch has to be scratched I will seriously consider you,' she lied stonily.

'What more do you want from me?' Gaetano asked silkily. 'I'm honest. I'm clean. I don't lie or cheat.'

'It doesn't stop you from being a four-letter word of a man,' Poppy told him roundly. 'I thought Italian lovers were supposed to be the last word in seduction. You just turned me off big time.'

'I was respecting your intelligence by not shooting you a line,' Gaetano traded with husky amusement that laced through his dark deep drawl in a sexy, accented purr.

Poppy pictured herself flipping over and slapping him so hard his perfect teeth rattled in his too ingenious head. Her own teeth gritted aggressively. Without warning she was also imagining easing back into the hard, allmale heat of him while his arms closed round her and his hips moved against hers. And that sensual imagery was so energising that she felt boiling hot all over. Her nipples swelled and prickled and the heat in her pelvis mushroomed. Her face burned with shame in the darkness. Wanting was wanting, she reasoned with the sexual side of her nature, but it wasn't enough on its own. Gaetano wasn't the man for her, she reminded herself doggedly.

'You know, if you were a nice guy—'

'When did I ever say I was a nice guy?' Gaetano cut in sharply.

'You didn't,' Poppy conceded grudgingly, turning over to pick out the powerful silhouette of his head and shoulders in the dim light. 'But you shouldn't be thinking about your sex life. Right now you should be worrying more about how your grandfather is going to feel when this engagement falls through. Because he's making such an effort to be welcoming and accepting of someone like me, I think he'll be devastated when our relationship comes to nothing.'

'Allow me to know my own grandfather better than you.'

'You're too focused on your career plan to see beyond it. What I saw today was that Rodolfo was incredibly happy about you getting engaged. How could he be anything other than upset when it breaks down?'

Gaetano grimaced and flung his dark head back against the pillows. She didn't understand. How could she? He could hardly tell her that she was supposed to bomb as a fiancée so that her disappearance from his life again would be more worthy of celebration than disappointment. Time would take care of that problem. After all, she had most likely been on her very best behaviour at her first meeting with his grandfather and sooner rather than later she would probably let herself down.

'You used to swear a lot,' he remarked out of the blue.

'I picked it up at school because everyone used bad language. For a while I did it deliberately because I was being bullied and I was desperate to fit in,' she confided.

'Did it make a difference?'

'No,' she admitted with a wry laugh. 'Nothing I wore or did or said could make me cool. Being plump with red hair and living at Woodfield Hall with "those posh bastards" was a supreme provocation to the other pupils.'

'What did the bullies do?'

Thinking of her getting bullied, Gaetano was experiencing an extraordinary desire to pull her into his arms and comfort her. But he didn't do comforting. Indeed he was downright unnerved by that perverse impulse and he actually shifted as far away from her as he could get and still be in the same bed.

'All the usual. Name calling, tripping me up, nasty rumours and messages and texts,' she recited wearily. 'I hated school, couldn't wait to get out of there. Once I was out, I stopped swearing as soon as I realised it offended people.'

He was tempted to tell her that she had never been plump. She had simply developed her womanly curves before she shot up in height. But right then he didn't want to talk and he didn't want to think about curves, womanly or otherwise. His hunger for her was making him uncomfortable and that infuriated him because Gaetano had never hungered that much for one particular woman. Beautiful women had always been pretty much interchangeable for him. It was the challenge, he told himself impatiently. He only wanted her because she was saying no. But that simplistic belief didn't ease his tension in the slightest. It was, he decided grimly, likely to feel like a *very* long engagement.

First thing in the morning, Poppy looked amazing, Gaetano conceded hours later, studying her from across the bedroom. Her red hair streamed like a banner across

the pale bedding, framing her delicate face and the rose-
bud pout of her lips. A narrow shoulder protruded from
below his slipped tee shirt and the sheet was pushed
back to bare one leg from knee to slender ankle. And
that easily, that quickly, Gaetano had a hard-on again
and gritted his teeth in annoyance. What the hell was
it about her? He felt like a man trying to fight an invisible illness!

'Poppy…?'

She shifted in the bed, lashes fluttering up on luminous green eyes. 'Gaetano…?' she whispered drowsily.

'I left that prompt sheet I meant you to study last
night on the desk in my home office. I'll see you at Rodolfo's party at three.'

Poppy sat up in a panic. 'What will I wear?'

'Your usual clothes. Be yourself,' he reminded her
as he vanished out of the door.

Poppy scrambled out of bed to follow him. 'Where
are you going?'

Gaetano swung round and sent her a pained appraisal. 'Work…the bank.'

'Oh…' Having asked what appeared to be a stupid
question, Poppy ducked hastily back into the bedroom
and went for a shower while planning her own day.

First of all she had to go and buy the ingredients for
her present for Rodolfo's seventy-fifth. She could only
hope that she wasn't getting it wrong in the gift department. After that she had a rather more pressing need to
attend to: finding work for herself. She had just about
enough money in her purse to make Rodolfo's cake but
she had nothing more and no savings to fall back on.

The sleek granite-topped kitchen had a fridge packed with food and a very large selection of chocolate cereals that made her smile. Gaetano had remembered her preference. She ate while she studied the prompt sheets he had mentioned. It was like a CV written for a job: qualifications listed, sports pursuits outlined, not a single reference to any memorable moments. He just had no idea of the sort of things that a woman in love would want to know about him, Poppy reflected ruefully. When was his birthday? What was his favourite colour?

She texted him to ask.

Gaetano suppressed a groan when his phone buzzed yet again and lifted it to see what the latest irrelevant question was.

Who was the first woman you fell in love with?

He had never been in love and he was proud of it.

What do you value most in a woman?

Independence, he texted back.

As Poppy walked round the supermarket with her shopping list she raised her brows. If he liked independent women why did he always date clingy airheads? So, she asked that too and they began to argue by text until she was laughing. Gaetano had an image of himself that did not always match reality. She could have told him that he dated clingy airheads because they did as they were told, accepted his workaholic schedule and made few demands.

Noticing a 'help wanted' sign in the window of a café she called in, enjoyed an interview on the spot and was hired to work a shift that very evening. Relieved to have solved the problem of being broke, she returned to the town house by the separate entrance at the side and proceeded to mess up Gaetano's basically unused kitchen with her baking session. She settled the cake into the cake carrier she had bought for the purpose and set the birthday card on top of it before going to get changed.

She wore a tartan skirt with black lace stockings and high heels. Gaetano wolf-whistled the instant he saw her. 'Wow...' he breathed with quiet masculine appreciation. 'Your legs are to die for...'

'Really?' Poppy grinned and then frowned doubtfully. 'Is this phase one of the Italian seduction routine?'

'You're very suspicious.'

'I don't trust you,' Poppy told him truthfully. 'I think being sneaky would come naturally to you.'

'I've never had to be sneaky with women,' Gaetano told her truthfully.

The drawing room was crowded with guests when they arrived. The instant Poppy saw the fancy cocktail-type frocks and delicate jewellery that the other women sported and the stares that her informal outfit attracted, she paled in dismay. She stuck out like a sore thumb and hated the feeling, squirming discomfiture taking her by storm and reminding her of her days at school when no matter how hard she'd tried she had always failed to fit in. Remembering that Gaetano had urged her to be herself was not a consolation because her unconventional appearance *had* to be an embarrassment to him. How could it be anything else?

Gaetano's grandfather made a major production out of welcoming them and announcing their engagement. Poppy's guilt over their deception sent colour flying into her cheeks but she saw only satisfaction in Gaetano's brilliant smile and from it she deduced that everything was going the way he had planned.

But Poppy was wrong in that assumption. She served Rodolfo with the strawberry layer cake with mascarpone-cheese icing that was his favourite and which she had learned to bake at his wife's side. His eyes went all watery and he gave her an almost boyish grin as he took up the cake knife she passed him and cut himself a large helping.

'So, when's the big day?' he asked Poppy within Gaetano's hearing.

Gaetano tensed. 'We haven't set a date as yet...'

'You don't want to risk a treasure like Poppy getting away,' his grandfather warned him softly, shrewd eyes resting on his grandson's lean, darkly handsome face. 'I don't believe in long engagements.'

'We don't want to rush in either,' Poppy remarked carefully, instinct sending her to Gaetano's rescue.

'Next month would be a good time for me before I head off to Italy for the summer,' Rodolfo pointed out calmly.

'We'll talk it over,' Gaetano fielded smoothly.

'And when you get back from your honeymoon,' the old man delivered cheerfully, 'it will be as CEO.'

Gaetano nodded, thoroughly disconcerted and fighting not to betray the fact that he knew that his promotion was now a *marriage* step away from him. He studied Poppy from below his black lashes. Against all the odds, Rodolfo adored her. Trust Poppy to bake his grandmother's signature cake. She couldn't have done anything more likely to please and impress. She had ticked his grandfather's every box. Not only was she beautiful, kind and thoughtful, she could actually *cook*. Gaetano experienced a hideous 'hoist with his own petard' sensation and wondered how the hell he was going to climb back out of the hole he had dug.

CHAPTER FIVE

'Why are you in such a hurry?' Gaetano frowned as Poppy sped away from him towards the bedroom. His grandfather had outmanoeuvred him and he needed to have a serious conversation with his fake fiancée.

'I have to get changed and get out in the next…er… ten minutes!' she exclaimed in dismay, hastening her step after checking her watch.

Gaetano took his time about strolling down to the bedroom where Poppy was engaged in pulling on a pair of jeans, lithe long legs topped by a pair of bright red knickers on display. Her face flushing, she half turned away, wriggling her shapely hips to ease up the jeans. The enthusiastic stirring at his groin was uniquely unwelcome to Gaetano at that moment. 'Where do you have to be in ten minutes?' he asked quietly.

'Work. I picked up a waitressing shift at the café round the corner. I'll be back by midnight,' she told him chirpily.

In the doorway, Gaetano went rigid, convinced that he could not have heard her correctly. 'You applied for a job as a *waitress*…' his dark deep drawl climbed tellingly in volume and emphasis as he spoke that word '…while you're pretending to be engaged to me?'

'Why not? Bartending is better paid but the café was closer and the hours are casual and flexible and that would probably suit you better.'

Brilliant dark eyes landed on her with the chilling effect of an ice bath. 'You working as a waitress doesn't suit me in *any* way.'

'I don't see why you should object,' Poppy reasoned, thrusting her feet into her comfy ankle boots. 'I mean, you're still working and what am I supposed to do with myself while you're busy all day? It's not even as if pretending to be your fiancée is a full-time job.'

'As far as I'm concerned, it *is* full-time and you will go to the café now and tell them that you're sorry but you won't be working there tonight,' Gaetano told her with raking impatience. '*Diavelos!* Do I have to spell every little thing out to you? I'm a billionaire banker. You can't work in a café or a bar for peanuts while you're purportedly engaged to me!'

An angry flush had lit up Poppy's cheeks. 'Then what am I supposed to do for money?'

'If you need money, I'll give it to you,' Gaetano declared, pulling out his wallet, relieved that the problem could be so easily fixed. But seriously, where was her brain? Working as a waitress while living in a mansion?

Poppy backed away a step and then snaked past him in the doorway to trudge down to the hall. 'I don't want your money, Gaetano. I *work* for my money. I don't take handouts from anyone.'

'But I'm the exception to that rule,' Gaetano slotted

in grimly as he followed her with tenacious resolve. 'While you are engaged to me, you are not allowed to embarrass me by working in a low-paid menial job.'

Outraged by that decree, Poppy whirled round to face him again, the hank of hair from her ponytail falling over her shoulder in a bright colourful stream. 'Is that a fact?' she prompted. 'Well, I'm sorry, you're out of luck on this one. As far as I'm concerned, any kind of honest work is preferable to living off charity and I don't care if you think waitressing is menial—'

'We have a deal!' Gaetano raked at her with raw bite. 'You're breaking it!'

'At no stage did you ever mention that I would not be able to take paid work,' Poppy flung back at him in furious denial. 'So, don't try to deviously change the rules to suit yourself. I'm sorry if you see me working as a waitress at Carrie's coffee shop as a major embarrassment. Don't you have enough status on your own account? Does it really matter what I do? I would remind you that I am an ordinary girl who needs to work to live and that's not about to change for you or anyone else!'

'It's totally unnecessary for you to work…in fact it's *preposterous*!' Gaetano slammed back at her loudly, dark eyes flaring as golden as the heart of a fire now, his anger unconcealed. 'Particularly when I have already assured you that I will cover your every expense while you are staying in London.'

'Just as I've already told you,' Poppy proclaimed heatedly, 'I will *not* accept money from you. I'm an independent woman and I have my pride. If our positions were reversed, would you want me keeping you?'

'Don't be ridiculous!' Gaetano roared back, all control of his temper abandoned in the face of her continuing refusal to listen to him and respect his opinion. Never before in his life had a woman opposed him in such a way.

More intimidated than she was prepared to admit or show by the depth of his anger and the sheer size of him towering over her while he gave forth as if he were voicing the Ten Commandments, Poppy brought up her chin. 'I'm not being ridiculous,' she countered obstinately. 'I'm standing up for what I believe in. I don't want your money. I want my own. And as only a few people know I'm engaged to you, I don't see how it's going to embarrass you. Especially as you don't embarrass that easily.'

'And what's that supposed to mean?' he demanded.

Poppy dealt him an accusing look. 'You should've given me some pointers on what to wear at the birthday party. Once I saw how the other women were dressed, I felt stupid.'

Gaetano shrugged. 'It wasn't important. I want you to be yourself,' he repeated dismissively. 'As for the waitress job—'

'I'm keeping it!' Poppy incised, lifting her chin combatively because she was needled by his assurance that being the odd one out in the fashion stakes at the party was something she should simply be able to shrug off. Had that been a rap on the knuckles? Was she oversensitive? Too prone to feeling inadequate?

'And that's your last word on the subject?' Gaetano growled as she yanked open the front side door, which serviced his wing of the house.

'I'm afraid so,' Poppy declared before she raced off at speed, pulling the door shut behind her.

'If you don't watch out, you'll lose her,' a voice said from behind Gaetano.

In consternation, he swung round to focus on his grandfather, who was wedged in the doorway communicating between the two properties. 'How much of that did you hear?' Gaetano asked tautly.

'With this door open I couldn't help overhearing the last part of your argument,' Rodolfo Leonetti advanced. 'I'll admit to hearing enough to appreciate that my grandson is a hopeless snob. She was correct, Gaetano. There can never be shame in honest work. Your grandmother insisted on selling her father's fish at a stall until the day she married me.'

'Your wife was raised on a tiny backward island in a different era. Times have changed,' Gaetano parried thinly.

Rodolfo laughed with sincere appreciation. 'Women don't change that much. Poppy's not interested in your money. Do you realise how very lucky you are to have found such a woman?'

In silence, Gaetano jerked his aggressive chin in acknowledgement. He was still climbing back down from the dizzy heights of the unholy rage Poppy's defiance had lit inside him, marvelling at how angry she had made him while being disconcerted by his loss of control. His lean hands flexed into fists before slowly loosening again.

'And as her temper seems to be as hot as your own it may well take some very nifty moves on your part to keep her,' his grandfather opined with quiet assurance as he strolled back through the communicating door.

Gaetano struck the wall with a knotted fist and swore long and low beneath his breath. Poppy set his temper off like a rocket, not a problem he had ever had with a woman before. That's because you date 'clingy airheads', a voice chimed in the back of his mind, an exact quote of Poppy's text that sounded remarkably like her. He gritted his teeth, tension pulling like tight strings in his lean, powerful body to tauten every muscle group. It was stress caused by the lack of sex, he decided abruptly. A wave of relief for that rational explanation for his recent irrational behaviour engulfed him. Gaetano didn't like anything that he couldn't understand. Yet Poppy fell into that category and he knew he didn't dislike her.

Poppy worked her shift in the café, her mind buzzing like a busy bee throughout. Had she been too hard on Gaetano? It was true that he was a snob but what else could he be after the over-privileged life he had led since birth? But Rodolfo's clear desire to rush his grandson into marriage had shocked Gaetano and naturally that had put him in a bad mood, she conceded ruefully. Evidently when Gaetano had suggested their fake engagement he had seriously underestimated the extent of his grandfather's enthusiasm for marrying him off. Only an actual wedding was going to satisfy Rodolfo Leonetti and move Gaetano up the last crucial step of his career ladder. An engagement wasn't going to achieve that for him, which pretty much meant that everything Gaetano had so far done had been for nothing.

When Poppy finished work, she was astonished to glance out of the window and see Gaetano waiting outside for her. Street light fell on his defined cheekbones, strong nose and stubbled jaw line. One glance at his undeniable hotness and he took her breath away. Why had he come to meet her? Colour washing her face, she pulled her coat out of the back room and waited for the manager to unlock the door for her exit. Gaetano's gaze, dark, deep-set and pure gold, flamed and he moved forward.

'What are you doing here?' she asked to fill the tense silence.

'You can't walk back to the house on your own at this time of night,' Gaetano told her.

'Well, I suppose you would think that way,' Poppy remarked, inclining her head to acknowledge his bodyguards ranged across the pavement mere yards from them. Gaetano was never ever alone in the way that other ordinary people were alone. 'Why didn't you just send one of them to look out for me?'

'I owed you,' Gaetano breathed, unlocking the sleek sports car by the kerb. 'I was out of line earlier.'

'You get out of line a lot…but that's the first time you've admitted it,' Poppy said uncertainly.

Gaetano swung in beside her and in the confined space she stared at him, her breath hitching in her throat, heartbeat thumping very loudly in her eardrums. Black-lashed eyes assailed hers and she fell still, her mouth running dry. He lifted a hand, framed her face with spread fingers and kissed her. Her hand braced on a strong masculine thigh as she leant closer, helplessly hungry for that connection and the heat and pressure of his strong sensual mouth on hers. Her body went haywire, all liquid heat and response as his tongue delved and tangled with hers, and a deep quiver thrummed through her slender length. The wanting gripping her was all powerful, racing through her to swell her breasts and ignite a feverish damp heat between her thighs. In a harried movement, Poppy yanked her head back and forced her trembling body back into the passenger seat. 'What was that for?' she asked shakily.

'I have no excuse or reason. I can't stop wanting to touch you.'

'It wasn't supposed to be like this…with us,' she mumbled accusingly through her swollen lips.

Long brown fingers circled over the top of her knee and roved lazily higher, skating up her inner thigh. 'Tell me, no,' Gaetano urged in a harsh undertone.

'No,' she framed without conviction, legs involuntarily parting because with every fibre of her being she craved his touch.

'You're pushing me off the edge of sanity,' Gaetano growled, shifting position to claim her mouth again. With little passionate nips and licks and bites he took her mouth in a way it had never been taken and sent hot rivers of excitement rolling into her pelvis.

Long fingers stroked over the taut triangle of fabric stretched tight between her thighs, lingering to circle over her core. A warm tingling sensation of almost unbearable excitement gripped her and she bucked beneath his hand, helplessly, wantonly inviting more. Give me more, her body was screaming, shameless in the grip of that need. The fabric that separated her most sensitive flesh from him was a torment but he made no attempt to remove or circumvent its presence. She ground her hips down on the seat, nipples straining and stiff and prickling, the hunger like a voracious animal clawing for more inside her. That hunger was so terrifyingly strong and her brain felt so befogged with it she shivered, suddenly cold and scared of being overwhelmed.

'This is not cool,' Gaetano whispered against her lips. 'We're in a car in a public street. This is not cool at all, *bella mia*.'

'It's just lust,' she tried to say lightly, dismissively, and she tried to summon a laugh but found she couldn't because there was nothing funny about the power of the physical urges engulfing her or the nasty draining aftermath of blocking and denying those urges.

'Lust has never made me behave like a randy teenager before,' Gaetano growled. 'Around you I have a constant hard-on.'

'Stop it…*stop* talking about it!' Poppy snapped, ramming her trembling hands into the pockets of her flying jacket.

'That's impossible when it's all I can think about.' With a stifled curse he fired the engine of the car. 'But we have more important things to discuss.'

'Yes. Rodolfo called your bluff,' she breathed heavily, struggling to return to the real world again.

'That's not how I would describe what he did. I've been mulling it over all evening,' Gaetano admitted grittily. 'I'm afraid you hit the target last night when you accused me of ignoring the human dimension. I'm great with figures and strategy, not so good with people. But this afternoon looking at Rodolfo and listening to him talk I saw a man aware of his years and afraid he wouldn't live long enough to see the next generation. All my adult life I've read him wrong. I thought all I had to do to please him was to become a success and be everything my father wasn't but it wasn't enough.'

'How wasn't it enough?'

'Rodolfo would have been a much happier man if I'd married straight out of university and given him grand-children,' Gaetano breathed wryly.

'Why regret what you can't change? Obviously you didn't meet anyone you wanted to marry.'

'No, I didn't *want* to get married,' Gaetano contra-dicted drily. 'I've seen too many of my friends' mar-riages failing and my own parents fought like cat and dog.'

Poppy grimaced and said nothing. Gaetano was very literal, very black and white and uncompromising in his outlook. He had probably decided as a teenager that he would not get married and had never revisited the de-cision. But it did go some way towards explaining why he never seemed to stay very long with any woman be-cause clearly none of his relationships had had the op-tion of a future.

'At some stage you must have met at least *one* woman who stood out from the rest?' she commented.

'I did…when I was at university. Serena ended up marrying a friend and I was their best man. They divorced last year,' Gaetano volunteered with rich scorn. 'When I heard about that, I was relieved I had backed off from her.'

'That's very cold and cynical. For all you know you and she could have made a success of marriage,' Poppy commented tongue in cheek, mad with curiosity to know who Serena had been and whether he still had feelings for her now that she was free. Her face burned because she was so grateful he had not persevered with the wretched woman. She was just then discovering in consternation that she couldn't bear to think of Gaetano with *any* other woman, let alone married to one. When had she become that sensitive, that possessive of him? She had no right to feel that way and that she did mortified her. Was this some pitiful hangover from her infatuation with him as a teenager?

As she walked into the hall Gaetano pushed the door open into a dimly lit reception room. 'Before I went out I ordered supper for us. I thought you'd be hungry because unless you ate while you were working, you missed dinner.'

She was strangely touched that it had even occurred to Gaetano to consider her well-being. But then Poppy wasn't used to anyone looking out for her. In recent years she had acted as counsellor and carer for her family. Neither her mother nor her brother had ever had the inclination to ask her how she was coping working two jobs or whether she needed anything. Removing her coat, she sank down into a comfy armchair, glancing round at the stylish appointments of the spacious room. An interior designer had probably been employed, she suspected, doubting that such classy chic was attainable in any other way. She poured the tea and filled her plate with sandwiches.

For a few minutes she simply ate to satisfy the gnawing hunger inside her. Only slowly did she let her attention roam back to Gaetano. The black stubble framed his jaw, accentuating the lush curve of his full mouth, and he could work magic with that mouth, she conceded, inwardly squirming at that intimate thought and the longing behind it while ducking her head to evade the cool gold intensity of his gaze. Her body, still taut and tender from feverish arousal, recalled the stroke of his fingers and she tingled, dying inside with chagrin that she had lost her control to that extent.

'So, what do you want to talk about?' she prompted in the humming silence.

'I think you already know,' Gaetano intoned very drily.

'You have to decide what to do next,' Poppy clarified reluctantly, disliking the fact that he read her with such accuracy and refused to allow her to play dumb when it suited her to do so.

After all, so much hung on the coming discussion and it was only natural that she should now be nervous. Of what further use could she be to Gaetano? Their fake engagement was worthless because Rodolfo Leonetti wanted much more than a fake couple could possibly deliver. They couldn't set a wedding date because they weren't going to get married. And if she was of no additional value to Gaetano, maybe he wanted her to leave his home and maybe, quite understandably, he would also expect to immediately stop paying the bills for her mother's treatment at the clinic? A cold trickle of nervous perspiration ran down between Poppy's breasts and suddenly she was furious with herself for not thinking through what Rodolfo's declaration would ultimately mean to her and the lives of those who depended on her.

'I had no problem deciding what to do next. I'm very decisive but unfortunately what I do next is heavily dependent on what you decide to do,' Gaetano admitted quietly, disconcerting her while his extraordinarily beautiful eyes rested on her full force.

'What *I* decide...?'

'Only a fake fiancée can become a fake bride!' Gaetano derided, watching her pale.

'You can't seriously be suggesting that we carry this masquerade as far as a wedding!' Poppy exclaimed with a look of disbelief.

'Rodolfo likes you. He's really excited and happy about our relationship,' Gaetano breathed grimly. 'In fact it's many years since I saw him this enthusiastic about anything or anyone. I would like to give him what he wants even if it's not real and even though it can't last.'

'You love your grandfather. I understand that you don't want to disappoint him, but—'

'We could get married for a couple of years while I continue to pay for your mother's care.'

Poppy leant forward to say sharply, 'If Mum does well, she will probably be released from the clinic next month.'

Gaetano shook his handsome dark head slowly as if in wonder at her naivety. 'Poppy… Jasmine is most probably a long-term rehabilitation project. To stay off alcohol for the foreseeable future she's going to need regular ongoing professional support.'

It was true, Poppy conceded painfully. What Gaetano was saying was true, *horribly* true, but until that moment Poppy had not thought that far ahead. Indeed she had dreamt only of the day when she hoped and prayed that her newly sober parent would walk out of the clinic and back into the real world. Sadly, however, the real world offered challenges Jasmine Arnold might struggle to handle. And Poppy already knew that she did not have the power to stop her mother drinking because she had already tried that and had failed abysmally.

'If you agree to marry me I will faithfully promise to take care of your mother's needs for however long it takes for her to regain her health and sobriety,' Gaetano swore. 'At the same time I will make it possible for you to return to further education. That would mean that by the time we divorce you would be in a position to pursue any career you chose.'

Poppy sucked in a steadying breath because he was offering to deliver momentous benefits and security. But she still didn't want to sell herself out for the money that would empower her to transform her mother's life and give them both the best possible chance of a decent future. 'I can't take your money or your support. It's immoral,' she argued jaggedly. 'Stop trying to tempt me into doing what I know would be wrong.'

'I'm offering you the equivalent of a job. All right…'

Gaetano shifted an expressive bronzed hand in the air with the fluid arrogance that came as naturally as breathing to him. 'Taking on the role of being my wife would be an unusual job but it's not a job you *want*, so why shouldn't you be paid for sacrificing your freedom? Because make no mistake—you *would* be giving up your freedom while you were pretending to be my wife.'

'Fooling your grandfather, faking and pretending. It wouldn't be right,' Poppy protested vehemently.

'If it makes Rodolfo genuinely happy, why is it wrong?' Gaetano fired back at her in challenge. 'It's the best I've got to offer him. I can't give him the real thing. I can't give him a real marriage when I don't want one. Marrying you, a woman he has readily accepted and approved, is as good as it's likely to get from his point of view.'

Poppy was pale and troubled. 'You're good in an argument,' she allowed ruefully. 'But I'm never going to win a trophy for my acting skills.'

'You don't need to act. Rodolfo likes you as you are. Think about what I'm offering you. You can reclaim your life and return to being a carefree student,' Gaetano pointed out, his persuasion insidious. 'No more fretting about your mother falling off the wagon again, no more scrubbing floors or serving drinks.'

'Shut up!' Poppy told him curtly, leaping to her feet to walk restively round the room while she battled the tempting possibilities he had placed in front of her.

Gaetano studied her from below heavily lashed eyelids. She would surrender, of course she would. She had had a very tough time coping with her mother over the past couple of years and it had stolen her youthful freedom of choice. As a teenager she had been ambitious and he could still see that spirited spark of wanting more than her servant ancestors had ever wanted glowing within her.

'And how long would this fake marriage have to last to be worthwhile?' she demanded without warning.

Gaetano almost grinned and punched the air because that was when he knew for sure that he had won. 'I estimate around two years with three years being the absolute maximum. By that stage both of us will be eager to reclaim our real lives and I would envisage that divorce proceedings would already have begun.'

'And you think a divorce a couple of years down the road is less of a disappointment for Rodolfo than a broken engagement?'

'At least he'll believe I *tried*.'

'And of course your ultimate goal is becoming CEO of the Leonetti Bank and marrying me will deliver that,' Poppy filled in slowly, luminous green eyes skimming to his lean, darkly handsome features in wonderment. 'I can't believe how ambitious you are.'

'The bank is my life, it always has been,' Gaetano admitted without apology. 'Nothing gives me as much of a buzz as a profitable deal.'

'If I were to agree to this…and I'm not saying I *am* agreeing,' Poppy warned in a rush, 'when would the marriage take place?'

'Next month to suit Rodolfo's schedule and, for that matter, my own. I won't be here much over the next few weeks,' Gaetano explained. 'I have a lot of pressing business to tie up before I can take the kind of honeymoon which Rodolfo will expect.'

At that disconcerting reference to a honeymoon a tension headache tightened in a band across Poppy's brow and she lifted her fingers to press against her forehead. 'I'm very tired. I'll sleep on this and give you an answer in the morning.'

Gaetano slid fluidly out of his seat and approached her. 'But you already know the answer.'

Poppy settled angry green eyes on his lean, strong face. 'Don't try to railroad me,' she warned him.

'You like what I do to you,' Gaetano husked with blazing confidence, running a teasing forefinger down over her cheek to stroke it along the soft curve of her full lower lip.

In all her life Poppy had never been more aware of anything than she was of that finger caressing the still-swollen surface of her mouth. But then, as she was learning, Gaetano couldn't touch any part of her body without every nerve ending standing to attention and screaming for more of the same. Her breathing fractured in her throat and sawed heavily in and out of her chest. His fingertip slid into her mouth and before she could even think about what she was doing she laved it with her tongue, sucked it, watched his brilliant eyes smoulder and then his outrageous long black lashes lower over burning glints of gold.

'Are you offering to let me have you tonight?' Gaetano enquired, startling and mortifying her with that direct question.

Her luminous eyes flew wide. 'I can't believe you just asked me that!'

'And I can't believe that you can still try to act the innocent when you're teasing me,' Gaetano riposted.

'You touched me first,' she reminded him defensively, her cheeks scarlet as she thought of what she had done with his finger and the expectation he had developed as a result. 'Are you always this blunt?'

'Pretty much. Sex requires mutual consent and I naturally dislike confusing signals, which could lead to misunderstandings.'

Poppy stared up at him, momentarily lost in the tawny blaze of his hot stare. He wanted her and he was letting her see it. Her whole body seized up in response, her nipples prickling while that painful hollow ached at the heart of her. She tore her gaze from his, dropped her eyes and then, noticing the sizeable bulge in his jeans, felt pure unashamed heat curling up between her thighs.

'If you're not going to let me have you, sleep in one of the spare rooms tonight,' Gaetano instructed. 'I'm not a masochist, *bella mia*.'

'Spare room,' Poppy framed shakily, the only words she could get past her tight throat because it hurt her that she wanted to say yes so badly. She didn't want to be used 'to scratch an itch', not her first time anyway. Surely some day somewhere some man would want her for more than that? Gaetano only wanted the release of sex and would probably not have wanted her at all had they not been forced into such proximity.

Gaetano let her reach the door. 'If I marry you, I'll expect you to share my bed.'

Wide-eyed, Poppy whirled round to gasp, 'But...'

'I'm too well-known to get away with sneaking around having affairs for a couple of years,' Gaetano asserted silkily. 'If we get married it should look like a happy marriage, at least at the start, and there's no way I'd be happy in a sex-free marriage. Is that likely to be a deal-breaker?'

'I'll think it over.' Her heart-shaped face expressionless, Poppy studied the polished floor. She wanted to discover sex with Gaetano but she wasn't about to confess that to him. *That* was private, strictly private. Her body burned inside her clothing at the thought of that intimacy. Meaningless, sexual intimacy, she reminded herself doggedly. And it disturbed her that even though she knew it would mean nothing to him she still wanted him...

CHAPTER SIX

POPPY SANK INTO the guest-room bed and rolled over to hug a pillow. She was incredibly tired but so wired she was convinced that she would not sleep a wink.

She was going to marry Gaetano Leonetti. Gorgeous, filthy rich, super-successful Gaetano. Who sent her body into spasms of craving with a single kiss. If she was honest with herself, she really hadn't needed a night to think it over. He would help her protect her mother and he would support her getting back onto a career path. Really, marrying Gaetano would be win-win whichever way she looked at it, wouldn't it be?

As long as she didn't get too carried away and start acting as if it were a real marriage. As long as she didn't fall for Gaetano. Well, she wasn't about to do that, was she? He was almost thirty years old and had never been in love. The closest he had come to love was with a woman who had married his friend. And he had acted as best man at their wedding, which didn't suggest to her that it had been very close to love at all. Gaetano might be planning to marry her but he wasn't going to love her and he wasn't going to keep her either. It would be a temporary marriage and it would make Rodolfo happy…at least for a while, she thought guiltily, because faking it for the older man's benefit still troubled her conscience. He was such a kind, genuine sort of man and so unlike Gaetano, who kept the equivalent of a coffin lid slammed down hard on his emotions.

While Poppy was ruminating over her bridegroom's lack of emotional intelligence, Gaetano was subjecting himself to yet another cold shower. She *had* to marry him. There was no alternative. Just at that moment in the grip of a raging inferno of frustrated lust he felt as though he would spontaneously combust if he didn't get Poppy spread across his bed as the perfect wedding gift. The definitive wedding gift, with those ballerina legs in lace stockings, those pert little breasts in satin cups, that voluptuous pink mouth pouting as she looked up at him with those witchy green spellbinding eyes. He groaned out loud. He couldn't credit that he had barely touched her when he wanted so much more.

But if they married, a few weeks down the matrimonial road he'd be back to normal, he told himself bracingly. The challenge would be gone. The lust would die once he could have her whenever he wanted her. He would soon be himself again, cooler, calmer, back in control, fully focussed on the bank. How was it possible that just the fantasy of sinking into Poppy's wet, willing body excited him more than he had ever been excited? What was it about her?

Maybe it was the weird clothes, maybe he had a secret Goth fetish. Maybe it was her argumentative nature, because he had always thrilled to a challenge. Maybe it was her cheeky texts that made him laugh. The fact she could still blush? That was strange. Every time he mentioned sex she went red, as if he had said something outrageous. She couldn't possibly be that innocent, although he was willing to allow that she might well have considerably less experience between the sheets than he had acquired.

Gaetano shook Poppy awake at the ungodly hour of six in the morning, obstinately and cruelly ignoring her heartfelt moans to insist that she join him for breakfast. After a quick shower and the application of a little make-up, Poppy teamed a black dress enlivened with a red rose print with high heels and sauntered down to the dining room. Gaetano was already ensconced with black coffee, a horrendously unhealthy fry-up and the *Financial Times*.

She was gloriously conscious of his attention as she helped herself to cereal and took a seat at the other end of the table, her ruby cluster ring catching the light. Gaetano put down the newspaper and regarded her levelly, dark golden eyes steady as a rock and full of an impatience he didn't need to voice.

'Yes, I'll marry you,' Poppy told him straight off.

'Does that mean I get to share my bed with you tonight?' was Gaetano's first telling question.

'You are incredibly goal-orientated about entirely the wrong things!' Poppy censured immediately. 'You can wait until we're married.'

'Nobody waits until they're married these days!'

'I haven't had sex before. I want it to feel special,' she told him stubbornly.

His expressive dark eyes flared with incredulity. 'I refuse to credit that. I saw you with Toby Styles…'

'I hate you!' Poppy launched at him in a sudden tempest of furious embarrassment, her pale skin flushed to her hairline. 'Of all the moments I don't *want* to be reminded of, you have to bring that one up and throw it at me!'

'Well, it was one of those unforgettable moments that did seem fairly self-explanatory. I saw you sidling out of the shrubbery covered in blushes and grass stains,' Gaetano commented with grudging amusement. 'So, why lie about it? This is purely about sex, *bella mia*, and I'm all for full bedroom equality. Whether or not you're a virgin or a secret slut matters not a damn to me.'

Poppy compressed her lips. 'If you must know—although it's none of your blasted business—I did plan to have sex that day with Toby but I changed my mind because it wasn't what I really wanted.' No, what she had really, *really* wanted that day, she acknowledged belatedly, was to wander off into the shrubbery and be ravished by Gaetano, who had dominated her every juvenile fantasy. Sadly, however, Gaetano hadn't been an option.

'Poor Toby…' Gaetano frowned.

'He was very decent about it,' Poppy muttered in mortification. 'He's married to one of my friends now.'

'But there must have been someone since then?'

'No.'

Gaetano continued to stare at her as if she were a circus freak. 'But you're so full of passion…'

Only with you. The words remained unspoken.

Gaetano lifted his coffee with a slightly dazed expression in his shrewd gaze. 'I'll be the first...*really*?'

Poppy shrugged a shoulder. 'But if you think it's likely to be a turn-off I can always go and look for a one-night stand.'

'Don't even think about it,' Gaetano growled.

'That was a joke.'

'It's not a turn-off, simply a surprise,' Gaetano admitted flatly. 'OK, I'll wait until we're married if it's so significant to you. But I think you're making an unnecessary production out of it.'

Her body was all he wanted from her, Poppy interpreted painfully. At least if she was his legal wife, it would feel less demeaning, wouldn't it?

'I'll organise a gynae appointment for you,' Gaetano continued briskly. 'Reliable birth control is important. We don't want any slip-ups in that department when we're not planning to stay together.'

'Obviously not,' she agreed, sipping with determination at her hot-chocolate drink while thinking for the very first time in her life about having a baby. She had always liked children, always assumed that she would become a mother one day, but she reckoned that day lay a long way ahead in her future.

'And whatever you do,' Gaetano warned with chilling precision, 'don't go falling for me.'

'And why would I do that?' Poppy demanded baldly, her cheeks hotter than hell in fear of him mentioning that so mortifying teenaged crush again. 'Having sex with you is not going to make me fall in love with you.

I know you think you're fantastic in bed, Gaetano, *but* you're not fantastic enough *out* of bed.'

Infuriatingly, Gaetano did not react badly to that criticism. 'That's good because that's one complication I can do without. I hate it when women fall for me and make me feel that it's my fault.'

Well, that was frank, and forewarned was forearmed, Poppy told herself squarely. 'It's probably your money they're falling for,' she suggested in a tone of saccharine sweetness. 'You have yet to show me a single loveable trait.'

'*Grazie al cielo*...thank goodness,' Gaetano responded in a tone of galling relief. 'I don't want you to get the wrong idea about me *or* this marriage.'

'I won't. This marriage will be like one of those business mergers. You are *so* safe,' Poppy declared brightly. 'You will merely be the first stepping stone on my sexual path.'

Gaetano was taken aback to discover that he didn't want to think of a string of other men enjoying her along that particular path. In fact it gave him a slightly nauseated sensation in the pit of his stomach. The acknowledgement bemused him and he put it down to the simple fact that as yet he had not enjoyed her either. He was thinking too much about something relatively unimportant, he reflected impatiently. Sex was sex and his wedding night would provide the cure for what was currently afflicting him. Since when had he ever attached so much consequence to sex? Even so, it had been entirely right to have the conversation with

Poppy to ensure that they perfectly understood each other's expectations.

'I'll make a start on the wedding arrangements today,' Gaetano completed smoothly.

'You look beautiful,' Jasmine Arnold told her daughter warmly as she emerged from her bedroom in her wedding dress.

The older woman was attending her daughter's wedding with a member of the clinic support staff. Although Poppy could see a big improvement in her mother's appearance and mood, she knew how hard it was for Jasmine to return to Woodfield Hall where she had been so depressed. And while Poppy had asked her mother to walk her down the aisle, her brother was doing it instead because Jasmine could not face being the centre of that much attention.

Poppy quite understood the older woman's reluctance because hundreds of guests were attending the wedding being staged to celebrate Gaetano's marriage at Woodfield Hall. The Leonetti men had always got married in the church in the grounds of their ancestral home and neither Rodolfo nor Gaetano had seen any reason to flout tradition. Indeed Gaetano had expected Poppy to move straight into the main house as though she already belonged there but Poppy had returned to the small service flat where she had grown up, determined to move back and forth as required.

'I'm still hoping that you know what you're doing,' Damien muttered in an admission intended only for Poppy's ears as he emerged from his own room, smartly

clad in his hired morning suit. He looked relieved when
he registered that his mother and her companion had
already left for the church. 'You've always had a thing
for Gaetano...'

'As I've already explained, this is only a business
arrangement.'

'Maybe it is...for him.' Her brother sighed. 'But if
it's only business why are you always checking your
phone and texting him?'

'He expects regular updates on the wedding arrangements.'

'Yeah...like his staff can't do that for him,' Damien
responded, unimpressed.

But it was true, Poppy reflected ruefully. Gaetano
was hyper about details and had a surprising number
of strong opinions about bridal matters that she had
mistakenly assumed he wouldn't be interested in. Although, as he had warned her, she had barely seen him
since the month-long countdown to the wedding had
begun, they had stayed in constant contact by phone
while Gaetano flew round Europe. Poppy had ignored
his opinion of the casual job she had taken and had kept
up regular shifts at the café.

Now she climbed into the limousine waiting in the
courtyard to collect the bride and her brother. The chapel was barely two hundred yards away and she would
have much preferred to walk there but Gaetano had vetoed that option, saying it lacked dignity.

In the same way he had vetoed the flowers she'd
wanted to wear in her hair and had had a family diamond tiara delivered to her. He had also picked the

bridal colour scheme as green, arguing that that particular shade would match her eyes, which had struck Poppy as ridiculously whimsical for so practical a male. And to crown his interference he had acted as though he were her Prince Charming by buying her wedding shoes the instant he saw them showcased in some high-fashion outlet in Milan. Admittedly they were gorgeous, even if they were over-the-top dramatic—delicate leather sandals ornamented with pearls and opals that glimmered and magically shone in the light. In fact Gaetano had embarrassed his bride with his choice of shoes because her selections had been considerably less fanciful. Her dress was cap-sleeved and fitted to the waist, flaring out over net underskirts to stop above her slender knees. In comparison to the Cinderella shoes, the dress, while being composed of beautiful fabric, was plain and simple in style.

'Are you nervous?' Damien prompted.

'Why would I be? Well, only because the Leonettis have invited hundreds of people,' she admitted.

'Including most of the estate staff and locals, so you can't fault Gaetano there. The rich are going to have to rub shoulders with the ordinary folk.' Damien laughed.

Poppy smiled because Gaetano had kept the last promise he had made before their engagement. Within a week Damien would be starting work as a mechanic in a London garage staffed by other former offenders. Her brother's happiness at the prospect of a complete new start somewhere he would no longer be pilloried for his past had lifted her heart. Not that her heart needed lifting, she told herself urgently. If her family was happy, *she* was happy. In stray moments between the wedding arrangements and spending time with Rodolfo, who got lonely in his big empty mansion, she had started looking into the option of training as a garden designer and that gem of an idea looked promising.

Closing her hand into the crook of her brother's arm, she looked down the aisle to where Gaetano had turned round to see her arrival and she grinned. My goodness, how ridiculous all this pomp and ceremony were for a couple who weren't remotely in love, she thought helplessly. But Gaetano certainly looked the part of bridegroom, all tall, dark and handsome, black curls cropped to his head in honour of the wedding, the usual stubble round his jaw line dispensed with, his bronzed, handsome features clean-shaven. His dark eyes glittered gold as precious ingots in the sunlight filtered by the stained-glass window behind him. He looked downright amazing, she conceded with a sunny sensation of absolute contentment.

When Poppy came into view, she took Gaetano's breath away. Her waist looked tiny enough to be spanned by his hands and, as he had requested, her glorious hair tumbled loose round her shoulders in vibrant contrast to the white dress that displayed her incredible legs. And she was wearing the shoes, the shoes *he* had bought for her, having known at a glance and feeling slightly smug at the knowledge that they were the sort of theatrical feminine touch the unconventional Poppy would appreciate.

The priest rattled through the ceremony at a fair old pace. Rings were exchanged. Poppy trembled as

Gaetano eased the ring down over her knuckle, glancing up to encounter smouldering golden eyes that devoured her. Colour surged into her face as she thought of the night ahead but there was anticipation and excitement laced with that faint sense of apprehension. She had decided that she was glad that Gaetano would become her first lover. Who better than the male she had fallen for as a teenager? After all, no other man had yet managed to wipe out her memory of Gaetano. There would be someone else some day, she told herself bracingly as Gaetano retained her hand and his thumb gently massaged the delicate skin of her inner wrist with the understated sensuality that seemed so much a part of him.

'You made me wait ten minutes at the altar but you were definitely worth waiting for,' Gaetano quipped as they walked down the aisle again.

'I warned you I'd be late,' Poppy reminded him. 'Knowing you, you'd have preferred to find me waiting humbly for you.'

'No, waiting naked would have been sufficient, late or otherwise,' Gaetano whispered only loud enough for her ears. 'As for humble—are you kidding? You've never been the self-effacing type.'

Rodolfo hugged her outside the chapel, his creased face wrinkled into a huge smile. 'Welcome to the family,' he said happily.

A beautiful blonde watched with raised brows of apparent surprise as, urged on by the photographer, Poppy wound her arms round Gaetano's neck and gazed at him as if he were her sun, her moon and her stars. She was great at faking it, she thought appreciatively as Gaetano smiled down at her with that wonderful, charismatic smile that banished the often forbidding austerity from his lean, darkly handsome features.

'Congratulations, Gaetano,' the blonde intercepted them as they made their way to the limo to be wafted back to the hall.

'Poppy…meet Serena Bellingham. We'll catch up later, Serena,' Gaetano drawled.

'Is she the one you almost married?' Poppy demanded, craning her neck to look back at the smiling blonde who rejoiced in the height, perfect figure and face of a top model.

'Oh, don't do it. Don't make something out of nothing the way women do!' Gaetano groaned in exasperation. 'I didn't *almost* marry Serena and, even if I did, what business is it of yours? This isn't a real wedding.'

The colour ebbed from below Poppy's skin to leave her pale. She felt oddly as though she had been slapped down and squashed and she felt enormously hurt and humiliated but didn't understand why. But, unquestionably, he was right. Theirs was not a normal wedding and she was not entitled to ask nosy personal questions about exes.

As if he recognised that he had been rude, Gaetano released his breath in a slow measured hiss. 'I'm sorry. I shouldn't have said that.'

'No, it's OK. I'm just naturally nosy,' Poppy muttered in an undertone.

'Serena is a very talented hedge-fund manager. She may come and work for Leonettis now that she's single again. Her ex was envious of her success, which is—apparently—the main reason their marriage failed.'

Poppy pictured Serena's cloyingly bright smile and her tummy performed a warning somersault. It sounded as though Gaetano had spoken to Serena recently to catch up. Confidences had been exchanged and that sent the oddest little current of dismay through Poppy. She suspected that if the beautiful blonde went to work for Gaetano, it wouldn't entirely be a career move. But even if that was true, what business was it of hers to judge or speculate? She was Gaetano's wife and soon she would also be Gaetano's lover yet she had not, it seemed, acquired any relationship rights over Gaetano, which suddenly struck her as a recipe for disaster.

Woodfield Hall was awash with guests and caterers. Jasmine Arnold approached her daughter to ask if it would be all right if she took her leave. Newly sober, Poppy's mother did not want as yet to be in the vicinity of alcohol. Understanding, Poppy hugged the older woman and they agreed to talk regularly on the phone. As Gaetano joined her Poppy smiled at one of her few school friends, Melanie, who was now married to Toby Styles, the estate gamekeeper.

Overpowered by Gaetano's presence, the small brunette gushed into speech. 'You and…er… Mr Leonetti? It's so romantic, Poppy. You know,' Melanie said, addressing Gaetano directly, 'the whole time we were growing up Poppy never had eyes for anyone but you.'

Gaetano responded wittily but Poppy was already trying not to cringe before Toby grinned at her. 'Nobody knows that better than me,' he teased.

Kill me now, Poppy thought melodramatically when Gaetano actually laughed out loud and chatted to the couple about their work on the estate as if nothing the slightest bit embarrassing had been shared. And of course, why would it embarrass Gaetano to be reminded of Poppy's adolescent crush?

As they mingled she noticed Rodolfo chatting to Serena Bellingham. The blonde was wreathed in charming smiles. Poppy scolded herself for thinking bitchy thoughts. And why? Just because Serena had once shared a bed with Gaetano? Just because Serena had the looks, the social background and the education that would have made her the perfect wife for Gaetano? Or because Gaetano had once freely chosen to have a relationship with Serena when he had merely ended up with Poppy by accident and retained her for convenience?

Deliberately catching her eye, Serena strolled over to Poppy's side. 'I can see that you're curious about me,' she drawled in her cut-glass accent. 'I'm Gaetano's only serious ex, so it's natural…'

'Possibly,' Poppy conceded, determined to be very cautious with her words and ashamed of the explosive mixture of inexcusable envy and resentment she was struggling to suppress.

'We were too young when we first met,' Serena declared. 'That's why we broke up. Gaetano wasn't ready to commit and I was, so I rushed off and married someone else instead.'

'Everyone matures at a different rate,' Poppy remarked non-committally.

'Maturity is immaterial,' Serena responded with

stinging confidence. 'You and Gaetano won't last five minutes. You don't have anything to offer him.'

Disconcerted by that sudden attack coming at her out of nowhere, Poppy froze. 'That's a matter of opinion.'

'But you'll do very well for a short-lived *first* marriage. Gaetano is the last man alive I would expect to stay married to a Goth bride. You don't fit in and you never will…'

As that bitingly cold forecast hit her Poppy was silenced by Gaetano's arm closing round her spine. She encountered a suspicious sidewise glance and her temper flared inside her. Evidently, Gaetano was so far removed from the reality of Serena's barracuda nature that it was Poppy he didn't trust to behave around Serena. Entrapped there in Gaetano's controlling hold, Poppy silently seethed and brooded over what Serena had said.

Sadly, the blonde's assurance that Poppy would never fit in as Gaetano's wife had cut deep—particularly because Poppy had quite deliberately made conventional choices when it came to what to wear for her wedding day. Why had she done that? she suddenly asked herself angrily. And there it was—the answer she didn't want. She had done it for Gaetano's benefit in an effort to please him and make him proud of her, make him appreciate that the housekeeper's daughter could get it right for a big occasion. Serena's automatic dismissal of all that Poppy had to offer had seriously hurt and humiliated her.

Fortunately from that point on their wedding day seemed to speed up and race past. Poppy's throat was sore and she put that down to the amount of talking she had to do. She ate little during the meal even though she was trying to regain the weight she had lost in recent months while she had worked two jobs. Unfortunately her appetite had vanished.

She changed into white cropped trousers and a cool blue chiffon top for their flight to Italy. The luxurious interior of the Leonetti private jet stunned her into silence. She studied the glittering ruby cluster nestling next to the wedding band on her finger and Serena's wounding forecast of her marriage seemed to reverberate in her ears. *You don't fit in and you never will.*

And why should that matter when they didn't plan to stay married? Poppy asked herself wearily, unsettled by the nagging insecurities tugging at her. Why should she care what Serena thought? Or what Serena truly wanted from Gaetano? She reckoned that Serena was already planning to be Gaetano's second, rather more permanent wife. So what?

It wasn't as though she had any feelings for Gaetano beyond tolerance, Poppy reminded herself. Lust was physical, not cerebral.

CHAPTER SEVEN

'STOP... STOP THE CAR!' Poppy yelled as the Range Rover wound down the twisting Tuscan country road.

Startled, Gaetano jumped on the brake. He frowned in astonishment as Poppy leapt out of the car at speed and assumed that she felt sick. But to his surprise and that of the security men climbing out of the car behind, Poppy ran back down the road and crouched down.

Bloodstains and dust had smeared her white cropped jeans by the time she stood up again cradling something hairy and still in her arms as tenderly as if it were a baby. 'It's a dog...it must've been hit by a passing car.'

'Give it to my security. They'll deal with this,' Gaetano advised.

'No, we will,' Poppy told him. 'Where's the closest veterinary surgery?'

The dog, a terrier mix with a pepper and salt coat and a greying snout, licked weakly at her fingers and whined in pain. Fifteen minutes later they were in the waiting room at the local surgery while Gaetano spoke with the vet in Italian.

'The situation is this...' Gaetano informed Poppy.

'The animal is not microchipped, has no collar and has not been reported missing. Arno can operate and I can obviously afford to cover the cost of the treatment but it may be more practical simply to put the animal to sleep.'

'Practical?' Poppy erupted.

'Rather than put the dog through the trauma of surgery and a prolonged recuperation when the local pound is already full, as is the animal rescue sanctuary. If there is no prospect of the dog going to another home—'

'I'll keep him,' Poppy cut in curtly.

Gaetano groaned. 'Don't be a bleeding heart for the sake of it.'

'I'm not. I *want* Muffin.'

His gorgeous dark eyes widened in surprise, black lashes sky-high. *'Muffin?'*

'Ragamuffin… Muffin,' she explained curtly.

'But I can buy you a beautiful pedigreed puppy if you want one,' Gaetano murmured with unconcealed incredulity. 'Muffin is no oil painting and he's old.'

'So? He needs me much more than a beautiful puppy ever would,' Poppy pointed out defiantly. 'Think of him as a wedding gift.'

Having made arrangements for Muffin's care, they drove off again.

'You've become so cold-hearted,' Poppy whispered ruefully, studying his lean dark classic profile. 'What happened to you?'

'I grew up. Don't be a drama queen,' Gaetano urged. 'When you care too much you get hurt. I learned that from a young age.'

'But you're shutting yourself off from so many good things in life,' she argued.

'Am I? Rodolfo enjoyed a long and happy marriage but he was so wretched after my grandmother passed that he too wanted to die.'

'That was grief. Think of all the happy years he enjoyed with his wife,' Poppy urged. 'Everything has a downside, Gaetano. Love brings its own reward.'

Gaetano voiced a single rude word of disagreement in Italian. 'It didn't reward my mother when the husband she once adored ran round snorting cocaine with hookers. It didn't reward me as her son when her super-rich second husband persuaded her to forget that she had left a child behind in England. But you'll be glad to know that my mother's second husband *loved* her,' Gaetano continued with raw derision. 'As she explained when she tried to foolishly mend fences with me a few years ago, Connor loved her so much that he was jealous of her first marriage and the child born from it.'

Poppy had paled. 'That's a twisted kind of love.'

'And there's a lot of that twisted stuff out there,' Gaetano completed in a chilling tone of finality. 'That's why I never wanted anything to do with that kind of emotion.'

Poppy knew when to keep quiet. Of course, his outlook was coloured by his background, she reflected ruefully. Her parents had been happily married but his had not been. And his mother's decision to turn her back on her son to please her second husband had done even more damage. Poppy had been surprised that Gaetano's mother had not been invited to the wedding but Rodolfo had simply shrugged, saying only that his former daughter-in-law rarely returned to England.

Gaetano turned off the winding road onto a lane that threaded through silvery olive groves. Woods lay beyond the groves, occasionally parting to show views of rolling green hills and vineyards and an ancient walled hilltop village. Gaetano indicated another track to the left. 'That leads down to the guest house where Rodolfo spends his summers.'

'We'll have to be careful to stay in role with your grandfather staying so close,' Poppy remarked.

'La Fattoria, the main house, is over a mile away. He won't see us unless we visit. He is very keen not to intrude in any way on what he regards as our honeymoon,' Gaetano said drily.

'So this property has belonged to your family for a long time,' she assumed.

'Rodolfo bought it before I was born, fondly picturing it as the perfect spot for wholesome family holidays with at least half a dozen children running round.' Gaetano sounded regretful on the older man's behalf rather than scornful. 'Sadly I was an only child and my parents only ever came here with parties of friends. The house was signed over to me about five years ago and I had it fully renovated.'

A magnificent building composed of creamy stone appeared round the next corner. It was larger than Poppy had expected but she was learning to think big or bigger when it came to Leonetti properties, for, while the family might only consist of Rodolfo and his one grandson, the older man did not seem to think in terms of small or convenient. Glorious urns of flowers adorned the terrace and a rotund little woman in an apron, closely followed by a tall lanky man, appeared at the front door.

'Dolores and Sean look after La Fattoria.' Gaetano introduced the friendly middle-aged Irish couple and their cases were swept away.

Poppy accepted a glass of wine and sat down on the rear terrace to enjoy the stupendous view and catch her breath in the sweltering heat. She was feeling incredibly tired and had tactfully declined Dolores's invitation to do an immediate tour of the house. Worse still, she was getting a headache and she had an annoying tickle in her sore throat that had made her cough several times and was giving her voice a rough edge. It was just her luck, she thought ruefully. She was on her honeymoon in Tuscany in the most gorgeous setting, with an even more gorgeous man, and she was developing a galloping bad cold.

The master bedroom was a huge airy space with a tiled floor and a bed as big as a football pitch. The bathroom was fitted out like a glossy magazine spread and she revelled in the wet room with the complex jet system. Everything bore Gaetano's contemporary stamp and the extreme shower facilities were not a surprise. She had been feeling very warm and the cold water gushing over her before she managed to work out how to operate the complicated controls cooled her off wonderfully. Clad in a light cotton sundress, she wandered back downstairs.

Black hair curling and still damp from the shower, Gaetano joined her on the terrace to slot another glass of wine into her hand. 'From our own award-winning winery,' he told her wryly. 'Rodolfo takes a personal interest in the vineyard.'

Poppy surveyed him from below her lashes. He was so beautiful, she found it a challenge to look anywhere else. His spectacular black-lashed eyes were reflective as he leant gracefully up against a stone pillar support to survey the panoramic landscape, his lithe, lean, powerful body indolently relaxed. A faint shadow of black stubble roughened his strong jaw line, accentuating the wide sensual curve of his mouth. A tiny nerve snaked tight somewhere in her pelvis as she thought of how long it had been since he kissed her and whether a kiss could possibly be as unbelievably good as she remembered it being. Likely not, she told herself, for she had always been a dreamer. How else could she have imagined even as a teenager that Gaetano Leonetti would ever be seriously interested in her?

And yet, here she was, a little voice whispered seductively, Gaetano's wedding ring on her finger, and mortifyingly that awareness went to her head like the strongest alcohol. But their marriage still wasn't real; it was *still* a fantasy, the same little voice added. She had been a fake fiancée and a fake bride and now she was a fake wife. In fact just about the only thing that wouldn't be fake between them was their wedding night.

The very blood in her veins seemed to be coursing slowly, heavily. She finished her wine and set down the glass, insanely aware of the tightening prominence of her nipples. She lifted the tiny handwritten menu displayed on the table, glancing with a sinking heart through the several courses that were to be served.

'You know, I'm not remotely hungry and I don't think I *could* eat anything,' Poppy confided truthfully. 'I hope that's not going to offend Dolores...'

Gaetano glanced at her, eyes flaming golden as a lion's in the sunset lighting up the sky in an awesome display of crimson and peach. Mouth suddenly dry, she stopped breathing, frowning as he strode back into the house and disappeared from view. A few minutes later she heard a noisy little car start up somewhere and drive away. Gaetano reappeared to close a hand over hers and tug her gently back indoors.

'Do we have to eat in some stuffy dining room?' She sighed.

'No, we don't have to do anything we don't want to do,' Gaetano told her, bending down to lift her up into his arms. 'I've sent Sean and Dolores home. We're on our own until tomorrow and I am much hungrier for you than for food.'

'You can't possibly carry me up those stairs!' Poppy exclaimed.

'Right at this moment I could carry you up ten flights of stairs, *bellezza mia*,' Gaetano admitted, darting his mouth across her collarbone so that her head fell back to expose her slender white throat and her bright hair cascaded over his arm. 'Congratulations on being the only woman smart enough to make me wait...'

'Wait for what? *Oh*...' Poppy registered with a wealth of meaning in her tone while distinctly revelling in being carried as though she were a little dainty thing, which, in her own opinion, she was not.

Gaetano settled her down on the bed. Helpfully she kicked off her shoes and wished she had taken a pain-killer for her sore throat and head. But she couldn't possibly take the gloss off the evening by admitting that she was feeling under par, could she? And she would have to admit it to get medication because she had packed nothing of that nature, indeed had only brought her contraceptive pills with her. She wasn't about to make a fuss about a stupid cold, was she?

He ran down the zip on her dress but only after kissing a path across her bare shoulders and lingering at the nape of her neck where her skin proved to be incredibly sensitive and she quivered, her insides turning to liquid heat beneath his attention.

'I have died and gone to heaven…' Gaetano intoned thickly as the dress dropped unnoticed to the carpet, exposing his bride in her ice-blue satin corset top and matching knickers.

'This is your wedding present,' Poppy announced, stretching back against the smooth white bedding with a confidence that she had never known she could possess.

Of course it would be different once he started removing stuff and nudity got involved, she conceded rue-fully. For now, however, having guessed that Gaetano would be the type of male who found sexy lingerie that enhanced a woman's figure appealing, Poppy felt like a million dollars. Why? Simply because somehow Gaetano always contrived to look at her as if she had the most amazing female body ever and that had done wonders for her self-image.

'No, *you* are my wedding present,' Gaetano told her with conviction. 'I've been counting down the hours until we were together.'

Her luminous green eyes widened in surprise and she bit back the tactless retort that anyone would consider that a romantic comment. After all, Gaetano was fully focused on sex and neither romance nor commitment would play any part in their marriage. And wasn't that all she was focused on as well? As Gaetano came down on the bed beside her, his shirt hanging loose and unbuttoned to display a sleek, bronzed, muscular six-pack, Poppy was entranced by the view. He was stunning and, for now, he was hers. Why look beyond that? Why try to complicate things?

Loosening the corset one hook at a time, Gaetano ran a long finger down over the delicate spine he had exposed and then put his mouth there, tracing the line below her smooth ivory skin. 'You are so beautiful, *gioia mia.*'

Poppy hid a blissed-out smile behind her tumbling hair and closed her eyes as he eased off the light corset and lifted his hands to cup her breasts. Her back arched, her straining nipples pushing against his fingers until he tugged on the tender buds and an audible gasp escaped her.

Gaetano lifted her and turned her round to face him. 'I want to be your first,' he breathed in a roughened undertone. 'It will be my privilege.'

'Careful, Gaetano…you're sounding nice.' Now outrageously aware of her naked breasts, Poppy crossed her arms to hide them.

'I may be many things, but nice isn't one of them,' Gaetano growled, pulling her down on the bed beside him and covering her pouting mouth hungrily with his own. Unbridled pleasure snaked through her as his tongue merged with hers. An electrifying push of hunger gripped her as his hands shifted to toy with her breasts. He pushed her back against the pillows and lowered his mouth to her pouting nipples.

'Palest pink like pearls,' Gaetano mused, stroking a tender tip with appreciation as he gazed down at her.' I wondered what colour they would be…'

Her green eyes widened. 'Seriously?' she prompted.

'And they're perfect like the rest of you,' he groaned, lowering his head to lick a distended crest. 'You were so worth waiting for at the church.'

Poppy wasn't quite as pleased as she would have assumed she would be by having that much appreciation directed at her physical attributes. Gaetano was interfering with her fantasy, that fantasy that she had not even acknowledged was playing at the back of her mind, the fantasy in which Gaetano loved her and appreciated her for all sorts of other reasons that went beyond lust.

'And so were you,' Poppy told Gaetano, deciding to turn the tables as she sat up to dislodge him and pushed him back against the pillows. He studied her with questioning dark golden eyes semi-veiled by black curling lashes. She spread her fingers across his hard pectoral muscles, stroking down over his sleek ribcage to his flat abdomen.

'Don't stop now,' he husked.

Her fingers were clumsy on his belt buckle and the button on the waistband of his trousers, her knuckles nudging against the little furrow of dark hair that disappeared below his clothing. She reached for the zip. Her lack of expertise was obvious to Gaetano and the oddest sensation of tenderness infiltrated him as he noted the tense self-consciousness etched in her flushed face.

'Why do I get the feeling this is a first for you?'

'Everyone is a learner at some stage…' she framed jerkily.

Gaetano yanked down his zip for himself and then tossed her back flat on the bed again while he divested himself of his trousers and his boxers. 'If you touched me now, it would all be over far too fast,' he told her thickly. 'That's why I'm going to do most of the touching and you will lie back and let me do the work.'

'If you think of it as work, I don't think you should bother.'

'Nothing would stop me now. I can hardly wait to be inside you.' Gaetano leant over her, his urgent erection pushing against her hip. 'Having you in my bed has been my fantasy for weeks.'

'Fantasy never lives up to reality,' Poppy said nervously. 'I don't want to be a fantasy.'

'Sorry, it's *my* fantasy,' Gaetano traded, stroking a wondering hand down over the slender curve of her hip to the hot, damp secret at the heart of her.

Her hips jerked and her eyes shut as he traced between her thighs. Her breath snarled in her throat. She was so sensitised that she shuddered when he circled her clitoris with his fingertip. Her whole body was climbing of its own volition into a tight, tense spiral of growing need. Even the brush of a finger against her tight entrance was almost too much to bear. Her hips pushed against the mattress, her heart thumping like thunder inside her chest as he shimmied down the bed, fingertips delicately caressing her inner thighs as he pushed her legs back, opening her.

'No, you can't do that!' she gasped in consternation.

'*Stai zitto…*' he told her softly. 'You don't get to tell me what to do in bed.'

The flick of his tongue across torturously tender nerve endings deprived her of voice and then of thought. Her head shifted back and forth on the pillows, the thrum of hunger building up through her body to a siren's scream of need. She gasped, she cried his name, she moaned, she lost control so completely and utterly that when the explosive release of orgasm claimed her it took her by storm. And the world stopped turning for long minutes, her body still quaking with wondrous aftershocks while Gaetano looked down at her with satisfaction.

As Gaetano tilted her back she felt the smooth steel push of him against her still-throbbing core. The tight knot low in her pelvis made its presence felt again, the hollow ache of hunger stirring afresh. He slid against her, easing into her by degrees, straining her delicate sheath.

'You're so tight,' he groaned, pulling back again and then angling his hips for another, more forceful entrance.

The sharp stinging pain made Poppy flinch for a millisecond and then her body was pushing on past that fleeting discomfort to linger on the satisfying stretch and fullness of his invasion. A little moan broke low in her throat and she moved her hips to luxuriate in the throbbing hardness of his bold masculinity.

Gaetano swore in Italian. 'You feel like heaven,' he growled in her ear. 'Am I hurting you now?'

'Oh, no,' she told him truthfully.

And then he moved again, withdrawing and spearing deep enough to wring a cry of startled enjoyment from her. From that moment on her eagerness climbed in tune with Gaetano's every measured thrust. Her heart raced, her legs clamping round his lean hips as she lifted to him, matching his driving rhythm while the electrifying excitement continued to build. And when she reached that peak for the second time she plunged over it in a fevered delirium of intense quivering release and lay adrift in pleasure.

'That was amazing,' Gaetano muttered thickly, rolling over onto his back while curving an arm round her trembling body. '*You* were amazing, *bella mia*.'

Poppy felt totally exhausted and she was content to lie there in the circle of his arms and marvel at the sublime sense of peace she was experiencing. Belatedly, she acknowledged that her throat and head had now become seriously sore. She hoped that Gaetano wouldn't catch her cold and felt guilty for not warning him.

In fact she was just about to mention her affliction when Gaetano sat up to say quietly, 'Possibly part of the reason it felt so amazing was that it was the very first time I've had sex bareback.'

'Bareback?' she queried.

'I didn't use protection. I had a health check a couple of weeks ago to ensure that I'm clean and you're guarded against pregnancy,' he reminded her. 'I couldn't resist the temptation to try it.'

Poppy made no comment because she knew that he would be ultra-careful with her in the protection stakes because to be careless and risk a pregnancy would come at too high a price for either of them.

'I'm really hungry now…aren't you?' Gaetano admitted, thrusting back the sheet and vacating the bed.

'Not really, no.' Indeed the thought of forcing food past her aching throat made her wince. 'But I could murder a cup of tea.'

'You'll have to make it for yourself,' he warned her. 'I sent the staff home.'

'I've been making tea for myself since I was a child,' she told him wryly.

'I forgot.' Faint colour enhancing the exotic slant of his cheekbones, Gaetano frowned. 'Your voice sounds funny…'

'I'm getting a cold.' Poppy sighed. 'I hope you don't get it too.'

'I never catch colds.' Gaetano vanished into the bathroom and a moment later she heard the shower running.

Poppy was so exhausted that she really didn't want to move, but exhaustion was something she had become practised at shaking off and working through in recent months when she had spent all day cleaning Woodfield Hall and then had stood at the bar serving drinks all evening. Sliding out of bed, she went into the dressing room to pick an outfit and padded off to find another bathroom to use.

Gaetano hadn't hurt her much, she thought tiredly as she dressed. He had been considerate. He had made it incredibly enjoyable. Why did the knowledge that he had learned how to make sex enjoyable with other women stab her like a knife? She blinked, feeling hot and more than a little dizzy. Clearly she had caught an absolute doozy of a cold but she didn't want to be a burden by admitting to Gaetano that she felt awful. A good night's sleep would make her feel much better.

Casually clad in cotton palazzo pants and a tee shirt, she went downstairs, located the kitchen and put on the kettle. She heard Gaetano talking to someone and her brow pleated as she walked to the doorway to see who it was. She almost groaned out loud when she finally realised that he was talking into his phone in tones that sounded angry. As his brilliant dark golden eyes landed on her she froze at the chilling light in his gaze.

'What's wrong?' she asked, her voice fracturing into roughness.

Gaetano thrust his phone back in the pocket of his jeans and stared at her angrily, almost as if he'd never seen her before. 'That was Rodolfo calling to warn me about something some tabloid newspaper plans to print tomorrow. One of his old friends in the press tipped him off…'

'Oh..?' Poppy heard the kettle switching off behind

her and turned away, desperate to ease her sore throat with a hot drink.

Gaetano bit out a sharp, unamused laugh. 'When were you planning to tell me that you once worked as a nude model?'

Poppy spun back, wide-eyed with astonishment. 'What on earth are you talking about?'

'That filthy rag is going to print photos of you naked tomorrow. My wife *naked* in a newspaper for the world to see!' Gaetano launched at her in outrage. '*Madonna diavolo*...how could you cheapen yourself like that?'

'I've never worked as a nude model. There couldn't possibly be photos of me naked anywhere...' Poppy protested and then she stilled, literally freezing into place, sudden anxiety filling her eyes.

'Oh, you've just remembered doing it, have you?' Gaetano derided harshly. 'Well, thanks for warning me. If I'd known I would've bought the photos to keep them off the market.'

'It's not like you think,' Poppy began awkwardly, horrified at the idea that illegal shots might have been taken of her at the photographic studio while she was unaware. But what else could she think?

As something akin to an anxiety attack claimed her already overheated body Poppy found it very hard to catch her breath. She dropped dizzily down into the chair by the scrubbed pine table. 'I'm not feeling well,' she mumbled apologetically.

'If you think that feigning illness is likely to get you out of this particular tight corner, it's not,' Gaetano asserted in such a temper that he could hardly keep his voice level and his volume under control.

The mere idea of nude photos of Poppy being splashed all over the media provoked a visceral reaction from Gaetano. It offended him deeply. Poppy was his wife and the secrets of her body were his and not for sharing. He wanted to punch walls and tear things apart. He was ablaze with a dark, violent fury that had very little to do with the fact that another scandal around his name would once again drag the proud name of the Leonetti Bank into disrepute. In fact his whole reaction felt disturbingly personal.

'Not feigning,' Poppy framed raggedly, pushing her hands down on the table top to rise again.

'I want the truth. If you had told me about this, I would never have married you,' Gaetano fired at her without hesitation.

Poppy flopped back down into the seat because her legs refused to support her. She felt really ill and believed she must have caught the flu. He would never have married her had he known about the photo. Who would ever have thought that Gaetano, the notorious womaniser, would be that narrow-minded? And why should she care? And yet she *did* care. A lone stinging tear trickled from the corner of her eye and once again she tried to get up and leave but she couldn't catch her breath. It was as though a giant stone were compressing her lungs. In panic at that air deprivation her hands flailed up to her throat, warding off the darkness that was claiming her.

Gaetano gazed in disbelief at Poppy as she virtually

slithered off the chair down onto the floor and lay there unconscious, as pale and still as a corpse. And all of a sudden the publication of nude photos of *his* wife was no longer his most overriding concern…

CHAPTER EIGHT

'No, I don't think that my wife has an eating disorder,' Gaetano bit out between gritted teeth in the waiting room.

'Signora Leonetti is seriously underweight, dehydrated…in generally poor physical condition,' the doctor outlined disapprovingly. 'That is why the bacterial infection has gained such a hold on her and why we are still struggling to get her temperature under control. That she contrived to get through a wedding and travel in such a state has to be a miracle.'

'A miracle…' Gaetano whispered, sick to his stomach and, for the very first time in his brilliantly successful, high-achieving life, feeling like a failure.

How else could he feel? Poppy had collapsed. His wife was wearing an oxygen mask in the IC unit, having drugs pumped into her. All right, she hadn't told him how she was feeling but shouldn't a normal, decent human being have *noticed* that something was wrong?

Unfortunately he clearly couldn't claim to be a normal, decent human being. And his analytical mind left him in no doubt of exactly where he had gone wrong.

He had been too busy admiring his bride's tiny waist to register that she was dangerously thin. He had been too busy dragging her off to bed to register that she was unwell. And when she had tried to tell him, what had he done? *Porca miseria*, he had shouted at her and accused her of feigning illness!

'May I see her now?' he asked thickly.

He stood at the foot of the bed looking at Poppy through fresh eyes, rigorously blocking the sexual allure that screwed with his brain. Ironically she had always impressed him as being so lively, energetic and opinionated that he had instinctively endowed her with a glowing health that she did not possess. Now that she was silent and lying there so still, he could see how vulnerable she really was. It was etched in the fine bones of her face, the slenderness of her arms, the exhaustion he could clearly see in the bluish shadows below her eyes.

And what else would she be but exhausted? he asked himself grimly. For months she had worked two jobs, managing the hall and working at the bar. She had been so busy looking after her mother and her brother that she had forgotten to look after herself. He suspected that she had got out of the habit then of taking regular meals and rest. And even when both food and rest had been on offer in London she had *still* chosen to work every day at that café. In truth she was as much of a workaholic in her proud and stubborn independence as he was, he acknowledged bleakly. He could only hope that he was correct in believing that she did not suffer from an underlying eating disorder.

'Your grandfather is waiting outside…' a nurse informed him.

'There was no need for you to leave your bed,' Gaetano scolded the older man. 'I only texted you so that you would know where I was.'

'How is she?' Rodolfo asked worriedly.

And Gaetano told him, withholding nothing. 'I've been a pretty lousy husband so far,' he breathed in grim conclusion, conceding the point before it could be made for him.

'You have a steep learning curve in front of you.' His grandfather sighed. 'But she's a wonderful girl and well worth the effort. And it's not where you start out that matters, Gaetano…it's where you end up.'

Rodolfo could not have been more wrong in that estimate, Gaetano reflected austerely. Where you started out mattered very much if you had previously blocked the road to journey's end. His marriage was not a marriage and the relationship was already faltering. He had put up a roadblock with the word divorce on it and used that as an excuse to behave badly. He had screwed up. He had been shockingly selfish and with Poppy of all people, Poppy who had trailed round after him and his dog, Dino, on the estate when they were both kids. And what had she been like then?

Like an irritating little kid sister. Kind, madly affectionate, his biggest fan. He exhaled heavily. He had had more compassion as a boy than he had retained as an adult and he had not lived up to Poppy's high expectations. Worse still, he had taken advantage of her despair over her family's predicament. He had forced through the terms he wanted, terms she should have denied for her own sake, terms only a complete selfish bastard would have demanded. But it was a little too late to turn that particular clock back.

Was the selfishness a Leonetti trait? His father had been the ultimate egotist and his mother had never in her life, to his knowledge, put anyone's needs before her own. Had his dysfunctional parents made him the ruthless predator that he was at heart? Or had wealth and success and boundless ambition irrevocably changed him? Gaetano asked himself grimly.

Poppy surfaced to appreciate that her head had stopped aching. She discovered that she could swallow again and that her breath was no longer trapped in her chest. She opened her eyes on the unfamiliar room, taking in the hospital bed and the drip attached to her arm before focusing on Gaetano, who was hunched in the chair in the corner.

Gaetano looked as if he had been dragged through hell and far removed from the sophisticated, exquisitely groomed image that was the norm for him. His black curls were tousled, his jaw line heavily stubbled. His jacket was missing. His shirt was open at his brown throat and his sleeves were rolled up. As she stared he lifted his head and she collided with glorious dark golden eyes.

Snatches of memory engulfed her in broken bits and pieces. She remembered the passion and the pleasure he had shown her. Then she remembered his fury about the nude photos, his refusal to credit that she was ill. But she remembered nothing after that point.

Gaetano stood up and pressed the bell on the wall. 'How are you feeling?'

'Better than I felt when I fainted…er…did I faint?'

'You passed out. Next time you feel ill, *tell me*,' he breathed with grim urgency.

Poppy grimaced. 'It was our first night together.'

'That's irrelevant. Your health comes first…*always*,' he stressed. 'I'm not a little boy. I can deal with disappointment.'

She was relieved to see that his anger had gone. A nurse came in and went through a series of checks with her.

'Why did I pass out?' Poppy asked Gaetano once the nurse had departed.

'You had an infection and it ran out of control. Your immune system was too weak to fight it off,' he shared flatly. 'From here on in you have to take better care of yourself. But first, give me an honest answer to one question…do you have an eating disorder?'

'No, of course not. I'm naturally skinny…well, I have lost weight over the last few months,' she conceded grudgingly.

'You have to eat more,' Gaetano decreed. 'No more skipping meals.'

'I didn't eat on our wedding day because I wasn't feeling well,' she protested.

'Am I so intimidating that you couldn't tell me that?' Gaetano asked, springing restively upright again to pace round the spacious room.

'Come on, Gaetano. All those guests, all that fuss. What bride would have wanted to be a party pooper?'

'You should have told me that night,' Gaetano asserted.

Poppy's lashes lowered over her strained eyes. 'You weren't in the mood to hear that I was ill.'

'*Dio mio!* It shouldn't have mattered how I felt!'

A flush drove away her pallor but she kept her gaze firmly fixed on the bed. 'We had an agreement.'

'That's over, forget about it,' Gaetano bit out in a raw undertone.

She wondered what he meant and would have questioned him but the doctor arrived and there was no opportunity. Gaetano spoke to the older man at length in Italian. Breakfast arrived on a tray and she ate with appetite, mindful of the doctor's warning that she needed to regain the weight she had lost. She was smothering a yawn when Gaetano lifted the tray away.

'Get some sleep,' he urged. 'I'm going back to the house to shower and change and bring you back some clothes. As long as you promise to eat and rest, I can take you out of here this evening.'

'I'm not an invalid…' Uneasy with his forbidding attitude, Poppy fiddled with her wedding ring, turning it round and round on her finger. 'What's happened about the photos you mentioned?'

Gaetano froze and then he reached for the jacket on the chair and withdrew a folded piece of paper. 'It was a hoax…'

The newspaper cutting depicted a reproduction of a calendar shot headed Miss July. In it Poppy was reclining on a chaise longue with her bare shoulders and long legs on display while a giant floral arrangement was sited to block any more intimate view of her body.

'I kept my knickers on,' she told him ruefully. 'But I had to take my bra off because the straps showed. I was a student nurse on the ladies' football team. We did the charity calendar to raise funds for the children's hospice. There was nothing the slightest bit raunchy about the shots. It was all good, clean fun...'

Dark colour now rode along Gaetano's cheekbones. 'I know and I accept that. I'm sorry I shouted at you. When Rodolfo showed me that photo in the newspaper I felt like an idiot.'

'No, you're not an idiot.' Just very *very* possessive in a way Poppy had not expected him to be. *My* wife, he had growled, outraged by the prospect of anyone else seeing her naked.

'You have an old-fashioned streak that I never would have guessed you had,' Poppy remarked tentatively.

'What is mine is mine and you are mine,' Gaetano informed her in a gut reaction that took control of him before he could even think about what he was saying.

That gut reaction utterly unnerved him. What the hell was wrong with him? *Mine?* Since when? Only weeks earlier he would have leapt on the excuse of inappropriate nude photos to break off their supposed engagement. He had not intended to stay engaged to Poppy for very long at all, had actually been depending on her to do or say something dreadful to give him a good reason to reclaim his freedom. How had he travelled from that frame of mind to his current one? All of a sudden she felt like his wife, his *real* wife. Why was that? Sex had never meant that much to Gaetano and had certainly never opened any doors to deeper connections. But he had wanted Poppy as he had never wanted any woman before and that hunger had triumphed.

Poppy went pink. 'Not really...'

'For as long as you wear that ring you're mine,' Gaetano qualified.

Poppy hadn't needed that reminder of her true status, hadn't sought that more detailed interpretation. Her heart sank and she closed her eyes to shut out his lean, darkly handsome features. It was no good because she still saw his beautiful face in her mind's eye.

'Lie down, relax,' Gaetano urged. 'You're exhausted. I'll be back later.'

You're mine. But she wasn't. She was a fake bride and a temporary wife. Casual sex didn't grant her any status. Suppressing a groan, she shut down her brain on her teeming thoughts and fell asleep.

Late that afternoon, she left the hospital in a wheelchair in spite of her protests. In truth she still felt weak and woozy. Gaetano lifted her out of the chair and stowed her carefully in the passenger seat before joining her.

She was wearing the faded denim sundress Dolores had packed for her.

'I need to organise new clothes for you,' Gaetano told her.

'No, you don't. When this finishes we go our separate ways and I won't have any use for fancy threads.'

'But *this* isn't going to finish any time soon,' Gaetano pointed out softly.

Poppy studied his bold bronzed profile. So far they had enjoyed the honeymoon from hell but he was bearing up well to the challenge. His caring, compassionate husband act was off-the-charts good but she guessed that was purely for Rodolfo's benefit. They were supposed to be in love, after all, and a loving husband would be upset when his bride fell ill on their wedding day. Lush black lashes curled up as he turned his head to look at her, blue-black hair gleaming in the bright light, spectacular golden eyes wary.

'What's wrong?' he prompted.

'I should compliment you. You can fake nice to the manner born,' she quipped.

His wide sensual mouth compressed. For once there was no witty comeback. 'Dolores is planning to fatten you up on pasta. I also mentioned that you're passionate about chocolate.'

Chocolate and Gaetano, she corrected inwardly.

She collided with his eyes and hurriedly looked away, struggling not to revel in the sound of his dark, deep, accented drawl and the high she got from the sheer charisma of his smile. Awareness shimmied through her like an electrical storm. Something low in her tummy had turned molten and liquid while her breasts were swelling inside her bra. He had taught her to want him, she thought bitterly, and now the wanting wouldn't conveniently go away. That hunger was like a slow burn building inside her.

When they returned to La Fattoria, Gaetano insisted

that she went straight to bed and dined there. He ignored her declaration that she was feeling well enough to come downstairs and urged her to follow medical advice and rest. A large collection of books and DVDs were delivered mid-evening for her entertainment and although Poppy was tired she deliberately stayed awake waiting for Gaetano to come to bed. She drifted off around one in the morning and wakened to see Gaetano switching out the light and walking back to the door.

'Where are you going?' she mumbled.

'I'm sleeping next door,' he said wryly.

'That's not necessary.' Poppy had to fight to keep the hurt note out of her voice. She had been looking forward to Gaetano putting his arms around her again and she was disappointed that it wasn't going to happen.

'I'm a restless sleeper. I don't want to disturb you,' Gaetano countered smoothly.

Poppy's heart sank as if he had kicked it. Maybe if sex wasn't on the menu, Gaetano preferred to sleep alone. And why would she argue about that? It was possible that Gaetano had already had all he really wanted from her. She had heard about men who lost sexual interest once the novelty was gone. One night might have been enough for him. Was he that kind of lover? And if he was, what did it matter to her? It wasn't as if she were about to embarrass herself and chase after him, was it? Why would she do that when their eventual separation and divorce were already set in stone?

So, it didn't make sense that after he had gone she curled up in the big bed feeling lonely and needy and rejected. Why on earth was she bothered?

* * *

'You shouldn't be down here keeping an old man company,' Rodolfo reproved as Poppy poured his coffee and her own. 'No cake?'

'Cinzia's putting it on a fancy plate to bring it out. You're getting spoiled,' Poppy told him fondly, perching on the low wall of the terrace.

His bright dark eyes twinkled. 'Nothing wrong with being spoiled. You spoil me with your cakes but Gaetano's supposed to be spoiling you.'

Poppy's luminous green eyes shadowed. 'He does but I've let him off the honeymoon trail for a few hours to work. It keeps him happy…'

'You look well,' Gaetano's grandfather said approvingly. 'On your wedding day you looked as though a strong breeze would blow you over, now you look…'

'Fatter?' Poppy laughed. 'You can say it. I'd got too thin and I look better carrying a little more weight. Dolores has been feeding me up like a Christmas turkey.'

Hands banded round her raised knees, Poppy gazed out over the valley, scanning the marching rows of bright green vines. The property referred to as the guest house was a substantial building surrounded by trees and it had a spectacular view. It had always been Rodolfo's favourite spot and when he had tired of his late son's constant parties at the main house he had built his own bolt-hole.

Cinzia, who looked after the guest house and its elderly occupant, brought out the lemon drizzle cake that Poppy had baked.

Poppy and Gaetano had been in Tuscany for a whole

month, days fleeing past at a speed she could barely register. As soon as she had regained her strength, Gaetano had begun taking her out sightseeing. Her brain was crammed to bursting point by magnificent artworks and architectural wonders. But the memories that lingered were of a rather more personal variety.

Her delicate gold earrings were a gift from Gaetano, purchased from one of the spectacular goldsmiths on the Ponte Vecchio in Florence. In Pisa they had strolled through the magical streets to dine after the daily visitors had left and he had told her that in bright light her red hair reminded him of a gorgeous sunset. In Lucca they had walked the city walls in the leafy shade of the overhanging trees and Gaetano had briefly held her hand to steady her. In Siena she had proved Gaetano wrong when he'd told her that climbing more than four hundred steps to the top of the Torre del Mangia would be too much for her and he had laughed and given her that special heart-stopping smile that somehow always rocked her world. And in the Grotta del Vento he had whipped off his jacket and wrapped it round her when he'd seen her shiver in the coolness of the underground cave system.

Personal memories but not the romantic memories of a newly married couple, Poppy conceded unhappily. There was no sex. There had been no sex since she had taken ill and he refused to take hints. And she refused to count as romantic all the many evenings they had talked long and late at the farmhouse after a beautiful leisurely meal because every evening had ended with them occupying separate beds.

Indeed, Gaetano only got close to her in his grand-father's presence, clearly as part of his effort to keep up the pretence that they were a normal couple, and then he would close his arms round her, kiss her shoulder or her cheek, act as if he were a touchy-feely loving male even though he wasn't. His determined detachment often made Poppy want to scream and slap him into a normal reaction. What had happened to the sex-hungry male who couldn't keep his hands off her?

And while Poppy was lying awake irritating herself by wondering how to tempt Gaetano without being too obvious about it and scolding herself for being so defensive, another bigger worry slowly began to percolate in the back of her mind. At first she had told herself off for being foolish. After all, they had only had sex once and she had conscientiously taken the contraceptive pill from the first day it was prescribed to her. When her period was late she had believed that her illness or even the change of diet or stress could have messed up her menstrual cycle. As the days trickled past her subdued sense of panic had steadily mounted and she was very glad that she was visiting the doctor the following day for an official review following her release from hospital a month earlier. She would ask for a pregnancy test then just to be on the safe side. And of course she would soon realise that she had been foolishly worrying over nothing. There was no way she could possibly be pregnant.

Leaving Rodolfo snoozing in the shade, Poppy clicked her fingers to bring Muffin gambolling to her side as she strolled back to the main house.

Muffin had made a full recovery from his injuries and had been inseparable from Poppy from the day Gaetano had brought him back from the vet's and settled the little terrier in his wife's lap. The dog ran ahead as Poppy walked below the trees enjoying the cool shade rather than the heat of late afternoon. She smiled at the colourful glimpses of poppy-and-sunflower-studded fields visible through the gaps between the trees.

Since the wedding she had talked to her mother and brother every week on the phone. Damien was happy in his new job while her mother had renewed contact with Poppy's aunt, Jess, who had stopped seeing her sister when she became an alcoholic. Now there was talk of Poppy's mother going to live with her sister in Manchester after she was released.

That idea left Poppy feeling oddly abandoned and she told herself off for her selfishness because it was not as if she herself would be in a position to set up home with her mother any time soon. No, Poppy was very conscious that she had a long, hard haul ahead of her faking being happily married to Gaetano for at least a couple of years. And if she was miserable, well, she accepted that that was her own fault as well. If her emotions made her miserable it was because she had failed to control them. Her craving for Gaetano's attention had been the first warning sign, missing him in bed after only one night the second. From that point on the warning signs had simply multiplied into a terrifying avalanche.

If Gaetano held her hand, she felt light-headed. If he touched her she lit up inside like a firework. If he smiled her heart soared. Her adolescent crush had grown into something much more dangerous, something she couldn't control and that occasionally overwhelmed her. She had fallen madly, insanely in love with the husband who wasn't a husband. It wasn't fair that Gaetano should be so beautiful that she found intense pleasure in simply looking at him. It was even less fair that he was such entertaining company and had wonderful manners. Nor did it help that he took great pains to ensure that she ate well and rested often, revealing a caring side she had only previously seen in play around his grandfather. It was all a cheat, she kept on telling herself. It was a cheat because he wasn't available to her in any way even though she loved him.

She *loved* Gaetano. She was ashamed of that truth when he had warned her not to make that mistake long before he'd even married her. How had she turned out so predictable? It was not as if she believed in the pot of gold at the end of the rainbow. She was not a dreamer now that she had grown up. She knew that no happy ending awaited her and she would cope as long as she contrived to keep her emotional attachment to herself because she would die a thousand deaths before she allowed Gaetano to even suspect how she felt. He hadn't asked for love from her and he didn't want her love. No way was he getting her love for free so that he could pity her.

A fancy sports car that didn't belong to Gaetano's collection was parked outside La Fattoria. Poppy smoothed down her exotic black and red sundress, one of the designer garments Gaetano had purchased for her weeks ago. It was cutting-edge style and edgy enough to feel comfortable to her, so she had acquiesced to the new wardrobe, mortified by the suspicion that for her to insist on continuing to wear cheap clothing would embarrass Gaetano. No, he might deserve a kick for seducing her with unforgettable enthusiasm and then stopping that intimacy in its tracks, but she still cringed at the idea of embarrassing him in public.

Gaetano saw his wife from the front window, her show-stopping long legs silhouetted beneath the thin fabric of her dress. It was see-through, and it killed him to see her legs and recall that one indescribably hot night when he had slid between them. Feeling his trousers tighten, he gritted his teeth. The sooner he was out of their marriage and free again, the more normal he would feel.

In truth nothing had felt normal since their wedding. Being around Poppy without being able to touch her was driving him insane. He had a high sex drive and he had never tried to suppress it before. But for the first time in his life with a woman he was trying to do the right thing and it was hurting like a bitch. Poppy deserved more than he had to give. But inexplicably Poppy had got under his skin and since he had laid eyes on her no other woman had attracted him. Although he'd satisfied himself sexually with her, he still desired her, which was a first for him. The thrill of the chase had gone, but the hunger lingered, ever present, ever powerful. There was something about her that affected him differently from other women. She didn't irritate him, she didn't make demands, she didn't care about his money. In the strangest of ways she reminded him of his grandmother, who had been as at home with staff as she was with visitors. Poppy's easy charm was spread wide and he no longer marvelled that Rodolfo idolised her and the household staff couldn't do enough for her. Even that ugly little dog was her devoted slave.

'Sorry… I needed to freshen up,' Serena announced as she walked back into the drawing room. 'I got blown to bits. I forgot to tie my hair back before I drove over.'

Gaetano studied the smooth golden veil of Serena's hair. He had never seen her with a hair out of place. Poppy's hair got madly tangled, but she didn't care. It had been wild that night in bed, he recalled, fighting off arousal as he pictured that vibrant mane tumbled across the pillows, her lovely face flushed and full of satisfaction, satisfaction *he* had given her.

Poppy entered and froze at the sight of Serena. 'Sorry, I didn't realise you had company.'

'Oh, I'm not company. I'm one of Gaetano's oldest friends,' Serena reminded her. 'How are you, Poppy? I would have called in sooner, but it is your honeymoon, after all.'

'Are you staying round here?'

'Didn't Gaetano tell you that my parents have had a house near here for years and years? We first met at one of his parents' parties when we were teenagers,' Serena told her with a golden-girl smile of fond familiarity aimed at Gaetano.

Serena was the wicked witch in the disguise of a beautiful princess, Poppy decided bleakly. Serena knew exactly where to plunge the knife and twist it in another's woman's flesh. She loved to boast of how well, how intimately and how long she had known Gaetano. 'Fancy that,' she said non-committally.

'I'm actually here to beg for a favour,' Serena confided cutely. 'I met Rodolfo in the village last week and he told me that Gaetano was flying to Paris for a conference tomorrow. May I come too? As you know I'm looking for a new job and I could use the introductions you'd give me.'

'Of course. I'll pick you up on the way to the airport,' Gaetano suggested calmly.

Hell no, Poppy thought, watching Serena look at Gaetano with a teasing girly smile and a shake of her golden head that sent the silken strands tossing round her perfect face. Her teeth ground together.

'Are you coming too?' Serena asked Poppy.

But Poppy could see that somehow Serena had already established that Gaetano would be travelling to Paris alone. 'No, I'm afraid I have an appointment to keep,' Poppy admitted.

'I wish you'd agreed to reschedule that. I wanted to accompany you,' Gaetano reminded her with detectable exasperation.

Poppy wrinkled her nose. 'It's only a check-up.'

And she didn't want him attending the doctor's surgery with her because she didn't want him present for the discussion of the pregnancy possibility.

'I could cancel and come to Paris with you,' she heard herself offer abruptly, because she really didn't want Serena getting the chance to be alone with Gaetano.

'You need to keep that appointment,' Gaetano countered levelly. 'In any case, I'll be back by evening.'

'I'll look after him,' Serena assured her smugly and Poppy wondered unhappily if the other woman somehow sensed that Gaetano's marriage was not quite normal. Or was it simply that the beautiful blonde could not imagine a male as well educated and sophisticated as Gaetano marrying an ordinary woman without there being some hidden agenda?

She had paled at Serena's self-satisfaction. Gaetano had not been with a woman in a month. Naturally Poppy didn't want him on board his private jet with a man-eater like Serena. Serena was already putting out willing and welcome signals as bright as traffic lights. But what could Poppy possibly say to Gaetano to inhibit him in such a marriage as theirs? He didn't belong to her. She didn't own him.

There were other ways of holding onto a man's attention though, she reasoned abstractedly. There was using sex as a weapon, exactly the sort of manipulative behaviour she had looked down on *before* she fell in love with Gaetano. Now, all of a sudden confronted by Serena studying Gaetano as though he were one of the seven wonders of the world, Poppy's stance on the moral high ground felt foolish and dangerous. Pride wouldn't keep her warm at night if Gaetano succumbed to Serena's advances and embarked on an affair with her. An affair that Poppy suspected would soon be followed by divorce and remarriage because she didn't believe that Serena would accept being hidden in the background or that Gaetano would resist the chance to acquire a woman who would make a much more suitable wife.

* * *

Gaetano released his breath in a slow hiss when Poppy joined him for dinner in a black halter-necked dress that outlined her lithe, slender figure. His intense dark gaze rested briefly on the taut little buds of her breasts that were clearly defined by the thin fabric and he compressed his lips round his wine glass. Look, *don't* touch, he told himself grimly.

'I've been wondering,' he remarked. 'What made you choose nursing?'

Surprised by the topic, Poppy lifted and dropped her bare shoulders. 'I like caring for people. Being needed makes me feel useful.'

'Your family certainly needed you,' Gaetano said drily.

The main course was served. After eating in silence for a few minutes Poppy said, 'I'm thinking of doing something other than nursing when the time comes.'

'Such as?' Gaetano prompted impatiently.

'Gardening,' she admitted in a defensive tone.

'Gardening?' Gaetano repeated with incredulity.

'I always discounted my interest in growing things because I come from several generations of gardeners. But I suppose it's in my blood,' Poppy opined wryly. 'Of course if I'd ever mentioned it I would have found myself working for your family and I didn't want that.'

'I've never understood why not. We're good employers.'

'Yes, but working on the estate means real old-fashioned service.'

'And what is bartending but service?' Gaetano watched her turn to lift her water glass and his attention dropped to the firm, full, pouting curve of her breast revealed by her dress. He shifted tensely in his seat.

'There's not that same sense of inequality between employer and employee that there is on the estate. I can't explain it but I've never accepted that you are superior to me simply because you were born into wealth and privilege.'

'Have I ever made you feel that way?'

Poppy pushed away her plate and stood up. 'You can't help it. Your parents raised you like that.'

'Where are you going?'

'For a walk—it's a beautiful evening. I'll have space for dessert by the time I come back,' she told Sean, who was hovering to remove their plates.

'I'll come too.' Gaetano sprang upright.

Poppy was as restless as a cat on hot bricks, which was hardly surprising when she had set herself the objective of somehow seducing Gaetano before his flight to Paris. Sadly discussing her career aspirations and the class system wouldn't get her any closer to him and she wasn't very deft at flirting. If all else failed, she thought ruefully, she would simply slip into bed with him and pray that his libido cracked his detachment.

'That's a daring dress,' Gaetano observed. 'The split in the skirt shows me your thighs at every step and I can see the curve and shape of your breasts. Don't wear it anywhere more public…'

Poppy was relieved that he had actually noticed the provocative outfit because it meant that she wasn't yet fading into the wallpaper as far as he was concerned. Her high heels crunched through the gravel. A finger danced up her exposed spine like a flame licking at her bare skin and she shivered, snatching in a breath as he flicked the knot at the nape of her neck. 'If I pulled that loose…'

'The whole thing would probably fall off,' she completed.

Gaetano groaned out loud. 'Don't tempt me.'

'I didn't think you could be tempted any more.'

'Temptation runs on a continuous loop around you.'

Poppy glanced at him with disbelieving eyes. 'Then why have you been keeping your distance?'

'It should've been that way from the start, *bellezza mia*. I was a selfish bastard to insist on sex.'

'So, tell me something new,' Poppy invited.

After a moment of telling silence, Gaetano's stunning dark golden gaze locked to her flushed face in near wonderment at that response before he burst out laughing. 'Well, that's telling me…'

'If you wanted lies you married the wrong girl.'

'Obviously,' Gaetano conceded, lounging back against an aged stone pedestal table at the viewpoint where the land fell away to reveal the panoramic landscape beyond the garden. Poppy gazed out at the beautiful countryside, her hair glowing like a live flame against her ivory skin as the sun went down.

'I'm not being fair to you,' Poppy muttered with sudden awkwardness. 'I wanted sex too!'

'Maybe when we were actually having it but not before,' Gaetano qualified.

'Oh, for goodness' sake, Gaetano... I couldn't *wait* to rip your clothes off!' Poppy flung back at him in exasperation. 'I didn't stay a virgin until this age by not knowing what I wanted. I'm not some easily led little rag doll. Stop talking as if you took advantage of a naïve kid!'

'But I *did* take advantage of you.' Gaetano reached out to grip both her hands in emphasis and prevent her from her constant pacing back and forth in front of him. 'You were a virgin and I'm a natural predator. What I want I take. And I very much wanted you.'

Poppy took a step closer to his lean, powerful body. 'How much is "very much"?'

He brought her hands down lightly to the revealing bulge at his groin. Her fingertips fluttered appreciatively over the hard jut of his erection and he jerked in surprise at that intimate caress. His golden eyes smouldering with erotic heat, he pulled her up against him and crushed her ripe pink mouth beneath his, his tongue darting and delving deep to send tiny shudders of shocking arousal coursing through her lower body. Liquid heat pooled between her thighs.

'You're a tease,' Gaetano told her darkly.

'No, I'm a sure thing,' Poppy contradicted, helpless in the grip of the need throbbing and pulsing through her trembling length.

She felt the sudden give at her neck as he tugged loose the tie of her dress. As the bodice dropped to her waist his hands closed to her hips and he lifted her up onto the stone table before reaching below the skirt to close his hands into the waistband of her lace knickers and yank them down.

'Out here?' she whispered, shaken by the concept as he dug her discarded underwear into his pocket with single-minded efficiency.

'Out here because I couldn't make it back indoors... and I believe I can promise you a very active night,' he husked, bending her backwards to capture a rosy nipple between his lips and lash it with his tongue while his fingers stroked and teased the delicate pink folds at her core.

'I want you,' she framed jaggedly, her breath strangled in her throat by a responsive gasp as his thumb rubbed over her and then a long finger tested her readiness.

He slid a single digit into her lush opening and her body jackknifed, spine arching, hips lifting off the cold stone surface. And the coldness below her only added to the intense heat punching through her quivering body, steamrollering over her inhibitions and heightening every sensation to an unbearable level.

'So wet, so tight,' Gaetano growled, yanking down his zip with a lack of cool that even in the state he was in astounded him. On some level the hunger was so all-consuming that he honestly thought he might die of overexcitement if he didn't get inside her.

His mouth roved between the straining mounds of her perfect breasts, tugging at the swollen buds, arrowing lower, letting her feel the long, slow glide of his tongue while he pulled her to the edge of the table to position her.

He plunged in and drove the breath from her body with the intensity of his entrance. She whimpered as he stretched her, her body clenching round him like a hot velvet glove.

'*So* good,' Gaetano ground out between gritted teeth as he pulled back and slammed back into her with delicious force.

Poppy couldn't think, she could only feel and she was riding a torrent of excitement she couldn't control, her entire being pitched to crave the peak of his every powerful thrust. The heat and the hunger and the pleasure all melded together into one glorious, overwhelming rush of sexual ecstasy. Her climax claimed her in an explosive surge of intense sensation and her teeth bit into his shoulder as the exquisite convulsions shook her violently in his arms.

In the aftermath she was as limp as a floppy doll. He fed her feet back into her underwear, retied her dress and lifted her down to the ground again where she swayed, utterly undone by the sheer primal wildness of their joining.

'Did I hurt you?'

'No, you blew me away,' she whispered truthfully.

'You bring out the animal in me, *delizia mia*,' he admitted raggedly, pressing his sensual mouth to the top of her down-bent head in what felt like a silent apology.

'And I like it,' Poppy admitted shakily. 'I like it very much.'

'What the hell have we been playing at, then, for the last few weeks?' he demanded.

Poppy shot him a teasing glance. 'You were depriving me of sex. Why, I have no idea.'

But Gaetano was in not in the mood to talk. He was already painfully aware of the lack of logic in his recent behaviour. He couldn't answer his own questions, never mind explain or defend his decisions to her. He had honestly believed that for once he was doing the honourable thing and that she would appreciate his restraint. Evidently he had got that badly wrong. She was accusing him of depriving her. *Diavelos*...no doubt it was sexist but he was the one who had felt most deprived. And being deprived of the joy of her body had eased his conscience.

His brooding silence nagged at Poppy's nerves. Perhaps even though he enjoyed the physical release of her body he had preferred the distance provided by their lack of intimacy. Maybe he was worried she was getting too attached. Maybe she wasn't as good an actress as she liked to believe.

'It was just sex, you know,' she mumbled as lightly as she could. 'It doesn't have to mean anything.'

'I know,' Gaetano fielded drily while also knowing that he could never, ever have imagined having a wife who would admit that she had just used him for sex.

It felt wrong to him and downright offensive but he was willing to admit that getting married to Poppy and living with her while struggling to stay out of her bed had played merry hell with his values. One hint of encouragement from her and he had shelved honour without a backward glance. In fact he'd been a pushover, he conceded grimly. He craved her like a drug. He was already thinking of early nights, dawn takeovers and afternoon siestas, hopefully the kinkier, the better, because his bride was still on a wonderful learning curve. Did it really matter if she only wanted him for sex?

Why complicate something simple? She was right. It was just sex, not something he had ever felt the need to agonise over or attach labels to. *Maledizione!* What was she doing to his brain? Why was he dwelling on something so basic?

CHAPTER NINE

'I BELIEVE THE medication you received in hospital may have disrupted your birth control. Of course, no contraceptive pill is foolproof either. It's an interesting conundrum,' Mr Abramo remarked as if the development were purely one of academic interest. 'Fortunately you're in much better health than you were a month ago…absolutely blooming, in fact!'

Poppy's smile felt stiff because she was still in shock. She was pregnant, one hundred per cent with no room for error pregnant and Gaetano was likely to go into even greater shock over that reality. One night, one bout of passion, one baby. Obviously, Gaetano would feel that he had been very unlucky. What were the odds of such a development? What would he want to do? How would he react? She was already praying that he would not hope that she might be willing to consider a termination.

While it was true that she hadn't planned on a baby, she still wanted the child that was now on its way. Her baby and Gaetano's, a little piece of Leonetti heritage that even Gaetano couldn't take off her again, divorce or otherwise. A little boy, a little girl, Poppy wasn't fussy about the gender. Indeed she was getting excited about the prospect of motherhood and feeling guilty about the fact. How could she dare to look forward happily to an event that would probably seriously depress and infuriate Gaetano, who preferred to plan everything and liked to believe that he could control everybody and everything in his life? The baby would be a wildly out-of-control event. And Gaetano had been frank from the outset that he did not want to risk a conception when they were planning to part. Having foreseen that scenario, he had set out to prevent that situation arising.

Before her conscience could claim her and stifle her natural impulses, Poppy paid a visit to a very exclusive baby shop in Florence where without the smallest encouragement she purchased an incredibly expensive shawl and a tiny pair of exquisite white lace bootees. When she emerged again, clutching a cute beribboned bag, she saw her pair of bodyguards exchanging knowing looks and, scolding herself for her mindless compulsion, made a hurried comment about needing wrapping paper for her gift.

When she returned to La Fattoria for lunch, Gaetano was still in Paris. But he might well have fallen asleep during the flight there, Poppy thought with a wicked little smile. Quite deliberately she had exhausted him. A sexually satiated tired male was unlikely to be tempted by the offer of sex on the side. She had kept him up half the night and had awakened him at dawn in a manner that he had sworn was the ultimate male fantasy.

His response had been incredibly enthusiastic. But then Gaetano had remarkable stamina, she reflected sunnily. She ached all over. She ached in places she hadn't known she could ache but it had all been in a good cause. Surely Serena could no longer be considered a threat?

Given the smallest excuse, Gaetano would have abandoned Serena at the airport. Her incessant flirtatiousness had begun to irritate him during the flight back. Raunchy jokes about bankers and the mile-high club had fallen on stony ground. Gaetano had partied on board when he'd acquired his first private jet but those irresponsible days were far behind him now that he was in the act of becoming the new CEO of the Leonetti Bank. He was quietly satisfied by the attainment of that long-held ambition but he had spent far more time choosing a gift for Poppy during a break between meetings than he had spent considering his lofty rise in status. Ironically now that he had that status it meant less than he had expected to him. His focus in life had definitely shifted in a different direction.

Poppy got sleepy in the late afternoon and went for a nap. She lay on the bed wondering about how best to share her news with Gaetano and tears prickled her eyes because she feared his reaction. He wasn't likely to be happy about her pregnancy and she had to accept that. It would drive them apart, not keep them together. Fate had thrown them something that couldn't be easily worked around.

Gaetano was strangely disappointed when Poppy didn't greet him downstairs as Muffin did. Muffin hurled himself cheerfully at Gaetano's legs, refused to sit when told and barked like mad. Muffin didn't discriminate. Everyone who came through the front door received the same boisterous, undisciplined welcome. Dolores informed Gaetano that Poppy had gone up to lie down and concern quickened the long strides with which he mounted the stairs. Suddenly Gaetano was worrying about what the doctor might have told his wife about her health because taking forty winks in the evening was more Rodolfo's style.

As Gaetano entered the bedroom, Poppy, roused by Muffin's barks, pushed herself up on her elbows and smiled, tousled red hair falling round her sleep-flushed face.

'I exhausted you last night,' Gaetano assumed with a wolfish grin of all-male satisfaction as he stood at the foot of the bed. 'I wondered what you were doing in bed and started worrying about what Mr Abramo might have said but that was before I remembered that you had another very good reason to need some extra rest.'

'It's the heat. It makes me feel drowsy.' Butterflies danced to a jungle beat in her tummy while she studied him.

In his beautifully tailored designer suit, Gaetano was a vision of masculine elegance and sex appeal. He was gorgeous with dark stubble outlining his strong jaw line and those intense dark eyes below his extraordinary lashes. Her breasts tingled and heat simmered low in her pelvis.

'It's weird because I've only been away a few hours...

but I missed you,' Gaetano confided in a constrained undertone. 'What did Mr Abramo have to say?'

Poppy tensed and swung her legs off the side of the bed so that she was half turned away from him. 'He had some news for me after the tests,' she told him tautly.

'What sort of news?' Gaetano prompted, shedding his jacket and jerking loose his tie while wondering if she would consider him excessively demanding and greedy if he joined her on the bed.

'Unexpected news,' Poppy qualified tightly. 'You're going to be surprised.'

'So, go ahead and surprise me,' Gaetano urged, unsettled by her uncharacteristic reluctance to meet his eyes and shelving the sexual trail to force his brain to focus.

'I'm pregnant.' She framed the words curtly, refusing to sound apologetic or nervous, putting it out there exactly like the fact of life it was.

'How could you possibly be pregnant?' Gaetano shot at her with an incredulous frown. 'If it had only just happened, it would be too soon to know and the one and only other time…it isn't possible…'

'It *is* possible. I fell ill that same day and I missed taking my pill. Mr Abramo also believes the drugs I was given could have interfered with my birth control,' she told him flatly.

'You got pregnant on our wedding night?' Gaetano queried in astonishment. 'From *one* time? What are you? The fertility queen?'

'You didn't use a condom,' she reminded him.

'There shouldn't have been a risk.'

'If you're having sex there's always a risk,' she pointed out ruefully. 'The odds weren't good that night because I ended up in hospital. In any other circumstances we'd probably have got away with it.'

'Pregnant,' Gaetano repeated, expelling his breath on a long slow hiss as he paced over to the windows, the taut muscles in his lean behind and long, powerful legs braced rigid with tension. 'You're pregnant.'

Although there was little expression in his dark, deep drawl Poppy took strength from his lack of anger and his ability to joke. Gaetano was dealing with it, *wasn't he*? He was good in a crisis, very cool-headed and logical and what they had right now was undeniably a *huge* crisis. A baby nobody had counted on was on the way, a baby she would nonetheless love and protect to the best of her ability.

Gaetano was still feeling light-headed with shock. A baby! He was going to be a father? *Dio mio*…he was in no way prepared to be a parent. Having a child was a massive responsibility. It had proved a challenge too much for his own parents and even Rodolfo had struggled with the test of raising Gaetano's good-for-nothing father. How the hell would he manage? What did he have to offer a child?

'Gaetano?' Poppy probed in the tense silence.

He swung round and raked long brown fingers through his cropped black hair in a gesture of frustration. 'A baby… I can't believe it. That's some curve ball to be thrown.'

'Yes,' Poppy agreed stiffly. 'For both of us.'

'In fact it's a nightmare,' Gaetano framed, shocking

her with that assessment, which was so much more pessimistic than her own.

Poppy stiffened but fought not to take that comment too personally. 'Not much I can do to change your outlook if that's how you feel.'

'I don't like the unexpected, the spontaneous,' he admitted grimly. 'A baby will turn our lives upside down.'

'But there's a positive side as well as a negative side,' Poppy murmured.

'Is there?' Gaetano traded in stark disagreement. 'We had a divorce planned.'

Poppy lost colour and screened her eyes. A *nightmare*? That had been a body blow but that his second comment on their situation should refer to their divorce was even tougher. But what had she expected from him? A bottle of champagne and whoops of satisfaction? It could have been a lot worse, she told herself urgently. Gaetano could have lost his temper. He could have tried to imply that the pregnancy was somehow more her fault than his. But then possibly he hadn't reached that stage yet. After all, he was still pretty much stunned, studying her with brilliant dark eyes that had an unusually unfocused quality. *We had a divorce planned.* He had gone straight for the jugular.

'But, obviously I couldn't possibly leave you to raise my child alone,' Gaetano completed without skipping a beat. 'Looks like we're staying together, *bella mia.*'

Poppy stiffened at his bleak intonation. 'So, you're suggesting that we should forget about getting a divorce now?'

'What else would I suggest?' Gaetano asked very

drily. 'You're carrying the next generation of the Leonetti dynasty. Nobody expects you to do that alone, least of all me. Even though I had two parents they did a fairly rubbish job of raising me. To thrive, our child will need both of us and a stable home to grow up in.'

'But it's not what we planned,' Poppy reminded him while anger simmered like a pot bubbling on the hob beneath her careful surface show of calm.

There was nothing to be gained from losing her temper, she told herself fiercely, but his practical approach was downright insulting. Yes, she agreed that ideally a child should have both parents and a steady home but at what cost? If the parents themselves made sacrifices that resulted in unhappiness how could that be good for anyone? Poppy did not want an unwilling husband and reluctant father by her side. That was not a cross she was prepared to bear for years knowing that it wouldn't benefit anyone. If that was the best Gaetano had to offer, he could keep it and the wedding ring, she thought painfully. She wanted more, she *needed* more than a man who would only keep her as a wife because she had fallen pregnant.

'We couldn't possibly make a bigger mess of our marriage than my parents did,' he pointed out wryly. 'We can only try our best.'

'As a goal, that just depresses me, Gaetano,' Poppy admitted.

'How? We'll continue on as we are now but at least we won't be living a lie for Rodolfo's benefit any longer.'

'No, *you* won't need to live a lie any longer,' Poppy agreed tightly as she walked towards the door.

'Where are you going?'

Powered by a furious mix of anger and pain, Poppy ignored the question and stalked up the stairs to the next floor where the luggage was stored. From the room used for that purpose she grabbed up two cases.

From his stance on the landing, Gaetano stared at her in bewilderment. 'What on earth are you doing?'

'Your nightmare is leaving you!' Poppy bit out squarely.

'I did not call you a nightmare,' Gaetano argued vehemently.

'No, you called the baby I'm having a nightmare, which was worse,' Poppy countered fiercely. 'This baby may be unplanned and a big unexpected surprise but I love it already!'

'*Dio mio*, Poppy!' Gaetano exclaimed as she yanked garments out of the built-in closets in the dressing room, hangers falling in all directions. 'Will you please calm down?'

'Why would I calm down? I'm pregnant and my husband thinks it's a nightmare!'

'I didn't mean it that way.'

'And you seem to believe that I have no choice but to stay married to you. Well, here's some news for you, Gaetano… I can have a baby and manage perfectly well without you!' Poppy slung at him from between gritted teeth. 'I don't *need* you. I deserve more. I don't intend to stay married to a guy who's only with me because he thinks it's his duty!'

'That's not what I said.'

'That's exactly what you said!' Poppy slammed a case

down on the bed and wrenched it open. 'Well, this particular nightmare of yours is taking herself off. There's got to be better options than you waiting for me.'

Standing very still, Gaetano lost colour and watched her intently. 'There probably is. But I want very badly for you to stay.'

'No, you don't, not really,' Poppy reasoned thinly. 'You think our baby would be the icing on the cake for Rodolfo but you don't want to be married and you don't want to be a father.'

'I *do* want to be married to you.' Gaetano flung back his shoulders and studied her with strained dark eyes. 'And I know that I can learn how to be a good father. I meant that the situation of being unprepared for a child was a nightmare. I'm not good with surprises but I can roll fast with the punches that come my way. And believe me, watching you pack to leave me *is* a hell of a punch.'

The firm resolution in that response surprised her. She paused to roughly fold up a dress before thrusting it into the case, sending an unimpressed glance at his lean, darkly handsome face. She wasn't listening to him, she told herself urgently. She had made her decision. It was better for her to leave him with her head held high than to consider giving him another chance... wasn't it?

'Is it? Are you really capable of changing your outlook to that extent? Accepting being married without feeling that you're somehow doing me a favour and settling for second best?' she queried with scorn. 'Accepting our child as the gift that a child is?'

'I know that I was difficult when I married you.' Gaetano compressed his lips on that startling admission. 'I'm not easy-going but I am adaptable and I do learn from my mistakes. *Dio mio, bella mia*…my attitude to you has changed most of all.'

'How?' Poppy prompted, needing him to face up to the major decision he was trying to make for both of them. She didn't want Gaetano deciding that they should stay married and then changing his mind again because he felt trapped by the restrictions. She had to know and understand exactly what he was thinking and feeling and expecting. How else could she make a decision?

His wide sensual mouth twisted. 'I don't want to discuss that.'

'Why not?'

'Because sometimes silence is golden and honesty can be the wrong way to go,' he framed grudgingly. 'And knowing my luck, I'll say the wrong thing again.'

'But you should be able to tell me anything. We shouldn't *have* secrets between us. How has your attitude to me changed?' Poppy persisted, curiosity and obstinacy combining to push her on.

Gaetano glanced heavenward for a brief moment and then drew in a ragged breath. 'I asked you to pretend to be engaged to me because I thought you would be a huge embarrassment as a fiancée.'

Shock gripped Poppy in a debilitating wave only to be swiftly followed by a huge rush of hurt. 'In what way?'

'I was the posh bloke who made unjustified assumptions about you,' Gaetano admitted, his deep voice raw-edged with regret. 'I assumed you'd still be using a lot of bad language. I expected you to be totally lost and unable to cope in my world. In fact I believed that your eccentric fashion sense and everything about you would horrify Rodolfo and put him off the idea of me getting married, so that when the engagement broke down he would be relieved rather than disappointed...'

Gaetano had finished speaking but his every word still struck through the fog of Poppy's shell-shocked state like lightning on a dark stormy night. She felt physically sick.

Gaetano had watched the blood drain from below her skin and fierce tension now stamped his lean dark features. 'So that's the kind of guy I really am, the kind of guy you get to stay married to and the father of your future child. I know it's not pretty but you have earned the right to know the truth about me. Most of the time I'm an absolute bastard,' he stated bleakly. 'I tried to use you in the most callous way possible and it didn't once occur to me to wonder how that experience would ultimately affect you...or Rodolfo.'

Poppy wrapped her arms round her slim body as if she were trying to hold the dam of pain inside her back from breaking its banks. She couldn't bear to look at him any longer. He had seen from the outset how unworthy she was to be even his fiancée and he had planned to use her worst traits and the handicap of her poor background as an excuse to dump her again without antagonising his grandfather. In short he had handpicked her as the fake fiancée most likely to mortify him.

Poppy cringed inside herself. His prior assumptions appalled her, for she had not appreciated how prejudiced he had still been about her. Shattered by his admission, she felt humiliated beyond bearing. He had seen her flaws right at the beginning and had pinned his hopes on her shaming him. How could he then adapt to the idea of staying married to her for years and years? Raising a child with her? Taking her out in public?

'The moment I picked you to fail was the moment that I sank to my all-time personal low,' Gaetano confessed in a roughened undertone. 'I got it horribly wrong. You *showed* me how wrong my expectations were. You proved yourself to be so much more than I was prepared for you to be and I became ashamed of my original plan.'

'But you didn't need to tell me this once we went as far as getting married,' she whispered brokenly, backing in the direction of the door, desperate to lick her wounds in private.

'You've always been honest with me. I'm trying to give you the same respect.'

'Only a couple of months ago you had *no* respect for me!' Poppy condemned with embittered accuracy.

'That changed fast,' Gaetano fielded, moving a step closer, wanting to hold her so badly and resisting the urge with a frustration that coiled his big hands into fists. 'I *learned* to respect you. I learned a lot of other stuff from you as well.'

Feeling as though he were twisting a knife in her heart, Poppy voiced a loud sound of disagreement and snapped, 'You didn't learn anything...you never do. You're dumb as a rock about everything that really matters from giving Muffin a second chance at life to raising our child!' she accused. 'How could I ever trust you again?'

Poppy stalked out of the door and he fought his need to follow her. He didn't want her racing down the stairs and falling in an effort to evade him. 'Muffin trusts me,' he murmured flatly to the empty room. *Muffin?* Muffin who couldn't even tell him and Rodolfo apart? Admittedly, Muffin wasn't the sharpest tool in the box.

Gaetano groaned out loud. Maybe he should have kept on pretending to be a better man than he was but Poppy would only have found him out in the end. Poppy had a way of cutting through the nonsense to find the heart of an issue and see what really mattered. Just as Gaetano had finally seen what really mattered. Unfortunately that single instant of inner vision and comprehension had arrived with him pretty late in the day. He wasn't dumb as a rock about emotional stuff. He simply wasn't very practised at it. It wasn't something he'd ever bothered with until Poppy came along.

Poppy pelted out into the cool night. She needed air and space and silence to pull herself back together. The garden was softly lit, low-sited lights shining on exotic leaves and casting shadows in mysterious corners. Her face was wet with tears and she wiped her cheeks with angry hands. Damn him, damn him, damn him! What he had confessed had wounded her deeply. She loved Gaetano and he had always been her dream male. Handsome, brilliant, rich and glitzy, he had met every requirement for an adolescent fantasy. Now for the first time she was seeing herself through his eyes and it was so humiliating she wanted to sink into the earth and stay hidden there for ever.

He had only remembered the highly unsuitable bold girl with the potty mouth, and eccentric clothes, who could be depended on to embarrass him. And being Gaetano, who was never ever straightforward when he could be devious, manipulative and complicated instead, he had hoped to utilise her very obvious faults to frighten Rodolfo out of demanding that his grandson marry. And ironically, Rodolfo himself had set Poppy up for that fall by advising Gaetano to marry 'an ordinary girl'. And just how many ordinary girls did a jet-setter like Gaetano know?

None. Until Poppy had stumbled in that night at Woodfield Hall, to demand his attention and his non-existent compassion.

An embarrassment to him? No conventional dress sense, a dysfunctional family, no idea how to behave in rich, exclusive circles. Well, nothing had changed and she would never reach the high bar of social acceptability. Poppy shuddered, sick to her stomach with a galling sense of defeat and failure. She had never cared about such things but evidently Gaetano did. Even worse, Gaetano was currently offering to stay married to his unsuitable bride because she was pregnant.

She sat down on one of the cold stone seats sited round the table and her face burned hot in spite of the cool evening air when she remembered what had happened on that table only the day before. Gaetano was like an addiction, toxic, dangerous. He had gone from infuriating her to charming her to making her fall very deeply in love with him. And yet she had still never guessed how he really saw her. The gardener's daughter with the unfortunate family. It hurt—oh, my goodness, it *hurt*. But he had been right to tell her because she had needed to know the truth and accept it before she could stop weaving silly dreams about their future. So, how did she stay married to a male who had handpicked her to be an embarrassment?

The answer came swiftly. In such circumstances she could *not* stay married to Gaetano. Regardless of her pregnancy, she needed to leave him and go ahead with a divorce.

'Poppy…'

Poppy stiffened. He must have walked across the grass because she would have heard his approach had he used the gravel paths. She breathed in deep, stiffening her facial muscles before she lifted her head.

'Should I have kept it a secret?' he asked her in a raw undertone.

He knew she was upset. His dark eyes were lingering on her, probably picking up on the dampness round her eyes even though she had quickly stopped crying. He noticed too much, *knew* too much about women. 'No,' she said heavily. 'It was better to tell me. I don't like you for it and it'll be hard to live with what I now know but you can't build a relationship on lies and pretences.'

Gaetano stilled in the shadow of the trees, his white shirt gleaming, his spectacular bone structure accentuated by the dim light. 'Don't leave me,' he framed unevenly. 'Even the idea of being without you scares me. I wouldn't like my life without you in it.'

Poppy couldn't imagine Gaetano being scared and she imagined his life would be a lot more normal and straightforward without her in it. Their child deserved better than to grow up with unhappily married and ill-matched parents. A divorce would be preferable to that. She would give Gaetano as much access as he wanted to their child but she didn't have to live with him or hang round his neck like an albatross to be a good parent. They could both commit to their child while living separately.

'I can't stay married to you,' she told him quietly. 'What would be the point?'

'I'm not good with emotions. I'm good at being angry, at being passionate, at being ambitious but I'm no good at the softer stuff. I lost that ability when I was a kid,' Gaetano admitted grittily. 'I loved my parents but they were incapable of loving me back and I saw that. I also saw that in comparison to them I felt *too* much. I learned to hide what I feel and eventually it became such a habit I didn't have to police myself any more. Emotion hurts. Rejection hurts, so I made sure I was safe by not feeling anything.'

Involuntarily, Poppy was touched that he was talking about his parents in an effort to bridge the chasm that had opened up between them. He never ever talked about his childhood but she would never forget his determined non-reaction when his dog had died, his stark refusal to betray any emotion. 'That makes sense,' she conceded.

'The only woman I ever loved after my mother left was my grandmother.'

'I thought at some stage you and *Serena*...'

'No. I walked away from her because I felt nothing and I knew there should be more.'

Poppy bowed her head, wondering why he was trying to stop her from walking away from him.

'I'm not quite as dumb as a rock,' Gaetano asserted heavily. 'But I was all screwed up about you long before we even got to the wedding. Unfortunately marrying you only made me ten times more screwed up.'

'Screwed up?' Poppy queried, shifting uncomfortably on her hard stone seat.

'I got really involved with the wedding.'

'Yes, that was a surprise.'

'I wanted it to be special for you. I became very possessive of you. I assumed it was because we hadn't had sex.'

'Obviously,' Poppy chimed in because he seemed to expect it.

'In fact I was really only thinking in terms of sex.'

Poppy sent him a rather sad smile. 'I know that... it's basically your only means of communication in a relationship.'

'You're the only woman I've ever had a relationship with.'

Poppy stared at him, green eyes luminous in the light. 'How can you say that with your reputation?'

'All those weeks after your illness when I didn't touch you but we were together all the time...that was like my version of dating,' Gaetano told her darkly. 'The affairs I had with women before you went no further than dinner followed by sex or the theatre followed by sex or—'

'OK… I've got the picture,' she cut in hurriedly, her gaze clinging to the dark beauty of his bronzed features with growing fascination. 'So…your version of dating?'

'I wanted to get to know you—'

'No, you were on a massive guilt trip because I fell ill. That's why you didn't sleep with me again and why you spent so much time entertaining me.'

'I'm not a masochist. I spent so much time with you because I was enjoying myself,' Gaetano contradicted. 'And I didn't touch you again because I didn't want to be selfish. I thought you would be happier if I made no further demands.'

Poppy sent him a withering appraisal. 'You got it wrong.'

'Poppy…let's face it,' Gaetano muttered heavily. 'I got *everything* wrong with you.'

Her tender heart reacted with a first shard of genuine sympathy. 'No, the sex was ten out of ten and your version of dating was amazingly engaging. You made me happy, Gaetano. You definitely win points for that.'

'I bought you something today and it wasn't until I bought it and realised what it symbolised that I finally understood myself,' he framed harshly, pulling a tiny box from his pocket.

Poppy studied the fancy logo of a world-famous jeweller with surprised eyes and opened the box. It was a ring, a continuous circlet of diamonds that flashed like fire in the artificial light. She blinked down at it in confusion.

'It's an eternity ring,' Gaetano pointed out very quietly.

A laugh that wasn't a laugh at all was wrenched from Poppy. 'Kind of an odd choice when before you came home and I made my announcement you were set on eventually getting a divorce,' she pointed out.

'But it expresses how I feel.' Gaetano cleared his throat in obvious discomfiture. 'When you talk about leaving me, it tears me apart. Because somewhere along the line, somehow, I fell in love with you, Poppy. I know it's love because I've never felt like this before and the idea of losing you terrifies me.'

'Love…' Poppy whispered shakily.

'Never thought it could happen to me,' Gaetano confided in a rush. 'I didn't want it to happen either. I didn't want to get attached to anyone and then you came along and you were so perfect I couldn't resist you.'

'P-perfect?' she stammered in a daze.

Gaetano dropped down on his knees in the dew-wet grass and reached for her hand. He tugged off the engagement ring and threaded on the eternity ring so that it rested beside her wedding ring. 'You're perfect for me. You get who I am, even with my faults. The money doesn't get in the way for you, doesn't impress you. You keep me grounded. You make me unbelievably happy. You make me question my actions and really think about what I'm doing,' he bit out. 'With you, I'm something more, something better, and I need that. I need you in my life.'

Her lashes fluttered. She could hear him but she couldn't quite believe him, there on his knees at her feet, his hand trembling slightly in hers because he was scared, he was scared she wouldn't listen, wouldn't accept that he really loved her. And that fear touched her down deep inside, wrapping round her crazy fears about Serena and the terrible insecurities that had sent her running out of the house and sealing them for ever. Suddenly none of that existed because Gaetano *loved* her, Gaetano *needed* her...

'I love you so much. I couldn't stand to lose you and my first thought when you told me you were pregnant was, "She'll stay now," and it was a massive relief to think that even though you didn't love me you would stay so that we could bring up our child together.'

'I do love you,' Poppy murmured intently, leaning forward to kiss him.

'You're not just saying it because I said it first?' Gaetano checked.

'I really, *really* love you.'

'Even though I don't have a single loveable trait?' he quoted back at her quick as a flash.

'You grew on me like mould,' Poppy told him deadpan.

Gaetano burst out laughing and sprang upright, pulling her up into the circle of his arms. 'Like mould?' he queried.

Poppy looked up into his beautiful eyes and her heart did a happy dance inside her. 'I like cheese,' she proclaimed defensively.

'Do you like your ring?'

'Very much,' she told him instantly, smiling up at him with a true sense of joyful possessiveness. 'But I like what it symbolises most of all. You didn't want to let me go, you wanted to keep me.'

'And I intend to keep you for ever and ever. Anything less than eternity wouldn't be enough, *amata mia.*'

'The baby was a shock, wasn't it?' She sighed, walking back towards the house with him hand in hand.

'A wonderful one. Our little miracle,' Gaetano said with sudden rueful humour. 'It took one hell of a baby to get in under my radar, so I'll be expecting a very determined personality in the family.'

Gaetano halted at that point to claim a kiss. And Poppy threw herself into that kiss with abandon. He pressed her back against a tree trunk, his body hard and urgent against hers and a rippling shudder of excitement shimmied through her slender length.

'Let's go to bed,' she suggested, looking up at him with bold appreciative eyes.

'We haven't had dinner yet and a mother-to-be needs sustenance,' Gaetano told her lazily, trailing her indoors and out to the terrace where the table awaited them.

But neither of them ate very much. Between the intense looks exchanged and the suggestive conversation, it wasn't very long before they headed upstairs at a very adult stately pace, which broke down into giggles and a clumsy embrace as Poppy rugby-tackled Gaetano down onto the floor of their bedroom. By the time they made it to the bed and he had moved the suitcase she had left there they were kissing passionately and holding each other so tightly that it was a challenge to remove clothes. But they managed through kisses and caresses and mutual promises to make love with all the fire and excitement that powered them both and afterwards they lay with their arms wrapped round each other, secure in their love and talking about their future.

Poppy glanced out of the front window and saw her children with Rodolfo. Sarah was holding his hand and chattering, her little face animated below her halo of red curls. Benito was pedalling his trike doggedly in front of them, ignoring the fact that the deep gravel on the path made cycling a challenge for a little boy.

Sarah was four years old and took after her mother in looks and her father in nature. She already knew all her numbers, was very much a thinking child and tended to look after her little brother in a bossy way. Benito was two, dark of hair and eye and as lively as a jumping bean. He was on the go from dawn to dusk and generally fell asleep during his bedtime story in his father's arms.

Sometimes, or at least until she looked at her expanding family, Poppy found it hard to credit that she had been married for five years. Gaetano might have been a late convert to family life but he had taken to it like the proverbial duck to water. He adored his children and rushed home to be with them and it was thanks to his persuasion that Poppy was carrying their third child. Third and last, she had told him firmly even though she liked the way their family had developed. In retrospect she was glad they hadn't waited and that Sarah had taken them by surprise and not having too big a gap between the children meant that they could grow up with each other.

But, at the same time, Poppy was also looking forward to having more time to devote to her own interests. She had taken several landscape designer courses over the years and was planning to set up a small landscaping firm. She had redesigned the gardens at La Fattoria to make them more child-friendly and had already taken several private commissions from friends, one of which had won an award. The gardens at the London town house and at Woodfield Hall both bore her stamp and when she wanted to relax she was usually to be found in a greenhouse tending the rare orchids she collected.

Gaetano was CEO of the Leonetti Bank and when he travelled, Poppy and the children often went with him. He put his family first and at the heart of his life, ensuring that they took lengthy breaks abroad to wind down from their busy lives. Poppy's mother, Jasmine, had made a good recovery and was now training as an addiction counsellor to help others as she had been helped. She lived in Manchester with her sister but she was a frequent visitor in London, as was Poppy's brother. Damien, backed by Gaetano, had recently started up a specialist motorcycle repair shop.

In fact there wasn't a cloud in Poppy's sky because she was happy. Sadly, Muffin had passed away of old age the year before and he had been replaced by a rescued golden Labrador who enjoyed rough and tumble games with the children.

'Guess who…' A pair of hands covered her eyes while a lean, hard body connected with hers.

Poppy grinned. The familiar scent of Gaetano's cologne assailed her while his hands travelled places nobody else would have dared. 'You're the only sex pest I know,' she teased, suppressing a moan as the hand that had splayed across her slightly swollen belly snaked lower and circled, sending sweet sensation snaking through her responsive body.

Gaetano spun his wife round and she reached up to wind her arms round his neck. 'Sorry, I slept in this morning and missed seeing you.'

'You were up with Benito last night when he had a nightmare, *amata mia*,' he reminded her. 'That's why I didn't wake you.'

Poppy teased the corner of his wide sensual mouth with her own, heat warming her core. She wanted to drag him to the bed and ravish him. Her hunger for him never went entirely away. He shrugged off his jacket and stared down at her with smouldering dark golden eyes. 'Share the shower with me…'

'Promise not to get my hair wet,' she bargained.

'You know I can't.' An unholy grin slashed Gaetano's lips. 'Sometimes you get carried away. Is that my fault?'

'Absolutely your fault,' his wife told him as she peeled off her dress.

Gaetano treated her to a fiercely appreciative appraisal. 'Did I ever tell you how amazingly sexy you look when you're pregnant?'

'You may have mentioned it once or twice—'

'Sometimes I can hardly believe you're mine. I love

you so much, *amata mia*,' Gaetano swore passionately, gathering her up into his arms with care and kissing her breathless.

'I love you too,' she said between kisses, happiness bubbling through her at the sure knowledge that she was going to get her hair very wet indeed.

* * * * *

'You're so...so...'

'I know what you're going to say. You're going to tell me that I'm *so arrogant*... I prefer *confident*.'

Delilah laughed, and just like that Daniel kissed her—and this time his kiss wasn't lingering and explorative. This time it was hungry and demanding. He manoeuvred her so that they had stepped out into the darkness and his mouth never left hers.

She'd been kissed before, but never like this. His hunger matched hers, and she whimpered and coiled her fingers into his hair, pulling him into her and then arching her head back so that he could kiss her neck, the side of her face, the tender spot by her jawline.

She was shocked by the need pouring through her in a tidal wave that eclipsed every preconceived notion she had ever had about the nature of relationships.

When he pulled away, she actually moaned. 'And you wonder why I'm nervous.'

The Italian Titans

Temptation personified!

Theo and Daniel De Angelis have never wanted for anything. These influential Italians command empires and conduct every liaison on *their* terms…until now.

Because these enigmatic tycoons are about to face their greatest challenge in the most unlikely of forms— two gorgeous girls with demands of their own!

Find out what happens next in:

Theo's Story:
Wearing the De Angelis Ring
January 2016

Daniel's Story:
The Surprise De Angelis Baby
February 2016

THE SURPRISE
DE ANGELIS BABY

BY
CATHY WILLIAMS

Published in Great Britain 2016
By Mills & Boon, an imprint of HarperCollins*Publishers*
1 London Bridge Street, London, SE1 9GF

© 2016 Cathy Williams

ISBN: 978-0-263-92099-4

Printed and bound in Spain
by CPI, Barcelona

Cathy Williams can remember reading Mills & Boon Modern Romance books as a teenager, and now that she is writing them she remains an avid fan. For her, there is nothing like creating romantic stories and engaging plots, and each and every book is a new adventure. Cathy lives in London and her three daughters—Charlotte, Olivia and Emma—have always been, and continue to be, the greatest inspiration in her life.

Books by Cathy Williams

Mills & Boon Modern Romance

The Wedding Night Debt
A Pawn in the Playboy's Game
At Her Boss's Pleasure
The Real Romero
The Uncompromising Italian
The Argentinian's Demand
Secrets of a Ruthless Tycoon
Enthralled by Moretti
His Temporary Mistress
A Deal with Di Capua
The Secret Casella Baby
The Notorious Gabriel Diaz
A Tempestuous Temptation

The Italian Titans

Wearing the De Angelis Ring

One Night With Consequences

Bound by the Billionaire's Baby

Seven Sexy Sins

To Sin with the Tycoon

Protecting His Legacy

The Secret Sinclair

Visit the Author Profile page at
millsandboon.co.uk for more titles.

CHAPTER ONE

COULD THE DAY get any better?

Daniel De Angelis stepped out from the air-conditioned comfort of his black chauffeur-driven Mercedes and removed his dark sunglasses to scan the scenery around him.

Frankly—perfect. Brilliant sunshine glinted on the calm turquoise water of the Aegean Sea. He'd never made it to Santorini before, and he took a few minutes to appreciate the scenic view of the bowl-shaped harbour from where he stood, looking down on it from a distance. He could even make out the vessel he had come to snap up at a bargain price.

It looked as picture-perfect as everything around it, but that, of course, was an illusion. It was semi-bankrupt, on its last legs—a medium-sized cruise ship which he would add to his already vast portfolio of conquests.

He knew down to the last detail how much money it had lost in the past five years, how much it owed the bank, how much its employees were paid, how discounted their fares were now they were desperate to get customers… He practically knew what the owners had for their breakfast and where they did their food shopping.

As with all deals, big or small, it always paid to do his homework. His brother, Theo, might have laughingly referred to this extravagant purchase as nothing more than a toy—something different to occupy him for a few months—but it was going to be a relatively expensive toy, and he intended to use every trick in the book to make sure he got the best possible deal.

Thinking about his brother brought a grin to his face. Who'd have thought it? Who would have thought that Theo De Angelis would one day be singing the praises of the institution of marriage and waxing lyrical about the joys of love? If he hadn't heard it with his own ears when he had spoken to his brother earlier in the week then *he* wouldn't have believed it.

He looked around him with the shrewd eyes of a man who knew how to make money and wondered what he could do here. Exquisite scenery. Exquisite island, if you could somehow get rid of the hordes of annoying tourists milling around everywhere. Maybe in the future he would think about exploiting this little slice of paradise, but for the moment there was an interesting acquisition at hand, and one which would have the benefit of his very personal input—which was something of a rarity. He was relishing this break from the norm.

Then there was his successful ditching of the last woman he had been dating, who had become a little too clingy for comfort.

And, last but not least on the feel-good spectrum, a sexy little blonde thing would be waiting for him when his time was up on that floating liner so far from paradise…

All in all this was going to be something of a holiday and, bearing in mind the fact that he hadn't had one of those in the longest while, Daniel was in high spirits.

'Sir? Maybe we should head down so that you can board the ship? It's due to leave soon…'

'Shame… I've only been here for a few hours.' Daniel turned to his driver, whom he had brought with him from the other side of the world on an all-expenses-paid, fun in the sun holiday, with only a spot of driving to do here and there. 'I feel Santorini could be just the place for me… Nice exclusive hotel somewhere… Kick back and relax…'

'I didn't think you knew how to do that, sir.'

Daniel laughed. Along with his brother and his father, Antonio Delgado was one of only a few people in whom he had absolute trust, and in fairness his driver probably knew more about his private life than both his brother *and* his father, considering he drove him to his numerous assignations with numerous women and had been doing so for the past decade.

'You're right.' He briskly pulled open the car door and slid inside, appreciating the immediate drop in temperature. 'Nice thought, though…'

In truth, kicking back by the side of a pool with a margarita in one hand and a book in the other wasn't his thing.

He kicked back in the gym occasionally, on the slopes occasionally and far more frequently in bed—and his women all ran to type. Small, blonde, sexy and very, very obliging.

Granted, none of them stayed the course for very long, but he saw that as just an occupational hazard for a man whose primary focus—like his brother's—had always been on work. He thrived on the pressure of a high-octane, fast-paced work-life filled with risk.

He had benefited from the privileges of a wealthy background, but at the age of eighteen, just as he had done with Theo, his father, Stefano De Angelis, had told him that his fortune was his to build or not to build as the case might be. Family money would kick-start his career up to a certain point, but that would be it. He would fly or fall.

And, like Theo, he had flown.

Literally. To the other side of the world, where he had taken the leisure industry by storm, starting small and getting bigger and bigger so that now, at not yet thirty, he owned hotels, casinos and restaurants across Australia and the Far East.

He had acquired so much money that he could spend the remainder of his life taking time out—next to that pool with a book in one hand and a margarita in the other—and *still* live in the sort of style that most people could only ever dream of. But work was his passion and he liked it that way.

And this particular acquisition was going to be novel and interesting.

'Don't forget,' he reminded Antonio, 'you're to drop me off fifteen minutes away from the port.'

'It's boiling out there, sir. Are you sure you wouldn't rather enjoy the air-conditioning in the car for as long as possible?'

'A little discomfort won't kill me, Antonio, but I'm deeply touched by your concern.' He caught his driver's eye in the rearview mirror and grinned. 'No, it's essential that I hit the cruise ship like any other passenger. Arriving in the back seat of a chauffeur-driven Merc isn't part of the plan.'

The plan was to check out the small cruise liner incognito. The thing hadn't made a buck in years, and he wanted to see for himself exactly where the myriad problems lay. Mismanagement, he was thinking. Lazy staff, incompetence on every level...

He would spend a few days checking out the situation and making a note of who he would sack and who he would consider taking on as part of his team when the liner was up and running in its new format.

Judging from the list of airy-fairy scheduled activities, he was thinking that the entire lot would be destined for unemployment.

Five days. That was the time scale he had in mind, at the end of which he would stage his takeover. He didn't anticipate any problems, and he had big plans for the liner. Forget about woolly lectures and cultural visits while on board substandard food was served to passengers who frankly wouldn't expect much more, considering the pittance they were paying for their trips.

He intended to turn the liner into one of unparalleled luxury, for a wealthy elite whose every whim would be indulged as they were ferried from golf course to golf course in some of the most desirable locations in the world. He would decide on the destinations once the purchase was signed, sealed and delivered.

As with every other deal he had successfully completed, Daniel had utter confidence that he would succeed with this one and that the ship would prove to be a valuable asset. He had never failed and he had no reason to assume that this would prove the exception.

At the port, with the shiny black Merc behind him and a battered backpack bought especially for the purpose slung over his shoulder, he cast a jaundiced eye over the motley crew heading onto the liner.

Already he could see that the thing was in a deplorable state. How could Gerry Ockley, who had inherited this potential goldmine from his extremely wealthy father, have managed so thoroughly to turn it into something that no self-respecting pirate would have even considered jumping aboard to plunder? How the hell could he ever have imagined that some wacky cultural cruise would actually turn a profit?

True, it had taken over eight years to run it into the ground, but he would have thought that someone—bank manager...good friend...concerned acquaintance...*wife*— would have pointed him in the right direction at some point.

The liner was equipped to hold two hundred and fifty passengers comfortably, in addition to all the crew

needed. Daniel figured that at present it was half full—
if that.

He would be joining it halfway through its trip and,
ticket at the ready, he joined the chattering groups of
people, mostly in their mid-fifties and early sixties, who
were gathering in preparation for boarding.

Did he blend in? No. When it came to anyone under
the age of thirty-five, as far as he could tell he was in the
minority. And at six foot two he was taller than nearly
everyone else there.

But he was in no doubt that he would be able to fend
off any curious questions, and he was tickled pink that he
would be travelling incognito for the next few days. Was
that really necessary? Possibly not. He could always have
stayed where he was, in his plush offices in Australia, and
formulated a hostile takeover. But this, he thought, would
afford him the opportunity of removing at least some of
the hostility from his takeover.

He would be able to tell Ockley and his wife exactly
why he was taking over and exactly *why* they couldn't refuse him. He would be able to point out all the significant
shortcomings of their business and he would be able to
do that from the advantageous perspective of someone
who had been on board their liner. He was being kind,
and in the process would enjoy the experience. The fact
that the experience would be reflected in his offer would
be a nice bonus.

He could feel inquisitive eyes on him as the crowd of
people narrowed into something resembling an orderly
queue. With the ease born of habit he ignored them all.

His appearance matched his battered backpack. He was
just a broke traveller on a cut-price cultural tour of the
Greek islands and possibly Italy. His hair, a few shades
lighter than his brother's, was slightly longer than he normally wore it, curling at the nape of his neck, and as he

hadn't shaved that morning his face was shadowed with bristle. His eyes, however, the same unusual shade of green as his brother's, were shrewd as they skimmed the crowds. He had tucked his sunglasses into his pocket.

The sun was ferocious. He could feel himself perspiring freely under the faded polo shirt and realised he shouldn't have worn jeans. Fortunately, he had a few pairs of khaki shorts in the backpack, along with an assortment of tee shirts, and those should do the trick in the blistering sun once he was on board the liner.

He switched off the thought, his mind already moving to work, planning how he would co-ordinate the work to be done on the liner and the time when it would be ready to set sail in its new, improved condition. He would charge outrageous prices for anyone lucky enough to secure a ticket, and he had no doubt that people would be queuing to pay.

Done deal.

He hadn't felt this relaxed in ages.

Delilah Scott eyed her mobile, which was buzzing furiously at her, and debated whether she should pick it up or not.

Her sister's name was flashing on the screen, demanding urgent attention.

With a little sigh of resignation she answered, and was greeted with a flurry of anxious questions.

'Where on earth have you been? I've been trying to get through to you for the past two days! You know how I worry, Delly! It's mad here, with the shop… I can't believe you've decided, just like that, to extend your holiday! You *know* I'm depending on you getting back here to help… I can't do it on my own…'

Delilah felt her stomach churn into instant nervous knots.

'I—I know, Sarah,' she stammered, gazing through the tiny porthole of her very small cabin, which was just big enough for a single bed, the very barest of furniture, and an absolutely minuscule en-suite shower room. 'But I thought the added experience would come in handy for when I get back to the Cotswolds... It's not like I'm on *holiday*...' she tacked on guiltily.

'You *are* on holiday, Delly!' her sister said accusingly. 'When you said that you'd be doing some teaching for a fortnight, I never expected you to send me an email telling me that you'd decided to extend the fortnight into *six weeks*! I *know* you really needed to get away, Delly...what with that business with Michael...but *still*... It's *manic* here...'

Delilah felt the worry pouring down the phone line and experienced another wave of guilt.

Back home, Sarah was waiting for her. Building work which was costing an absolute arm and a leg was set to begin in two weeks' time, and she knew that her sister had been waiting for her to get back so that they could weather it together.

But was it too much to take a bit of time off before the dreadful drudgery of normal life returned? She had just completed her art degree, and every single free moment during those three years she had been in that tiny cottage with her sister, worrying about how they were going to survive and counting the takings from the gallery downstairs in the certain knowledge that sooner or later Dave Evans from the bank was going to lose patience and foreclose.

And then there had been Michael...

She hated thinking about him—hated the way just remembering how she had fallen for him, how he had messed her around, made her feel sick and foolish at the same time.

She definitely didn't want to hear Sarah rehashing that horrible catastrophe. Delilah loved her sister, but ever since she could remember Sarah had mothered her, had made decisions for her, had worried on her behalf about anything and everything. The business with Michael had just fed into all that concern. Yes, it was always great to have the comfort of someone's love and empathy when you'd just had your heart broken, but it could also be claustrophobic.

Sarah cared so much…always had…

Their parents, Neptune and Moon, both gloriously irresponsible hippies who had been utterly and completely wrapped up in one another, had had little time to spare for their offspring. Both artists, they had scratched a living selling some of their art, and later on a random assortment of crystals and gems after their mother had become interested in alternative healing.

They had converted their cottage into a little gallery and had just about managed to survive because it was slap-bang in the middle of tourist territory. They had always benefited from that. But when they had died—within months of one another, five years previously—sales of local art had already begun to take a nosedive and things had not improved since.

Sarah, five years older than Delilah, had been doing the best she could, making ends meet by doing the books for various people in the small village where they lived, but it had always been understood that once Delilah had completed her art degree she would return and help out.

As things stood, they had taken out a substantial loan to fund renovations to the gallery, in order to create a new space at the back where Delilah would teach art to anyone local who was interested and, more importantly, other people, keen on learning to draw and paint, who would perhaps attend week-long courses, combining sightseeing in the picturesque Cotswolds with painting indoors and outdoors.

It was all a brilliant if last-ditch idea, and whilst Delilah had been totally in favour of it she had suddenly, when offered the opportunity to extend her stay on board the *Rambling Rose*, been desperate to escape.

A little more time to escape the finality of returning to the Cotswolds and to breathe a little after her break-up from Michael.

Just a little more time to feel normal and relaxed.

'It'll be brilliant experience for when I get back,' she offered weakly. 'And I've transferred most of my earnings to the account. I'll admit I'm not on a fabulous amount, but I'm making loads of good contacts here. Some of the people are really interested in the courses we'll be offering...'

'Really?'

'Honestly, Sarah. In fact, several have promised that they'll be emailing you for details about prices and stuff in the next week or so.'

'Adrian's just about finished doing the website. That's more money we're having to expend...'

Delilah listened and wondered whether these few weeks on the liner were to be her only window of freedom from worrying. Sarah would not countenance selling the cottage and Delilah, in fairness, would have hated to leave her family home. But staying required so many sacrifices that she felt as though her youth would be eaten up in the process. She was only twenty-one now, but she could see herself saying goodbye to her twenties in the never-ending task of just making ends meet.

She had had a vision of having fun, of feeling young when she had been going out with Michael, but that had been a very narrow window and in the end it had just been an idiotic illusion anyway. When she thought about him now she didn't think of *fun*, she just thought of being stupid and naïve.

She knew that she was playing truant by extending her stay here, but the responsibilities waiting for her wouldn't be going anywhere…and it was nice not being mothered by her sister, not having every move she made frowningly analysed, not having her life prescribed because Sarah knew best…

She hung up, relieved to end the conversation, and decided to spend what remained of the evening in her cabin.

Maybe she would ask a couple of the other teachers on the liner—young girls, like herself—to have something to eat with her in the cabin, maybe play cards and joke about some of the passengers, who mostly reminded her of her parents. Free-spirited ageing hippies, into all sorts of weird and wonderful arty pastimes and hobbies.

Tomorrow, she would be back to teaching, and she had a full schedule ahead of her…

Daniel stretched. Peered through the porthole to a splendid view of deep blue ocean. The night before he had enjoyed an expected below average meal—though not sitting at the captain's table. That sort of formality didn't exist aboard this liner. It seemed to be one big, chattering, happy family of roughly one hundred people, of varying ages, and fifty-odd crew members who all joined in the fun. He had mixed and circulated but he knew that he'd stuck out like a sore thumb.

Now, breakfast…and then he would begin checking out the various classes—all of which seemed destined to make no money. Pottery, poetry writing, art, cookery and a host of others, including some more outlandish ones, like astronomy and palm reading.

Today he ditched the jeans in favour of a pair of low slung khaki shorts, a faded grey polo shirt and deck shoes, which he used on his own sailing boat when he occasionally took to the sea.

He paused, in passing, to glance in the mirror.

He saw what he always saw. A lean, bronzed face, green eyes, thick dark lashes, dirty blond hair streaked from the Australian sun. When he had time for sport he preferred it to be extreme, and his body reflected that. Boxing sessions at the gym, sailing on his own for relaxation, skiing on black runs...

It was after nine, and on the spur of the moment he decided to skip breakfast, pulling a map of the liner from his pocket and, after discarding some of the more outrageous courses, heading for the section of the liner where the slightly less appalling ones were taking place.

He had no idea what to expect. Every single passenger seemed to be an enthusiastic member of some course or other, and as he made his way through the ship, his sharp eyes noting all the signs of dilapidation, he peered into full classes. Some people were on deck, enjoying the sun, but it had to be said that the majority had come for the educational aspect of the cruise.

It took all sorts, he thought as he meandered through the bowels of the liner.

Inside the ship, as outside, it was very hot. The rooms in which the various courses were being taught were all air-conditioned, and for no better reason than because his clothes were beginning to stick to him like glue, he pushed open one of the doors and stepped inside.

In the midst of explaining the technique for drawing perspective, Delilah looked up and...

Her breath caught in her throat.

Lounging indolently by the door was the most stunningly beautiful man she had ever seen in her life. He definitely hadn't joined the cruise when they had started.

He must have embarked in Santorini, a late member of the passenger list.

He was tall. *Very* tall. And built like an athlete. Even wearing the standard gear of nearly every other passenger on the liner—longish shorts and a tee shirt—it was impossible to miss the honed muscularity of his body.

'May I help you?'

Everyone had turned to stare at the new recruit and she smartly called them back to attention, and to the arrangement of various little ceramic pots they had been in the process of trying to sketch.

Daniel had been expecting many things, but he hadn't been expecting this. The girl looking at him questioningly was tall and reed-slender and her hair was a vibrant shade of copper—a thousand different shades from red through to auburn—and had been tugged back into a loose ponytail which hung over one shoulder.

He sauntered into the room and looked around him at the twenty or so people, all seated in front of canvasses. A long shelf at the back held various artists' materials and on the walls several paintings were hanging—presumably efforts from the members of the class.

'If I'm interrupting I can always return later...'

'Not at all, Mr...?'

'Daniel.' He held out his hand and the girl hurried forward and briefly shook it. 'I joined the cruise yesterday,' he expanded, 'and I haven't had time to sign up to any of the courses...'

'But you're interested in art?' That brief meeting of hands had sent a sharp little frisson skittering through her and it was all she could do to maintain eye contact with him. 'I'm Delilah Scott, and I'm in charge of the art course...'

Up close, he was truly spectacular. With an artist's eye she could appreciate the perfect symmetry of his lean face. The brooding amazing eyes, the straight nose and the wide, sensual mouth. His hair looked sun-washed— not quite blond, but nothing as dull as brown—and there was something about him…something strangely charismatic that rescued him from being just another very good-looking guy.

She would love to paint him. But right now…

'I can explain the course that I run…'

She launched into her little set speech and edged slightly away, because standing too close was making her feel jumpy. She'd had enough of men to last a lifetime, and the last thing she needed was to start feeling jumpy around one now.

'Of course I don't know what standard you're at, but I'm sure you'll be able to fit in whether you're a complete beginner or at a more intermediary level. I can also show you my qualifications… You would have to return later to get the proper lowdown, because as you can see I'm in the middle of taking a class and this one will last until lunchtime… But perhaps you'd like to see some of the work my class have been doing…?'

Not really, Daniel thought, but he tilted his head to one side and nodded with a show of interest.

She was as graceful as a ballerina. He liked women curvy and voluptuous. This girl was anything but. She was willowy, and dressed in just the sort of appalling clothes he disliked on a woman. A loose ankle-length skirt in a confusing number of clashing colours and a floaty top that left way too much to the imagination.

Personally, he had never been a big fan of having to work on his imagination when it came to women. He liked to see what he was getting, and he'd never had any trouble in finding beautiful women keen to oblige. Small, tight clothes showing off curves in all the right places… Girls who were in it for fun, no-strings-attached relationships. True, the occasional woman might get a little too wrapped up in planning for a future that wasn't going to happen, but that was fine. He just ditched her. And not once had he ever felt a qualm of guilt or unease about doing that because he was straight with every single one of them upfront.

He wasn't ready for marriage. He wasn't even in it for anything approaching long term. He didn't want a partner to meet his family and close friends and start getting ideas. He didn't do home-cooked meals or watching telly or anything remotely domesticated.

He thought of Kelly Close and his lips thinned. Oh, no, he didn't do *any* of that stuff...

As far as Daniel De Angelis was concerned, at this point in his life work was way more important than women, and when and if he decided to tie the knot— which was nowhere in the near future, especially as Theo was now happily planning a big wedding himself, thereby paving the way for Daniel to take his time getting there— he intended to marry someone who didn't just see the benefits of his bank balance.

He'd had his brush with a scheming gold-digger and once was plenty enough. Kelly Close—an angelic vision with the corrupt heart of a born opportunist. He slammed the door on pointless introspection. Enough that she had been a valuable learning curve. Now he had fun. Uncomplicated fun with sexy little things, like the blonde who would be waiting for him when he jumped ship.

Delilah Scott was showing him around the room, encouraging him to look at what the aspiring artists had already accomplished while they had been on the cruise.

'Fascinating,' he murmured. Then he turned to her before she could conclude the tour. 'So—lunch. Where shall we meet and what time?'

'Sorry?' Delilah asked in confusion.

'You said you wanted to give me the lowdown on the course. Over lunch sounds good. When and where? I'm guessing there's only one restaurant on the liner?'

Delilah felt a rush of heat swamp her and sharply brought herself back down to earth. 'Did I say that? I didn't think I had. You're more than welcome to just turn up tomorrow morning for the class, or you could join in right now if you like… There's lots of paper…pencils…'

Those amazing green eyes, the opaque colour of burnished glass, made her want to stare and keep on staring.

'I intend to spend the morning considering my options,' Daniel inserted smoothly. 'Checking out what the other courses are…whether they're more up my street… I'll meet you for lunch at twelve-thirty in the restaurant. You can tell me all about your course and see whether it fits the bill or not…'

Not his type, but eye-catching all the same. Skin as smooth as satin, sherry-coloured eyes, and she was pale gold after time spent in the sun. And her mouth… Its full lips parted now as she looked at him.

'I don't think there's any need for me to explain the course over *lunch*…'

'You're in the service industry… Surely that implies that you have to serve the customer? I'm just after some information…'

'I know that, but…'

But Michael had left her wary of men like this one. Good-looking men who were a little offbeat, a little off the beaten track…

Eight months ago Michael Connor had sauntered into her life—all long, dark hair and navy blue eyes and a sexy, sexy smile that had blown her away. At twenty-seven, he already had a fledgling career in photography, and he had charmed her with the amazing photos he had taken over the years. He had wined and dined her and talked about taking her to the Amazon, so that she could paint and he could take pictures.

He had swept her away from all her miserable, niggling worries about money and held out a shimmering vision of adventure and excitement. Two free spirits travelling the world. She had fallen in love with him and with those thrilling possibilities. She had dared to think that she had found a soul mate—someone with whom she could spend the rest of her life. They had kissed, but he hadn't pressed her into bed, and now she wondered how long he would have bided his time until deciding that kissing and cuddling wasn't what he was in it for.

Not much longer—because he'd already had a girl-friend. Someone in one of those countries he had visited. She'd chanced upon the fact only because she had happened to see a text message flash up on his screen. When she had confronted him, he'd laughed and shrugged. So he wasn't the settling down type…? He had an open relationship with his girlfriend so what was the big deal…? He had lots of women…he was single, wasn't he? And he'd hung around with *her*, hadn't he? She hadn't *really* thought that they were going to get married and have two point two kids and a dog, had she?

She had misread him utterly. She'd been taken in by a charming facade and by her own longing for a little adventure.

She'd been a fool.

Her sister had always sung the praises of stability and a good old-fashioned guy who could provide, whose feet were firmly planted on the ground. She'd seen no virtue in their parents' chaotic lives, which had left them with debt and financial worries.

She should have paid more attention to those sermons.

'I won't occupy a lot of your time,' Daniel murmured,

intrigued by this woman who didn't jump at the offer of having a meal with him.

Delilah blinked, ready to shake her head in instant refusal.

'There's a bar... We can have something light and you can tell me all about your course. You can sell it to me.' He flung his hands wide in a gesture that was both exotic and self-deprecating at the same time. 'I'm caught on the horns of a dilemma...' Again, he found it weirdly invigorating to actually be in the position of trying to *persuade* a woman to join him for a meal 'You wouldn't want to drive a man into the arms of learning palmistry, would you?'

Delilah swallowed down a responding smile. 'I suppose if you really think it's that important...'

'Great. I'll see you in the bar at twelve-thirty. You can hone your pitch before we meet...'

Delilah watched as he strolled out of the room. She felt as though she had been tossed into a tumble drier with the speed turned to high and she didn't like it. But she'd agreed to meet him and she would keep their meeting brief and businesslike.

She could barely focus on her class for the next three hours. Her mind was zooming ahead to meeting Daniel in the bar. And sure enough when, at a little after twelve-thirty, she hesitantly walked into the small saloon bar, which was already filling up with passengers whose courses had likewise ended for the morning, there he was. Seated at a small table, nursing a drink in front of him.

He was eye-catching—and not just because he was noticeably younger than everyone else. He would have been eye-catching in any crowd. She threaded her way through to him, pausing to chat to some of the other passengers.

Daniel watched her with lazy, deceptive indolence. He hadn't boarded this third-rate liner for adventure. He had boarded it for information.

He looked at her narrowly, thoughts idly playing through his head. She seemed to know everyone and she was popular. He could tell from the way the older passengers laughed in her company, totally at ease. He was sure that she would be equally popular amongst the staff.

Who was worth keeping on? Who would get the sack immediately? He wouldn't need any of the teachers on board, but the crew would be familiar with the liner, would probably have proved themselves over a number of years and might be an asset to him. It would certainly save him having to recruit from scratch and then face the prospect of some of them not being up to the task. When it came to pleasing the wealthy there could be no room for error.

Would *she* be able to help him with the information he needed? Naturally he wouldn't be able to tell her why...

Not for a second did Daniel see this as any form of deception. As far as he was concerned he would merely be making the most of a possible opportunity, no harm done.

He rose as she finally approached him.

'You came,' he said with a slashing smile, indicating the chair next to him. 'I wasn't sure whether you would. You seemed a little reluctant to take me up on my offer.'

'I don't normally fraternise with the passengers,' Delilah said stiffly as she sat down.

'You seemed familiar enough with them just then...'

'Yes, but...'

'What can I get you to drink?'

His eyes roved over her colt-like frame. He watched the way her fingers nervously played with the tip of her ponytail and the way her eyes dipped to avoid his. If he had had the slightest suspicion that she knew who he was he might have wondered whether her shyness was some kind of act to stir his interest—because women, in his company, were usually anything but coy.

'Just some juice, please.' Delilah was flustered by the way he looked at her—as though he could see straight into her head.

Juice in hand, and with a refill of whisky for him, he returned to settle into the chair and looked at her.

'So, you wanted to know about the course…'

Delilah launched into chatter. She found that she was drawn to look at him, even though she didn't want to. It wasn't just that he was a passenger—something about him sent disturbing little chills racing up and down her spine and sent her alarm bells into overdrive.

'I've brought some brochures for you to have a look at…'

She rummaged in her capacious bag and extracted a few photocopied bits of paper, which she self-consciously thrust at him. Several had samples of her work printed inside, and these he inspected, glancing between her face and the paintings she had done at college.

'Impressive,' he mused.

'Have you seen any other courses that interest you? Aside…' She allowed herself a polite smile. 'Aside from the palmistry?'

'I'm tempted by astronomy… When it comes to stars, I feel I could become something of an expert…' Daniel murmured. His last girlfriend had been an actress. Did that count? 'But, no…' He sat back briskly, angling his chair so that he could stretch his legs to one side. 'I'm only here for a week. Probably just to take in a couple of stops. I think I'll go for yours…'

A week? Delilah felt an inexplicable surge of disappointment, but she pinned a smile on her face and kept it there as she sipped some of the orange juice.

'Well, I can't guarantee I can turn you into Picasso at the end of a week… I mean, most of the other passengers

are here for the full month, and then we have more joining us when we dock at Naples…'

'Seems a bit haphazard,' Daniel said. 'Put it this
way—I managed to get a place at the last minute, and
for whatever duration I chose…'

'It's…it's a little more informal than most cruises, I
guess,' Delilah conceded. 'But that's because it's a fam-
ily-run business. Gerry and Christine *like* the fact that
people can dip in and out…'

'Gerry and Christine?'

Ockley. He knew their names, knew how far into debt
they were. Little wonder people could dip in and out of
the cruise at whim. Any business was good business when
it came to making ends meet.

'They run the cruise ship. Actually, it's theirs, and
they're great.'

She felt herself relax, because he was so clearly interested in what she was saying. He was just another keen
passenger, and if his looks made her a bit jittery then that
was *her* problem and, after the debacle with Michael, it
was one she could easily deal with.

'Are they? In what way?'

'Just very interested in all the passengers—and the
crew have been with them for ages.'

'Is that a fact…? And I guess you know all the crew…?'

'They're wonderful. Devoted to their jobs. They all
love the fact that they're pretty much allowed free rein
with what they do… Of course they all follow the rules,
but for instance the chef is allowed to do as he likes and
so is the head of entertainment. I've been very lucky to
get this job…' She guiltily thought of her sister, but she
would be back home soon and all would be fine.

Daniel saw the shadow cross her face and for a few
seconds was intrigued enough to want to find out more
about the woman sitting in front of him. But there was no

time in his busy, compacted schedule for curiosity about a random stranger, however strangely attractive he might find her. He had to cut to the chase.

'So…' He carried the conversation along briskly. 'Tomorrow…what time do we start…?'

CHAPTER TWO

'NOW HAVE A look at the jug. George…see how it forms the centre of the arrangement? With the other two pieces in the background? So that the whole forms a geometric shape…? If you could just make the jug a teeny bit smaller, then I think we're getting there!'

For the umpteenth time Delilah's eyes skittered towards the door, waiting for it to be pushed open by Daniel.

Her calm, peaceful enjoyment of her brief window of freedom appeared to have disappeared the moment she had met the man. She had been knocked sideways by his looks, but more than that he had a certain watchfulness about him that she found weirdly compelling…

She was seeing him through the eyes of an *artist*, she had told herself, over and over again. The arrangement of his features, the peculiar aura of authority and power he emanated was quite unlike anything she had ever seen before in anyone.

She had laughingly told herself that she was reading far too much into someone who was probably a drifter, working his way through the continent. Someone who had managed to accumulate sufficient money to buy himself a few days on the liner so that he could pursue a hobby. Most of the passengers were in their fifties or sixties, on the cruise for the whole time, but there were a number who, like him, were on the cruise for a limited period of time, taking advantage of one or other of the many courses offered while enjoying the ports before disembarking so that they could continue travelling.

He was a traveller.

But she still found herself searching out the door every two minutes, and when—an hour after the class had begun—he pushed it open and strolled into the room she drew her breath in sharply.

'Class!' Everyone instantly stopped what they were doing and looked at Daniel. 'I'd like to introduce a new recruit! His name is Daniel and he's an aspiring artist, so I hope you'll welcome him in and show him the ropes if I happen to be busy with someone. Daniel… I've set aside a seat for you, with an easel. You never mentioned what level you feel you might be at…?'

Daniel didn't think that there was *any* level that might apply to him. 'Basic.' He smiled, encompassing every single person in the room, and was met with smiles in return, before their attention reverted to their masterpieces in the making.

'In that case, why don't you start with pencil? You can choose whichever softness you feel comfortable with and perhaps try your hand at reproducing the arrangement on the table in front of the class…'

She was extremely encouraging. She had kind things to say about even the most glaringly amateurish efforts. She took time to help and answered all the questions thrown at her patiently. When he told her, as he stared at the empty paper pinned to his easel, that he was waiting for inspiration to come and that you couldn't rush that sort of thing, she didn't roar with laughter but merely suggested that a single stroke of the pencil might be all the inspiration he needed.

He thought that he might have been a little more interested in art at school if he'd had *her* as his teacher instead of the battleaxe who had told him that the world of art would be better off without his input. Not that she hadn't had a point...

He'd managed something roughly the shape of one of the objects on the table by the time the class drew to an end, but instead of heading out with everyone else he remained exactly where he was, watching as she tidied everything away.

Delilah could feel his eyes on her as she busied herself returning pencils and foam pads and palette knives to the various boxes on the shelf. She'd been so conscious of him sitting there at the back of the class, sprawled out with his body at an angle and doing absolutely nothing, from what she could see. She'd barely been able to focus.

Now she turned to him and smiled politely. 'Won't you be joining the other passengers for some lunch?' she asked as she began the process of dismounting the easels and stacking them away neatly against the wall, where straps had been rigged to secure them in place.

Daniel linked his fingers behind his head and relaxed back into the chair. 'I thought you could give me some pointers on my efforts today...' He swivelled the easel so that it was facing her and Delilah walked slowly towards it.

'I'm sorry you haven't managed to accomplish a bit more,' she said tactfully. 'I was aiming for more of a *realistic* reproduction of the jugs...it's important to really try and *replicate* what you see at this stage of your art career...'

'I don't think I'll be having a career in art,' Daniel pointed out.

'So this is just a hobby for you...? Well, that's good, as well. Hobbies can be very relaxing, and once you become a bit more familiar with the pencil—once your confidence starts growing—you'll find it the most relaxing thing in the world...'

'Is that what *you* do to relax?' he asked, making no move to shift.

'I really must get on and tidy away this stuff…'

'No afternoon classes?'

'The afternoons, generally speaking, are downtime for everyone. The passengers like to go out onto the deck, or else sit in the shade and catch up with their reading or whatever homework's been set…'

'And what do *you* do?'

'I… I do a little painting…sometimes I sit by the pool on the top deck and read…'

Daniel enjoyed the way she blushed. It was a rare occurrence. The women he dated had left their blushing days far behind.

'I thought we might have lunch again today,' he suggested, waiting to see what form her refusal would take. 'As you can see…' he waved in the vague direction of his easel '…my efforts at art are crap.'

'No one's efforts at art are anything but good. You forget that beauty is in the eye of the beholder…'

'How long are you going to be on the liner for?'

'I beg your pardon?'

'Are you here for…?' He whipped out the crumpled cruise brochure from his shorts pocket, twisted it in various directions before finding the bit he wanted. 'For the full duration of a month?'

'I can't see what this has to do with the course, Mr… er… Daniel…'

'If you're going to be on the course for the full duration I *might* be incentivised to stay a bit longer than a week.'

Complete lie—but something about her appealed to him. Yet again she was in an outfit more suitable for one of the middle-aged free spirits on the cruise ship. Another flowing skirt in random colours, and another kind of loose, baggy top that worked hard at concealing her figure—which, he saw as he surreptitiously cast his eye over it, was as slender and as graceful as a gazelle's.

The libido he had planned on resting while he was on the ship stirred into enthusiastic life as he wondered what the body under the unappealing clothes might be like.

He went for big breasts. She was flat-chested—that much he could see. He went for women who were small and curvy—she was long and willowy. He liked them blonde and blue-eyed. She was copper-haired and brown-eyed.

Maybe it was the novelty… But whatever it was he was happy to go with the flow—not forgetting that she could also be a useful conduit to the information he wanted.

'Don't you have the rest of your travel plans already sorted out?' Delilah was irritated to find herself lingering on the possibility that this man she had spent about fifteen seconds with might stay on for longer than he had originally suggested.

'I try not to live my life according to too many prearranged plans,' Daniel murmured, appreciating the delicate bloom of pink in her cheeks. 'I guess we probably have that in common…'

Delilah grimaced. 'I wish that *was* like me,' she said without thinking. 'But unfortunately you couldn't be further from the truth.' She reddened and spun round, away from those piercing unusual eyes. 'Of course,' she said, 'it would be lovely if you stayed on a bit longer. I'm sure you could become an able artist if you put all your efforts into it.'

She knew that the cruise ship was running at a loss. All the crew knew that. Gerry and Christine had not kept it a secret from them at all. In fact on day one they had called a meeting and apologised straight away for the fact that they couldn't be paid more. None of the teachers on board had protested. They were there because they loved what they did, and the fact that there was sun and sea in the mix was enough for all of them.

But the Ockleys had suggested that if they could try and persuade some of the passengers to prolong their stay, or even tempt interested holidaymakers into hopping on board for a couple of days to try their hand at one of the many courses... Well, every little would help.

'Persuade me over lunch,' Daniel suggested. It felt like a challenge to get her to comply—and since when had he ever backed down in the face of a challenge? 'Unless, of course, you find my company objectionable...?'

Realistically, he didn't even countenance that.

'I had lunch with you yesterday because you wanted to find out about the course.'

Delilah did her best to dredge up the memory of her disaster of a relationship with Michael and to listen to the warning voice in her head reminding her that she was still recovering from a broken heart—which, by defini-tion, meant retreating from men, taking time out, paying attention to the value of common sense.

'So? What does that have to do with anything? We've talked about the course and now I'd like to find out whether you think I'm a suitable candidate to be on it. I wouldn't want to be accused of wasting your time...so why the hesitation?'

'Perhaps a quick lunch,' she agreed—for Gerry and Christine's sake.

Daniel smiled slowly. 'Shame the choice of food is so limited,' he said, rising to his feet and giving his effort at drawing the jug a cursory glance.

If he had really been interested in learning how to draw then she would have had to commit to an indefi-nite period of time explaining to him how he might set about improving his skills, because he clearly had none.

Fortunately he had no intention of spending too long on that particular subject.

'And it's below average…'

'Sorry?' Delilah, in the act of washing her hands, turned round and frowned. 'What do you mean?'

'From what I've sampled, the food onboard doesn't exactly set the culinary world alight, does it?'

He moved to stand by the door and watched as she gathered her bag—some sort of tapestry affair that could have held the kitchen table and sink. Again, her hair was pulled back, with strands escaping round her face, and she absently shoved the stray strands behind her ear.

'It's okay…' she said cautiously.

'You don't want to rat on your fellow crew members,' Daniel murmured, with a hint of amusement in his voice. 'I understand that. But just between the two of us, I've been disappointed with what I've been served so far…'

'I don't think the passengers come for the food…'

'It's all part and parcel of the package,' Daniel said expansively. 'You said that the chef is allowed free rein…?'

'But he has to stick to a budget,' Delilah qualified uncomfortably. 'Anyway, it doesn't really matter, does it? I mean, if you're *really* unhappy, then perhaps you should mention something to Christine…'

'Who is the head chef?'

'Stan…and he works really hard to do the best he can with the money he's allotted…' She tripped along behind him, riveted by the long, lean lines of his muscular body.

'Don't worry,' Daniel said in a placating voice.

They had reached the bar and, as usual, people were tucking in to the offerings in a desultory fashion. Salads… baguettes with a variety of fillings…jacket potatoes…

It beggared belief that the owners of the liner had got their mismanagement down to such a fine art. Had they *no* concept of the importance of good food onboard a cruise liner, where the passengers did not have the option of scouting around for alternative restaurants?

'I'm not going to accost your pal in front of the chip-fryer...'

'Can I tell you something?' She reached into her bag for her wallet and insisted that she paid for his drink, as he had paid for hers the day before. This wasn't a date.

Daniel was chuffed. He couldn't remember the last time any woman had offered to pay for anything for him—not that he would have allowed it. But, no...the offer had never been made anyway. And yet this girl, who clearly bought her clothes from charity shops, was offering to buy him a drink. He was oddly touched by that. If only she knew!

His inherent cynicism quickly rose to the surface. If only she knew how much he was worth, then there was no chance in hell that she would be dipping into her wallet to buy him anything.

Once upon a time, in the tragic wake of his mother's death, he had foolishly allowed his emotions their freedom. He had fallen for Kelly Close's sympathetic ear. He had harboured no suspicions about the sweet-natured primary school teacher who had been into doing good and giving back to the community. He'd enjoyed lavishing gifts on her, enjoyed basking in her shyly endearing acceptance of whatever he bought for her.

Until he'd glimpsed the band of pure steel underneath the shyness when she had ditched her job and suggested that they make their arrangement permanent. It had occurred to him then, belatedly, that when you got past all the coy dipping of the eyes and trembling, grateful smiles, she had managed to acquire quite a substantial nest egg of priceless jewellery—not to mention the studio apartment he had bought her because the lease on her own flat had supposedly expired, and the countless weekends away.

At that point he had tried to pull back and bring some common sense to bear on the proceedings. He had discovered then that gold-diggers came in all different shapes and sizes and, his guard temporarily down, had realised that Kelly Close had found her way through the cracks in his armour and staged a clever assault, with her eventual aim being a wedding ring on her finger and a claim to his vast inheritance should they ever divorce. Which, he had seen very quickly, would have happened sooner rather than later.

A clean severing of the ways, however, had turned into a cat fight. Threats of a kiss-and-tell exposé to the tabloids had resulted in money changing hands—a vast sum of money, which had hit him at the worst possible time. In return he had managed to secure a contract with a privacy clause, prohibiting her from ever mentioning his name in public, but the emotional cost to him had also been steep.

With his brother and his father in another country, he had at least been spared the horror of either of *them* knowing about the unholy mess and the financial cost to him because he had taken his eye off the ball. But he had learnt a valuable lesson, and now, whilst it cost him nothing to be generous with his money, he made damn sure not to be generous with his emotions. Those he kept firmly under wraps. Considering his women exited their relationships with him better off by furs and diamonds and cars, he didn't think it was an unfair trade-off.

'What?' he asked.

Their eyes tangled and he didn't look away. But she was desperate to. He could see it in those sherry-coloured eyes and in her sudden flush. She wanted to look away but she was drawn to look at him.

What would she be like under those clothes? What noises did she make when she made love? What would it feel like to touch her between her legs...to hold her small breasts in his big hands...to lick her nipples...?

He cleared his throat, got a grip. He liked the fact that he never lost control when he was with a woman. *Never.* He had no idea why he kept veering off in that direction now. Was it the salty tang of the sea air? He was here on a fact-finding mission and yet he felt as though he was playing truant from real life. Was that it?

'I've known lots of art students...' She tiptoed around her words, not wanting them to sound offensive. Artists could sometimes be very sensitive souls. 'And you're nothing like any of them...'

'I'm very glad to hear it,' Daniel drawled. He immediately sideswiped a sudden twinge of guilt at his masquerade. 'I pride myself on being one of a kind.'

'That's what I mean,' Delilah blurted out. 'You'd never hear an artist come out with something as arrogant as that.' She pressed the palms of her hands against her cheeks, mortified. 'I'm so—so sorry...' she stammered.

When Gerry and Catherine had made noises about the crew trying to persuade their guests into prolonging their stay, she didn't think that one of the methods they would have advised using would have been insults. Delilah was horrified at what she had said. She was not the sort who ever did anything but encourage.

Having grown up with her wildly unorthodox background, she knew only too well the frailty of human beings—the way they could be lovable and exasperating at the same time. She had seen the way her sister had made allowances for their mum and dad, and she, too, had fallen into line, doing the same. She also knew how hurtful unintentionally blunt statements could be. Her mum had once told Sarah, without meaning to offend at all, that too much maths was turning her into a very boring person. Delilah didn't think that her sister had ever forgotten that stray remark, which had been accompanied by a merry laugh and a fond ruffling of her hair.

She impulsively rested her hand on his and Daniel looked at her earnestly.

'I think I'll survive,' he said, making no move to remove his hand.

She had beautiful fingers. Long and slim and soft—the fingers of an artist or a musician. He was tempted to ask if she played any instruments…

'In fact, you aren't the first person to have told me that I can sometimes be a little arrogant,' he confessed, with such a rueful, charming, self-deprecating smile that Delilah could feel all her bones begin to melt.

Which made her yank her hand away at the speed of light. Her heart was beating so fast that she would have bet that if everyone in the bar fell silent they would all hear it.

'But I prefer to think of it as being self-confident…' he expanded softly. 'Now, if you insist on buying a drink for me, then I will graciously accept—but on one condition…'

'What's that?' She barely recognised her voice, which sounded high-pitched, girlish and breathless. She cleared her throat. She was a teacher, being paid to do a job. He was her *pupil*. She was also sworn off men.

Her ego had been battered and bruised by her experience with Michael. She wondered whether, instead of toughening her up the way it should have, it had somehow made her more vulnerable to someone like this guy, with his smooth charm and his insanely sexy good looks… Or was he the equivalent of a strong dose of pick-me-up tonic? Was that light, musing, flirtatious banter just a soothing balm, restoring her fragile self-confidence, making her feel good about herself?

And if it was then why should she be nervous around

him? It wasn't as though she was going to actually let him get under her skin, was she? He was nothing more than a passing stranger whose innate charm made her feel better about herself.

She relaxed when she looked at it in that light. It made sense.

'I buy you dinner.'

'What for?'

'Why not?' Daniel frowned.

'You've already bought me lunch. Twice. So that we could talk about the course I offer and your contribution.' She was doggedly determined not to let a couple of non-dates and a dinner invitation—extended because he was obviously a very sociable animal, probably accustomed to an abundance of female company—go to her head. 'I don't see the point of dinner. What do you want to talk about now?'

'Good God…what sort of an answer is *that*?'

Delilah thought it was a very good answer to give a guy who was probably bored by the lack of female eye candy on the ship. A bit of mild flirting might do her the power of good, but it was important for him to realise that she wasn't easy. She was probably over-thinking the whole thing, because she knew that she was no supermodel—and he was good-looking enough to have supermodels banging on his door even if he wasn't made of money. But still…

'How old are you?' Daniel asked, while she was still in the middle of getting her thoughts together.

'Twenty-one, but…'

'We're not at *school*, Delilah… Do you mind if I call you by your first name? We're two adults on a cruise ship. I think it's fair to say that accepting a dinner invitation from me doesn't actually require hours of mental debate and indecision. It's a simple yes or no scenario…'

'Of course, but...' But why did it feel so *dangerous*? Like he said, they were both adults—and why not?

'Besides...' He leaned forward, drawing her into an intimate circle where only the two of them existed. 'I was given a little money before I...er...embarked on this adventure, and I promised myself that I would spend it buying dinner for a beautiful woman...'

Delilah felt a thrill of forbidden pleasure race through her at his blatant flattery. He was so utterly serious that she could feel herself going hot and cold. Gripped with sudden panic and confusion, she tried to remember if she had ever felt like this when she had been with Michael— or had that been more of a slow-burning attraction? The meeting of two minds, connected, she had thought at the time, at the same level? Of course he had been a very attractive man, too, but certainly not in this full-on, sledge-hammer-to-the-ribs kind of way.

Two different situations, she told herself, frowning. This was pure lust—her body reminding her that whilst her emotions had been knocked for six, she could still respond to other men. Reminding her that she would recover from the blow she had taken and that being physically attracted to another man was the first step. This was a healthy and positive reaction to someone with drop-dead good looks.

'Surely you wouldn't insult me by throwing my invitation back in my face? And I thought we could make it something a bit more special than the buffet in the restaurant...'

Daniel hadn't actually tried the buffet, but judging from what he had sampled of the other meals, he didn't think it would be too hard to top it.

'What would that be?' Delilah asked, curiosity getting the better of her.

'I'd like to see you with your hair loose,' he heard

himself say—which surprised him as much as it surprised her.

Delilah's hand flew to her hair and her eyes widened. 'I beg your pardon?'

'Tonight. Have dinner with me. Dress up…wear your hair loose… I have money to blow and I've never been one to hang on to money if I can spend it. I'm going to ask your head chef to prepare a meal especially for us, and I intend to pay him way over the odds for it. Of course I'll make sure I clear it with the captain and his…er… wife first…'

He had no doubt at all that they would accept his offer with alacrity, and it would afford him the opportunity to see exactly what standard the head chef was capable of cooking to. As with all the other members of the crew, he would be more than happy to keep the chef in gainful employment if he was up to scratch. He might be on the verge of staging a hostile takeover, but that didn't mean he couldn't be fair in certain areas.

To his complete mystification she continued to look dubious, even though he could sense that she wanted to take him up on his offer. Even though he could sense that there was a part of her that was drawn to him…

'I'd bet that Stan…that is his name, isn't it?…would love nothing more than to practise the skills he's learnt without having to consider a budget…'

'Isn't it a bit extravagant to blow a lot of money on a meal when you've still got travelling to do…? I mean, I'm assuming this is just a single leg of your journey…'

'I'm very touched by your concern,' Daniel said gently, 'but I'm more than capable of looking after my finances… So what time will you be ready to join me? It's going to be a stunning night. The water is as calm as a sheet of glass. I think I'll get a table laid out for us in a secluded corner of the deck outside… Dining under the stars has always been something of a dream for me, and when else would I be likely to get the chance?'

Delilah wondered how much money he had to spend. She couldn't fight the fact that it was incredibly flattering, and a bit of flattery was just so seductive to her at this point in time. What was the harm in responding to it? As long as she remained in control everything would be fine—and she knew that she was more than capable of remaining in control. She might not be very experienced, but she was experienced enough to know that she would never risk making an idiot of herself again.

'Just dinner,' she said quickly.

'As opposed to dinner and...what?'

Unaccustomed to this sort of sexual banter, Delilah flushed and cleared her throat. 'I don't feel comfortable accepting an invitation from you when I know that it's going to cost the earth,' she offered lamely, only just rescuing herself from launching into a ridiculous speech about sex not being on the agenda because she wasn't looking for any kind of relationship and she wasn't the sort of girl who went in for meaningless flings.

'Hardly *the earth*,' Daniel pointed out drily. 'I'll pay the going rate for a good meal in Sydney. Or London. Or New York. Plus a little extra for the setting, of course...'

He named a figure that made her eyes water.

She had no idea what it felt like to spend that much money on a single meal in one reckless go. Her parents had seldom eaten out. In fact her mother had been a terrible cook and Sarah had usually done the cooking duties in the house. Delilah could remember meals, but they had all been basic, with food bought on a budget, because her parents had never had more than a couple of dimes to rub together. And then later, at art college, she had scraped by and so had everyone else she had known.

Even when she had been going out with Michael they had gone out on the cheap.

This seemed so generous…so impulsive…so *tempting*… Would it be so very wrong to accept? Would a couple of hours of being made to feel better about herself really hurt?

'I would offer to pay half, but there's no way I could afford it,' she said—and if that was the end of that, then so be it, she thought. Though her mind was already leaping ahead to the seductive prospect of being made to feel desirable and attractive by a man like him. 'I mean, I earn… Well, not much, in actual fact…because…'

'Because they're not making much money on this liner…?'

'Times are tough,' she said vaguely. 'The economy isn't booming and cruises aren't the sort of things that people race to throw money at…'

Too true, Daniel thought wryly. Especially ill-conceived cruises with sub-standard food that only seemed to attract ageing hippies with limited disposable incomes…

He was mentally making a note of everything she said and everything he saw, because when it came to putting in an offer there was no way he would allow the Ockley couple to try and pull a fast one by pretending their cruises were anything but loss-making ventures.

'Besides…' Delilah thought of the money she was currently sending to her sister, trying to pull her weight in paying off the interest on the loan they had secured from the bank for their building work.

Daniel tilted his head to one side and looked at her narrowly. 'Besides what…?

'Nothing. Okay. Well, why not? Dinner might be nice… And maybe,' she tacked on dutifully, 'I could persuade you to extend your stay on the ship…?'

'Maybe,' Daniel said, non-committal.

He thought that *that* kind of conversation would hit a roadblock in under thirty seconds. No, this evening would be about finding out about the cruise and her fellow crew members.

And finding out about *her*. She'd been on the verge of saying something about where her limited income went and he had to admit that he was curious. Unlike the women he had dated in the past, she was reluctant to try and engage his attention by bombarding him with every single detail about herself. That in itself fired up his curiosity.

'And you can tell me about your travels,' she said wistfully. 'Where you're planning on heading to next…'

'That's easy. London.'

'Really?'

'I have some…some business to attend to over there…'

'What do you do?' Delilah asked with interest. 'I mean, what's your profession?'

'I work in the leisure industry.'

Which was absolutely true. Although in fairness she probably wouldn't get close to suspecting the role he actually played. Not so much *working* in the industry as running and dominating it…

'That probably explains how you managed to get the time off to do a little drifting,' she said with a smile. 'I guess if you worked in an office your manager mightn't be too thrilled if you told him that you wanted time off to explore the artist in you…'

Daniel laughed. He was rarely bothered by a guilty conscience, but he couldn't help feeling another twinge of guilt at his deliberate manipulation of the truth.

'I don't have a manager,' he murmured. 'Funny, but I've always found it galling to obey someone else's orders.'

Delilah laughed, her eyes tangling with his. He was *so sexy.* He had that indefinable sexiness that came with not caring what other people thought about you. He didn't give a damn if she or anyone else thought that some of the things he said were arrogant. She got the feeling that he wouldn't care what *anyone* thought about him.

Her heart picked up speed. The way he was looking at her, his eyes narrowed and brooding, sent little thrills of pleasure racing up and down her spine.

Why shouldn't she allow herself to feel like a woman again? Surely if she didn't then Michael would end up having the last word?

Yes, Sarah had told her that she had to learn from her experience and *make sensible choices* when it came to men, and Delilah knew that her sister was right. But the sensible choice held as much attraction as a bout of flu, and wicked rebellion flared inside her.

She licked her lips in a gesture that Daniel thought was unconsciously erotic.

'No one likes taking orders from other people,' she said breathlessly. 'I guess we'd all like to be able to do our own thing, but unfortunately that's not how life is.'

Daniel looked around him before settling his gaze back on her flushed face. 'This strikes me as a pretty loose situation for you,' he pointed out. 'Didn't you tell me that you're all allowed to do your own thing on the liner, without constraints?'

'Yes, but I'm only here for a few weeks,' she reminded him.

'And then what? Going to hitch a ride on another cruise ship?'

'If only…'

Daniel leaned forward, intrigued. 'So tell me…?'

'There's nothing to tell.'

From a young age she had learnt that there were just

too many kids who were happy to snigger behind her back. She and Sarah had been the sisters with the weird parents. They'd learned that the less they'd said about their home life, the better, so they had kept themselves to themselves. The habit was so deeply engrained that even now, as a young adult, Delilah automatically shied away from confiding.

So what was it about *this* guy that made her want to open up?

And why did the thought of acting against her better judgement in accepting his invitation feel so appealing?

'I should be heading back to my cabin...' She barely recognised her voice and took a few steadying breaths. 'I... I'm going to do some preparation for my class tomorrow and...and...grab a bit of this beautiful weather... We should be at another port the day after tomorrow... It will be nice to just sit and soak up the sun with my book... You know... It's all go, go, go when we dock...and my students expect me to have clever things to say about all the places of culture that we visit...so...'

Daniel smiled slowly. 'So...' He sat back and thought that he needed to use the afternoon productively himself. Various deals going on required his attention. Time, as they said, was money. 'Seven sharp,' he murmured. 'Out on the deck. Far from the crowds...'

'You haven't got permission yet...' Delilah pointed out.

'Oh, I'll get permission,' he drawled.

'Because everyone listens and obeys when you talk?'

She'd said that jokingly, but there had been a thread of seriousness behind the jest and she wasn't all that surprised when he looked at her, eyebrows raised.

'Without exception...' he replied, deadly serious.

CHAPTER THREE

DELILAH HADN'T CATERED for dining under a starry sky with an Adonis. When she thought of guys at all now she vaguely assumed that the one meant for her would be a little dull, a little staid and a *lot* reliable. She'd had her brush with adventure and had pronounced herself jaded with love, only interested in a guy who would never use her, let her down or make inflated pie-in-the-sky promises he had no intention of keeping because he had girlfriends in every other port.

She hadn't been looking for racing pulses and sweaty excitement, and she couldn't quite believe that racing pulses and sweaty excitement had found *her.*

Consequently she possessed nothing in her wardrobe that was remotely suitable for dining with a man like Daniel. He hadn't talked about his love life, but she imagined him with lots and lots of beautiful women—the female equivalent of him. Head-turning model-types who wouldn't wear long skirts and baggy tops.

Somehow, despite his artistic inclinations, she couldn't picture him actually *going out* with an artist. At least, none of the artists *she* knew.

In the end at precisely six-thirty, after a quick shower in her cramped en-suite bathroom, she extracted the dressiest of her outfits from the single unit wardrobe.

Another long skirt, but black, and a fitted tee shirt with sleeves to the elbows—also black.

At five foot ten, she owned no high shoes at all, so she slipped on a pair of ballet pumps, giving a welcome rest to her flip-flops.

She left her hair loose.

Even in the brief length of time it had been exposed to the blistering sun it had lightened in colour. She was accustomed to tying it back. It was just more practical. Now, staring at her reflection in the mirror, she realised that the long, unruly hair she had always wished she could tame didn't look half bad.

Heart beating madly, she made her way to the outer deck to find him—she had had no idea where exactly he might be.

The sky was velvety black and pricked with tiny glittering stars. As he had said the ocean, dark and fathomless, was as still as a sheet of glass. The air was balmy, salty, indescribably fresh.

The sound of the passengers inside was barely discernible out here. There were a few couples strolling around, but most had confined themselves to the upper deck, which was more brightly lit and allowed easier access to the entertainment taking place inside.

Tonight, someone was doing a cabaret, and Delilah guiltily thought that it was a true indication of the finances of the liner that the person singing was really not terribly good—but then, as with Stan, Alfie, who was in charge of entertainment, was working on a tight budget.

Having managed to secure a charming and very secluded spot on the liner, Daniel was waiting for Delilah to track him down.

As predicted, it had been no bother getting the whole set-up arranged, and it had given him an excellent opportunity to acquaint himself with Gerry Ockley—a genial, bearded guy who clearly lacked any business acumen.

Perhaps his wife was a top-notch accountant, but Daniel doubted it.

The man had been only too happy to accept his very generous offer, and in fact had been more than willing to open up about the general finances of the liner.

Daniel brushed aside a few momentary misgivings about his planned takeover, about the fact that his aim was to get the liner at a knock-down price. When it came to business he had never felt sorry for any of the companies he had taken over. The bottom line was that a company could only be taken over if it was doing badly, and if it was doing badly then it was usually the result of bad management from the top down.

What was there to feel sorry about?

It was a dog-eat-dog world when it came to business. People got their chances, and if they screwed it up then who was to blame the predators for moving in?

But even so... On this particular occasion...

'You've found me...' He stood up, banishing unwelcome thoughts.

Delilah was staring open-mouthed at the table, the chairs, the linen cloth, the wine chilling next to him in an ice-cold bucket.

'Wow...'

'It was the best they could offer,' Daniel murmured as he pulled a chair out for her, 'given the circumstances...'

'It must have cost the earth...' She sat down and thought that it couldn't possibly get more romantic than this.

He was in a pair of dark trousers and a black polo shirt, and in the shadowy darkness he was just impossibly good-looking. When he rested those amazing eyes on her she could feel her skin tingle and her thought processes shut down. She felt like a different person...a person who was

still wonderfully alive and not nursing disillusionment...
She felt young again...

It was heady stuff, and when he poured her a glass of
chilled wine she drank it far too quickly.

'Like I said... I enjoy spending money...' Which was
the absolute truth—and he was generous to a fault when
it came to women.

His eyes roved over her face—the full mouth, the look
of fresh-faced innocence—and all of a sudden he felt impossibly jaded.

'I hope it's not money from...er...ill-gotten gains...'
She could already feel that single glass of wine shoot to
her head.

Daniel pretended to be outraged. 'You're not implying
that I'm a *criminal*, are you?'

'No. I was just...just teasing you. It seems so wildly
extravagant.'

Daniel thought that she had no idea what *wildly extravagant* entailed, and he really liked that.

'Hasn't any man ever been "wildly extravagant" with
you?' he mused, and Delilah laughed.

'No!'

'Why not?'

He'd joined this cruise on a fact-finding mission, but he
decided that he'd found out sufficient facts to be going on
with and that it was much too tempting to find out more
about the woman opposite him, blushingly sipping her
wine, which he had topped up.

'Because...' She lowered her eyes and then laughed
softly. 'Don't tell me you're really interested...?'

'Why wouldn't I be?'

'Because...' This flirty little game felt exotic and daring. 'Because I bet you have loads of girls scampering
behind you. And men who have loads of girls scamper-

ing behind them don't really spend time listening to what they have to say.'

'I'm offended!' Daniel laughed, enjoying the conversation and the novelty of a woman who didn't care what she said to him and wasn't trying to impress.

'No, you're not.' She smiled.

'Do you have a boyfriend? And if you have why hasn't *he* done anything wildly extravagant for you?'

He fancied her. He didn't know why, because she wasn't his type, but he didn't intend to question it.

He just knew that he had spent too much of the night before thinking about her…

And she was jumpy around him—coming close and then backing away. She fancied him as much as he fancied her, and God knew she was probably wondering why—just as he was.

He thought of the sexy little number who would be waiting for him and decided on the spot that he would have to dispatch her. Right now he couldn't get his head around any other woman but the one now shyly sneaking glances at him.

'No.' She'd tensed up. 'I don't. And wildly extravagant gestures wouldn't be what I would look for in a boyfriend, anyway. I don't go for that sort of thing.'

Daniel raised his eyebrows. 'You're more into the dull-as-dishwater types? Who always make sure never to waste a single penny on something unless it has a practical purpose? You shock me, Delilah. I thought, as you're an artist, you would be wild and reckless…'

'Wild and reckless ends in tears.' She gulped down a bit more wine and realised that she was on her third glass. 'But you're teasing me, aren't you?'

'Am I?'

'My parents were wild and reckless,' she confessed. Usually Daniel could spot the incipient beginnings of a long-winded tale, at which point he would tactfully change the subject—because long-winded tales from women always seemed to ask for similarly long-winded tales from *him*, but this time he had no inclination to do so.

'Were they?' he encouraged.

'Sorry, I don't normally talk about myself...' She started to apologise in advance, breaking off as Stan approached, in full chef garb, to regale them with the various dishes on offer.

Daniel had been right in thinking that the chef would be thrilled to bits to cook something that wasn't dictated by a strict budget. Delilah hadn't seen him this enthusiastic since she had boarded the liner.

Choices made, Daniel sat back and looked at her expectantly.

'You were going to tell me about your wild and reckless parents?' he said.

'They were artists... Neptune and Moon.'

'Come again?' He felt his lips twitch.

'Neptune and Moon. They gave themselves those names before we were born, actually...'

'We...?'

'My sister, Sarah, and me.' She smiled. Sarah had been dismissive of their parents' crazy names, but she, Delilah, had secretly loved them because they'd sounded so ethereal and glamorous.

It suddenly clicked why she loved this cruise so much—loved working aboard the ship. It was full of people just like her parents. The formerly wild and reckless, who had been tamed only by advancing years.

Sarah, five years older, had always preached caution. She had been the mother figure, taking over where Moon had so gaily left off. She had advocated the sensible path, had kept a cautionary eye on the boys who had occasionally come to the house. And Delilah had fallen into line, turning to her sister for practical advice and to her parents for fun.

It should have been the other way around, but it hadn't been. Neither she nor her sister would have changed it for the world, but an unconventional upbringing carried its disadvantages. Maybe a yearning for fun guys was ingrained in her—like those women who just kept falling for bad boys who broke their hearts. Maybe that was why she was here, sitting in this impossibly romantic setting with this impossibly sexy guy.

It was a disturbing thought but she pushed it aside—because she wasn't going out with him. She might be having fun with someone inappropriate but she was tougher now, and not about to make the same mistake twice.

Besides, Michael had never shown any real interest in *her*—had never asked any questions about her childhood or her past. He had been a 'live for the moment' type of guy, which she could now see was part and parcel of his egocentric personality. Their conversations had all revolved around *him*—*his* exploits, *his* big plans.

'Are you going to tell me that they're on this cruise with you?' he asked drily, and she shook her head.

'My mother died five years ago,' she said quietly, 'and my father within six months afterwards. Sarah and I think it was from a broken heart. They were so attached to one another it was just inconceivable that one could exist without the other.'

'A lonely life for you kids—having parents who were so wrapped up in one another...'

She looked at him, startled. 'That's what my sister thinks, but I've never looked at it that way.'

She told him about some of the ventures her parents had been involved in, about the friends who had dropped by and remained in the cottage for weeks on end. Summer evenings when a party of three had turned into a party of ten, with someone fetching a guitar. She missed all that, even though at the time she had found it a little embarrassing—at least when compared to the very staid behaviour of her friends' parents.

She barely noticed their starters being brought for them, although she *was* aware of really enjoying what she ate.

'It's nothing *like* the stuff he cooks for the masses!'

She was relieved to get on to a less personal topic, because she found that she could have carried on blathering about herself till the cows came home. He made a good listener. *Too* good.

Too good a listener. Too good-looking a specimen. And he seemed to reach parts of her that she'd never even known existed. Sitting here, close to him, it felt as if every inch of her body was tuned in to him—as if she'd been plugged into a socket and been wired. Everything was amplified. Her breathing...the staccato beats of her heart...the little pulse in her neck... And between her legs there was a place that tingled and throbbed... It was crazy.

Daniel's keen eyes noted every minuscule reaction. She had a face that was as transparent as glass, and she was too inexperienced to have absorbed the ability to hide her emotions.

Her pupils were dilated, her full lips half parted.

Did he want to get tangled up with someone who was inexperienced? It made no sense. In fact, it defied all common sense.

But they were adults. *She* was an adult. And the way she had been looking at him for the past hour...

'What did you think of the starter?' she asked quickly, because her whole body was in danger of going up in flames.

She wondered whether it hadn't been a gigantic error

of judgement to accept this date with him. It was one thing to opt for daring and reckless and to tell herself that it was okay—because why should she continue in a deep freeze just because she had been hurt once?—but it was quite another when she had no idea what the repercussions might be.

She was vulnerable and he was dangerous.

Did that make him more exciting or less so?

Daniel sat forward, temporarily breaking the spell.

'Excellent,' he said truthfully. 'And I'm expecting the main course to be just as good. The guy obviously has a great deal of skill, even if he can't display any of it because he can't afford good ingredients...'

'It's the same with Alfie, the head of entertainment,' Delilah confided, leaning forward with a soft smile. 'He's hired a young girl to sing. Maria. But she's actually only here so that she can get in a bit of travelling before she goes to university. He plucked her when we docked in the port before Santorini. I don't think he auditioned anyone else. He doesn't have much money to play with, and I think he felt that people wanted more than just to listen to him every night on the piano... She's decorative, but way out of her depth when it comes to doing cabaret...'

'And the other teachers on the cruise? Are they as inspired as you?'

'That compliment sounds a little overblown,' she said drily, and Daniel laughed.

'You're a brilliant artist.'

'Thank you very much. I'm also very cheap, because I've only just graduated. As have a couple of the others. The rest are doing it because they love what they're teaching and don't really need the money because they're retired.'

Their main courses were brought and, as he had predicted, they were as delicious as his starter had been.

Stan, he thought, was *not* going to hit the dole queue. Little did he know it, but Stan—the chef on a budget—was about to hit the jackpot instead. Fat pay cheque and guaranteed work on the liner once it had been updated, modernised and restored to fully operational opulence.

He would find out about the remainder of the crew in his own good time. Right now he was far too absorbed in present company.

'And what are you going to do once you're through with your stint here?' he asked.

Delilah shrugged, suddenly shy of continuing the conversation, suddenly wanting him to stop right there. She was a talented artist who should be finding that the world was her oyster. Not a talented artist who would be returning to the middle of nowhere to bury herself in country life, trying to make ends meet so that the she and her sister could keep the cottage on, walking the sensible path because she had been burnt once.

'Who knows?' she said gaily. 'What about you?'

'I told you... London for me. At least for a month or so. I have a family visit to make...and work to be done... and then Australia...'

'What family visit?' she asked with interest.

London... He would bum around and make some money there, she reckoned, before taking an adventurous path to the other side of the world, seeing lots of exotic and interesting places in between.

'My brother has just found true love and become engaged...'

For a second she frowned at the tone of his voice. 'Why do you sound so cynical?'

'Learning curve...' he said neutrally. 'It's a beautiful thing.'

Theo was about to marry a girl from a similar background and so, Daniel knew, would he. Not because he was in any danger of having his relationship arranged for him, as his brother's had been—against his will—but because he knew what it felt like to get involved with someone who only had your bank balance in mind. A wealthy woman was an independent woman. There would be no danger of opportunism. Which was why it was fine for him to fool around with sexy little starlets and aspiring glamour models—there was no way any of them would make it past the starting post.

He'd loved and been hurt, Delilah thought with a little stab. And he wasn't about to launch into an emotional explanation. The shutters had dropped and for a second she'd been locked out. She'd just finished telling him all about herself and now she realised that she barely knew a thing about *him*.

'Are you close to your brother?' she asked, reluctantly eating the last tasty morsel of steak on her plate. 'What about your parents? Do they worry about you having such a nomadic lifestyle?'

Daniel had the grace to flush. 'Close to my brother? Yes. Always have been. Parents? Just my father. My mother died several years ago.'

He didn't bother with the *nomadic lifestyle* assumption because he had to have the least nomadic lifestyle on the planet. Yes, he travelled—but rarely simply for pleasure. And when he did travel for pleasure it was for very brief windows of time during which he didn't laze around and relax. He stretched himself and his body to the max.

'And what does your brother do?' She tried and failed to imagine what his brother looked like. Surely not nearly as drop-dead gorgeous?

'He's...er...in business...'

Delilah laughed that melodic laugh that made him want to smile.

'Sounds like your family is the exact opposite of my

own,' she said, waving aside the coffee that had been brought to them but tucking in to some of the chocolates. 'Although Sarah's very traditional.'

She leant in to confide in him.

'Right now she's supervising some work that's due to begin on the cottage where we live. Where we've always lived, actually. Our parents were hopeless with all things financial, and since they died we've been struggling just to make ends meet. Thank goodness Sarah is practical. She studied business at college, and if it weren't for the money she makes doing the books for some of the local businesses, well... Of course I send as much money back to her as I can, and it's been brilliant that I've managed to get hold of some work so soon after leaving art college...'

Daniel said nothing. What was there to say? He was here to buy the liner on which she worked in order to send money back to keep her home fires from being snuffed out.

'I'm talking too much about myself...' Delilah reddened. How could she have let herself get so carried away? Why would this gorgeous guy, travelling the world with only his backpack for company, be interested in *her* mundane family history? 'Can I ask you something?'

Daniel fixed watchful eyes on her. She knew nothing about his background, the immense wealth that was attached to the De Angelis name, but he was always wary of the unexpected. He had a feeling that she would not conform to type. He could economise with the truth, but it would be a harder task to lie to her outright.

'You can ask whatever you like,' he drawled. 'Just so long as I reserve the right to say *no comment.*'

Her brows pleated in a frown, because that seemed a peculiar response, but she shrugged it aside and smiled. 'I know we've only just met, but...'

She hesitated on an indrawn breath and for a second Daniel felt a twinge of disappointment.

He'd liked her shyness, the way she blushed and looked away when he stared at her for too long. He'd liked the way she didn't advertise her availability. He was so accustomed to women coming on to him that it had appealed to him that she hadn't. It had nothing to do with money. She thought he was some kind of loser—a drifter bumming around from one destination to the next with no discernible income.

No, she hadn't come on to him even though he knew without a trace of vanity that he was good-looking. Now he wondered if it had all been a ploy she would use to seduce him.

'But…?' he queried, his voice a shade cooler.

'I wondered whether I could paint you.'

Surprise deprived him of an immediate answer, allowing her time to rush into hasty speech.

'I don't mean that I want you to sit for the class,' she elaborated.

Daniel immediately relaxed. 'I'm breathing a sigh of relief even as you say that.'

'And it would have to be out of my working hours, of course. It's a huge imposition, but I think you'd make an amazing…er…subject to try and capture on canvas…'

'I'm flattered,' Daniel murmured, enjoying her obvious discomfort over making the simple request.

'You have very good bone structure,' she informed him quickly.

'I don't think any woman's ever used *that* as a chat-up line with me before…'

'I wasn't chatting you up.'

Hot and flustered, Delilah dived into the remainder of her wine and wondered whether she would be able to walk in a straight line by the time they left the table.

'Please feel free to say no. It was just an idea, but it would entail you having to waste some of the gorgeous sunshine while you pose for me. I know that you only plan on being on this cruise for a few days, and you probably don't want to waste your precious time sitting still...'

'I've always found sitting still difficult,' Daniel agreed. 'But in this instance I'm willing to make an exception.'

She smiled at him with open delight.

'But of course,' he said slowly, watching her face with leisurely thoroughness, 'there is such a thing as quid pro quo. I sit for you and in return you do something for me...'

'If it's to return your dinner invitation in a similar fashion, then there's no chance of that happening.' She laughed.

'I really like the way you laugh,' Daniel said, distracted. 'Your face lights up.'

'I don't think any man has ever used *that* chat-up line with me before...' She parroted what he had said earlier, at which point she realised that she had definitely drunk too much. She *had* to have drunk too much, because this was outrageous flirting—and outrageous flirting was something she had never done...not even with Michael...and it was something she definitely shouldn't be doing now.

Daniel looked at her with lazy intensity. She was as skittish as a cat on a hot tin roof and the urge to take her, to make love to her, ripped through him with astounding force.

He was used to getting what he wanted without putting much effort in. Women went to ridiculous lengths to get his attention. They threw themselves at him with shameful abandon. He couldn't remember the last time he'd had to work at trying to get a woman into bed, but right now, even knowing from the blush on her cheeks that she fancied him, he still hesitated.

He was almost tempted to indulge in that rarely practised art form known as *courting*, but time wasn't on his side and he wasn't even sure if he could subdue the force of his desire in order to take things slowly, one step at a time.

'What do you want me to do?' she pressed on.

The sultry night air… The black ocean all around them… The stars above… She was on a high.

'I'll tell you in a little while.'

He tossed his linen napkin on to his plate and looked around to see Stan, peering at them anxiously from behind the glass windows.

Delilah could only gape as he beckoned the chef across with a practically invisible inclination of his head, but she was thrilled when he proceeded to compliment him on everything they had been served. Thrilled when he quizzed him about his background in cooking, apparently interested in hearing all about where Stan had trained and what had brought him to the liner.

Dnaiel might not divulge a lot about himself, but somehow his restraint was a…

A turn-on…

Compared to him, Michael—who had always been eager to promote himself and had never tired of talking about the exciting life he'd lived, taking photographs in exotic places—seemed immature and empty.

Somehow Daniel didn't glory in his exploits.

He was clearly used to dealing with different people of different cultures and in different situations, but his anecdotes weren't laced with self-praise. It was odd that she was only now fully recognising that trait in Michael, seeing him for what he really was, and it felt good—like an achievement.

'Are you *sure* you can afford this?' she whispered, when Stan had eventually cleared the table and left, visibly puffed up by Daniel's effusive praise.

'Have you *never* been wined and dined before?' He laughed, standing up and waiting for her to get to her feet.

'Do fast food restaurants count?'

He laughed, reached for her hand and tucked it into the crook of his elbow.

Delilah's state of heightened excitement escalated a couple of notches. She could feel the ripple of sinew and muscle in his forearm and the outside lights danced over his face, throwing it into wildly exotic angles.

They strolled towards the railings and peered down at the endless ocean.

This had been a bloody good idea, Daniel thought, with a feeling of wellbeing. *Inspired*, in fact. He hadn't banked on any sort of sexual entanglement, but now that the possibility had surfaced he certainly wasn't going to run away from it.

But first things first…

He turned round so that he was leaning against the railing, with his back to the ocean, and pulled her gently towards him. He registered an initial resistance before she yielded, although her body remained stiff.

'Relax,' he urged, with a smile in his voice.

'You should know something,' Delilah said in a rush. 'I've just come out of a relationship and it didn't end very well. So I'm not… I'm not looking for anything… I shouldn't be doing this at all…'

'You're not doing anything.'

'I'm here…on a date…with *you*…'

'What did he do?'

'He strung me along,' she said painfully.

'That,' said Daniel, 'is something I would never do. I've always made it a policy to lay my cards on the table, and when it comes to women I don't string them along. If you're not looking for a relationship, trust me—neither am I. This is a harmless attraction.'

He was right—*so why didn't it feel that way?* she wondered.

'Harmless?'

'No strings attached,' he soothed. 'And without strings attached there's no emotional involvement. It's only when emotions are in the mix that complications begin. I've been there, done that, and I'm a convert to the uncomplicated arrangement...'

He made it sound so easy, and his conviction liberated her from her misgivings. Who cared whether it was a good idea or a bad idea? She could spend all night analysing the rights and wrongs and then he'd be gone, and she knew that she would regret not having had the courage to take what he was offering.

And wasn't he just echoing what she had been thinking anyway? He'd been upfront and honest with her. He was passing through and she was here, in a bubble, with no one looking over her shoulder.

She tentatively wrapped her arms around him, glad that it was deserted on this section of the deck.

'I'm only here for a few days, Delilah...'

'I know that.'

'You'll only be able to paint me for those few days.'

'I know that, too.'

'And here's where I get to the thing I want from you in return for sitting for you...'

'Yes?' Her voice was a breathy whisper.

'You. I want *you*, Delilah...'

There was just no way that bluntly spoken statement could be invested with anything romantic at all, and yet...

It went to her head with like an injection of adrenaline directly into her bloodstream.

'That's the trade?' she framed in a shaky voice.

'Never let it be said that I don't know how to strike a deal while the iron's hot...'

He dipped his head and his lips met hers in an unhurried, all-consuming kiss. His tongue meshed with hers and it was the most erotic experience she had ever had. Even though his hands remained clasping the rail on either side of him…even though it was only that long, lazy kiss that was doing the damage.

Delilah stroked the side of his lean, beautiful face and heard herself say, *'Okay…'*

CHAPTER FOUR

DELILAH HAD NO idea how she managed to focus at all the following day. Her routine had been disrupted by the liner putting in to dock at Olympia.

Before Daniel had boarded the cruise ship she had diligently looked at the itinerary and made copious notes about all the exciting places of cultural interest they would be visiting. Part of her responsibilities covered introducing interested passengers to new experiences. Bearing in mind she had not travelled at all, and that every single sight would be as fresh to her as to them, she had worked doubly hard to make sure that she had all the relevant facts and figures at her disposal.

Olympia...site of the Olympic Games in classical times...held every four years from the eighth century BC to the fourth century AD...all in honour of the great god Zeus...

She had done all her homework on the Greek gods and Greek mythology. She could have passed an exam.

But as it was, the only thing filling her head as they disembarked was the guy who had allowed her to scuttle back to her cabin the evening before alone, with just a chaste kiss on her cheek as a reminder of his lips.

'You need to think about my proposal...' he had

drawled in his dark, sexy voice, while his eyes had remained fastened to her face, draining her of all her willpower. 'I need to know that we're going to be on the same page…'

He didn't do long-term. He didn't do commitment. He wasn't looking for a relationship. He was looking for a bit of fun and he wanted his fun to be with *her*…

The thought of the *having fun and clearing off* situation he was proposing should have left her stricken with terror after Michael, but she had squared away her misgivings. Daniel had been right when he'd said that no one could get hurt when emotions weren't involved—that was true.

Desire, as she was finding out fast, was a stand-alone emotion. That had come as a revelation to someone who had always thought of love and desire in the same breath. She wanted him, he wanted her, and there was something so wonderfully clean and clear-cut about that. It was nothing like the muddle of hopes and dreams and forward-planning she had so foolishly felt with Michael.

Right here and right now this was liberating.

Now, in the bright, burning sun, Daniel was part of the group she had opted to show around the ancient ruins. How was she supposed to deliver her spiel when she could feel his eyes following her every move? Could see him listening to every word she said with his head tilted?

He was the very picture of keen amateur interest—even though, unlike some of the others, he had not brought his sketchpad with him. Notwithstanding that, she knew what was running through his head. She could just *tell* whenever their eyes met and his gaze lingered on her.

She and Daniel would share a cabin bed for a few days and then he would disappear for ever.

He hadn't even tried to package up the deal in attractive wrapping paper.

He had told it like it was—told her to expect nothing more.

He was a textbook example of just the sort of guy she should be avoiding. No promise of anything long-term. No mention of love.

But she had underestimated the force of her own body and the way it was capable of responding to something that made no sense.

She would return to the Cotswolds, where she could count eligible guys on the fingers of one hand, and she would settle down with someone more suitable. Of course she would. There would be all the time in the world for her to invest her love in Mr Right. But how would she feel if she did that and always thought about the Mr Wrong she had decided to avoid? The Mr Wrong who would be just the sort of replacement therapy she was in need of?

The group lunched at a charming little café close to the site they had been exploring and later, with the sun still burning down, late in the afternoon, made their way back to the liner.

'I'm disappointed you didn't take your sketchpad with you.' She turned to Daniel once they were back on the liner, joining all the others also making their way back on and then dispersing into various groups, or going to one of the bars to relax before the evening meal.

It had been a hot, tiring day, but he still managed to look amazing. In a plain white tee shirt, some khaki shorts, loafers and sunglasses, he looked like one of the Greek statues come to beautiful life.

'I thought about it, but then concluded that I would have much more fun watching you.'

He couldn't credit the level of his excitement at the prospect of sleeping with her. The detailed report he had been putting together, which would highlight all the reasons why the Ockley couple would find themselves without an option when it came to selling to him, had taken a back seat.

For the first time in living memory work wasn't uppermost in his mind.

Delilah, captivated by the slow-burning desire she could see in the depths of his green eyes, was finding it hard to tear her gaze away.

'I… I should go and change… Have a look at some of the sketches my class have done…'

'Boring.'

'I beg your pardon?'

'Give me the sketches and I'll mark them out of ten. Even without the benefit of a degree in art I could tell you that Miranda and Lee need to pay more attention in perspective class…'

Her lips twitched and she struggled not to laugh. 'Maybe I could meet you…later…?'

Daniel leant against the wall, drawing her into an intimate circle that enclosed just the two of them, and Delilah looked shiftily around her.

'We're not breaking any laws,' he said, with an edge of impatience.

'Yes, I know. But…'

'But what? So *what* if some of the people in your class think that we're having a fling? What do you think they're going to do? Report you to the principal?'

'It's not that,' she said sharply. 'The fact is that I'll be staying on after you leave this liner, and I don't want to have people whispering about me behind my back.'

Daniel raked his fingers through his hair and shook his head. 'Why do you care what people think?'

'Don't you?'

'Of course not. No, I tell a lie. I care about what my father and my brother think of me, but beyond that why should I?' Their eyes met, and when she dipped her head to look away he tilted it back so that she was looking at him, his finger gently on her chin. 'Okay,' he conceded, 'why don't you tell me where you are and I'll come to you under cover of darkness...like a thief in the night...'

'Tell you where I am...?' Her mouth went dry at the thought of that, in a mixture of excitement and nervousness.

'Your cabin?' he said drily. 'Unless you're bunking down in a sleeping bag out on the deck?'

'I...'

'Are you having second thoughts?' *Because,* he might have added, *there's a limit to the amount of chasing I intend to do.* He'd never had to chase. Frankly, an attack of nerves—the whole three steps forward, two steps back thing—was something he could do without.

But he wasn't sure whether his rampant libido was capable of walking away.

'No, I'm not having second thoughts.' Delilah had made up her mind and she wasn't going to backtrack.

He smiled and found himself relaxing, which only made him realise that he'd tensed up at the thought of her changing her mind.

'But...' She sighed.

'You're nervous?' he intuited, and she looked at him sheepishly. 'You're not the kind of girl who accepts propositions from strange men you meet on cruise liners...? And especially not when you're supposedly recovering from a broken heart...'

'I was in love with the idea of *being* in love,' she said slowly. 'I wanted excitement and adventure, and when Michael came along it felt like I'd found that...'

'Rule number one,' Daniel drawled, 'is that you don't talk about your ex when you're with me. He's history— and good riddance from the sound of it.'

'Is that the approach you took when *your* heart was broken?' she asked tentatively.

'Another rule—we don't talk about my exes either. But, just for your information, my heart wasn't broken. The bottom line is that whatever doesn't kill you makes you stronger.'

'You're so...so *confident*...' Delilah was frankly in awe of his pragmatic approach.

Daniel shrugged coolly. 'You don't get anywhere by dithering or dwelling on past errors of judgement. You learn and you move on.'

'When you say stuff like that it shows me how much I don't know about you... I mean, I don't know anything other than you're travelling and your next stop is London before you head off to the other side of the world...'

But then she'd thought she'd known Michael because he had talked a lot about himself, and she hadn't at all, had she?

'What else do you want to know? And do you want to have this long and meaningful conversation over there?' He nodded to the outer deck and to a clump of deckchairs, all of which were empty.

Did she want more facts about him? Delilah felt that she knew *the essence* of the man, and knew that she had been drawn to him not just because of the way he looked but because he was incredibly funny, incredibly intelligent and so thoughtful and considerate in the way he had listened to her without interruption. The way he was interested in everything she had to say.

'I have a very small cabin,' she said shyly. 'All of the crew do...'

'Then come to me,' Daniel murmured. 'I can't say it's a palatial suite, but there's a double bed... My feet have a tendency to hang over the edge, but they probably don't cater for men as big as me... And don't be nervous. Who says I'm accustomed to picking up strange girls I meet on cruise liners…?'

'Are you telling me that *you're* nervous?'

'I can say with my hand on my heart that I have never been nervous when it comes to sex…'

'You're so…so…'

'I know what you're going to say. You're going to tell me that I'm so *arrogant*—I prefer the *confident* description.'

Delilah laughed, and just like that he kissed her. And this time his kiss wasn't lingering and explorative. This time it was hungry and demanding.

He manoeuvred her so that they had stepped outside onto the deck and his mouth never left hers.

She'd been kissed before, but never like this, and she'd never felt like this before either. His hunger matched hers and she whimpered and coiled her fingers into his hair, pulling him into her and then arching her head back so that he could kiss her neck, the side of her face, the tender spot by her jawline.

Her whole body was on fire, and right here, right now, she couldn't have cared less who saw her.

She lost the ability to think, and along with her ability to think, she also lost her inhibitions. She'd taken her time with Michael, wanting to make sure that they had something really lasting and special before she slept with him, and it was puzzling that she just wanted to fly into bed with Daniel even though there was nothing between them but lust.

She couldn't get enough of him, of his mouth on her mouth, on her bare skin, setting her aflame. She wanted to touch. Was *desperate* to touch. Not just his beautiful face but all of him. And she was shocked by the need pouring through her in a tidal wave that eclipsed every preconceived notion she had ever had about the nature of relationships.

When he pulled away she actually moaned—a soft little broken moan—before reluctantly opening her eyes and staring right up at him.

'You're beautiful,' Daniel told her roughly, and Delilah laughed shakily.

'I bet you say that to all the women you chase…'

'I don't chase women.'

'Because they chase *you*?'

Daniel smiled slowly, his silence telling her that she had hit the nail on the head. He was a man who didn't have to run after women. He was a guy who didn't have to try.

He was a guy who probably needed someone who played hard to get—but she wasn't good at playing games, and besides this wasn't a normal relationship…was it?

This wasn't one of those relationships that was built to last from its foundations up. There wasn't going to be a slow burn, or a gradual process of discovering one another and really getting to know one another. That had been *her* learning curve, and what a fool she'd been.

This wasn't what she had spent her formative years expecting.

This was a blast of the unexpected, powering through her and obliterating all the signposts she had always taken for granted when it came to relationships.

'And you wonder why I'm nervous…' she sighed on a heartfelt whisper.

If he knew that she had never slept with a man before then he would run a mile. Men who were in danger of being knocked down by the stampede of women eager to climb into bed with him would have no concept of an inexperienced woman, and they wouldn't have any patience with one.

She didn't want him to run a mile.

Just acknowledging that shocked her, but she was honest enough not to flinch from the truth.

This was pure lust, and sleeping with him felt necessary and inevitable.

'Don't be,' he told her softly. 'Just because women chase me it doesn't mean that I make comparisons... Now, I'm going to go and have a much needed shower, and my cabin number is...'

He whispered it into her ear and she shivered.

Just the fact that they were pre-planning this sent a delicious frisson rippling through her.

She almost didn't want him to leave, but she was hot and sticky as well.

She watched him disappear back into the body of the liner and her heart was thudding so hard in her chest that she wanted to swoon like a Victorian maiden.

Delilah had no idea what a man who looked like Daniel saw in her, but she made sure to do her utmost to look her very best before she joined him in his cabin.

He liked her hair, so she left it loose and blow-dried it into glossy waves. She wore no make-up aside from some mascara and a little lip gloss, and thankfully the sun had turned her skin a pale biscuit-brown. As for clothes...

Instead of her usual long skirts she wore one of the only two pairs of trousers she had brought with her. Having anticipated a shorter stay on the liner, she'd found her scant supply of clothes had had to stretch for far longer than she'd bargained for, but these tan trousers hadn't yet seen the light of day and they looked okay, twinned with a cropped vest that showed off her slender arms and just a sliver of tanned belly.

When she stood back from the mirror she realised that

the artist had gone—at least for the night. She briefly wondered whether he might have preferred her artist image, but swatted that temporary misgiving away.

Nerves took hold of her as she made her convoluted way to his cabin. Many of the rooms were empty, waiting for the occasional new passenger who might want to hop on board—not that there had been very many of those, despite the brilliant deals advertised. And she knew, as she wound her way to his section of the ship, that he was in one of the best cabins—probably an upgrade.

Gerry and Christine were generous to a fault, and most of the passengers had been offered upgrades at very little extra cost.

She could barely breathe as she tentatively knocked on the door, pushing it open as he told her to enter.

Outside, darkness had abruptly fallen, another starry, moonlit night, and through the portholes of his cabin she could see the stars twinkling in the sky and the whisper of a crescent moon illuminating the sea with a ghostly radiance.

He'd changed into cream trousers, low slung on his lean hips, and a cream tee shirt, and he was barefoot.

Delilah discovered that she was finding it hard to catch her breath and the Victorian maiden swoony feeling was beginning to get hold of her again.

She inhaled deeply and made a conscious effort not to twist her hands together in a giveaway gesture of nervousness.

God, he was beautiful. That streaky dirty blond hair was slightly too long but somehow emphasised the sharp contours of his face, adding depth to the fabulous green eyes and accentuating the bronzed skin tone that spoke of some exotic heritage in his gene pool. No wonder he needed to carry a large stick with him at all times to fight the women off.

'Are you going to tear yourself away from the door any time soon?' Daniel strolled towards her and gently propelled her into the cabin and closed the door behind her.

He'd taken one very long, very cold shower, and even that hadn't been able to stanch the unfamiliar excitement of anticipation. Always in control, he had now surrendered to the novelty of *not* being in control. The unread email messages on his computer remained unread. His mobile phone was switched off so that he wouldn't be interrupted by someone wanting something from him. His attraction to her had happened so fast and hit him so hard that he could only blame the fact that he was far removed from his comfort zone of wealth and luxury.

'You've ordered room service?' Delilah finally managed to croak as she stared down at the table, which had been set for two.

'Stan again rose to the occasion. Of course I could have just ordered something from the room service menu. but...' He shrugged, unable to tear his eyes away from her.

She'd always hidden the glorious figure he'd glimpsed beneath her baggy clothes. Even earlier, when they had visited the site of the ruins, she had worn a long skirt and flip-flops and yet another loose, floaty top. 'It's the best thing if you want to keep cool,' she had told him when he had asked her whether she wasn't scared of tripping over her skirt and doing untold damage as they clambered around.

She wasn't wearing camouflage gear now.

Caramel skin...those strangely captivating eyes... long russet hair tamed into sexy waves...so, so...long. Way too long to be fashionable, but incredibly, *incredibly* spectacular...

And she wasn't wearing a bra. He could see the firm roundness of her small breasts pushing against the thin, tight vest. Could practically see the circular outline of her nipples…

Feeling as hot and bothered as a horny teenager on his first date, he spun away and reached for the bottle of champagne which was chilling in an ice bucket.

'And—and bubbly,' she stammered, watching him expertly open the bottle. 'You didn't have to…to go to all this trouble…' She fiddled with the thin gold chain she wore round her neck—a birthday present from her parents a million years ago.

'Allow a man to be indulgent…' He held out a champagne flute to her, but before she could drink he curved his hand over her satin-smooth cheek and watched her for a few seconds without saying anything.

'You're staring…' Delilah breathed, but the feel of his hand on her was strangely calming.

'You do that to me,' Daniel husked. 'You make me want to stare.'

He'd always gone for the obvious in women—much to his brother's perpetual amusement. Plenty of time to settle for the prissy, classy clothes of the wealthy, well-bred woman of means he would eventually marry. Prissy and classy wasn't fun, and in the meanwhile he intended to have a fun-filled diet.

This woman couldn't have been more restrained in her choice of clothing, but the effect on him was dramatic.

Delilah sipped the champagne and watched him warily over the rim of her glass. Wanting to be here didn't mean that she had the courage to match her desire.

'I thought we'd have something light to eat.' Daniel broke the bubble of heightened silence and pulled out a chair for her. 'Unless you've already grabbed something? No? Thought not…'

She was still nervous. That in itself was a bad sign, because it meant that she wasn't exactly into transitory sex—which was what he wanted—despite what she'd said. But he had given her his speech and that had been sufficient to ease his conscience.

Both adults and due warning. Job done.

Which nevertheless still left the fact that she was nervous, and he found that he was willing to go against the grain, willing to move at her pace within reason. In a peculiar way, he was willing to court her...

'Stan has prepared salad stuff...crayfish and lobster... two things that go perfectly with champagne...'

Delilah sat. Her eyes were fairly popping. What had she expected? Not this. Maybe she'd thought that he would greet her half naked at the door, Tarzan-style, before slinging her over his shoulder and heaving her off to his bed. There was, after all, something raw and elemental about him.

He might not be on the lookout for any kind of relationship, but he was putting a lot of effort in, and she knew instinctively that he was taking things slowly because he sensed that she was nervous.

And that warmed her, because it said so much about him.

'He'll miss you when you go,' she said lightly, helping herself to salad, the little pulse in her neck fluttering with awareness as he sat down opposite her.

His cabin was at least five times the size of hers. It was comfortable, but not luxurious, and even with her untrained eyes she could see the hallmarks of Gerry and Christine's straitened financial circumstances. The room needed a good overhaul.

Through the doorway she could glimpse the bed, and she quickly averted her eyes, determined not to become a victim of stage fright.

'You've spoiled him by letting him cook whatever he wants, no expense spared...'

'Are you going to deliver another sermon on my extravagance?'

Delilah blushed. 'No, I'm not. You're not careful, and that's nice. My sister and I have spent so long just trying to make ends meet that I've become accustomed to being careful all the time when it comes to money.'

'You spend a lot of time talking about your sister...'

Excellent salad, he mentally noted. Another point in Stan's favour—and his sous chef as well. Two jobs safe. And from what he'd seen some of the rest of the crew were diligent and efficient and, having spoken to them, he'd seen they knew the ropes.

'She brought me up,' Delilah said simply.

'And where were your parents when this sisterly bringing up was taking place?'

He was fascinated by the guileless transparency of her face. She smiled, dipped her eyes, blushed, fiddled with her champagne flute... Her broken heart hadn't been able to kill off her naturally warm, shy disposition.

Was it unreasonable to expect his next woman to have those appealing traits?

Then he remembered that this woman knew nothing about him. She wasn't out to impress him. He felt that had she known just how wealthy, how powerful, how influential he was, she would probably be a lot more forward in trying to grab his attention and hold it.

'Like I said, our parents were so wrapped up in one another that they didn't have a lot of time for us. I mean, they were fabulous parents, and very, very loving in their own scatty way, but they were unconventional. They really didn't see the point of school.' Delilah smiled. 'Despite the fact that they both went to art college. They had a lot of faith in the University of Life.'

'But they were fun?' Daniel guessed.

'Gosh—absolutely. On the one hand it was embarrassing when I was a kid, because of the way they dressed, but on the other hand they weren't all buttoned up like the rest of the parents…and that was kind of great…'

Daniel pushed back his chair and linked his fingers behind his head.

Every scrap of his attention was focused on her and Delilah could feel herself wanting to open up, like a bud blossoming under the warmth of sudden sunshine.

'And you're looking for the same kind of overpowering love…? You thought you'd found it, and it turned out that you hadn't, but that hasn't really put you off, has it?'

'Security, stability…those are the things that are important in a relationship…'

'Because you fell for the wrong guy? Because your sister told you so?'

'No! Maybe… Well, not in so many words…'

'But deep down you're not falling for it. That's why you're here with me. Deep down you don't see why you shouldn't have the fireworks and the explosions…which is what your parents had…'

'You don't understand. They really were *so* involved in one another. There'd be days when Mum would just forget to shop for food, and Sarah was always the one who shouldered the responsibility for bringing a bit of normality into the house… Sometimes, they would get one of their friends to babysit us for a week or so, while they went on a hunting mission for crystals or artefacts, and at least once a year they blew what little money they'd managed to make on a trip to India…you know, to bring stuff over for the shop…'

Neptune and Moon, Daniel thought wryly. The names said it all.

But the sisters had seen the situation through different eyes. It was obvious that sister number one was a practical bore, who had drilled into sister number two the importance of being earnest and then really hammered it home when Delilah had strayed off the tracks...

And then quite suddenly he thought about his own situation.

Theo, he knew, had been affected by the relationship of their parents and by their mother's death in ways that he, Daniel, perhaps hadn't. They'd both been devastated, had both witnessed their father's slow, inexorable decline— the way the energy had been sapped out of him, the way he had withdrawn from active life, unable or unwilling to cope after the rock on whom he had depended had been taken from him.

That had toughened Theo and shown him a road he would make sure to avoid—the road that led to any sort of emotional commitment.

Daniel couldn't help grinning at the way *that* particular situation had eventually played out, considering his brother was now loved up, locked down and proud of it.

He, Daniel, had found solace in the wake of their mother's death and the sudden upheaval in their household in another way. He had buried his emotions so deeply after Kelly Close that he doubted he would ever be able to find them again. That suited him.

Taken aback by that rare bout of introspection, he closed his hand over Delilah's and slanted her a devastating smile.

'Word to the wise?' he said wryly. 'Your sister's probably got the hang of it by steering you clear of all those fairytale stories of Prince Charmings sweeping lonesome Cinderellas off their feet so that they can live happily ever after in that mythical place known as cloud nine... Have fun and then marry the guy who makes sense.'

Was that his way of reiterating his warning? Of telling her that she had to look elsewhere for romance? She'd already got that message, and there was no way she would

be idiotic enough to look for it with someone like *him*.
Oh, no.

But, yes, she *did* believe in all that burning fireworks
and explosions stuff—even if her sister didn't… It might
be called lust, and not love, but she still wanted it and he
was right—that was why she was here with him now.

Surprised by just how much she had confided in him,
and made uneasy by her lack of restraint, she took a deep
breath and caught his eyes.

'I didn't come here to talk,' she murmured huskily.

This, Daniel thought, was more like it. This was the
kind of language he understood.

He stood up, pulled her to her feet and slowly drew her
against him. 'I like the outfit, by the way…'

He kissed her long and slow, until her whole body
was melting. His tongue, meshing lazily with hers, was
doing wonderful things, making her want to press herself
against him so that there wasn't an inch of space between
their bodies. He curved his hand over her bottom and then
loosely slipped it underneath the waistband of her trousers, just a few delicate fingers running against her skin.

'And I'm going to like it even more when you're out
of it and it's lying on the ground…'

CHAPTER FIVE

SHE FALTERED AS he led her towards the bed she had glimpsed through the door that separated the small sitting area from the sleeping area.

Her mouth went dry and she hesitated—watched, fascinated by his complete lack of inhibition, as he began to undress.

He'd done this lots of times. There was certainty in the way he pulled the tee shirt over his head, exposing his hard, muscled torso, and self-confidence in the way he kept his eyes on her, a half smile playing on his mouth. He was a man who, as he had told her, had never been nervous when it came to sex.

This was his playing ground and he was the uncontested master of it.

Her eyes followed his hand as it reached for the zipper of his trousers and rested there for a few seconds.

'This,' he drawled, strolling towards her, 'is beginning to feel a little one-sided…'

Her courage disappearing faster than water draining down a plughole, Delilah gulped.

'Shall we get into bed?' she whispered, by which she meant under the covers, where she could wriggle out of her clothes in as inconspicuous a manner as possible.

Daniel raised his eyebrows and placed both hands on her shoulders.

They'd spent so much time talking—way more than

he had ever spent talking with any woman, and certainly way more than he had ever spent with any woman before sex. In fact, when he thought about it, conversation rarely served as an appetiser before the main course. Usually by the time he and whatever hot date he happened to be with hit the bedroom clothes would have been off and action would be about to happen—no exchange of words needed.

Hot, hard and urgent.

When, he wondered, were her nerves going to be banished? He'd had an erection from the second she'd walked into the cabin and he was in danger of having to have a very cold shower if he was to get into anything resembling a comfortable state.

'I like my women to be naked *before* we get into bed,' he said gently. 'Jumping into the sack with someone who's fully clothed, right down to her shoes, somehow takes the edge off the whole business... In other words it's a mood-killer...'

He slipped his hands under her tee shirt and Delilah tensed.

'I don't like games when it comes to sex,' he told her, his voice cooling by the second, because her body was as rigid as a plank of wood. 'I have no time for any woman who thinks that she can tease me and then pull away...'

'That's not what I'm doing.'

'Then would you care to explain why you've suddenly turned into a statue?'

Delilah dropped her head and was grateful for her long, loose hair, because it shielded her face from his piercing eyes.

'I've never done this before...' She reluctantly looked up at him with clear eyes and Daniel frowned.

'When you say that you've *never* done this before...'

'You're my first,' she told him bluntly, waiting for him to recoil in horror—but he didn't. Although she had no idea what he was thinking, because when their eyes tangled again she could see that the shutters had dropped.

'You're telling me that you're a virgin?'

'It's not *that* unusual,' she flared defiantly.

'But you were involved with someone...'

'I... We...we were taking it slowly. Look, I don't want to talk about this—'

'Too bad. You're a virgin, Delilah.' He raked frustrated fingers through his hair. 'I don't do virgins.'

'You don't *do* a lot of stuff, do you?' She found that she couldn't bear the thought of him walking away from her—not after she had convinced herself that this was the right thing to do, the thing she wanted and needed to do. 'Why don't you just come right out and say it? You're just not attracted to me now!'

She made to turn away but his grip was holding her in place. He was holding her very gently, applying almost no pressure, but he was strong. *Very* strong.

'Touch me and you'll see that for the nonsense it is,' he told her roughly.

She fixed her eyes on his hard chest—his small, flat brown nipples, the dark gold hair spiralling down to where he had begun unbuttoning his trousers before stopping.

Heat poured through her, settling damply between her legs.

Her eyes flared and, feeling her very slight tremble, Daniel knew that what he should do right now was gently let her go. Perhaps give her a rousing pep talk on waiting for the right guy to come along, with whom she could share the precious gift of her virginity.

It wasn't in his brief to take it—even if it had been offered to him. Virginity equalled vulnerability, and that equalled all sorts of unknown complications.

He had laid out the ground rules but she was a novice

to the game, so how was she supposed to know where he was coming from? She already thought him to be someone he wasn't. The situation was complicated enough as it stood, without her finding that she had got in over her head because of the sex.

He'd never had a problem jettisoning any of the women he had dated in the past. They had all been experienced, had all known the score. If some of them had been disappointed that they hadn't been able to convert him, then tough. All was fair in love and war.

His gut instinct told him that it would be different with Delilah if she turned sex into something it wasn't and would never be.

'You're not saying anything,' she muttered. 'I suppose you're horrified…'

Tears of humiliation sprang to her eyes and she gulped them back. She only had herself to blame. She had punched above her weight and this was where it had got her. It was to be expected. Any man who looked like a Greek god with a wealth of sexual experience behind him…any man who kicked off his affairs by telling the woman involved that he wasn't in it for the long term… was a man who would have no time for virgins.

'Not horrified…' Daniel corrected. 'Flattered. Turned on. Why would I be horrified?'

The more he thought about it, the more turned on he became. Her first… He physically ached to touch her, to show her just how fantastic sex could be… Even though the downside still continued to niggle away at the back of his mind…

He guided her hand to his bulging erection and grinned with a ridiculous surge of satisfaction as her eyes widened and her breathing hitched.

He was a big boy—a *very* big boy—and she was touching the evidence of just how turned on he was.

'But…' His voice was unsteady as he ploughed on with a conversation he knew he had to have. He'd had it before, but this time he had to make sure that she understood and accepted where he was coming from.

'But…?' Delilah whispered.

'You have no idea what you're doing to me right now,' he told her shakily.

He raked his fingers through his hair and shook his head, as though he might be able to clear it and regain some control over the situation. He'd never felt so out of control in his life before. It was as if he'd suddenly found himself stranded on foreign soil, with no landmarks to show him the direction he needed to take.

'Why me?' he asked flatly.

Delilah's breath hitched. 'If it's going to be a question-and-answer session about the fact that I didn't sleep with Michael, then I get the picture. I'm going to go now, and we can both pretend that this never happened. I told you I don't want to talk about it and I don't.'

She turned away. She'd had her reasons for keeping Michael at bay, even though she had supposedly been head over heels in love with him and planning their future, but she couldn't remember what they were now. Daniel's blunt incredulity made her decision to hold off sleeping with her ex feel freakish.

Daniel didn't answer. Instead he propelled her towards the bed and urged her down. Like a rag doll, she flopped onto it before sitting upright and drawing her knees to her chin, wrapping her arms around herself.

'It's not the most difficult question in the world to answer, Delilah.'

The dark, velvety tones of his voice washed over her soothingly, but she was still as tense as a bowstring and she huddled into herself as he, too, sat on the bed, though not within touching distance of her.

'I just don't see what that has to do with anything,' she told him mutinously.

'I'm not your Prince Charming,' Daniel said, without bothering to mince his words. Tough love. Or something like that. At any rate the laying of cards on the table, so that all misunderstandings could be avoided.

He was giving her a choice, and he couldn't be fairer than that, could he?

The mere fact that he was giving her a choice at all, when really he should be extricating himself from a possibly awkward situation in the making, was a little unnerving, but he fought down that unwelcome thought.

'Why would you think that you are?' Understanding dawned. 'Because I've chosen to sleep with you?' she said slowly. 'And you're so big-headed that you think the only reason I would do that is because I'm the sort of idiot who wants her fairytale ending to be with you…'

She swung her legs over the side of the bed before he could reach out to stop her and stood, shaking, arms tightly folded, staring at him and glaring.

'Of all the conceited, smug and, yes, *arrogant* men in the world, you just about have to take the biscuit!'

Taken aback by her anger, Daniel likewise vaulted upright, and they stood facing one another with the width of the bed separating them.

'What's a man supposed to think?' he demanded gruffly.

'Do you want to know *why* I chose to sleep with you?'

'You mean aside from the sizzling, irresistible attraction to me that you're powerless to fight…? The sort of sizzling, irresistible attraction you never felt for your loser ex…?'

Delilah blinked, because just like that the atmosphere between them had shifted.

Her whole body tightened and tensed, hyper-aware of

him, of his glorious masculine beauty, as he stood there, looking steadily at her, his thumbs hooked into the waistband of the trousers he hadn't got around to removing.

Antennae on red-hot alert, Daniel could almost feel something physical in the change in the air. Her eyes were still angry and accusing, but she was clutching herself just a little bit tighter, and her body was just a little bit more rigid—as though she had to use every ounce of willpower not to shatter into a thousand pieces.

'Did it never occur to you that you might be my adventure? The sort of adventure I need right now...at this point in time?' she flung at him.

He frowned. 'Explain.'

'Why should I? This was a big mistake...'

'Physical attraction is never a big mistake,' he said, in complete contradiction to what he had been thinking earlier.

Covering the small cabin in a couple of strides, he was looming over her before she had time to take evasive action. Not that her legs felt as though they could do any such thing. In fact, her legs were being very uncooperative at the moment, seemingly nailed to the floor, unable to move an inch, never mind take evasive action.

'Tell me what you meant when you said that I was your adventure.'

Delilah's heart was beating so fast and so hard that she could scarcely catch her breath, and she inhaled deeply in an attempt to establish some calm inside. Everywhere she looked her eyes ran slap-bang into something that set her nervous system hurtling towards meltdown.

Stare straight ahead and her vision was filled with the sight of his steel-hard, bronzed torso... Raise her eyes and she met his green, sexy ones... Look past him and what did she see? The bed. At which point the images that cluttered her head were enough to make her breathing go funny all over again.

'I went through something I thought was right, but it was only because I wanted it so badly to *be* right,' she whispered.

She found the safest point in the cabin and stared at it—it happened to be her feet. Not for long, though, because he raised her head so that she couldn't avoid looking at him.

'I felt like I'd spent my youth worrying about keeping the gallery afloat and worrying about Sarah working just to stand still. Michael was like a blast of fresh air, and it felt like he brought all sorts of exciting possibilities to my life. Maybe that was what I fell in love with. Maybe I was just desperate for a future that wasn't so…*predictable*. I'm only twenty-one, for heaven's sake! But it didn't work out, and I came here just to get away from…from everything. It was supposed to be just for a couple of weeks, but my art course proved so popular that I couldn't resist staying on—because when I return to the Cotswolds all I'm going to be doing is helping my sister in a last-ditch attempt to get the shop going, so that we have sufficient income to live on without having to worry about money all the time.'

Daniel had never had to worry about money. He and Theo had been born into privilege. Sure, his father had sent them both on their way to make their fortune, but they hadn't left the nest empty-handed. He had no doubt that both he and his brother would have succeeded whatever their backgrounds, because they both had the same drive, the same high-octane ambition that had fuelled their father and propelled him into making his fortune, but the fact remained that they had been born with silver spoons in their mouths.

Golden spoons, if he were to be perfectly honest.

He'd never delved into the details of any of his girl-friends' backgrounds, preferring to live in an uncluttered present which was mostly about sex, and of course the expensive fripperies that accompanied his very brief liaisons. Hearing about the sort of life Delilah was returning to brought into sharp relief the great big space between them.

It wasn't just the fact that she was green for her years, an innocent compared to his vastly more experienced self, but she was also, from the sound of it, broke.

Their worlds were so completely different that he might have been looking down at someone from another planet.

Under normal circumstances their paths would never have crossed, and yet now that they *had* crossed something about her had got to him and wasn't letting him go—wasn't allowing the voice of logic and reason to have a say.

'Have you ever been to the Cotswolds, Daniel?'

'I can't say that the countryside has ever done much for me…' he murmured.

'It's very beautiful. But very quiet. In winter, people hibernate. I love it there, but it's so quiet. It's a place where adventure would never happen to someone of my age.'

'You can't be the only young person there…'

'You'd be surprised how many of them move down to London to see a bit of the bright city lights before they return to the country to have kids and raise families.' She sighed. 'I wouldn't be able to do that because I have a duty to help Sarah, and that's something I want to do anyway, but…'

'But here you are, with one bad experience behind you—although from the sounds of it you don't need any sticking plaster—and here *I* am. And before you return to fulfil your sisterly obligations you don't see why you can't sleep with me on the rebound—have yourself a little fun and excitement before you take up your responsibilities with your sister... *I'm* your bright city lights before you return to the country...'

Did he like that? Daniel wasn't sure.

'That's more or less it.' She squashed the hint of defiance trying to creep into her voice. 'So if you think that I'm in any danger of falling for you, turning you into my Prince Charming, then you're way off track. That's not it at all. I've decided to...to... That you could be the one to...'

'To teach you the many and varying ways of enjoying love...?'

Delilah's mouth tightened, but her heart flipped at the slow smile playing on his lips.

The man was utterly incorrigible—and she had to admit, grudgingly, that that was just part and parcel of his overwhelming appeal.

'I may not be experienced,' she muttered, 'but that doesn't mean I don't have my head well and truly screwed on.'

'By which you mean...?'

Without her even realising he had taken her hand and led her back to the bed, and Delilah sank back against the pillows, not knowing whether she was relieved that this adventure was going to happen or terrified that this adventure was going to happen.

She was still fully clothed, her feet dangling off the bed, and before he joined her he knelt and removed her sandals, easing them off her feet in a gesture that was curiously delicate and erotic at the same time.

How odd that it was just the sort of thing a real-life Prince Charming might have done...

'…that I'm not the sort of catch you have in mind for yourself…?'

Daniel raised his eyes to hers and she shrugged and smiled and nodded all at the same time.

He was her adventure—someone she was prepared to have fun with, but certainly not the sort of man she would ever want as a permanent fixture in her life.

It couldn't be better. Could it? They were singing from the same song sheet and there was no way he should now be feeling as though his nose had been put out of joint by her admission.

'That's right,' she whispered.

She took a deep breath and held it, watching as he lowered his head to hers in slow motion. His kiss feathered her mouth, lingered, deepened, and at the same time he began removing her top. He cupped one small breast and then gently eased his hand underneath her stretchy bra. She shuddered against him.

'Feel good…?'

He breathed the question into her ear and Delilah gasped out a response, because now he was playing with her nipple and sending delicious shivers straight down from her breasts to the place between her legs which was growing wetter by the second.

'Want me…?' he asked. 'Because if I'm to be your rebound adventure, then I need to know that it's an adventure that you really want…'

'I want you, Daniel…' Her eyes fluttered open to meet his. He had the most amazing lashes. Dark and long and in striking contrast to his light hair.

'Good,' Daniel murmured with intense satisfaction. 'Now, I want you to relax. Don't worry. I'm not going to hurt you.'

Aren't you? she thought in sudden confusion. But the thought vanished as quickly as it had come and she settled back into the soft duvet with a sigh as he hoiked up the top, taking the bra with it so that her breasts were pushed free of the restricting fabric.

Her whole body shrieked in urgent response as he clamped his mouth over her nipple and began teasing it with his tongue, drawing it into his mouth, tasting the stiffened bud.

She had exquisite breasts. Small and neat, the nipples perfectly defined rosy-pink discs. Sexy breasts. Breasts a man could lose himself in.

Rampant desire was flooding through him, making him uncomfortable, making him wonder how the hell he was going to keep a lid on his natural urge to take her, fast and hard.

He straightened to pull her free of the top and the bra, and then for a few seconds stared down at her pale nudity, at the perfection of her slender body—the way the golden tan gave way to the paleness where her swimsuit had prevented the sun from touching her bare skin.

Her hair flowed over the pillow in an unruly mass and she had twisted her head to one side, squeezed her eyes shut, clenched her small fists at her sides.

He eased open her hands and she turned, opened her eyes, looked at him.

His erection was prominent against his trousers, pushing into a massive bulge that sent her senses spinning.

'Now we're both half naked,' he growled, 'shall we be really, really daring and go the whole way?'

Delilah smiled, and then nodded. Her natural instinct was to shield herself from his hungry gaze, but for some reason she wasn't feeling shy in front of him—something about the way he was looking at her...with blatant, open appreciation.

She wriggled sinuously and his nostrils flared. 'You

have no idea what you're doing to me,' he muttered in a wrenching undertone, and Delilah decided that she could happily cope with having that effect on him.

He vaulted upright and removed his trousers, and as he did so she propped herself up on one elbow and just... *stared*.

In fact, she found that she couldn't stop staring.

He removed his underwear, silky boxers, and she stilled. Although his erection had been visible underneath his trousers, now she could appreciate it in all its magnificent glory—and magnificent it really and truly was.

'I know I'm big...' He correctly interpreted her wide-eyed stare of apprehension. He perched on the side of the bed and grinned. 'But I won't hurt you. Promise. I'll be very, very gentle, and in the end you'll be begging me to go harder...'

He began easing off her silky trousers, tugging them down until she was left in just her underwear. Simple cotton pants that made him smile, because they was a world apart from the lacy lingerie women always but *always* wore for him.

But then there wasn't a single bone in her body that advertised herself, was there?

Underneath her clothes she was as unaffected as she was everywhere else, and he liked that. A lot.

He didn't immediately tug down her underwear, even though she was squirming, her own hands reaching to do the job for him. Instead he pressed the flat of his hand between her legs, feeling the dampness spreading through the cotton, and firmly began to massage her, knowing just where to apply pressure so that her squirming was now accompanied by soft groans and whimpers.

He didn't stop. He wanted her on the brink of tipping over the edge. He wanted her so wet for him that he would slide into her, and she would stretch and take all of him, and love every second of the experience.

He was going to make sure that nothing hurt.

Even if he had to dig deep to find the self-restraint he would need.

'Please, Daniel…' His hand down there was sweet, sweet torture. Her body was on fire and he just kept on rubbing, until she thought she was going out of her mind. 'If you don't stop…'

'If I don't stop what…? You'll come against my hand?'

'You know I will,' she panted. 'And I don't want it to be like this… It should…should…'

'There are no *shoulds* when it comes to making love,' Daniel admonished teasingly. 'It's all about what makes you feel good. Does this feel good?'

'Better than good…'

She could barely get the words out, and when he slipped that questing hand under her panties, so that he was rubbing her properly, finding the throbbing bud of her clitoris and teasing it remorselessly, she wanted to faint.

She spread apart her legs and her body found its own rhythm as she began to move, angling herself so that he could slip one finger, then two, into her, while making sure to keep pressure on her clitoris. Straining under the bombardment of sensation, unable to hold off any longer, even though she wanted to, Delilah tensed, arched, and with a keening cry came against his fingers.

It was beautiful, he thought, dazed at the ferocity of his reaction to seeing her reach orgasm. Colour flooded her cheeks and she was breathing fast and shallow, and as she raised her body off the bed he thrust his fingers deeper into her, extending her orgasm and deepening it. Her face was shiny with perspiration.

If he could stop himself from ejaculating like a bloody

horny teenager, then he could do anything, he figured—because right now that felt like the hardest thing in the world to achieve.

'It shouldn't have been like that.' Delilah was dismayed, because this was just more evidence of her inexperience, but he was smiling as he lowered himself alongside her.

'Shh…'

'But I want to…to give you pleasure as well…'

'You are.'

'Tell me what to do.'

'You can hold me,' he suggested. 'But just hold me,' he warned. 'Because I might come if you do much more. I'm *that* close to losing control…'

'I bet you never do.'

'Lose control? Never. You, however, are turning out to be the exception to the rule when it comes to getting me to that point. Now, I'm going to touch you everywhere… with my mouth…with my hands…very, very slowly. I just want you to enjoy the experience, Delilah, and stop thinking that there should be a certain way of doing things…'

'Is that an order?' she whispered. She raised herself up to plant feathery kisses all over his face, ending with his beautiful mouth, but that was as far as he would allow her to go.

Masterful.

That was the word that sprang to mind, and his mastery thrilled her to her very core.

He kissed her neck and then spent time on her breasts, giving her body time to subside from its orgasm, time to find its way to building back up to a new peak. He kissed her flat stomach and felt her suck in her breath, then trailed lower, gently parting her legs to accommodate him.

He settled himself between her legs and then rested

them over his shoulders, and then he kissed and licked and teased her in her most intimate spot—and she loved every second of it. She gave herself to his exploration with an abandonment she would never have believed possible. His tongue flicked over her clitoris and she stiffened as she began to melt.

But this time he didn't let her build up the momentum that would take her over the edge. Instead, he teased her. He aroused her. He took her so far and then away, so that she had time to catch her breath, and the more he did that, the more she pleaded with him to come into her.

And in the end he just had to—because he was losing too much of his self-control to do anything else…

His wallet was on the ground and he barely looked as he flipped a condom over his rock-hard erection.

She was tight and wet and he eased himself inside her gently, in a two steps forward, one step back process that gradually allowed her to relax, so that he could fit into her without her tensing.

When he was ready to sink deeper into her, to have his shaft fill her, so was she, and as he thrust in, pushing her up the bed, taking his time and being as gentle as he could, he heard and felt the long, low shudder of her reaching orgasm.

It took her over.

Delilah hadn't thought that this depth of pure, unfiltered sensation could even exist. It did. She had stretched for him and moulded around his bigness as though their bodies had been made for one another. She came over and over and over, just as he reared up, the tendons in his neck straining, and came into her.

Time stood still. When finally they were back on Planet Earth she curved into him with a sigh of pure contentment. 'That was… Thank you…'

The disarming charm of her words distracted him from

the pressing concern that his condom appeared to have split. He chucked it onto the pile of clothes on the ground and wrapped his arms around her, drew her against him.

Mind-blowing. That was the only way he could describe the experience. Had it been because of the situation? Because she'd come to him a virgin? Or had it been because she had no idea of his identity? No idea of who he really was and how much he was really worth?

For just the briefest of moments he was disconcerted by that—by the very thing that had turned him on: namely her ignorance of his monetary value. He was disconcerted by the fact that she didn't know the truth about him.

'There's no need to thank me,' he told her huskily. He pushed back some wayward strands of hair. 'But there's something just a little bit worrying I have to say...'

'What's that?'

'I think the condom may have split...is that a problem? By which I mean are you in a safe period? It's highly unlikely that anything unfortunate will happen, but I thought I'd mention it...'

Delilah thought quickly and decided that she was perfectly safe, even though there *had* been a little hiccup—what with the travel and the stress and the sheer excitement of being on the cruise liner.

'Perfectly safe,' she told him firmly, nestling into him and smiling as she felt him stir against her naked thighs.

Daniel couldn't credit that his body was already gearing up for a repeat performance—one which it would not have...not just yet...because chances were that she would be sore.

The surprising urgency of his response settled his mind on the very pleasant prospect of what remained of the rest of his incognito holiday aboard the liner.

'Good,' he murmured, although he was already thinking ahead, wanting her in ways he couldn't remember wanting any other woman for a very long time. 'Glad to hear it.'

Delilah didn't add the reassurance that it was rare for a woman to fall pregnant on her first sexual encounter. She had read enough magazines to know that that was a myth.

'Now, how do you think we should spend the rest of the evening?' he asked.

She giggled and moved against him, and he grinned.

'Your body will need to take a little rest. I'd suggest we share a shower, but the facilities here leave a lot to be desired when it comes to joint showers... All cabins should cater for couples who want to have sex in the bathroom, don't you agree?'

'I don't think I've ever been in a shower that can fit more than one very skinny person.' She couldn't stop herself from touching him. She touched his hair, stroked his cheek, drew over the fine lines at the corners of his eyes with her fingers...

Daniel thought of the vast bathroom at his house in Sydney. The vast bathrooms at all the places he owned. He liked big bathrooms. Small, cosy spaces didn't do it for him.

What would she think if she knew the truth about him?

Just like that the question sprang from nowhere, and he frowned. She'd turn into just someone else who was desperate to please him, he decided, which was why it was refreshing that she didn't know.

'One shower at a time,' he said, with audible regret in his voice. 'Then what about you telling me about *my* half of this deal...?'

'Deal?' Delilah looked at him, perplexed, and he burst out laughing.

'I like the compliment,' he said with satisfaction. 'You've forgotten that, in return for me getting my wicked and very, very enjoyable way with you, you get to paint me… Talk to me about that. You can even put me in whatever sexy pose you want, and I guarantee that by the time we're finished talking about that we'll both be ready to make love all over again…'

CHAPTER SIX

'IT LOOKS GOOD…' Lying on his bed, arms folded behind his head, Daniel looked at the half-finished portrait of himself.

Somehow Delilah had managed to squeeze an easel into a corner of the cabin, so that she could paint him without being observed by all and sundry.

Daniel thought that had been an inspired idea, considering the portrait of him showed him in the position he was in now—reclining half naked on the bed, with a swirl of duvet blatantly advertising the fact that underneath it he was wearing nothing at all.

'You're not supposed to talk.'

But she smiled, because they did a lot of talking while he was posing for her and she liked that. They didn't talk about anything in particular. The conversation ebbed and flowed, drifted in and out of topics, and although there were vast swathes of his life which she felt she knew precious little about, she still felt that she knew the whole man, the complete package—knew the things that made him laugh and the things that pissed him off.

For three hours every day, for a week and a half now, he had been her captive audience, and it had bred an easy familiarity between them that thrilled her to the bone. If this was what successful therapy was all about then she was a fervent fan, because she hadn't thought about

Michael once, and she hadn't thought about the gallery either.

And she still hadn't tired of just *looking* at him. She knew every angle of his face and every muscle and sinew of his beautiful, strong body.

'It's utterly boring, trying to maintain this pose, if I can't talk at the same time.'

Or work. Or make the important business calls that needed to be made. Or do any of the other things around which his life was normally focused.

The truth was that he had shoved work commitments to one side, only really catching up after she had left him late in the night to return to her cabin. It was a fairly hellish routine when it came to grabbing much sleep, but frankly he didn't care. He was having a good time, and he saw no reason why he shouldn't indulge himself a little. The world wasn't going to stop turning on its axis just because he didn't clock in for a conference call at a prearranged time, or because he delegated a call to one of his guys at Head Office.

He was enjoying her.

And after that first time, when nerves had almost got the better of her, she had opened up to him like a peach.

His eyes flared now as he watched her painting him, her expression one of ferocious concentration.

That ferocious concentration was somewhat diluted by the fact that she wore nothing as she sat at her easel painting him. That was part of *his* side of the deal—a little addendum he had tacked on, and one which she had agreed to without, it had to be said, much persuasion.

She had a glorious body. Having previously only gone for women who were curvy and big-breasted, like pocket-sized Barbie dolls, he found that he couldn't get enough of her slender length, her long, shapely legs, her colt-like grace, the sweep of her hair...

Jarring at the back of his mind was the thought that all too soon it would have to come to an end. He'd already outstayed his original allotted time. He'd visited two countries more than he'd planned on doing. He'd produced more laughable attempts at still-life painting than any man should ever have to do. And he'd had the most mind-blowing sex…

Every day. Every night. More than once a night.

Just thinking about that mind-blowing sex was making him harden, and he knew that very shortly he would have to have her.

Delilah could sense where his thoughts were going without even having to look at the darkening in his eyes. It was as if they were connected by some kind of invisible umbilical cord to one another. He wanted her. And she wanted him.

Her nipples pinched at the thought of it and she wasn't shocked when he levered himself off the bed and strolled towards her.

Their routine of painting took place after lunch, when her classes were over. A lazy time for both of them. The sun continued to shine outside and the deep blue ocean continued to spread around them like a never-ending swathe of navy blue silk, but the only thing she had room for in her head was *him*.

He occupied every waking moment of her thoughts and most of her sleeping ones, as well.

'This portrait will never get finished if you keep interrupting me like this…' She looked up at him and grinned, her body already gearing up to unite with his, liquid pooling between her legs in anticipation.

Her breath hitched as he touched himself, touched his big, hard erection.

'My muscles were seizing up,' he drawled. 'I'm a man who enjoys lots of exercise. Physical activity.'

'I can point you in the direction of the squash courts,' she suggested helpfully. 'They could do with a lick of paint, but they function fine, and I'm sure you could rustle up a suitable partner if you want to get some much needed exercise...'

'I have a feeling that the way I play might spell certain death for whoever happens to be playing against me. Some of the guys here look as though they may have dodgy tickers...'

Delilah laughed, on a breathless high. So much for getting that bit of his arm just right... She could barely concentrate when he was posing for her, and when he was standing in front of her as he was doing now, butt naked and aroused, it was impossible.

She swivelled on the chair so that she was facing him, and then she stood on her tiptoes and kissed him—a lingering kiss that was as sweet and seductive as honey.

You thrill me, she would have liked to have told him, but that was off-limits. She knew that without having to be told. That sort of thing was taboo. Words of endearment or any hint at all that this might be deeper and more significant than either of them had bargained for were never spoken.

It wasn't love—of course it wasn't—but it *felt* as if it should be more than just a two-week fling...

When she thought about him disappearing she felt physically sick, so she tried not to think about it.

Instead, she thought about the fact that he had already stayed on for longer than he had first said he would, and she couldn't help pathetically wondering what that meant.

'Nice...' Daniel murmured, smiling down at her. 'Much better than lying on a bed pretending to be a statue.'

'You make a terrible model.'

'And here I was thinking that you found me good-looking...'

'Lord, but you're conceited. And that's not what I meant. You're far too restless to make a good model. Even when you're trying to stay perfectly still I can *hear* your brain whirring and I know you're itching to get up…'

'How well you know me, my little artist. Now, shall we put that to the test?'

'Put what to the test?'

'Your knowledge of me… Tell me what I'm thinking I'd like you to do now…'

Afterwards, lying on his bed, both on their backs, with her head resting on his shoulder, the pressing question of his imminent departure again began playing on his mind.

This wasn't going to do.

He couldn't play truant from reality for ever, and that was what he'd been doing. Good fun, but the time to say goodbye had come.

Conference calls had been cancelled, delegated, postponed…in one instance flatly avoided…but the final grain of sand had sifted through the upturned egg timer and now he had to leave.

A new acquisition required his urgent attention, and decisions had to be made about an office block he intended to refurbish in Mayfair. He couldn't duck low for ever.

However sweet the temptation was.

He turned to the sweet temptation and stroked her breast, looking down and smiling with male appreciation at the way her nipple tightened under the brush of his finger.

Propping himself up on his elbow, he continued to feather his finger over the stiffened pink bud before lowering his head to tease it with his tongue, then his mouth, suckling on it, but not touching her anywhere else at all.

Driving her crazy with just his mouth clamped to her nipple.

She squirmed and fidgeted, her whole body yearning for his—a physical ache that needed to be sated.

She'd learned how to touch him, where to touch him, the places that turned him on, and she reached down to close her hand over his erection, moving it slowly but firmly, building a little pace until she could tell from the change in his breathing that he was as turned on as she was.

And this, Daniel thought, was how things had ended up where they had—how he had ended up staying far longer than he had anticipated or planned.

This senseless drive to have more and more of her.

He laid his hand over hers and gritted his teeth, willing his erection to subside, because he couldn't think straight when he was aroused. It was as if she took over his whole mind.

After a couple of minutes he flipped onto his back and stared for a few seconds at the ceiling of the cabin.

If he looked through the circular window he would see the clear turquoise sky and the sun shining down on the navy blue ocean. When he took to the water in Australia he sailed with purpose, pitting his skill against nature. He got up close and personal with the sea, felt the whip of breeze on his face, challenged the ocean's depths to do their worst.

It was nothing like this. He thought that perhaps this was what people meant when they said that they'd had a 'relaxing' holiday. This was what doing nothing was all about, and he realised that it was something he rarely did. He hadn't even suspected how enjoyable it could be.

'We need to talk.'

In one easy, fluid movement Daniel slipped out of bed

and stood by the side for a few seconds, looking at her flushed face, at the flare of dismay in her eyes.

Was he going to tell her everything?

When they'd started their fling he'd presumed that he would leave the ship, wave goodbye and she would never be any the wiser as to his true identity. A few hot nights of passion and then a parting of ways.

He would conduct his business transaction with the Ockleys either from London or Sydney. He'd got the information he needed about the liner, had seen for himself what the crew were like. He even had his offer formulated in his head. It was low, but then the liner was fairly run down and would hit the metaphorical rocks within the next year or so. It was an offer he knew they might resent, but would be compelled to accept. In his eyes, that amounted to what was *fair*.

He hadn't planned on staying for as long as he had.

He hadn't planned on a number of things.

He frowned and had a quick mental flashback of her laughing, head thrown back…her concentration in her art classes, patiently giving encouragement to everyone… her blushing and laughing whenever he touched her or whenever she touched him…

'You might want to get dressed…'

He knew that this was for his benefit rather than hers. He couldn't think straight when she was naked, and he needed to think straight. This was just another woman he was going to leave behind, and he tightened his jaw in preparation for his parting speech.

Delilah sprang out of the bed. Her heart was beating so hard that it felt as though it might explode right out of her chest.

It was going to end.

He'd never promised otherwise. Had never hinted at it. Now, however, she realised just how much she had hoped that there might be a future for them. She'd somehow become needy and clingy and it appalled her.

What had happened to all her grand theories about the nature of lust? What had happened to her conviction that she couldn't be hurt if she slept with him because you could only be hurt when you were in love? What had happened to her assumption that love could never enter the equation because he was just a bit of fun to take her mind off the bad time she'd had with Michael and the worrying time that lay ahead with all their money problems?

Thoughts swarming in her head like angry bees, she fought against the realisation that she had fallen in love with him.

With beautiful, intelligent, utterly charismatic Daniel —who was a commitment-phobe, who didn't want to put down roots, who was just taking a breather with her in between his travels...

Just by being himself he had made her see how shallow Michael had been and how unsuitable as a partner.

She dressed quickly, barely able to look at him, already bracing herself for his 'Dear John' speech.

And the worst of it was that she wanted to beg him not to deliver the speech—wanted to tell him that they worked so well together, that they should try and continue what they had...that they had something special.

Except it was only special *for her*, wasn't it...?

'I know what you're going to say.'

'Do you?'

He didn't think so.

'You're going to tell me that you're moving on...that you have places to go, people to see...' She gave a brittle laugh and stared at him, chin tilted at a defiant angle.

Daniel thought that he might miss those shapeless long skirts and baggy tops.

'I never led you to believe that this would be a permanent arrangement.' He shoved his hands into his trouser pockets and then ran his fingers through his hair. He wanted to walk…to burn off some of his restless energy…but the cabin was the size of a matchbox so he settled for dragging the chair from the fitted dressing table by the wall and sitting down heavily.

'I know,' Delilah said tightly.

She badly wanted to beg him to reconsider. Her hands were shaking and she pushed them into the deep pockets of her skirt and perched on the edge of the bed.

'I don't do long-term,' he told her in the sort of gentle voice that set her teeth on edge. 'And there's a reason for that.'

'You've had your heart broken.'

'I've had my heart *hardened*.' He sighed. 'What do you think of this cruise liner?'

'Sorry?' She raised startled eyes to his and wondered where this was going. Was that *it* for his goodbye speech? Didn't she deserve more? Maybe just a tiny bit of remorse?

'What do you think of this cruise liner? I mean the way it's run…its condition…the general state of its health?'

'I… Well… I don't know where you're going with this, Daniel.' When he didn't answer, she gave a little shrug and looked around her. 'It could do with some work,' she said, still bewildered. 'Everyone knows that. All the crew know that Gerry and Christine have been having a few financial problems…'

'They're heavily in debt. Your eyes would water if you knew how much they owed the bank. They inherited this liner from Gerry's parents. A very wealthy family, as it happens. Lots of fingers in lots of pies. This was just one of their concerns. Unfortunately Gerry Ockley may have inherited their wealth—which, frankly, was already dwindling by the time John Ockley kicked the bucket—

but he has failed to inherit his father's business acumen. The estate was evenly divided between three sons and he got the liner as part of his legacy. He turned a niche and nicely profitable service into something equally niche but sadly not nearly as profitable.'

Her mouth had dropped open. He knew every single illusion she had had about him was slowly being shattered, but he had to continue, and he told himself that shattered illusions weren't such a bad thing.

He'd grown from his, hadn't he? Shattered illusions allowed you to develop the sort of tough strength that helped you get through life. That was how it had worked for him. She would move on from this a much stronger person.

He banked down the tide of savage guilt that *he* was the one responsible for giving her this learning curve.

'I am Daniel De Angelis,' he told her softly. 'You think that I'm a traveller, interested in dabbling in a spot of art, but that's not strictly speaking the truth...'

'I don't know what you're telling me...' Delilah shook her head in utter bewilderment. She felt as though she had suddenly been transported into a parallel universe, where everything looked the same but nothing actually was.

Her warm, teasing, sexy guy had vanished and in his place was this stranger, with his remote, guarded eyes, saying stuff that she didn't understand.

'I didn't come here to do a course on art,' he ploughed on—relentless, remorseless.

She wished she could just put her hand over his beautiful mouth and stop the flow of words.

'I came here to inspect this liner...to find out where its failings lay...to see its condition first-hand and to do it without anyone knowing who I was... I wanted the element of surprise—no superficial tidying or paint jobs. I wanted to see it in all its downtrodden glory...'

'But *why*?' Delilah whispered, her voice barely audible.

'Because I intend to buy it.'

That flatly spoken statement swirled around her like thick toxic waste, penetrating her consciousness, and then she was tying up all the things that hadn't made sense about him—starting with that ridiculously extravagant dinner on the deck...their first *date*. What a joke!

Anger began a slow, poisonous burn.

'You're not poor at all, are you?' She knew that she was stating the obvious, but there was still a pathetic part of her that was clinging to the hope that this was all some kind of big joke.

'I am a billionaire,' Daniel said.

No beating around the bush. He looked for the signs he secretly expected to see. The flare of certain interest as her preconceived notions gave way to far more tempting prospects.

They failed to materialise.

And along with that realisation came another one.

He wasn't ready to let her go. Not yet. Eventually, yes. But not yet. He still wanted her.

So now she would know the truth about him—but the bottom line was that he was very, very, *very* rich, and that, in the end, would be the deciding factor.

Women were always predictable in their reactions to extreme wealth. They gravitated towards it like bears to a pot of honey. Once she'd recovered from the shock of his revelations she would surely see the advantages of continuing what they had—not least because it was what she wanted.

He still desired her, and she still desired him—it was simple as that when you cut through all the murky red tape.

Goodbye speeches weren't set in cement, were they? And he didn't want to walk away leaving behind unfinished business. He didn't want to find himself missing those long, shapeless skirts and baggy tops and wondering whether he should have continued what they had.

Practical to the very last drop of blood in his body, Daniel knew that the fact that she was broke would work in his favour. He wondered whether she would be insulted if he offered to help her and her sister out of their dire financial situation…

'Why did you get involved with me?' Delilah asked bluntly. She had to clench her fists to stop her hands from shaking uncontrollably. Like a jigsaw puzzle, the pieces were all coming together, thick and fast, and what she was beginning to see of the finished picture made her feel sick.

'I didn't intend to get involved with *anyone*,' Daniel told her truthfully.

'But here I was and so you decided *why not*? Because I guess you're the kind of guy who always takes what he wants, and I'm thinking that you maybe decided you could kill two birds with one stone. You wanted all sorts of information about the ship and the people who worked on it, and you decided that I might be able to help you out with some of that information.'

Her voice was rising, even though she was trying to keep it calm and controlled. She just knew that if she really let what he had just told her overwhelm her then she would fly at him, and she wasn't going to do that. She was going to walk away and leave him with the contempt he deserved.

But underneath it all she could feel her heart breaking in two.

She'd been the biggest idiot in the world. She'd wanted adventure and she'd got a hell of a lot more than she'd bargained for. She'd got a nightmare.

She should have listened to her sister and to her own common sense. You couldn't clear your head of one stupid mistake with a guy by jumping into bed the second someone else came around.

Daniel flushed darkly. Strictly speaking, there was an element of truth there… But hadn't events put a different spin on it? Things had changed. But he couldn't deny that he *had* seen her as a good conduit of information for him and now, thinking about that, he was prey to a certain amount of guilt.

'You lied to me all along,' she said tautly. 'You lied about who you were, and you lied about what you wanted from me… The only thing you said to me that was true was that you weren't going to be sticking around and that you weren't interested in long-lasting relationships… Aside from that, every single thing you said to me was a lie. All lies!'

'I didn't lie to you about wanting you.'

His husky voice penetrated her anger and she hated herself for the way her body weakened. Even hating him, he could still do that—still make her insides go to mush—and she hated him even more for being able to do that.

Keep it cold, and hang on to your self-control…

'So what do you intend to do now?' she demanded. 'Throw everyone overboard and take over the liner? Like some kind of pirate?'

He *looked* like a pirate. She should have listened to her instincts and followed them… Should have realised early on that he just didn't fit the profile of an itinerant traveller, aimlessly seeing the world and stopping off to indulge his love of art.

No wonder his efforts at drawing and painting had been so poorly executed. In fact little wonder that he had barely put paint to canvas in all the classes he had so dutifully attended.

'I'm not the bad guy here,' Daniel told her, outraged

at the attacks being levelled against him, even though he could understand some of her justifiable fury.

Hell, if she looked at the bigger picture she would see that he would be doing the hapless Ockleys a favour by buying them out!

'Oh, you're an absolute saint.' Delilah's voice dripped sarcasm.

'The Ockleys are going under,' Daniel informed her, even though he was distracted by her glorious beauty— all rage and tousled hair and pursed lips. 'They're on a fast track to bankruptcy and when that happens they'll get nothing for this ship. It'll be taken off their hands for a song. I intend to buy it and bring it back up to spec...'

'And you think that I'm supposed to *congratulate* you for that? You *used* me.'

'You're overreacting.'

Delilah resisted the strong temptation to throw something at him. His stupid portrait would do the trick.

But even as she thought that another treacherous thought crossed her mind.

That portrait would be all she had left of him when they parted ways. And she hated herself for wanting to hang on to it.

'So what happens to all the people who depend on this liner for their livelihoods?' she flung at him, slamming the door on her weakness.

'I'm not going to throw them overboard!' Daniel thundered. 'You're being dramatic! I... Okay, so I apologise if you think that you were used...' Dull colour highlighted his cheekbones. Apologies were something else he didn't do. 'I intend to keep the staff who are up to the job. They'll find that they're richly rewarded and working on a ship that's actually not hanging on to survival by the skin of its pants!'

'I hate you.'

'You don't hate me,' he said huskily. 'You want me. If I came over there right now and kissed you, you'd kiss me back and you'd want more...'

'You wouldn't dare...' She glared at him.

'You should know better than to lay down challenges like that to a man like me.'

The air was charged as they stared at one another in electric silence.

'I should have seen the signs,' she muttered. 'I should have known from the very first moment you had that meal arranged on deck and paid poor Stan extra money that you weren't who you said you were!'

'*Poor Stan* will be singing my praises when I tell him what sort of money he'll be getting when he works for *me*.'

'And I suppose you'll turn this ship into some awful, rowdy, drink-all-you-can cruiser for the under-thirties...?' she said scathingly.

'The opposite—'

'And all that rubbish you told me about not being the sort of guy who wants long-term relationships... I suppose you were just referring to *me*...' Hurt and bitterness had crept into her voice as she dispassionately joined up all the dots. 'You're just an opportunist who decided to take advantage of a vulnerable woman. And you knew I was vulnerable... You knew I'd just come out of a bad relationship—that I wasn't looking forward to going back to the Cotswolds and facing all those financial problems...'

Considering he had spent his life making sure to avoid opportunists, Daniel was enraged that she had flung him into that category.

'I don't *do* relationships,' he told her flatly. 'Nothing to do with you. And I didn't drag you kicking and screaming against your will into the nearest bed because you were *vulnerable*!'

'But you knew that I *was*!'

'I didn't take you for a coward, Delilah.'

'What does *that* mean?'

'Face up to the choices you made. You knew what you were getting into. You knew I wasn't in it for the long haul. You *chose* to sleep with me. That was the decision *you* made—and, trust me, if you'd decided against it I would never have tried to force your hand. So do me a favour and take responsibility for your decisions!'

'I just never thought that I was going to end up in bed with a liar! I thought I'd been there, done that. I thought you were *different*.'

Daniel's teeth snapped, but there was nothing he could say to that.

'And if you *were* to "do" a relationship,' Delilah inserted in a driven voice, 'then it certainly wouldn't be with someone like *me*, would it? Someone without money? Not when you're a billionaire who can buy a cruise ship the way someone might buy a pair of shoes!'

His silence was telling.

'I'm careful,' he gritted. 'I'm a target for gold-diggers. That's just the way it is.'

'I think I've heard enough now,' Delilah said quietly. She felt utterly drained, exhausted on every level. Her legs were like jelly and she hoped that when she stood up she wouldn't go crashing to the ground. 'I'm going to take my painting with me, if you don't mind.'

She began easing the canvas from the easel, her back to him, not looking at him, although she was aware of his presence with every atom of her body.

If he touched her now...

She knew that she had to get out of the cabin as fast as she could—because she didn't trust herself...didn't know what she would do if he touched her now...and the last thing she wanted was to give him any excuse for thinking that she was the kind of mug who was so smitten with him that she would melt in his arms like the fool she'd been.

No way.

'This doesn't have to end here,' Daniel said gruffly.

She spun round to look at him with an expression of scorn.

He *never* pursued a woman. And especially in a situation like this, when he was staring at a woman who wanted no more to do with him... Pursuit should *definitely* be off the agenda. But, hell, he still wanted her, and he was driven by his own physical impulse.

'I still want you,' he told her.

'So you said. But we can't always have what we want.'

'You have no idea what I could give you.'

'A brief fling?' she enquired with saccharine sweetness. 'A couple more weeks until you get tired of me?'

'You could have anything you want,' he intoned, shocked that he was going down this road. 'You say that you and your sister are short of cash? Struggling to make ends meet? I could help you with that. I could inject money into your business, pull out all the stops, get it to a place where you'd never have to worry about money again...'

Considering her sister didn't know a thing about Daniel,—thank heavens—Delilah wondered what she would think if she brought him home and produced him as their knight in shining armour.

What a laugh.

As if he could *ever* be her knight in shining armour.

And 'pull out all the stops'? Rescue them from their financial situation? How long before he started thinking that she was just another one of those gold-diggers who saw him as a target?

She walked towards the door and said cuttingly, 'I don't think so. I don't want you *or* your money. I'd appreciate it if you just left me alone for the remainder of your time on this liner. I don't want you to come to my classes, and if you see me in the bar or the restaurant feel free to ignore me.'

She couldn't believe that her voice was as cool and controlled as it was, when inside she was falling apart at the seams.

Sex.

That was what she meant to him and that was *all* she meant to him. He still wanted her, and he didn't see why his lies and deception should stand in the way of getting what he wanted—especially when he could throw his money into the ring and try and tempt her with it. Try and *buy* her with it.

Daniel looked at her frozen expression. He had been locked out and he wasn't going to beg.

'And what do you think your students and your fellow crew members are going to think?' he asked. 'Unless they're blind, they already know that there's something going on between us...'

Delilah hitched her shoulder in a dismissive shrug. 'Like you told me at the very beginning—who cares? Why should I care what other people think when I won't be seeing any of them again?'

She wondered how much longer he would stay on the liner and thought that it wouldn't be long. Off at the next stop, having pulled the plug on Christine and Gerry. When she left this cabin she wouldn't be seeing him again. She would make sure of that, however hard it might be.

She didn't look back at him as she let herself out of the cabin. She walked quickly—away from people, away from the possibility of anyone seeing her and guessing that something was wrong. She didn't want to bump into any of her students or any of the other crew members... didn't want them to ask her if she was okay.

She just wanted to get back to the safety of her own cramped cabin and give in to the tears that she was struggling to hold back.

She just wanted to go home.

CHAPTER SEVEN

DELILAH GAZED UP at the building in front of her. It wasn't one of those vast, impressive glass houses that broad-casted to the world that the worker bees inside were *very important* worker bees. By comparison this was a mod-est building, just three storeys high, a squat, square and rather old-fashioned red brick affair, away from the cha-otic hustle and bustle of the city.

She didn't want to be here, but she had had to jump through hoops to find the wretched place and now that she was standing in front of it she wasn't going to retreat without seeing him.

Which didn't mean that she wasn't as nervous as a kitten.

In a sudden burst of anxiety she spun away from the building and headed to the nearest coffee shop, where she would try and rally her mental troops.

The heat of the Mediterranean sun seemed like a long, long time ago. Much longer than two months, which was when she had said farewell to the liner and to the friends she had made there.

Everything had been so chaotic.

Like a hurricane, Daniel had swept through them all and changed their lives in one way or another.

For Christine and Gerry, after what she had privately admitted must have been a horrible, horrible shock to the system, because they had both viewed the money he had flung down on the table as a hostile takeover, things had actually turned out okay.

Faced with the brutal facts of their financial situation, they had been forced to get their heads out of the sand and abandon their optimism that the tide was going to change—that they just needed a couple of bumper seasons, that hordes of culture vultures were waiting out there to book passages on their once-in-a-lifetime cruise.

And, Gerry had told her, Daniel's offer had been pretty fair—which had somewhat eroded Delilah's assumption that Daniel's sole interest had been to plunder and take for the cheapest possible price.

Which, of course, didn't excuse the fact that he had used her and lied to her.

Most the crew were to be re-employed, back on the liner, with six months of paid leave while the cruise ship was being renovated, and their salaries were now so inflated that they were overjoyed at the change of ownership. Stan, as Daniel had told her, had been over the moon at the prospect of running his own kitchen, no expense spared.

The other tutors had thought nothing of losing their jobs. Some, like her, had been part-time recruits and the rest, all in their mid-fifties, had been happy enough to use their talents in other directions. The liner had not constituted their sole income.

No one had been left with the corrosive bitterness that she had been left with—but then she had been in a unique situation.

As predicted, she had seen nothing of him, and had no idea how long he'd remained on the liner before leaving. She had hidden away, taking meals in her poky cabin and scuttling to her classes in a state of dread that she might see him sprawled in his usual chair, doing something and nothing in front of his easel.

He had not reappeared.

So much for his heated pursuit. So much for all that rubbish about still wanting her. He had given it one shot and then shrugged his shoulders and walked away. Literally jumped ship.

Delilah had told herself that she was hugely relieved, but somewhere deep inside disappointment had gnawed away at her, making her situation even more awful and painful than it already had been.

Everything had dissolved. There had been tearful goodbyes and promises to keep in touch. Many of the students had expressed an interest in the business she and Sarah would be starting, which was something, at least.

She had put a brave smile on her face. Several people had asked her about Daniel, asked her whether she would be seeing him again, and she had laughed and told them that it had been nothing more than a pleasant holiday fling.

All lies.

She had fallen in love and was she ever going to recover? Was there a Mr Right? A Mr Sensible and Suited To Her? The sort of chap she should have been looking for after Michael, who was going to elbow Mr Utterly Wrong out of the spot in her heart which he continued to occupy?

Even after everything had gone quiet.

Even after she'd returned to the Cotswolds.

After she'd done her very best to clear her head of him.

She still missed him. She missed him so much that she had gone through all the motions of helping Sarah and enthusing about their project like an automaton.

She missed him so much that she hadn't paid a scrap of attention to the fact that she had skipped a period, and it had only been when she'd started feeling sick and nauseous at certain smells and when certain foods were presented to her that she had twigged.

She closed her eyes briefly and relived that moment when time had stood still. Two bright blue lines had marked the end of life as she knew it. She could still taste the fear, the panic, and see the blank fog of confusion that had crashed over her like a tsunami. Then, when the utter shock had subsided, had come the numbness of just not knowing what happened next.

She opened her eyes and through the window of the coffee shop watched the crowds outside, scurrying about their business.

She had managed to find out, from Christine, where he was and how long he would be there. They, of course, were in touch with him, finalising the sale of their liner.

'He's not the predator we first thought,' Christine had confided. 'And his plans for the liner sound really interesting. Nothing we could ever have hoped to do in a million years... Literally catering for the rich and famous—and would you believe he's actually told me and Gerry that we can have three weeks a year free cruising for the rest of our lives? A way of keeping in touch with our beloved *Rambling Rose*. He didn't have to do that...'

Delilah's brain had stopped functioning at the word *predator*. That was what he was. A predator. He had obviously charmed Gerry and Christine, but she had no doubt that he would have done a pretty shrewd deal and then wrapped it up in lots of glitzy packaging so that he came out of it smelling of roses.

They might have been charmed.

They might have ended up thinking that he'd been a real sport and given them a good deal.

But *she* knew better than to judge a book by its cover. He was one of life's takers. She felt that he could have told her at *any time* who he really was. But he hadn't. Hadn't even come close. He'd been perfectly happy to string her along and she knew why.

At the end of the day there was no way that he would ever allow himself to become involved with someone he considered his inferior.

He played around with women, but in the end they were all potential gold-diggers and therefore only worthy of short-term meaningless dalliances.

Of which she had been one. One of a long number. He'd practically said so himself.

Unfortunately, even with that perfectly sound reasoning, she had still spent weeks thinking obsessively about him. She'd resisted telling her sister about her escapade, because she hadn't wanted any I-told-you-so lectures, but it had been hard. Harder than hard.

And now... Everything came with consequences, and sometimes those consequences lasted a lifetime.

She drained her tea—lemon and ginger—and took a deep breath before heading back out towards the building.

Winter was well and truly in the air. The days were getting shorter and there was a biting feel to the air that penetrated all the layers of clothes she had put on.

Thick socks, jeans, her thermal vest, a loose, long-sleeved tee shirt, a jumper, the long scarf which could wrap three times around her neck and a woolly hat pulled right down over her ears.

She barrelled through the revolving door of the building—a bit of an anachronism considering the age of the property—and was ejected into a modern marble interior that seemed more suited to a five-star luxury hotel than an office block.

But then she imagined that Daniel never did anything by halves.

Cool shades of grey were interrupted by towering plants and a semi-circular reception desk, behind which three snappily dressed women dealt with visitors with the help of their sleek, slimline computers.

The place carried the unmistakable whiff of vast sums of money being made.

At a little after eleven in the morning there wasn't the usual early-morning throng of employees hurrying to get to their desks, but there were sufficient people coming and going to allow her a few moments of unobserved privacy, during which she thought. Thought about what lay ahead...

Should she have warned him of her arrival? Would he have scarpered rather than have a conversation with her? He was only going to be in London for a couple of months. Renovations, apparently, to the office block in which she was now standing, gazing hesitantly around her. This was her window to catch him before he disappeared to the other side of the world. She needed to talk to him, whether she liked it or not, and the element of surprise had seemed like a good idea.

But she still couldn't convert her resolve into action. Her head was telling her to get the whole thing over and done with...her feet were refusing to co-operate.

And she felt horribly underdressed for the surroundings. Everyone seemed to be in a suit and carrying a briefcase. These were people who didn't waste time dawdling. These were *Daniel's kind of people*.

Up ahead, to the left of the semi-circular reception desk, were three subtly camouflaged elevators. Towards the back she could just about glimpse what looked like a private courtyard, and she assumed the building was designed around it, so that the employees had their own little mini-park to it in during their lunch break if they didn't want to head outside and face the crowds.

Gathering her courage, she headed for the imposing reception desk.

Would he even be in?

He was.

The blonde behind the desk wasn't warm and welcoming, but she didn't ask too many intrusive questions and the one side of the conversation Delilah heard, which was obviously conducted with someone else—perhaps his secretary while he was in the country—was brief and productive.

She was given a visitor's pass, directed to the lifts—or the stairs, if she'd rather—and told to make her way to the far right wing of the building.

Apparently she wouldn't be able to miss his office because it occupied most of the right wing of the building to which she had been directed.

A Very Important Man.

She would be going to see a stranger—not the man in whose arms she had lain night after night, who had made love to her as though it was the only thing he wanted to do in the world, the only thing he'd been born to do...

And just like that she was reminded of what she had lost, for coming out of the elevator was a couple...

The dark-haired woman was small and curvy, and gazing up adoringly at the very tall, very muscular dark-haired man who was holding her close against him.

This, Delilah thought with a pang of intense longing, was the very picture of a couple deeply in love.

She brushed past them and the man glanced briefly at her, barely registering her presence. A jolt of pure shock washed through her.

Those eyes! The same arresting shade of green as Daniel's...

She turned, watching their progress out of the building. That must surely be Daniel's brother... A De Angelis who had actually opened himself up to falling in love... Because the tall, striking guy was clearly head over heels in love with the small, curvy brunette pressed to his side.

On the spur of the moment she veered away from the lift and headed towards the staircase…

Daniel pushed himself away from his desk and stood up, strolling to the window and gazing down absently at the very impressive courtyard, with its fountain and its benches and carefully tended grass, which in the depths of winter, at just after eleven in the morning, was completely empty.

He had planned on having lunch with his brother and Alexa. They had, indeed, come to see the new premises with the intention of dragging him off to one of the many wine bars scattered nearby. But that had been before his secretary had informed him that a certain Delilah Scott was in Reception, asking to see him.

He turned from the pleasant view outside and couldn't contain a certain amount of satisfaction—even if that satisfaction was tempered with disappointment.

Two months. She'd walked away from him. He got it that she'd been furious with him because he hadn't announced his identity. He'd apologised. But he might just as well have not bothered, because his apology had counted for nothing. Nor had she made any attempt to understand where he was coming from.

He was rich—very rich. Most women would have been overjoyed, after their initial annoyance, to swap a so-called drifter for a billionaire.

Not her.

And that was probably why she had lingered in his head for the length of time that she had.

Unfinished business.

It could have been avoided, and then he wouldn't be where he had been for the last couple of months…thinking about her, feeling lukewarm about getting in touch with a replacement, having cold showers on far too regular a basis…

He wondered how she was going to play it. Another little spurt of anger because he'd lied to her? Before a reluctant but inevitable move towards him?

Maybe she'd fabricate some excuse about 'just passing by' and deciding to look him up. Presumably she would have found out where his offices were via Christine and Gerry. She could have called in advance, but then that wouldn't really tie in with some random excuse about being in the vicinity, would it?

A darker thought occurred to him…

He'd offered to help her and her sister out of the financial difficulties they were experiencing. Had sufficient time elapsed that she'd had time to work out just how advantageous it would be to have him on board?

That would be disappointing, but he knew enough about women to believe that they were predictably susceptible to a bit of gold being dangled in front of them. Even the most self-righteous couldn't resist and, frankly, he hadn't met too many of those in his lifetime.

Sex for money.

No strings attached.

She was coming to take him up on the offer he'd made to her two months previously and it irked him that he was willing to let her back into his bed. He was, however, enough of a realist to accept that if he didn't she would probably continue to niggle away at the back of his mind, and that wasn't going to do.

Time was money, and he just couldn't afford the unnecessary distraction.

The office block was pretty much up and running, thanks to the amount of money he'd thrown at it. Work had begun on the cruise ship and, again, things were moving along swiftly because money talked.

He anticipated heading back to Sydney some time before Christmas, detouring via Italy so that he could spend part of the festive season with his father, his brother and Alexa.

He wondered how Delilah would accept what was now on the table—because the offer hadn't changed. A limited time in which they would indulge their mutual desire.

He gave it a couple of seconds before he responded to the knock on the door—time during which he resumed his seat behind the big mahogany desk.

Delilah, her nerves at screaming point, wanted to hide behind the secretary who was now standing by the imposing wooden door that separated her outer office from her boss's.

Smoked glass advertised Daniel's presence in his office, but all she could see was a shape.

She thought how lovely it would be if that door opened and she discovered that her memories of him were all rose-tinted and wildly exaggerated. How much braver she would feel if she discovered that he was shorter than she remembered…squatter…less *overwhelming*.

But as she was ushered into the office every single one of those hopeful conjectures was wiped out by the sight of him, sitting behind an absolutely enormous desk.

This was and wasn't the Daniel she had fallen in love with.

Same striking face…those mesmerising green eyes… and the towering, muscular body of someone genetically programmed to be lean, who worked out so that there wasn't a spare ounce of fat on him.

Same overpowering presence…

Her breathing was shallow as she absorbed all of that and then everything else that was different.

His hair was shorter, cropped close, but still the same dirty blond colour. His skin was bronzed, so that there was the same peculiar eye catching contrast between his colouring and his hair.

He was wearing a suit.

'What a surprise.' He broke the silence and nodded to the chair in front of his desk. 'Why don't you sit down? You look as though you're in danger of imminent collapse.'

Delilah licked dry lips and thankfully subsided into the chair. Now that she was here, actually in front of him, all the cool she had hoped to have at her disposal had vanished. She was a mess.

'What brings you to London?' *As if he didn't already know.* He sat forward, resting his forearms on the desk, fingers lightly linked, head tilted questioningly to one side as he looked at her in perfect silence.

'I... I needed to talk to you...'

'About what? The fate of all the crew aboard the liner? I could go into the details, if you'd like, but suffice to say they're all happy campers...' He smiled, but the smile didn't quite reach his eyes. He was remembering the strident moral high ground she had taken the last time they had been together.

'I... No, I haven't come to talk about that...but of course, yes...it seems that you've re-hired a lot of the original staff...which is really good...'

'So if you haven't come for a little catch-up, then why are you here, Delilah? The last time we spoke you were in high dudgeon, and if my memory serves me right you stormed out of my cabin shrieking that you never wanted to lay eyes on me again...'

He'd missed those floaty shapeless clothes, which were nothing like the dapper suits that surrounded him. She was as nervous as hell and he wasn't surprised. Humble pie never tasted good, and she had chewed off a very large slice.

'I wouldn't be here if I... I didn't have to be...' Delilah muttered. He wasn't going to make this easy for her. She couldn't blame him in a way. On the other hand, what would it cost him to be a just a little friendlier?

So there it was... That hadn't taken long... He should be pleased, considering he'd always been a guy to cut to the chase, as well...

'So...' he drawled, relaxing back into the chair and looking at her with brooding intensity. 'Your venture with your sister...'

'Sorry?'

'The project you and your sister have sunk all your savings into...taken out a hefty bank loan to finance...'

'What about it?'

'Oh, I'm just thinking aloud...playing around with the reason why you've shown up on my doorstep two months after you stormed out of my cabin...'

'I stormed out of your cabin for a reason! You lied to me...' She had told herself that she wasn't going to go down the road of rehashing what had happened between them and resorting to old accusations, because that wasn't going to go anywhere, but the expression on his face...

Daniel lifted one lazily imperious hand to halt her mid-accusation. 'Let's skip Memory Lane,' he advised coolly, 'and bring things back to the present. When I was told that you had shown up here and wanted to see me, I confess I was a little surprised—but it didn't take me long to figure it out...'

'Why *am* I here?' she questioned jerkily. Surely he couldn't be *that* clever at reading situations? But then the timeline should tell him something, shouldn't it?

'Money,' Daniel said succinctly.

'Sorry?'

Suddenly consumed with restless energy, Daniel vaulted upright and began striding through his office, which had been kitted out in a style that suited the age of the building. His office in Sydney was the last word in modern. This was all wood and rich tones.

Not that he noticed. He was so damned *alive* to her... huddled in the chair, watching him... He was half furious with himself for even seeing her when he knew why she had come, and half triumphant that she was here at all, in his office, on the verge of caving in.

'It took you a while...' He stopped dead in his tracks in front of her and leaned down, supporting himself by his hands on either side of her chair, caging her in so that she automatically flinched back, nostrils flaring as she breathed him in. 'But in the end you couldn't resist the lure of the big bucks...'

His forest-green eyes locked with hers and his proximity sucked the oxygen out of her lungs, leaving her gasping and panicked.

Delilah's mouth parted in bewilderment.

'You want money and I'm prepared to give it to you... We've already established what the trade-off is...' He straightened, returned to his chair behind the desk, but now he pushed it back and stretched out his long legs to one side. 'And, seeing that you've tracked me down to re-establish what we had, *I* get to choose the terms and conditions...'

Something not quite audible left her throat.

She marvelled that she hadn't foreseen this—hadn't predicted that someone as arrogant and downright egotistical as Daniel De Angelis would put a completely different spin on her unexpected arrival at his office.

He thought that she had come running back, tail between her legs, so that they could resume where they had left off! And that she'd done it because he'd dangled his wealth in front of her like a carrot!

'And what exactly are these so-called "terms and conditions"?' she asked with glacial politeness.

'You're mine for as long as I want you…' He smiled, enjoying the thought of what was to come. 'And when I say mine, I *mean* mine. You…here in London…for the next few weeks…at my beck and call… In return I guarantee that I will sort out all the financial problems you and your sister are currently experiencing…'

'What a thoughtful and generous man you are, Daniel De Angelis.' She could barely keep her voice steady. 'But it's not going to work.'

She sprang out of her chair, walked in jerky steps to the window and took a few deep breaths as she stared down at the courtyard she had glimpsed earlier when she had entered the building. It was impressive. Like everything else she had seen of the premises.

She thought back to the casual way he had arranged that supper on the deck for them, his nonchalant approach to money, the ease with which he had seemed to *own* his surroundings, the lazy charm which she had found so bone-meltingly impressive.

All the hallmarks of a man born into money, accustomed to getting what he wanted at the snap of his fingers.

'Why not?' He frowned. 'Maybe you want to fix a price? Have a piece of paper signed by me so that you know what you're letting yourself in for?'

'Do you know something?' Delilah said, her voice high and shaky. 'I'm beginning to wish that I'd never come here! I might have known that you'd think the worst of me! Do you really and truly think that I made the trip here because I wanted to ask you for *money*? Because I wanted to trade my body for *cash*?'

She pushed herself away from the window but she

couldn't be still, so instead she stalked through the office, her arms wrapped tightly around herself, her nails biting into the tender flesh of her forearms.

'I feel sorry for you,' she said through gritted teeth, pausing long enough to look at him but then looking away again, because even though she was seething with anger some detached part of her still couldn't help but appreciate his overpowering masculine beauty. 'You're so caught up thinking that every single woman must be interested in your money you won't even allow yourself to think that some might not give a damn!'

'I don't imply that they're *exclusively* interested in me because of my bank balance.' Daniel wasn't going to rise to the bait. He was too busy enjoying the hectic flush in her cheeks.

He realised that this was part of the reason why he hadn't been ready to bid her farewell ten days into their fling... She challenged him in ways other women didn't and never had. It was the sort of thing that would get tiring after a while, but he hadn't yet had his fill of it.

Delilah's colour deepened. Oh, she knew only too well what else there was about this man that attracted a woman. The way he smiled...the look and the smell and the feel of him...the way he touched...his fingers, his hands...the way his mouth traced your contours until you were going crazy with want...

She blinked back the slow motion reel of graphic images.

'I don't care about your money, Daniel, and I haven't come here to try and barter my body for cash...'

'That's an ugly way of phrasing things.'

'I'm being honest.'

She'd lingered on the word *honest* and he frowned at her.

'Are we going to go there again? I didn't board that

liner with the express purpose of finding a woman so that I could establish a relationship with her based on lies… And if you haven't come here because of the money, then why *have* you come?'

He smiled slowly at her, the sort of wolfish smile that made her toes curl.

'You've missed me…' he mused flatly. 'Have you? Missed me?'

There was just the briefest of hesitations but it was enough for him to get the message that, yes…she'd missed him.

'There's something you need to know.' She said this before she could let that hot, sexy look on his face deprive her of all conscious ability to string two words together. She wrung her hands and gazed past him, through the window to the leaden grey sky outside. 'You're probably going to hit the roof, but I couldn't *not* tell you.'

Daniel stilled.

For once his agile brain was trying and failing to join the connections that would point him in the direction of knowing what she had stored up her sleeve.

'Spit it out, Delilah,' he said, but something was telling him that, whatever she had to say, it would be something he didn't want to hear.

'I'm pregnant.'

That flat statement left behind it a deafening silence. She didn't want to look at his face because she didn't want to see the dawning horror.

Daniel's thought processes had closed down. For the first time in his life he couldn't get his head around what she had said. He wondered whether he had misheard her, but when he looked at her face, drained of colour, there was no mistaking the sincerity of what she had just told him.

Yet he still heard himself say, 'You're kidding?'

'Do you really think I've come all the way down here to see you as a *joke*?' Delilah exploded.

Sifting through the fog swirling round in his head, he caught himself drawing the conclusion that she hadn't missed him…probably hadn't given him a passing thought until she'd discovered…

'Are you sure?'

'Of course I'm sure! I did three tests, Daniel.'

'Tests aren't always right.'

'It must have happened that very first time…if you remember…'

'I remember.'

Suddenly the generous dimensions of his very large office seemed too small. *Pregnant.* She was pregnant. Having his baby. He'd not given even a passing thought to having a relationship, certainly not settling down, and now here he was: facing fatherhood.

Life as he knew it was at an end.

The silence swirled and thickened and he surfaced from his daze to see her rising to her feet.

'Where are you going?' he demanded, shooting up as well.

'I'm leaving you to think about it.'

'Have you *lost your mind*?' He looked at her in utter amazement. 'You've waltzed in here and dropped a bombshell and you're leaving so that I can *think about it*?'

'It's a shock…' Delilah mumbled, edging towards the door—but not nearly fast enough, because he was in front of her before she could reach it.

'That's the understatement of the year!'

'And before you launch into some stupid speech about me coming here to try and get money from you because I'm pregnant, I haven't. I came here to tell you because you have a right to know and that's it. I don't want *anything* from you.'

What she wanted was the one thing he was incapable of giving. Love. Affection. Joint excitement at the prospect of having a baby with her.

But having a baby with her was the equivalent of a bombshell being detonated in his life.

Nowhere in all her secret romantic fantasies had she ever envisaged her life turning out like *this*.

'I can't have this conversation here.' He flung on his coat, then moved to stand by the door, like a bouncer at a nightclub, waiting for her to follow him.

Did she want a conversation? No. But a conversation was going to be necessary—like it or not. Bombshells would do that...would instigate a question and answer session.

One thing, however... There was no way she was going to let him think that she would be turning into a freeloader just because she was carrying his baby... She wasn't going to be one of those *gold-diggers* he had to be so careful about, because he was such a rich and important human being!

'I have a train to catch,' she told him.

'And you'll catch it,' he replied, in a voice of steel, 'just as soon as we talk about this. You're not paying me a flying visit and then disappearing so that I can *think about it*...and you're certainly not jumping to any conclusions that my role in this is to have a little think and then wash my hands of the whole thing. Not going to happen. This bombshell is going to have permanent consequences—whether you like it or not...'

CHAPTER EIGHT

SHE FOUND HERSELF tripping along in his wake, out of the office building, out into the bleak grey winter and, after five minutes of walking through a confusing network of small streets, straight into the dark confines of an ancient quintessentially English pub.

Dark suited her.

'I don't make daytime drinking a habit,' he told her, settling her into a chair while he remained on his feet, 'but I feel that the occasion demands it. What would you like? And don't even *think* of doing a runner when I'm up at the bar...'

'I wouldn't...' Although the thought *did* hold a certain amount of appeal.

She watched him as he headed for the bar. He'd slung his coat over the back of a chair and she greedily and surreptitiously drank in the long, muscular lines of his body, sheathed in a handmade Italian suit of pale grey.

He was the last word in sophistication, and she couldn't help but notice how people turned and stared. He was drop-dead gorgeous, and it was a timely reminder of just how out of place she was in his world. This was the world in which *he* belonged. Not her.

'Good. You're still here.'

'I'm not going anywhere.' She took the proffered mineral water from him. 'I know we do probably need to talk, but I just want to repeat what I said to you in your office.'

She shot him a defiant look from under her lashes. God, he was so beautiful, so urbane and sophisticated and carelessly elegant, while she...

One glance at her clothes and she knew that she would be plunged into unwanted feelings of inadequacy and self-consciousness. This wasn't the cruise liner, where the standard uniform had been *dress down and casual*. This was the city, where big money was made, and there was no room for the casual look. This was *his* comfort zone.

'Not interested.'

'You need to know that I didn't come here because I want anything from you,' she repeated fiercely. 'I know you think that you're a hot catch, and that you have to be on permanent guard because there are gold-diggers out there just dying to take advantage of you—'

'No one takes advantage of me.' Daniel's mind was almost entirely consumed with a future in which he was a father. 'I'm wary because I'm a natural target.' Experience had taught him that.

'But not for me.'

'Speech over?'

Delilah gazed at him with helpless frustration. 'I thought you would have taken the news a lot more badly,' she confessed.

'You thought I'd throw a tantrum? Shout? Hit things? Not my style. This is a problem that has to be dealt with, and throwing a temper tantrum isn't going to get either of us anywhere. And before you tell me that it's *your* problem and nothing to do with me—'

'I never said that.'

'You implied it. So before you decide to venture down that road again I'll tell you straight away that this is *my* problem as well and you won't be going through it on your own.'

Tears rose readily to her eyes and she blinked them

back. She'd been feeling tearful ever since she had returned to the Cotswolds. She had put that down to the fact that she missed him, that she couldn't see a way forward with a life in which he didn't feature. Now she understood that, however much she had missed him, her hormones were all over the place.

But she still resented the way he insisted on describing the situation as a *problem,* a *bombshell.* What other awful adjectives could he dredge up? she wondered? *Disaster? Catastrophe? Nightmare?* Didn't he have *any* sensitivity at all?

'Where are you living?' he demanded bluntly.

'Back at home with Sarah.'

'And the building work?'

'There were a few delays,' Delilah muttered, feeling about as comfortable as someone being pinned to a chair and questioned with a torch shining on their face. 'Halfway through they discovered some rising damp which had to be treated, and then the whole cottage needed treating, so everything has ended up a little behind schedule...'

'Behind schedule and over-budget?' Daniel guessed shrewdly. 'And presumably in a state of upheaval?'

Delilah maintained a mutinous silence, but he raised his eyebrows until she eventually shrugged grudging agreement.

'Pregnant and trying to cope with building work and general chaos?'

'There's a time line. It'll all be done in four weeks. The builders have assured us of that...'

Daniel burst out laughing and she glared at him resentfully. 'Since when do assurances from builders count for anything?'

'*You're* having work done on the liner. Are you telling me that you don't trust the time scale?'

'I pay them so much that they wouldn't dare overrun by a second.'

'Well, bully for you.'

'I don't like the thought of you having the stress of living somewhere there are builders trooping in and out, in the depths of winter… Chances are the heating will be down at some point and it'll be beyond uncomfortable. Unacceptable.'

'Hang on just a minute—!'

'No, Delilah, *you* hang on just a minute.' He was deadly serious as his green eyes tangled with hers and he leant forward, elbows on the table, cradling his drink in one hand. 'You don't get to do what you want. You're carrying my baby and this stops being just about you.'

'I get that, but—'

'There are no *buts.*'

'I have responsibilities to my sister. We have a business to get off the ground.'

'The situation has changed.'

'You can't just lay down laws, Daniel!' She could feel the power of him steamrollering over her, knocking aside every objection she raised, inexorably pressing her into a corner from which she would have no escape route.

She could feel control of her life being taken away from her and she resented it—because this was a guy who wasn't doing it because he cared about *her*… This was a guy who was doing it in response to the bombshell that had been dropped at his door.

'What did you think would happen when you came here to see me?'

'I… I thought that I'd give you some time to think things over…'

'And how much time did you allot to that?'

'You're busy, and you'd made it clear that you and I were in it for the very short term. You enjoy your freedom. I thought you'd take a few days…maybe even a few weeks…and after that…'

'I'm all ears…'

He leaned closer towards her and the unique scent of him filled her nostrils, leaving her giddy, making her lose the string of what she'd been telling him.

'And after that we could reach some sort of arrangement—if you chose to keep in touch at all…'

Wrong thing to say. He looked at her with thunderous incredulity. *'If I chose to keep in touch?'*

'I'm not saying that you would have vanished without a backward glance…' she backtracked hurriedly. 'But there's no need for you to take an…er…an active role… Lots of men don't…'

'I don't believe I'm hearing this.'

'Daniel, you have an empire to run! I looked you up on the internet… You don't even live in this country! Of course you can take an interest, but forgive me for thinking that you might find it a little tiresome to commute from Australia every other weekend!'

'I have no intention of being a part-time father.'

Delilah looked at him in bewilderment, because she had no idea where he was going with this.

'Well, what are you suggesting?' she asked cautiously.

'Let's start with the small stuff.'

'Like what?'

'The matter of you moving out of the Cotswolds.'

'That won't happen,' she said bluntly. 'It can't.'

'Your sister must understand this change in circumstances.' He looked at her narrowly. 'Except,' he said slowly, 'she doesn't know…'

'Not yet.'

'Good heavens, Delilah!'

'Well…'

'Well? You think she's going to give you a long lecture on being irresponsible...?'

She fought against the urge to confide in him. They didn't have any kind of relationship! 'She might...'

'Does she even know about me?'

'Not exactly.'

'Is that your way of saying not *at all*?'

He was outraged and frankly insulted when she blushed and shrugged her shoulders. He could almost understand her not confiding in her sister just yet about the pregnancy. It was a huge thing, and from what she had told him about her sister a warm hug and congratulations wouldn't have been her first response. Yes, he got that she might have needed time to absorb the enormity of her situation and then steel herself for sharing that particular confidence.

But to have kept silent about *him*...

Sheer male pride, but how many women would have *hidden* the fact that they'd been seeing him? He was accustomed to women doing their best to get him along to events where they could show him off to all their friends and family!

'Why should I have told her about you?' Delilah said defensively. 'We had a little bit of fun and then we went our separate ways. It wasn't as though you were going to be a continuing part of my life!'

'Well, once the cat's out of the bag you will have to explain that you labouring on a building site in the Cotswolds isn't going to do.'

'And what about *you*?' she threw at him. 'Are you going to emigrate to London so that you can be a part of your baby's life?'

Of course not! she thought bitterly. He would dish out orders and commands, have no problem with utterly disrupting her life—as if it hadn't been disrupted enough already—but he would make sure that *his* remained relatively intact.

It would be a major decision. Daniel knew that. But was there much of a choice for him?

He knew what it was like to come from a closely bonded family, knew the importance of having a father there as a role model. It was something he would not deny his own child, whatever the cost.

'I am,' he said, coolly and smoothly, and Delilah's mouth fell open.

'How *can* you?' she asked. Caught on the back foot, she could only think that he was having her on.

'What do you mean?'

'You can't just walk away from your home in Australia…'

'Because you assume that I'm as selfish as you are?'

'That's not fair, Daniel! I have a responsibility to my sister!'

'You also have a responsibility to our child, and frankly to me as well—considering I'm the father. I can effect a hand-over process at my offices in Sydney. The world is such a global village now that it's fairly immaterial where a head office is based unless it happens to be specifically based somewhere for tax purposes. Coincidentally, I've just finished work on my London office—there's no reason why I can't operate from there and go out to the Far East as and when the occasion demands.'

He would miss his boat and the freedom of going sailing when time permitted. He would also have to start looking for somewhere to live. The family penthouse in Knightsbridge wasn't going to do.

'I am prepared to change continents. You are prepared to do *what*, Delilah? You came down here in the expectation that you would impart your information and then walk away, safe in the knowledge that I had been informed, your conscience cleared, and you could carry on as normal.'

'Hardly as *normal*!'

'You didn't expect me to want to do anything apart from maybe clock in now and again when I happened to be in the country. Am I right? Maybe set up a standing order so that you could be solvent—?'

'I don't want your money.'

Daniel overrode her interruption. If she imagined that life was going to be anything but *abnormal* now then she had another think coming, and he intended to make sure that she was given no room to squirm away from her responsibilities and the changes he knew were going to be inevitable, whether either of them liked it or not.

'Did you think that I would be a little taken aback that you were having my child but aside from that would allow you to vanish back up to the country, leaving me to get on with my life undisturbed?' He laughed mirthlessly.

'You enjoy your freedom!'

'Not to the extent that I would allow it to take precedence over my responsibilities.'

'I don't want to be your *responsibility*! Just like I don't want this pregnancy to be a *bombshell* or a *problem* that has to be fixed. Neither of us expected this, but at least *I'm* not looking at it as some sort of catastrophe that has to be put right!'

'I'm not going to get lost in an argument about semantics. We have to deal with this, and you have to take on board that it's something we'll be dealing with *together*. I'm going to move to London and so are you.'

His voice was cool and inflexible, as was his expression. She could dig her heels in and tell him to get lost but she knew he would keep her hostage in the pub until she gave in.

And, as he'd said, he was moving continents simply to

be able to see more of his child. She was uneasily aware that for her to refuse to move a few dozen miles would smack of mulish inflexibility.

She might not want him in her life because it would be hard. Seeing him would be a constant reminder of what she wanted and what she couldn't have—a constant reminder of the limitations of their relationship. But, extracting *her* from the equation, wouldn't it be a good thing for their child to have the presence of an interested and caring father?

And she would still be there for Sarah. She would be able to go up at least once or twice a week to help oversee the building project.

'I would have to find somewhere to rent in London.'

'Leave that to me,' Daniel said with silky assurance.

'And I would still want my independence,' she felt obliged to inform him, just in case he thought that he could call all the shots. That was a precedent she didn't want to encourage. He was so forceful, so overpowering, that it wouldn't take much for him to assume that what he said was irrefutable law. 'And of course I would expect you to…er…keep yours, as well…'

This was going to be a mature, civil arrangement, and it was important that he understood that, however much he was willing to adapt and contribute, she would not expect him to change each and every aspect of his life.

She wasn't going take what he offered and then cling like a limpet.

She wasn't going to let him suspect just how much she wanted from him and just how painful it was for her to accept that it was just never going to happen.

She was going to play it cool.

'What do you mean by that?'

'I mean that if you're willing to come all the way over here, so that you can have a hands-on relationship with our child, then I'm willing meet you halfway on that score and move to London—at least temporarily. I expect that as time goes on things might very well change on that front.' *Hope sprang eternal.* 'But I don't expect either of us to give up our lives entirely. You're free to carry on seeing other…er…women, and I'm free to…to—'

'Out of the question.'

'I beg your pardon?'

'The small stuff was the business of you leaving the Cotswolds. The slightly bigger stuff is the business of what I mean when I say that I want to play an active role in my child's life. That's something I can't do on an occasional basis.'

He paused so that she could digest what he was saying.

'We're not getting involved in a custody situation,' he informed her. 'You won't be out and about playing the singles game while I hang around and wait for some guy to bounce along thinking he's got paternal rights over my child. Nor will I be chasing behind women and kidding myself that I'm still a bachelor.'

Delilah could only stare at him. Bombarded by so much information, she was finding it difficult to sift through and pick out the salient points.

'And that's not going to happen,' he continued remorselessly, 'because we're going to get married.'

Delilah stared at him in utter shock. He was as cool as a cucumber, so cool that she wondered whether she hadn't imagined his outrageous suggestion.

'You've got to be kidding,' she said eventually, and he tilted his head to one side and looked at her.

'About as serious as the Bubonic Plague.'

'I'm not going to *marry* you!'

'Of course you are.'

'Oh, I am, am I? Are you going to drag me up the aisle and force me to say *I do*?'

Delilah was literally shaking with anger. Coming from a self-confessed commitment-phobe—a guy who had bluntly told her that he would only ever consider marrying into his own class, because there were so many gold-diggers out there and a guy like him couldn't be too careful—was she actually expected to take his proposal *seriously*?

'I won't have to. You're pregnant, and I can give you everything you could ever want. Both you and our child would benefit from every advantage money can buy. You would never have to work again, never have to worry about money again… You could have the sort of life you've probably only ever dreamt about…'

'It was never my dream to be rich—and I can't believe I'm hearing this!'

Daniel regarded her coolly. When she'd protested enough she would see the sense of what he was saying. She probably did now, even though she was still busy protesting.

'I have *never*,' she said in fevered whisper, 'dreamt of falling pregnant by a guy who isn't interested in a relationship! I have *never* dreamt about being someone's responsibility or putting them in a position they don't want because they've had a *bombshell* dropped in their life! And I have *never* thought that what I really want out of life is *money*.' She stood up, shaking like a leaf. 'I'm going to go now.'

'Over my dead body!' Daniel leapt to his feet.

After the token protest he had expected gratitude. Or at least some show of looking at the situation with common sense! Instead, she was acting as though he had insulted her in the worst possible way by suggesting marriage!

'You're being ridiculous!' He wanted to bellow, to shake some common sense into her. Instead, he held her by the arm as she was about to hail a taxi. 'You're not running away from me, Delilah!'

'I'll be in touch. But I won't be marrying you.'

'Why?' He raked frustrated fingers through his hair. He hadn't wanted to have this sort of conversation in his office, and he wanted to have it even less here. In the street. With the crowds swarming around them.

She looked at him with simmering resentment. 'You really don't understand, do you?'

'It makes sense.'

He looked down at her upturned face. The face that had haunted him for the past few weeks—ever since she had walked out of his life.

She still turned him on.

She was as obstinate as a mule, had rejected his offer for reasons he couldn't even begin to understand, was viewing the situation with just the sort of incomprehensible female logic he had never had any time for, and yet...

He still wanted her so badly it was like a physical ache.

And it wasn't just because this was unfinished business.

Could it be, in part, because she was carrying his child? Did he want to be a father? He'd never given it a passing thought, and yet he had to admit that there was something incredibly sexy about knowing that she carried his baby. Was it just some kind of primitive response to the evidence of his own virility?

He lowered his head and captured her mouth in an urgent kiss, his hand curving in the small of her back. He felt her melt against him. Briefly but completely. Then she pressed her palms against his chest and pushed herself away.

'Tell me that marriage doesn't make sense,' he said thickly.

Delilah was burning up, her whole body consumed by

a driving need that left her weak. How could she explain that that was *precisely* why it made no sense...*for her*.

'I'll...call you...'

'You don't have my number.'

'I have your office number.'

'That won't do. I want you to be able to reach me any time of the day or night.'

He was far from happy about her disappearing on him, and he wasn't the sort of man who had any patience at all when it came to waiting, but he could see the determination on her face and he knew that if he pushed it there was the danger that he would scare her off completely.

He gave her his number and watched as she put it into her contacts list. 'I need to be able to get in touch with you,' he said as she slipped her phone back into her bag.

Delilah looked at him with clear eyes. 'You never needed to before.'

'Things are different now.'

'I don't want to feel as though you're putting pressure on me.'

'Dammit, Delilah...!'

Their eyes met and for a few seconds her heart went out to him. He was just so endearing in his impatience, so appealing in the way he was looking at her, his green eyes alive with masculine frustration at this situation he couldn't immediately resolve.

The longing to touch him was so intense that she stuck her hands behind her back. That kiss he had dropped on her mouth was still burning, still making her realise how fast her brain cells could go into meltdown when she was with him.

'I... I'll call you,' she repeated as a black cab slowed to a stop alongside her. A black cab that would cost money she barely had.

What he was offering suddenly had such an appeal that

she had to fight against giving it house room in·her head. He might be able to take care of her financially…it was true that if she married him she would never have a single financial worry in the world again…but that would be replaced by even more worries—for how on earth could she live with him when she knew that she would be waging a daily war with her own foolish feelings?

What *he* would see as a viable solution, a marriage of convenience, *she* would see as an agonising union with someone who could never return the love she felt for him.

Theirs would be a marriage of such unequal terms that it would be devastating for her mental and emotional health.

'When? I need to know…'

'In a week's time…or so…' She pulled open the taxi door before she could become embroiled in yet another debate with him. She slammed it shut and quickly rolled down the glass. 'You need time to think, Daniel, and to come to terms with the fact that I won't be marrying you…'

And then the taxi was pulling away into the impatient traffic and she was leaving him behind, already feeling the loss.

She knew that she wouldn't tell Sarah anything—not until matters had been sorted between herself and Daniel. She would confess everything as soon as they had reached some sort of solution, but at the moment a solution seemed far from being set in stone.

Move to London…

He would rent somewhere for her and she would be seeing him on a regular basis. He would be there for his child and she would be an add-on. His life would continue without her in it. Another woman would come along to absorb his attention and she wondered how she would feel when that happened.

How would she feel when, finally, he found the woman he felt he could marry? Someone rich and sophisticated?

She tried hard not to let her imagination run away with her, but over the next few days it was impossible to rein it in.

She was distracted—suddenly very conscious of all the building work happening in the kitchen, very much aware of how the disruption was beginning to get more and more unbearable. And yet she couldn't bring herself to think about leaving Sarah to get on with the project on her own.

She felt like someone wandering around in thick fog, waiting for a pinprick of light to announce a safe haven somewhere.

It was exactly a week before she contacted Daniel.

She had to brace herself for the sound of his deep, sexy drawl but when she connected with him it still took her breath away, leaving her winded.

'About time,' were his opening words.

In the middle of an important meeting he rose, signalled with a curt nod of his head that his CEO was to take over, and left the conference room without a second thought.

He'd kept many a woman waiting for the phone to ring. He'd never had the shoe on the other foot and he hadn't liked it.

It had, however, given him time to think, and he'd done a fair bit of that. He'd also put some things in motion—because at the end of the day he was a man of action. There was just so much thinking he could do, and then he needed to go beyond that point.

'Perhaps we could meet...' Delilah suggested.

'Where are you?'

'At home, of course...'

'I'll send my driver to collect you.'

'No!' She had yet to breathe a word to her sister, and the thought of some flash chauffeur-driven car pulling up outside the cottage for her sent a shiver of horror down her spine. 'I… I can come down to London…'

'When?'

'Well…'

'I'm not good at hanging around, Delilah,' Daniel told her abruptly. 'Time's passing and we need to find a way forward on this.'

'I realise that…'

'Then I suggest you get on the first train down and be prepared to stay longer than five minutes. I will ensure that my driver collects you from the station.'

'I'm perfectly capable of meeting you somewhere,' Delilah inserted quickly, because she was already in danger of handing over all control of the situation to him. He wielded power so effortlessly that it was easy to fall in with his expectation that whatever he wanted, he was entitled to get.

But, predictably, she was met at the station three hours later by his driver, and ushered to a long, sleek Jaguar with tinted windows that took her away from the bustle of the station, beyond the city and out of it.

Anxiously she dialled Daniel's number and he answered instantly.

'Where are you?' she asked.

'Waiting for you. Don't worry. You haven't been kidnapped.'

'I thought we'd be meeting…er…closer to your office…'

'Have you packed a bag?'

'I can't stay long,' she said hurriedly. 'I've told Sarah that I need to go to London for the night…'

'You're going to have to break the news to her some time.'

'I know that! Where exactly am I being taken?'

'It's a surprise.'

'I've already had my fill of surprises,' she told him honestly. 'I don't think I can stand any more.'

But, seeing that she was in his car, without the option of a quick escape, she could only sit back and watch as the clutter of the city was left behind, giving way to parks, trees, less foot traffic. It was a rare winter's day… cold, but with clear blue skies, barely a cloud in the sky.

She was delivered to a Victorian house with neat black railings outside and shallow steps leading to a black door, which was opened before she had time to bang on it with the brass knocker.

'Is this your house? Do you live here?'

His keen eyes roved over her. She was wearing so many layers that it was impossible to see whether she had gained any weight or not, but just thinking about it fired him up in a way that was sudden and powerful.

He dismissed the driver and ushered her into the house.

'Come and have a look around.'

'Why?'

'Because this is where you and our baby will be living. Here. With me.'

Delilah planted herself squarely in front of him, arms folded. 'Didn't you hear a word I said? I'm not going to marry you! And just looking at where you live shows me how different we are, Daniel! I don't come from your world and I don't want to marry into it! I *know* how you feel about women who don't come from the same background as you.' She sighed. 'What happened between us on the cruise was never meant to last. I was never the sort of woman you would have been interested in long term and just because I'm pregnant it doesn't change that. We're two people on opposite sides of a great big divide—'

'Five bedrooms, four bathrooms, countless other rooms…plenty of room for three…'

'You're *not listening.*'

'You don't want to marry me. I heard you the first time. I'm also hearing a load of rubbish about the fact that I have money and you don't.'

'It's not rubbish,' she persisted.

'Money shouldn't dictate the outcome of this situation.'

'But it will, won't it?' Delilah said bleakly. 'The man I met on that cruise was a pretend person. The real guy is here…' She looked around at the grand proportions of the house, the flagstoned flooring, the toweringly high ceilings, the priceless art on the walls. 'I don't *know* this guy…'

Daniel looked at her with a veiled expression. 'You didn't bring much with you.'

'I told you I wouldn't be hanging around.'

'No matter. I can get my guy to drive up to the Cotswolds and get whatever's necessary…'

'Necessary for what? What are you talking about?'

'We're going round in circles,' Daniel told her coolly. 'And getting nowhere fast.'

'I don't mind discussing whatever financial arrangement you want to make for the baby…'

'We need to talk about far more than that…and we can't talk here…'

'You mean in your house?'

'I want to take you somewhere special…'

'Where? Why? It doesn't matter where we have this conversation…'

'You'll need a bag…enough clothes for a couple of nights… I have a house in the Caribbean, Delilah… I want to take you there… We can relax… If you don't want to marry me I can't force you, but maybe if we're away from these surroundings we might find it easier to talk…'

He raised both hands to forestall her protest.

'It's a big villa… You can choose whichever room you want… Instead of arguing and getting nowhere we can at least try and recapture our friendship in a stress-free environment. I can't imagine how you must have felt when you discovered that you were pregnant. Money worries and then an unexpected pregnancy on top of that…tough.'

He smiled wryly and made no move to invade her space.

'A few days of sea and sand and sun might help us both find a way forward…'

Delilah's eyes widened. Little did he know it, but *he* was part and parcel of her stress. Cooped up in a villa with him? Crazy. How was *that* going to relieve her stress?

And yet wasn't he right? She felt herself getting more and more stressed by the second here. The prospect of sand and sun and sea was suddenly as powerful as the glimpse of an oasis in the middle of a desert.

Friendship. That was what they should be aiming for. The longer they argued, the less likely that was going to be. But maybe in different surroundings… Not here in London which felt frantic and claustrophobic, and not in the Cotswolds, which were all tied up with her financial worries and stress…

She found herself nodding slowly. What harm could a couple of nights do? And maybe if she could become his friend and remove the emotional attachment she would be able to deal with the situation better…

CHAPTER NINE

'Is THIS HOW you usually travel?'

In the space of one day Delilah had gone from arguing in London to sitting aboard a luxury private jet. She felt like an intruder into a world that might have been a different planet altogether.

With Daniel sprawled next to her she should have been as nervous as a kitten, but somehow the minute the jet had taken off she had felt herself relax. Daniel snapped shut the lid of his laptop and angled his big body so that he was facing her.

So she didn't want to talk about marriage and was adamant that he was the last person she would walk down the aisle with?

He wasn't going to press it.

So she wanted to make a big deal of their differences?

He wasn't going to waste time arguing with her about it. After Kelly, he'd sworn that a convenient marriage with someone independently wealthy enough to ensure his billions weren't the star attraction was the only kind of marriage he would ever consider.

But life had a way of pulling the rug from under your feet—although he'd never credited that he could ever be the victim of *that*. Control every aspect of your life and there could be no nasty surprises. That had been the theory at any rate.

She'd given him a way out, and he knew that he could

have taken it and kept his freedom intact, but the second she had told him about the pregnancy he had known that freedom didn't stand a chance.

He wanted the whole marriage deal. He wanted his child to have both parents. He didn't want her to get involved with anyone else. He didn't want to share his child, with weekend visits and watching from the sidelines while some other guy played the daddy role.

He didn't want to share *her*.

'It doesn't tend to work when I'm in London,' he drawled, eyebrows raised. 'Troublesome getting from my house to my office in a private jet... I find the car a much better proposition.'

Delilah didn't want him to make her laugh. They were going to stay in his villa. They were going to try to become friends. She was going to have to learn to put a little distance between them. But being witty came naturally to him, and he wasn't doing it because he cared for her, or because he wanted to get anywhere with her.

'What did you tell your sister?' he asked curiously.

'I told her that I was pregnant,' Delilah said on a sigh. 'I just didn't know how much longer I could keep it to myself. I mean, if I'm going to be living in London so that you can visit the baby I had to give her some warning...'

The last thing Daniel wanted to hear was that his role was being downgraded to ex-lover with visiting rights, but arguing wasn't getting him anywhere. He gritted his teeth in a tight smile.

'And her reaction?'

'Shock. I thought she was going to faint on the spot.'

'I don't suppose her shock was as great as yours when *you* found out...'

'It was the last thing I was expecting,' Delilah agreed, staring past him through the small window. They had been served drinks as soon as the plane had taken off and she nursed the orange juice she had requested. 'I was terrified,' she admitted. 'When I thought about having a baby all I could see were problems. It was like looking down a tunnel and not seeing any light.'

She focused on him and thought... *He's a friend...an ex who, thankfully, hasn't shied away from his responsibilities...who wants to provide support...that's the main thing...*

'I never thought that I'd be a single mum. I mean, it never occurred to me at all. I thought that I might end up on the shelf—but a single mother? No...'

Daniel didn't remind her that he had asked her to marry him. He wasn't interested in hearing another litany of reasons why it would never happen.

'I didn't think you would be as supportive as you've been,' she admitted, flushing.

'Because I'm a bastard who lied to you...?'

She looked away, reminded of the idiot she'd been to have fallen in love with a man who had never been in it for the long haul.

'There's no point rehashing that,' she said with casual nonchalance. 'The main thing is that you're going to have an ongoing relationship with our child and us becoming friends is a good idea...'

She was so *aware* of him—sitting so close to her that she could just move her hand and touch his forearm, feel its muscled strength and the brush of the dark blond hair on his arms under her fingers.

Becoming friends felt like the hardest thing in the world to do, but she was going to have to do it. She wasn't going to marry him—would never marry a man who didn't love her—but she was going to have to get used to a different type of relationship with him, however hard that was going to be.

'Tell me about where we're going…' she encouraged vaguely. 'Which island is it?'

'You wouldn't have heard of it.'

'Because I'm not well travelled?' she suggested, her voice cooler. 'I did geography at school. I was actually okay at it. I do happen to know about the Caribbean, even if I don't have first-hand knowledge of any of the islands.'

'You wouldn't have heard of it because I own it.'

Delilah's mouth dropped open and she stared at him in amazed silence for a few seconds. 'You *own* an island?'

'Not exclusively,' Daniel admitted. 'It's a joint enterprise with my brother. Not that either of us has actually spent much time holidaying there.'

He was a billionaire—there was no point in trying to play it down.

She didn't say anything, and eventually Daniel broke the tense silence with a heartfelt sigh. 'You're going to tell me that it's just another example of these different worlds we inhabit.'

'It's true, though, isn't it?'

'I can't deny that I've never had much experience of financial stress. My brother and I came from a wealthy family and we've both managed to make fortunes of our own.'

'I don't know why we're bothering with this trip,' Delilah heard herself say. 'We could have sorted out the money angle back in London.'

'Back in London we couldn't sort anything out without an argument.'

'I wasn't trying to be argumentative. I was trying to be practical.'

'The truth is, I thought that you could do with the relaxation… I get it that this will have been as much of a shock to you as it is to me and stress isn't good during pregnancy. At least, I wouldn't have thought so…'

For Delilah, that made more sense. He wanted to de-stress her for the sake of the baby, and he had the sort of bottomless wealth that enabled him to do it in style. Most men would have had to make do with a meal out.

Lots of men in his position, she thought guiltily, wouldn't even have bothered with the meal out—wouldn't have thought further than grabbing the get-out clause she had offered and running away with it. But he wasn't *most men*. She wanted to hate him because he had lied to her and strung her along, but she grudgingly had to concede that there was a strong streak of honesty and decency in him. He hadn't shied away from taking responsibility and now here he was, taking her on a far-flung getaway so that she could de-stress!

She followed his reasoning. They were to become friends, and that was going to be easier away from the grit and grime of London and, yes, from the arguing.

'What does it feel like to own an island?' she asked, intrigued against her will. 'What on earth do you do with it when you're not there?'

'Rent it out,' Daniel told her. 'It commands a healthy amount of money…'

'But you don't get there often to enjoy it?'

'Work,' he said flatly. 'It's almost impossible to take the time out.'

Delilah shot him a dry look. 'What's the point of work-ing so much that you never get to relax and enjoy the stuff you can buy with all your money?'

Daniel watched her narrowly. When he'd gone to San-torini he'd watched all those tourists and, yes, somewhere at the back of his mind had noted the comparison between himself and the laid-back holidaymakers.

When did *he* ever get to relax? He rarely took time out, and when he did he preferred solitary forms of re-laxation. Sailing…skiing… Did sleeping with women count? Women were a physical release… But complete and utter relaxation? No… He hadn't ever sought them out to provide that.

'Have you ever taken a woman to the island?' she asked, hoping that it sounded like a perfectly reasonable matter-of-fact question.

'Never.'

'Why not?'

'I marvel that I'd managed to forget how many "No Trespassing" signs you like to barge past…' But his voice was wry rather than belligerent.

'Friends know things about one another.'

'Especially friends who have enjoyed fringe benefits…?'

Delilah went bright red, and just like that her body fell into its familiar pattern, with her nipples pinching and tightening, her palms growing clammy with perspiration, and between her legs that hot ache that seemed to control all her senses until it was the only thing she was aware of.

'That feels like a long time ago.' She casually dismissed his husky suggestive remark and offered him a bright smile. 'Things are different between us now.' She cleared her throat and slanted her eyes away from his. 'So, when you've been to this island you've gone on your own?'

'Why not? It's great for snorkelling. It's surrounded by a reef and the water is very clear and very calm, The fish are so lazy and tame that they'd share your lunch with you if you gave them half a chance.'

'And you prefer to do all that on your own…?'

'I don't need a woman to spoil the peace by demanding attention and shrieking every time a fish gets too close…' he drawled.

'So what if *I* shriek when a fish gets too close?'

'You're different,' he commented drily. 'You're not

just any woman. You're the mother of my child... You should try and get some sleep now. We don't land on the island... We land on a runway on the mainland and take a helicopter from there. It's a long trip, all told...'

In other words he was no longer interested in chatting and he wasn't interested in her nosy questions.

Delilah shrugged and turned away. She knew that he had reopened his computer and could hear the steady sound of his fingers brushing against the keyboard, composing emails, reviewing important documents, doing all those things that kept him so busy that he seldom took time out to relax.

It was another mark in his favour that he was taking the time out now, when he didn't have to.

He was doing it because she was different... She was no longer a woman...she was the mother of his child. Her status had been elevated, but she missed being a woman he couldn't keep his hands off...

In the end she slept through most of the flight. When she opened her eyes the sky was bright blue outside the window and she straightened and peered past him to the banks of white wispy clouds.

'Are you excited?' she asked breathlessly, and he smiled at her.

'I think you'll enjoy the place.'

'Do you get excited about *anything*, Daniel?' she heard herself persist.

'I have my moments...' he murmured, green eyes locked on hers. 'Your hair's all over the place...'

He itched to brush it back from her face. He'd watched her as she slept and the urge to touch her had been overwhelming. He had amazing detailed recall of every inch of her body. Even before she had turned up at his office and announced the life-changing news that she was carrying his child she had managed to get under his skin in a way no other woman ever had.

She had preyed on his mind after she'd left. Why? Because, he'd told himself, she was unfinished business and he was egotistical enough to want to finish with a woman rather than the other way around. Egotism wasn't a good trait, but it was something he could deal with.

So he hadn't been able to get her out of his head...

So he hadn't been interested in replacing her with any of the women in his proverbial black book, who would have been overjoyed to have taken up where Delilah had left off...

It was just because they'd met under unusual circumstances. It was just because she'd had no idea of his true identity and he'd relished the freedom that had given him.

After his experiences with Kelly he had erected so many defences systems around himself and around his emotions that he hadn't recognised when his defences had been breached and she had breached them.

And he didn't mind.

In fact he liked it—liked it that she wasn't intimidated by him or impressed by his money.

When she had shown up in his office he hadn't been tempted to get rid of her. He'd formulated all sorts of reasons for her being there and rehearsed all sorts of arguments as to why he would be willing to take her back to his bed...where it felt as if she belonged...

The bottom line was that he'd never stopped wanting her. And more than that...

He'd watched her sleep, head drooping on his shoulder. He'd felt the soft brush of her hair against his mouth. Hell...

How was he supposed to have recognised the signs of something that was more than lust? He'd been in total control of his emotions for so long—how could he have been tuned in to the signs of anything that ran deeper than that?

And wasn't that why he was so adamant that there was no way he was going to let her go? No way that she would be able to walk away from him into the arms of someone else?

Just the thought of another man laying a hand on her filled him with sickening, impotent rage, and he'd had a lot of thoughts along those lines when she had disappeared back up to the Cotswolds. Pride had stopped him from pursuing her. That would have been a step too far. But she was here now and she was going to stay.

For the first time in his life, though, he had no idea what the rules of this game were. She didn't want him. He couldn't get to her through his money because she wasn't greedy and she wasn't materialistic, and he had lied to her. She was willing to try and forge a truce with him, but he knew that if he wanted more then he would have to use every trick in the book to get it.

And he did want more.

He just wasn't sure what those tricks to get it might entail.

Proceeding slowly—something that was anathema to him—seemed to be the only approach.

Delilah shoved her hair into something less chaotic and edged as far away from him as was physically possible.

The plane was coming in to land and she craned her neck to drink in everything as it descended and then bumped along a runway that was bordered by small hangars and beyond that waving palm trees.

As soon as the engine purred to a complete stop the heat seemed to invade the small cabin space and she was glad that she'd worn something light…a pair of cotton trousers and a loose-fitting sleeveless top.

'I feel almost guilty being here,' she confided as they headed out of the plane to make a smooth connection with a waiting helicopter. People bustled around them... the captain stopped to chat with Daniel...their bags were trundled in searing heat to the helicopter.

'Don't,' he commanded, looking down at her. 'You're pregnant and I don't want you to be stressed over anything. Or to feel guilty because you're here. Did your sister try and imply that it was somehow *wrong* for you to take a few days away?'

He helped her into the helicopter and then heaved his big body in alongside her, the two of them cramped in the confined space. The door was slammed down, locking them into the sort of intimacy that fired up all her senses.

She licked her lips and shook her head. 'Of course not. She understands the turmoil I'm going through...'

'And she agreed that the ex-lover you refuse to marry should be the one to try and help you with that?'

Delilah was spared having to answer that by the loud whirring of the helicopter blades as the aircraft tilted up and buzzed like a wasp, hovering and then swooping along, offering a breathtaking sight of navy blue sea and turquoise sky.

'Well?' Daniel prompted as the helicopter whirred to a shuddering stop on the island.

The flight had taken a matter of minutes and here they were. It was lush and green and a four-wheel-drive SUV was waiting for them on the airstrip. As far as the eye could see there was untouched beauty and the smell of the sea was pungent and tangy. She breathed in deeply and slowly and half closed her eyes, enjoying the heat, the slight breeze and the unique tropical sounds of unseen insects and birds.

'I can't believe this is all yours.' She opened her eyes, turned full circle and gazed at him.

'It's a small island,' Daniel said drily, ushering her towards the car while, behind them, she heard the helicopter begin to whirr into life, ready to lift off and go back to the mainland.

'But still…it's just so amazing…'

Privately, Daniel had never been able to stay longer than a handful of days on the island. Boredom would inevitably set in, even though the water sports were second to none.

'What else is there? Just a villa? I can't believe you don't come here as often as you can…'

She looked at him and then through the car window and then back at him, not knowing where to feast her eyes. Swaying coconut trees lined the sides of the road and through the tall, erect trunks she could make out slivers of blue, blue sea.

When everything had been worked out between them and some sort of visiting timetable arranged, she wondered how she would ever be able to compete with this. She had a vivid image of their child coming to a place like this for a holiday and then returning to England to spend the rest of the time with her in whatever modest house she might be living in.

And then she imagined their child coming here with Daniel and whatever partner had entered his life—maybe even one of those 'suitable' women. Because, with a child, he would doubtless be anxious to settle down and find himself a wife.

Had she done the right thing? She had stood her ground and refused to let him sacrifice his life because a mistake had happened, because she had fallen pregnant. She had refused to compromise when it came to love and the right reasons for entering into a marriage with anyone.

But now doubts began to gnaw away inside her. Worriedly she shoved them aside.

Ahead of them, the bumpy road was taking them up a small incline, and as the Jeep rounded the corner her mouth dropped open at the sight of the sprawling villa ahead of them. Banked by coconut trees and every shade of green foliage she could possibly have imagined, it was a one-storeyed building that was circled by a wide, shady veranda. Impeccably maintained lawns surrounded it on all sides, and as the car ground to a halt a plump dark-skinned woman emerged at the front door and several other members of staff spilled out from behind her.

Delilah thought that this must be what it felt like to be a member of royalty. Daniel took it all in his stride. He chatted with the woman, Mabel—who, he explained, looked after the house and all the staff when it was occupied, and made sure it was kept up to scratch when it was empty, coming three times a week from the mainland to check everything over.

'Your bedroom...' he paused and nodded to one wing of the massive villa '...is there. Mine is in the opposite wing. I'll get Mabel to show you to your room and then we can have some dinner and hit the sack. It's been a long day.'

So this was what it felt like to be friends. This polite, smiling man, who had once touched every part of her body, was now offering her the hand of friendship— which she had insisted on—and she hated it.

'Tomorrow,' he said, 'I'll give you a tour of the island, but don't expect anything much longer than half an hour. There are plenty of coves and small beaches. We can have a picnic on one of them...'

'And talk about how we handle this situation?' Delilah said with a wooden smile. 'Good idea. And it was a good idea to come here,' she conceded truthfully. 'I haven't felt so relaxed since I found out that I was pregnant.'

Daniel inclined his head to one side and shoved his

hands in his pockets. Even with her clothes sticking to her, and clearly tired after the convoluted journey that had brought them here, she still had that impossible certain *something* that fired him up.

And she showed zero sign of wanting anything more than a civilised conversation about technicalities. The girl who had given herself to him with abandon was gone.

'You never told me what your sister said when you informed her that you would be coming here with me...'

'I didn't tell her that we would be going abroad.' Delilah flushed and looked away. 'I just told her that I needed to spend a few days in London because I needed to sort some stuff out with you, and that we would probably have to visit a lawyer at some point to make our agreement legal...'

'I see...'

He didn't. And what he heard was the sound of her walking away from him. The way she hadn't been able to meet his eyes when she'd said that spoke volumes. He had asked her to marry him and, whatever excuses she had come up with, the bottom line was that she didn't want him in her life, and she felt guilty about her rejection because she was fundamentally such a warm, caring, genuine person.

And there was nothing he could do about it except play this waiting game and hope.

Delilah drew her knees up and gazed out at the distant horizon, which was a dark blue streak breaking up the cloudless milky blue of the sky and the deeper, fathomless blue of the ocean. The sand underneath her was powdery white and as fine as icing sugar.

Ground up coral from the reef that surrounded the island and the reef itself were responsible for the wealth of tropical fish, which were as tame as Daniel had predicted—bright flashes of yellow and turquoise and pink that weren't afraid to weave around her in the water.

It was paradise.

She should have been over the moon.

She was surrounded by the most amazing natural beauty. Water so clear that you could wade out for absolutely ages and still see your feet clearly touching the sand. Staff on hand to serve their every whim. The food was exquisite…

And Daniel had been nothing but conscientious. No longer the flirty, charming guy who had teased her and made her laugh, but guarded and serious.

They had talked about financial arrangements and agreed that getting lawyers involved would be a waste of time, because it was important to maintain the friendship they were so successfully cultivating.

The friendship that had replaced the fun and the sex.

'You're going to get burnt.'

Delilah spun round to see him striding towards her, a towel casually draped over his broad, tanned shoulders, his bathing trunks low-slung and emphasising the glorious muscularity of his body.

They'd been on the island for two days, and it wasn't getting any easier trying to hide the effect he still had on her.

'I'll be fine.' She smiled tightly at him and quickly averted her eyes. 'We're only going to be here for another couple of days, and I'm not going to waste this sun by sitting in the shade all the time. Besides, I've lathered myself with sunblock.'

Daniel steeled himself against the cool dismissal in her voice and draped the towel on the sand and lay down next to her.

Two days and he'd got nowhere at all. He'd never felt so impotent in his life before, and he didn't know what to do about it. She smiled, listened to what he said, seemed to take an interest in all the boring historical facts he dished out about the island, asked questions about the staff and the running of the place, but the polite mask never slipped.

Because it wasn't a mask.

He should never have lied to her. It had seemed perfectly reasonable at the time—a harmless piece of fiction that he could turn to his advantage. Except things had got out of hand, and by the time she'd discovered the truth they had both overstepped more boundaries than he liked to imagine.

She had made inroads into him without his even realising it, and when she had walked away pride had stopped him from going after her.

She had had time to come to conclusions about him that he was helpless to set straight.

Frustration tore through him.

'This heat is fiercer than you think,' he gritted. 'And the last thing either of us needs is for you to come down with sunstroke.'

Delilah's temper flared and she welcomed it. After two days of stilted politeness she had a churning sea of emotion inside, desperate for an outlet.

'I don't think I need you telling me what I should and shouldn't do,' she snapped. 'I appreciate that you've taken time away from work to come here on a rescue mission to get me to relax, but don't worry… I won't set back your timetable for squeezing me in by inconveniently coming down with sunstroke…'

'There's no need for the drama, Delilah,' he drawled, his mouth tightly compressed.

'I'm not being dramatic,' she returned in a high voice. She could barely look at him, and was angrily aware of just how easy it would be to lose herself in his extravagant good looks.

Hadn't he demonstrated, without having to say a word, just how detached he had become from her?

She was overwhelmed by the hateful feeling that she was being patronised.

Or maybe it was more than that.

Her thoughts veered off at a dangerous tangent and a series of heated assumptions were made. She'd thought that he'd been wildly generous in asking her here on this little break, was being understanding about the stress she had been through. And even though she had constantly reminded herself that this wasn't about *her*, the gesture had fed into her weakness for him. That was why it had been unbearable dealing with his politeness—that was why every solicitous helping hand had been a dagger through her heart.

Because she hadn't seen him for what he was and truly accepted it.

He had dropped all talk of marriage and had distanced himself. Maybe he thought that if he was too much like the Daniel she had hopped into bed with she might be encouraged into getting ideas into her head. He had proposed out of duty and responsibility, but she was sure that he must be quietly relieved to have been let off the hook.

And then there was the fact that he had brought her *here*. Not just on a little weekend break somewhere, but *here*. To an island he *owned*, where everything from the cool, elegant bedroom, with its bamboo furniture, to the exquisite infinity pool overlooking the sea, was the very last word in what money could buy.

Had he wanted to remind her how far apart their worlds were?

He intended to take an active interest in his child's life, but was this his subtle way of showing her that with marriage no longer on the agenda they were, as she had painfully pointed out to him, poles apart?

Suddenly it seemed very important that they talk about all the things they had somehow not got around to discussing.

Rigid with tension, she looked at him, relaxing on the towel like a man without a care in the world. She stuck on her oversized sunglasses and took a couple of stolen seconds to just look at him, lying there with his eyes closed against the glare of the sun.

'We haven't really decided anything…' She broke the silence tersely. 'And I'd quite like to get things sorted so that I can enjoy the rest of my time here without all that hanging over my head.'

Daniel opened his eyes and looked at her. 'Where do you want to start?'

'I've agreed to move down to London to accommodate you, so I guess I should know what the living arrangements will be…' Delilah wondered whether that concession had been the worst decision of her life.

'You'll have an apartment or a house—whatever you want and wherever you want it to be.' Daniel loathed this conversation, which smacked of finality. 'And naturally you will have a generous allowance…'

'I'm not asking for money from you,' Delilah said in a stilted voice. 'You can just pay maintenance for our child, like any other normal person.'

'But I'm not *a normal person*, am I? I'm extremely wealthy. and neither my child nor the mother of my child will ever want for anything.'

'And if…it's early days yet…if for some reason this pregnancy doesn't work out…'

I'll still want you in my life… That was what Daniel thought, with shocking immediacy.

'Then you can have your apartment back and I'll return to the Cotswolds…'

Her heart constricted and she was ashamed to realise that she would rather see him and suffer than never see him in her life again. How pathetic was *that*?

She twisted the knife inside her. 'Although maybe I'll stay in London and find somewhere else to live. Sarah will have become accustomed to my not being around, and in London I can…'

'Find a better job? A better life? Better dating scene? Mr Right?'

Daniel smiled coldly and Delilah flinched, because he just didn't give a damn, did he?

'Maybe all of those things,' she returned defiantly. 'Why not? But I'm not going to think about that. We'll have a baby together and sort out the details and then we'll both be free to go our separate ways. Will you want whatever's agreed to be legally put into writing?'

'Will you?' Daniel enquired, restless with a savage energy that was pouring through him like toxic waste. 'Do you think I'm the kind of man to give you something with one hand while keeping the other hand free to snatch it all back at a later date?'

He vaulted upright in one swift, graceful movement and stared down at her.

With the glare of the sun behind him, his face was thrown into a mosaic of shadows and angles and she was grateful for the oversized sunglasses hiding her eyes.

'I'll email my lawyer today,' he said, with considerable cold restraint. 'And have something drawn up for signing as soon as we return to London.'

'And visiting rights?'

'As many as I like,' Daniel gritted. 'And I'm warning you, Delilah, if you fight me on this I'll fight you back. In the courts if necessary.' He smiled coolly. 'And now that we understand one another, and the details have been worked out, I'm going for a swim—you can enjoy what remains of our time here without anything "hanging over your head…'"

CHAPTER TEN

DELILAH WATCHED HIM worriedly as he swam out, further and further. until he rounded the cove and disappeared from sight.

Of course he knew this island like the back of his hand! Didn't he? He might only have come to the place a handful of times…fewer than that, probably…but he wasn't a complete idiot. Just the opposite. He would know all about currents and the dangers of getting out of his depth.

She waited for fifteen minutes, her eyes glued to the distant horizon, reluctant to go back into the house until she could see him swimming back towards shore.

The sun was fierce and after a while she sidled under a coconut tree, where she tried hard to relax although her eyes kept flickering to the shore.

Eventually, after half an hour, she gave up and trudged back up to the house—where the first person she bumped into was Mabel, who was busying herself with cleaning.

'Mabel…' She hovered, feeling foolish in her swim-suit and sarong. The staff who looked after the huge villa and took care of the sprawling grounds, were friendly and smiling but kept a respectful distance.

Mabel turned to her, her broad smile going some way to putting Delilah at her ease.

'You should get out of those wet clothes, miss. You

change and give them to me and they'll be back in your room by this afternoon.'

'Er... I just wondered... What's the sea like on the other side of the island?'

Mabel's smile wavered, and Delilah couldn't blame the poor woman for her confusion.

'Because...' She hunted for a reason that wouldn't sound completely crazy. 'Because it looks so...so tempting to just swim round the corner and see what the other beaches are like...'

'I wouldn't, miss...'

'Why not?'

'The sea out here is unpredictable, miss, and once you get past the reef... Well...'

'Well, what?' Delilah smiled encouragingly.

'Sharks, miss... Barracuda... All sorts of things... And the water ain't calm, like it is close to the shore. So it's best for you to stay in the cove—or else Mr Daniel can drive you to some of the other coves... I could make a nice picnic lunch...'

Delilah smiled weakly. She had never been a strong swimmer, and she knew that she was seeing all sorts of potential dangers in a situation that *she* would have found threatening. Daniel was a man of considerably more experience than her. He was muscular, athletic...a man built to overcome hazardous conditions.

Hadn't he told her about all those black runs he had skied down? The surging, stormy seas he had successfully navigated in his boat where he lived in Australia?

But when, after two hours, he still hadn't made an appearance, worry began to set in with a vengeance.

She couldn't relax by the pool. She'd spread her towel on a chair, but the gorgeous view of the ocean, the blue sky, the softly swaying coconut trees that bordered the and on both sides, could not distract her from the nig-gling suspicion that she had engineered an argument that had irritated him to the point where he had disappeared into the ocean. And God only knew where he was now.

Probably safe and sound and heading back to the house. When she looked at it logically, she thought he'd probably made it to the next beach and was calmly relaxing and thinking things through.

It wasn't as if they hadn't *needed* to talk about what they had talked about. Sooner or later they would have *had* to sit down and discuss future arrangements. And, frankly, hadn't she seen just the sort of person that he was? He had *threatened* her, for heaven's sake! Had told her that if she did anything to try and curtail his visiting rights he would fight her—and it hadn't been an empty threat.

He was willing to play the good guy, but there was no way he would allow her to cross him, so if he had stormed off in a rage because she hadn't carried on being amenable and pliable then *tough*.

They were both dealing with a difficult situation, and if she hadn't been firm and businesslike then she would have sleepwalked into him taking charge of everything. Just as he had tried to take charge when he had asked her to marry him!

Had she agreed to marry him—had she *given in* to that treacherous little voice in her head that had urged her to take what was on offer even if it wasn't ideal. because it was better than nothing and because it would allow her the forbidden luxury of still being a part of his life—she would have ended up as nothing more than an append-age, to be tactfully sidelined when the urge to sleep with other women became more pressing than the novelty of being a daddy.

That was precisely what would have happened—
although she conceded he would have been diplomatic
about it, would have made sure that any outside life was
kept far from the prying eyes of the press. But he wouldn't
have cared if *she* had known, because that would have
been the unwritten codicil when they took their wedding
vows. Marriage not for love but through necessity, and
therefore not a marriage at all—at least not in the way
she understood marriage to be!

And if she hadn't liked it—well, doubtless he would
have shown her that tough, uncompromising side of him
that she had already glimpsed.

She had a light lunch by herself in the kitchen. Mabel
fussed around her but asked no questions about Daniel
and why he wasn't there.

Delilah had no idea what she or any of the other members of staff thought about their peculiar sleeping arrangements. The fact they had come together but slept
on opposite sides of the house. Did they gossip about
that? Or maybe the super-rich who rented the property
had their own peculiar arrangements so everyone who
worked there was more than accustomed to odd sleeping
situations. Who knew?

At night, the staff were all either collected and taken by
boat back to the mainland or else they stayed in the collection of well-appointed little houses that formed a clutch at
one end of the island. By the time six-thirty rolled around
most of them had already disappeared.

There would be a delicious meal for herself and Daniel
waiting in the kitchen, she knew. He didn't like anyone
hovering around in the evening, waiting to collect their
plates, and so, after the first night, he had allowed all the
domestic staff to leave early—including the two girls who
worked in the kitchen.

With no sign of him, and with darkness encroaching in the abrupt way that it did in the tropics, Delilah could bear the tension no longer.

It was a small island, and she was sure that she would be able to make her way to the next beach without getting lost. In fact it was practically impossible to get lost. But it made sense to wait until the place was empty, because although the staff might not be curious she knew that they might set out on a search party if she went missing.

The temperature had cooled by the time she quietly let herself out, pausing only to get her bearings and then purposefully walking in the direction she hoped would take her to the adjoining cove. She had a powerful torch, although the moon was full and it was bright enough for her to see without switching the torch on at all.

She had no idea how long she walked. At some point it occurred to her that she should probably return to the house soon—fortunately she had made sure to keep the lights on, so that she could orientate herself without too much difficulty. It didn't matter if they'd become fainter. As long as she could make them out in the distance she knew that she could return safely.

Getting lost wasn't a problem. Becoming exhausted, however, was, and it was so lovely and balmy, with just the softest stirring of a breeze and the soothing sounds of little insects, like peaceful, harmonious background music, that she decided to rest.

She'd changed into a pair of jeans and a tee shirt, and she was perfectly comfortable when she found herself a little mound of grass, where she nestled down and rested her legs.

She dozed.

It was impossible not to, because an overload of stress

had tired her out even more than walking the miles she had covered without realising it.

A loud crashing through the undergrowth woke her up with the unwelcome ferocity of a bucket of ice-cold water, and for a few seconds she was completely disorientated. She could still see through the trees and the bushes, and she could still hear the harmless sounds of the insects and the distant repetitive rolling of the sea, but she had no idea where she was until it all came back to her in a rush.

Daniel was missing.

She didn't care what they had said to one another. She just wanted him to be *safe* and she didn't think he was.

She struggled to her feet, backing away from the approaching noise, the sound of something methodically making its way towards her, and only heard his voice when she had spun around vainly, searching for the lights that would advertise the location of the villa.

'What in God's name are you doing here?' Daniel thundered, bringing her to a stop and probably, she thought frantically, disturbing every single member of staff who had chosen to stay on the opposite side of the island.

He stood in front of her like an avenging angel, hands aggressively on his hips and his body leaning forward, taut with belligerent accusation.

'I…' Relief washed over her and she just wanted to race forward and throw herself into his arms.

'Midnight stroll on an island you know nothing about?' he roared.

'There's nothing dangerous here! You said so yourself! No snakes…no big lions or tigers! You laughed when I told you that I'd be terrified of scrambling through all this bush on my own!'

'So you decided to put it to the test and find out whether

it was true or not?' He took a few steps closer to her. 'I've been worried sick about you!'

'Then you shouldn't have just jumped in the sea and swum away like that!' Her heart was racing, every sense heightened to breaking point.

'Dammit, Delilah, why do you think I did that?'

'Because you didn't want to talk about…about the arrangements for after I have the baby…' *Not unless those arrangements suited him—not unless he could have exactly what he wanted without her putting up any arguments…*

'And why do you think *that* was?' Daniel asked roughly.

He raked his fingers through his hair and glared at her. Coming back to the villa…realising that she wasn't there…he'd never felt so panicked in his life before. He'd been sick with fear.

What if something had happened to her? It would have been *his* fault. His fault for laying it on too thick because he'd been in a situation he hadn't been able to handle. Had he forced her into running away? He'd wondered whether she had gone to the staff houses—gone to see whether she could get one of them to take her back to the mainland on one of the boats that were kept anchored there, to be used if the need arose.

'Forget about dangerous animals! You could have fallen! Hurt yourself! You don't know the layout of this place!'

'And how do you think *I* felt?' Delilah yelled accusingly. 'You just took off! You didn't come back. I… I was worried. You went swimming. Anything could have happened. I thought I'd come out here and look for you…see if you'd swum to another cove…'

She didn't reveal the other more terrifying scenarios

concocted in her imagination. That he was lying in one of the coves, washed up and half dead.

'I was frightened,' she confessed with a hint of defiance

Daniel looked at her, holding his breath.

'Were you?' He exhaled deeply. 'Because *I* was,' he muttered.

He took her hand and led her out of the clearing in which she had fallen asleep. It took them under ten minutes to get to one of the many coves scattered on the perimeter of the island, and during that brief walk there was nothing Delilah could find to say.

He had been worried.

Not about *her,* she made a point of telling herself About the baby she was carrying…

But he was holding her hand…

Was it because he was scared she might trip and fall and somehow hurt the baby? Was that it?

She was dismayed at how pleasurable it was to dwell on an alternative explanation…

'I had no idea how close I was to the sea,' Delilah said 'I mean, I could hear it but…'

'In the dark it's confusing just how far or how close you are because the island's so small…'

She shook her hand free and walked to the water's edge, kicking off her flip-flops so that the sea, as warm as bath water, could lap over her feet. She stared out at the ocean, silvery black and ominous, but every corner of her mind was tuned in to his presence behind her, and she drew her breath in sharply as she felt him approach her from behind, so that he was standing a few inches behind her.

'I shouldn't have disappeared,' he said softly.

'Where did you go for all that time?' She didn't turn

around. It was easier to talk like this, when she wasn't drowning in his eyes and having her brains scrambled.

'There's a very small inlet on the east side of the island. I remembered it from way back. I swam there. I needed to…think…'

'I'm not going to stop you from seeing our child. You didn't have to threaten me like that.'

'I know and I… I'm sorry. Will you look at me? I want to see your face when I…when I say what I feel I must say…'

Delilah slowly turned around and looked up at him reluctantly, because she really didn't want to hear what he had to say now that he had cooled down. She didn't want any more talk about signing things and lawyers.

'I'd never drag you through the courts,' he said gruffly. 'I said that in the heat of the moment because I was just so…so damned frustrated.' He shook his head but was driven to stare back at her, at her beautiful upturned face. 'I brought you here because…'

Delilah waited, confused, because he was a guy who was never lost for words. 'Because you wanted me to relax,' she reminded him.

'Because I wanted to take time out and show you that I could be the man you wanted…in your life permanently.'

'We've been through this…' But her heart still leapt, because she'd thought he'd stopped wanting to marry her. Yes, she'd told herself that she wasn't going to marry anyone for the wrong reasons… But it still kick started a thrilling response deep inside her, like a depth charge going off.

'We're good together, Delilah…and it's not just about the sex. Even though…' he couldn't stop his voice from lowering to a sexy, husky whisper that sent shivers racing up and down her spine…the sex is the hottest sex I've ever had…'

'You don't mean that,' she was constrained to point out. 'You haven't been near me since… Not that it matters… But all that lust stuff…'

'Have you wanted me to?' Daniel interjected. 'To touch you? Because I've wanted to—so very badly—but I didn't want to scare you away. You felt that you'd ended up with a man who'd lied to you and I couldn't take that back. But I wanted to… No, I *needed* to show you that I'm no bastard. I learnt a tough lesson years ago and it hardened me. I never thought that you or any other woman would ever come along and make me question all the things I'd taken for granted…'

'Things like what?' Delilah whispered.

'Things like how emotions could get the better of me… like how I could fall in love with someone and want her so badly that the thought of not having her near me every day for the rest of my life would be beyond endurance…'

'You *love* me?' She could barely whisper that in case she'd misheard.

'I love you and I want to marry you… And I want you to believe me when I tell you that I'll never lie to you again, that I'm good for you…'

She flung her arms around him. She wanted to hold him so tightly that he would never be able to leave. She wanted to superglue him to her.

'I love you so much, Daniel. You're everything that doesn't make sense, but I fell in love with you—and that's why I knew that I couldn't marry you. Because I hated the thought of you being trapped into being shackled to me when you weren't capable of attaching emotionally.' She pressed her head against his chest and felt the steady beating of his heart. 'You can't imagine how tempted I still was to accept your proposal…except then you stopped asking and I was gutted…'

She felt him smile into her hair. 'Like I said, I didn't want you diving for cover because I had no idea how far you'd dive, and I couldn't risk you going anywhere I couldn't follow. My darling, I love you so much… Will you do me the honour…?'

Delilah grinned. She didn't think she would ever stop grinning.

'Just try and stop me,' she murmured, brimming over with happiness.

* * * * *

If you enjoyed reading Daniel's story,
you'll love his brother Theo's:
WEARING THE DE ANGELIS RING
Available now!

MILLS & BOON®
The Sheikhs Collection!

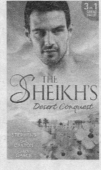

This fabulous 4 book collection features stories from some of our talented writers. The Sheikhs Collection features some of our most tantalising, exotic stories.

Order yours at
www.millsandboon.co.uk/sheikhscollection

MILLS & BOON®

Let us take you back in time with our Medieval Brides...

The Novice Bride – Carol Townend

The Dumont Bride – Terri Brisbin

The Lord's Forced Bride – Anne Herries

The Warrior's Princess Bride – Meriel Fuller

The Overlord's Bride – Margaret Moore

mplar Knight, Forbidden Bride – Lynna Banning

Order yours at
www.millsandboon.co.uk/medievalbrides